Beatitude

J.S. Wik

JK Publishing

Copyright

This book is a work of fiction, all characters names, places, and events are used fictitiously. Any resemblance is entirely coincidental.

Copyright © 2024 by J.S. Wik

As an independent author piracy can be extremely detrimental to my career. Please respect my copyright by not sharing, copying, or in any way using this file in a manner not intended.

Cover design by Sarah Kil Creative Studio
www.sarahkilcreativestudio.com

Please consider leaving a review to help other readers find this book.

Also By J.S. Wik

You can scan or click depending on which format you're reading.

Find more to read from J.S. Wik!
https://linktr.ee/JSWik

Since Beatitude is being released in June, which is Pride Month, it is dedicated to everyone that is a part of the LGBTQIA+ community and their allies! I hope the non-binary and queer representations in this book and this series helps you to feel seen, heard, and a bit more understood and accepted.

Forever an ally,

J.S. Wik

Newsletter Sign up

If you would like to be part of our Virtual Vacation Lovers community, and hear all about the incredible things J.S. Wik has coming up, simply go to the website below to sign up!
(You'll even get a free eBook out of it as a thank you!)

https://www.jswik.com

Trigger Warnings

I would hate for my readers to come across triggering subjects that would be emotionally difficult or potentially cause you harm. Read with caution if any of these are potential triggers for you. Your mental health matters!

- Date rape drug use

- Graphic violence (less than 15% of the book)

Contents

Newsletter Sign up

If you would like to be part of our Virtual Vacation Lovers community, and hear all about the incredible things J.S. Wik has coming up, simply go to the website below to sign up!
(You'll even get a free eBook out of it as a thank you!)

https://www.jswik.com

x

Chapter 1

Latitude

Noun; freedom of action or choice

Jackie walks through the large double front doors of Faith's home carrying two large suit cases and a duffel bag with the zipper bulging. Faith can't help but laugh at the sight. "This is all only for a week?" She asks. She's grateful for everything Jackie is doing for her, but moving in, even for a week is above and beyond anything she expected.

Struggling under the weight of the bag on her shoulder Jackie huffs. "I needed to make sure I had work clothes and clothes for whatever else we might be doing. Plus shoes, so many shoes, and shower stuff, hair products, and makeup. It all takes up space."

"Did you happen to bring any painting clothes?"

"What?" She asks in an exasperated tone with her eye brows squished together.

"You know, painting clothes, ones you're OK with getting paint on."

"I know what painting clothes are." She rolls her eyes. "What are we painting?"

Faith shrugs and simply says, "The house."

"What do you mean the house?" Jackie asks, looking around and finally setting her bag on the floor in the entryway.

"I've decided this house needs a refresh. I need to make it feel entirely different. Kind of like my new wardrobe. New clothes, new me…new paint, curtains, rugs, furniture, bedding, and décor, new house."

Jackie starts laughing, but stops immediately when she realizes Faith is entirely serious. "OK. I will have to pick up some painting clothes."

Faith's face lights up. "Thank you! I don't even have the paint yet. While you were packing up your entire house I was virtually redecorating mine." She turns her phone screen to show Jackie who smiles then she continues. "I think I'm going to enjoy redecorating this place even more than I did the first time." She looks around the large family room.

"Is there a guest bedroom you want me to stay in or should I put all this in your bedroom?"

"You can pick whichever room you'd like."

"Is there one that we won't be painting?"

"Well, we definitely won't be able to get to all of them in a week!"

"True. OK, I'm going to take my things upstairs." She hoists the duffel bag back up on her shoulder and grabs the handle of her luggage. Zeke sniffs at the strange things Jackie brought in the house, but jumps back as soon as they start rolling across the floor.

When Jackie comes back down the grand staircase she says, "You seem to be in better spirits than when I left. What's going on?" She asks with a puzzling look.

"Well, I boxed up some of my clothes to donate, and hung my new stuff in my closet. First though, I contemplated burning all of Jonathan's things, but I know that isn't the answer. Then while I was in my closet the idea to refresh the house hit me so I ran with it."

Jackie smiles. "I think it's a really good idea, Faith. Do we want to ask if Hope and Andy want to lend a hand as well?"

"Maybe. I still need to get everything. I don't mind painting. It isn't for everyone, some people loath it entirely."

"I don't mind it either, but I've known people who hate it too."

Faith looks down at her now black phone screen. "Jonathan would tell me to hire painters, but I want to do it myself."

"We're more than capable, and it'll be good for you. Besides it's his fault you're in this position anyways."

"I think it'll be good for me too. Don't remind me of all of the reasons my life is going to be different because of what Jonathan did. It's been in the back of my mind for nearly two weeks. This is the first glimpse of hope I've allowed myself since he was arrested."

Jackie sits down beside Faith on the couch. "Let me see what you've got so far."

Faith wakes her phone up once again bringing up all of the inspiration boards she worked on with each room labeled and leans in to show Jackie what she's done.

"Faith, these look amazing. I love how the colors are cohesive in their own way, even though they're in different rooms, but not so alike that every room looks the same."

"That's exactly what I'm going for. It's such a huge house, too much for me, really. I should just sell it, but I really don't want to."

"Then don't. Nothing says that you have to."

"It could make this all easier." Faith shrugs.

"How so? The way I see it you'll be adding more stress to your plate."

"I'm not going to do it. It's a thought that keeps popping up."

"Just talk to me before you do anything please. This isn't a time to be making any big decisions."

"What do you think I'm doing right now?" She chuckles then adds, "I'm kidding. I won't be moving, just redecorating!"

Jackie smiles. "You do really seem to be doing better."

"I do feel slightly less doom and gloom."

"That's a start."

Faith shakes her head with pride, having Jackie here will be a change for Faith, but a welcome one. They'll even be able to carpool to work at Hilltop Elementary where Faith teaches first grade and Jackie is the principal.

Faith pages through more of the inspiration boards and says, "Maybe we can run to the store tomorrow after school?"

"That sounds like a plan." Jackie agrees.

"I'm glad you're here. Thank you for this."

"For what?"

"For agreeing to help, for staying with me. For being my best friend."

"I'm happy to be all of those things, Faith. You have enriched my life beyond measure, I can't even begin to repay you for all of the ways you've helped me."

"No repayment necessary."

Faith looks around at the family room, dining room, and kitchen feeling hopeful for the change.

Chapter 2

Vastitude

Noun; *immensity, vastness*

Seven years ago

A few days have passed since Jonathan proposed and Faith is still on cloud nine. They've talked a little bit about the wedding and setting a date, but then Faith begins to feel overwhelmed with all of the things to plan and decide on.

Jonathan tried to suggest hiring a wedding planner, but Faith shut down his idea before he was even able to finish the sentence. She feels very strongly about planning her wedding herself. She needs to do a bit of research to know where to begin. Luckily there are a plethora of websites, blogs, and planners to choose from.

"According to the wedding app I downloaded we need to pick a date first." She says to Jonathan while looking at her phone screen. They finished eating dinner a little bit ago and are now sitting together in the living room.

Jonathan is sitting next to her on the couch watching the baseball game on the TV above the fireplace. He simply nods his head and says, "Hmhmm."

Faith feels frustration bubble up. "I'm not asking for much here, Jonathan, but a little interest in OUR wedding would be nice."

Jonathan turns to her surprised at her tone. "I'm so sorry, Faith! I wasn't meaning to ignore you. I'm really into the game! Strewn just hit a GRAND SLAM! I think they're going to win it!"

Faith squints at him then says, "I wish you were this enthusiastic about our wedding."

"I am." He turns and takes her hands in his. Looking directly into her eyes he continues, "I promise. It's just that the Stallions are playing so well! They're definitely making it to the play offs, maybe even the World Series!"

"I never did understand that. How can they call it the World Series when it isn't even the whole world? Besides, when did you start getting so into baseball?"

He takes a swig of his beer, turning back to the TV screen. "I blame it on your dad."

"Sure. That's an easy out, but I'm glad we got tickets to the game in September for him. He was so happy!"

"He really was! Now if they go to the World Series we'll have to get tickets for that too!"

Faith rolls her eyes. She might be annoyed, but seeing him so excited about this and the fact that it's something he can share with her dad does make her happy.

She turns her attention back to her phone screen, scrolling through all of the different things contained in the planning app.

During a commercial Jonathan says, "We can look at the calendar and pick a date after the game."

"I can live with that." She smiles at him grateful for his thoughtfulness.

"You'll probably want at least a year to plan, right? Isn't that what they say is the best amount of time to take to plan a wedding?"

"It is. A lot of that has to do with how long it takes to get a dress and the alterations, but also because some venues are booked out that far in advance. So once we pick a date we'll have to start thinking about where we would like to have it. What type of venue and then start looking for that."

"That's a lot."

"I've been telling you that." She rolls her eyes and laughs. "I can do it, but it will require input from you. I'm not doing this all on my own."

"I don't expect you to at all, Faith."

Just then the game comes back on so Faith goes back to her phone screen and Jonathan goes back to the TV. She's thinking of all the things they need to decide on yet such as the wedding party. Faith is sure Jackie will be her maid of honor, but isn't sure if Jonathan has even thought about his best man. Tom is really the only person that comes to mind, but it would be a little awkward since he and Jackie broke up five months ago.

Faith hasn't met or even heard of any other friends Jonathan might have to even consider for that role. It makes her feel a little anxious to bring it up. She doesn't want to point out his lack of friends, but she also doesn't want to not have anyone stand up in their wedding. She's always known Jackie would be by her side when she married the love of her life. She doesn't want to give that up because the man she is marrying doesn't have someone to stand up with him.

She finds and bookmarks some wedding dress designer websites. In the next month or so she'll start to make appointments for dress shopping. They'll need to decide on a date and venue before she'll be able to know what the design of her dress should be.

Suddenly, Jonathan jumps up from the couch shouting, "Yes!! Yes!! They did it!!"

Faith finds herself laughing at his outburst. He wouldn't have done this three months ago.

He turns, bending down, and takes her by the shoulders and kisses her fiercely. When he pulls away he has a big smile on his face and says, "Yeah, baby! Now they just have to keep it going!"

"I'm glad they won."

Jonathan sits down and pulls his phone out, pulling up the calendar. "We get to pick our date now." He smiles at her and asks, "I'm sure you've thought about this already, but when are you thinking?"

"Well, I know it's not quite a year off, but what do you think of April? Maybe towards the end of the month since the weather will be a little better."

"I kind of thought the summer would be easier because you won't have school and we'd be able to go on our honeymoon right away."

"I hadn't thought of that."

"We can always get married in April and schedule the honeymoon out a bit. I want to plan that. It will be a surprise."

"A surprise honeymoon?" Faith asks.

"Yes. It's not entirely unheard of."

"No, it's not."

"You trust me, right?"

"Of course I do."

"Then I will plan our honeymoon and it'll be a surprise for you."

"OK, Jonathan. Can we get back to the calendar? I don't want to get married on or too close to Jackie's birthday."

Jonathan looks down at his phone screen which has now turned black. He wakes it up and goes to April. "We want to get married on a Saturday right?" Faith nods her head and Jonathan continues. "We could do the thirtieth. That would be the closest to our dating anniversary, or we can go into May." He finishes and swipes into May.

Faith contemplates for a moment feeling as if she should just know what day would be the best for them to have their wedding. She knows the wedding is only one day and the marriage is what's important, but also, their anniversary will come around every year and that makes the date extremely important.

She looks at Jonathan. "Can we talk this through a little? I've got some thoughts I need to bounce off of you in order to figure it out."

"Of course. Start wherever you want."

"Well, we met in April, but technically we started officially dating in May."

"Right."

"So, either month kind of works in that respect."

"Yes, it does."

"I like the thirtieth of April because it's in between the two."

"So, April thirtieth then?" Jonathan asks curiously.

"I'm not done yet." Jonathan smiles at her and gestures for her to keep going. Faith takes a deep breath and then begins. "May was a very heavy month this year." Faith says thinking back to the pregnancy and miscarriage. "It would be nice to bring some light into the darkness I'm afraid will come that month. I will still be thinking of the baby and everything around the major milestones; like when we found out and first heard the heartbeat, but also when the miscarriage happened. A distraction from all of that would be nice and the wedding could provide exactly that."

"I like the idea of that." Jonathan says softly. He taps his finger on the screen to keep it awake.

Faith looks at the calendar on Jonathan's phone. "I kind of like the idea of the fourteenth." She offers. "That was the day we had the appointment and heard the baby's heartbeat for the first time, so the feelings associated with that day are mixed. This way they'll be so much happier."

"That was an incredible day. I'm sure it'll be even more so when I see you walking down the aisle towards me."

"So May fourteenth is it! I can't believe it! We picked our date!"

"Is it OK that it's less than ten months away?"

"Let's hope. We should start thinking about venues. That will really tell us if it'll be OK."

"Well, let's start with the location. Do we want to get married in Luna Shores? Or Caulfield, maybe? We can look into Sol Port too, if you want."

Faith hops up and goes to their office to grab her laptop. When she brings it back, she sits down next to Jonathan again and opens it. She searches 'Wedding venues near me' and a fair amount of options fill the screen.

She looks at Jonathan. "What feel are we going for?"

"What do you mean 'feel'?"

"Well, like the aesthetic or vibe. What are some words we want people to think or feel while they're at our wedding?"

"Oh, OK. I want it to be luxurious and opulent, but more like old money than new. I want grandeur, but not gaudy and in your face. It should be classy."

"OK. So as far as a venue goes we want something like an old ballroom or something similar."

"That would be perfect. What about Amethyst Hotel?"

Faith thinks back to Kansen Corp's holiday party. "The architecture is just right! I can call them during my lunch break from the café tomorrow and see what they have for availability." She says as she's pulling up the website for The Amethyst Hotel. "For now, I'm sure there's a way to contact them through their website."

"Great idea, Faith."

She scrolls through the pictures they have of weddings in their multiple ballrooms. Everything looks gorgeous and quite perfect for what Jonathan was describing.

"This looks exactly like what I said."

"Right."

"But what do you want, Faith? This isn't only about what I want. The wedding is ours."

"I agree. As for what I want, I think what you described sums it up pretty well. I don't want it to be flashy, but glamorous and decadent sounds perfect. Plus, after seeing these pictures," She gestures towards the bright screen in front of her. "this place is absolutely perfect."

"Great! Now we just have to hope they have availability for May fourteenth."

Faith clicks on the contact us tab and begins filling out the form they have specifically for weddings. "This way when I call they'll have most of the information already. Hopefully it will help things go faster."

"Is there anything else we need to decide?"

Faith laughs. "There are a ton of things we need to decide, Jonathan. Right this very minute, though, no. We should start thinking about the wedding party and the colors we want."

"I was thinking of the wedding party yesterday, actually. I'm not sure who I'd want to stand up with me."

"It isn't something you have to decide right now, but probably sooner rather than later. I'm going to have Jackie as my maid of honor obviously. I'd like to have Hope included somehow as well, but I don't want to make you have to choose two people when you're already having a hard time thinking of one."

"I appreciate that." He half smiles at her.

Faith decides to change the subject. "What do you think we should have for the colors?"

"I'll be wearing a black suit."

Faith laughs. "That's helpful. Thank you."

Jonathan smiles. "Is your dress going to be white?"

"Do you want our colors to be black and white?"

"I definitely don't want yellow or orange."

"No, I don't want that either. Although those colors could be beautiful, it's not what we're going for."

"Black and white is clean; crisp."

"True."

"It's classy too."

"That it is. I wasn't really serious, but maybe it can work." Faith looks back at her laptop screen and looks up weddings with black and white. Images of centerpieces with black candelabras and vases with white candles and flowers and guests dressed in black and white fill her screen.

Jonathan is looking too. "I'm convinced. Simple black and white is elegant."

"It really does." She smiles feeling her excitement building once again, overtaking the feeling of overwhelm. The pictures make it look so magical. All she can do is hope that she can make her wedding look so beautiful.

Chapter 3

Gratitude

Noun; the state of being grateful, thankfulness

Sitting at the large wooden desk in the office of Love's Café, Faith calls the Amethyst Hotel. It was all she could think about the entire morning, which of course was dragging on.

"Amethyst Hotel, Jamie speaking, how can I help you?"

"Hi, Jamie. My name is Faith. I am calling to inquire about possibly having our wedding and reception there."

"Let me transfer you to our events manager, Brenda. Hold please."

Faith hears a click and then a quick ring followed by a woman's voice saying, "Brenda speaking. How can I help you?"

She repeats exactly what she just said to Jamie before being transferred.

"Oh, yes. I saw your inquiry first thing this morning. From your answers I gather that you're still in the early stages of planning. Is that correct?"

Faith smiles. "It sure is." She hears Brenda's nails clicking on her keyboard.

"You put down a date of May fourteenth of next year." There's more clicking on the keyboard. "It looks like we actually have that date available."

Faith feels her heart pick up. "Really? It is?"

"It is!" Faith hears the smile Brenda wears through her voice.

"That's wonderful!"

"So, I will put you on the calendar for that day. We need to set up a meeting to go over your wedding details, but your date will be saved. I'll also email over the contract with pricing as well as menu options and a few other things for you to choose to help things along."

"That's perfect!"

Faith feels relieved to know the venue they really wanted is available and they won't have to find a new date.

They set up a meeting for the middle of August to go over everything else. Faith is hoping by that point they'll have a few more details figured out and a better understanding of what she's doing.

Faith texts Jonathan right away then sets her phone down. She leans back in the chair and puts her head back and closes her eyes for a moment imagining their wedding in the massive ballroom with the beautiful dim lighting that looks like it's lit with candles when there's a gentle knock on the door.

"Are you OK?" Jackie asks in a hushed voice. She's standing in the doorway to the office.

Faith opens her eyes smiling. She practically jumps out of the chair and moves in Jackie's direction who is walking towards her.

"I'm better than OK. We've got the Amethyst Hotel! She didn't say which room yet, but I'm assuming the big ballroom. Jackie, it's so beautiful and absolutely perfect!"

"Are you sure you don't want to call her back to make sure? It sounds like that's the one you really want."

"It's the only one that's big enough for the number of guests I estimated we would have. When she emails over the things she said she would, I'll mention it."

"OK. How is all of that going? Obviously you're happy about the venue."

"So happy! We picked a date. So I hope you don't have any plans on May fourteenth next year!"

"That's exciting. I'll have to check my calendar." Jackie says jokingly as she pulls her phone from the pocket of her sage green pants pretending to check.

"You're so funny." Faith says nudging her best friend.

"I'll be there with bells on…if that's what you want. Otherwise, hopefully, a pretty dress."

"No bells required." Faith makes a mental note to start looking at bridesmaid dresses as well as wedding dresses. "We're going with black and white." She tells Jackie as she pulls up the pictures she found last night and shows her the images on her phone screen.

"That looks gorgeous."

"I know! So elegant and classy."

"It is." Jackie pauses for a second looking at Faith with a curious expression. "I would have thought you would have wanted some color."

Faith laughs. "Me too! I actually made a joke with Jonathan about black and white which he didn't take as a joke. Then I saw these pictures and realized that we didn't need color."

"No matter what you choose it'll be beautiful."

"Thank you, Jackie."

"You're welcome. Is there anything I can help with?"

"Not right now. It took a bit to get to the colors and date with Jonathan. I hope planning the rest of it won't be this hard."

"It won't be. I'm more than willing to help!"

"I know, and I appreciate that so much!" Faith looks down at her thumb nail and rubs it as she leans against the side of the desk. "I want you to know you will be my maid of honor, if you accept. I'm not asking yet, though, not like this. Jonathan doesn't have anyone he's really thinking of having as a best man, so it's a little difficult."

"What about Andy?"

"I hadn't thought of that." Faith says contemplating how Andy might feel with the title being 'best man'. "We can just call them the best person. They did just recently meet though."

"But they've got some time to get to know each other before the wedding."

"That is true. It's a good idea! Thanks, Jackie. I'll mention it to Jonathan and maybe to Hope too. She'll know how they'll feel about it."

"Either way it's an honor and I'd much rather walk down the aisle with them than Tom." She practically spits his name out of her mouth.

"I know. I was worried that's who he was going to suggest."

"He didn't? I'm surprised."

"No. He didn't suggest anyone. He never really kept in touch with anyone he hung out with from high school. Which is probably a good thing. Now, all he does is work so it's not like he's got a ton of friends. And I've met some of his co-workers and would not want any of them in our wedding."

"I don't blame you." Jackie turns to walk out of the café office. "If there's anything I can do, just let me know! Oh and by the way, my answer is, yes! Of course!" She turns to look over her shoulder smiling and laughing as she walks out through the open door.

Faith doesn't want to shout after her since the café is busy for lunch. Instead, she goes back to the chair and starts a list on her phone adding bridesmaid dresses and finding a cute way of asking Jackie to be her maid of honor. She wasn't worried Jackie wouldn't want to, but she's grateful to have her in her corner for everything.

Hope walks into the office a few moments later and Faith asks, "I haven't talked to Jonathan about this yet. I kind of wanted to get your input on it first."

"OK…" Hope says with a worried but curious tone.

"How do you think Andy would feel about being Jonathan's best person?"

Hope smiles. "Well, they'll definitely appreciate the best person title, but they did just meet."

"I know. I thought the same thing. It was Jackie's idea. I was talking to her about Jonathan not really having anyone close enough for the job."

"Unless you guys are getting married in like a month there is time for them to get to know each other better."

"That's what Jackie said too!"

Hope laughs at that. "It really seems like Jackie and I have the same brain."

Faith laughs. "I hope you're not doing anything on May fourteenth next year."

"Not that I know of."

"Well you'll need to be at the Amethyst Hotel. I'm not sure what time yet."

"You're getting married at the Amethyst Hotel?"

"Yes, we are!"

"That's amazing, Faith! I'm so excited for you guys! As far as Andy and the best person thing goes, I think they'd be fine with it. Jonathan doesn't have to ask them yet. They should get to know each other a bit better first."

"I completely agree. I'll mention it to Jonathan, but maybe we should wait to mention it to Andy."

"Yes. That's exactly what I was thinking too."

Just then Jackie pops her head in the doorway. "Hey guys." She says holding a white bag of food. "I came and picked up my lunch. How are you doing, Hope?"

"I'm good! Just working. Are you looking for a summer job by chance?"

"Nope." Jackie chuckles and smiles at her.

Hope shrugs her shoulders. "It was worth a shot. We've been stupid busy and Georgina is on her first vacation like ever. We have Faith, so that helps at least."

"You're lucky to have her." Jackie says smiling at her best friend. "I've got to go before this gets cold."

Faith and Hope both say goodbye and Faith goes back out to tend to her tables in the Café.

Chapter 4

Amplitude

Noun; extent of dignity, excellence, or splendor

That night, at home after waitressing all day, Faith starts creating a workbook with spreadsheets to help her keep track of her wedding plans. She believes this will help keep everything organized. She adds a worksheet for the wedding dresses she likes with links to the websites they're on and one with a link to an inspiration board she started last night before bed.

When Jonathan comes home he finds Faith sitting cross leg on the couch completely entranced in her work with Zeke sleeping soundly on the floor beneath her. She looks up from her screen and smiles at him.

"How was your day?" She asks.

"It was OK. Not too busy. How was yours? I see you're busy at work."

"This isn't work. My day was good. Did you see my text about the Amethyst Hotel?"

"I did! That's exciting news, Faith."

"It is!"

"So if it's not work, what are you so enthralled with?"

"I've been creating a workbook with sheets to help me keep everything organized."

"You didn't want to buy a wedding planning planner or organizer?"

"I like this and besides, I can have it on my laptop and my phone. Plus, I won't have to carry a book around with me. Do you want to come see it?"

"Sure!" He sits down next to her on the couch watching the look on her face, he leans in to kiss her on the cheek. "You are so cute! I'm glad you're happy doing this." He gestures towards the screen.

"I am really enjoying it!"

She shows him all of the tabs she has set up so far and clicks the link to show him the board she created and all of the ideas and inspiration she's found.

"This all looks amazing! It's exactly what I described."

"Is there anything you don't like?"

"I don't think so, but it's also not like everything is going to be identical to what you showed me, right? It's all inspiration."

"Yeah, it's inspiration. I just didn't want to be set on something I really liked and then you didn't like it."

"I won't have that strong of an opinion on any of it, Faith. Kind of like how it was with decorating the house. I want to be included, but you're going to be making most of the decisions."

"I can live with that." Faith leans into Jonathan and he puts his arm around her.

"Our wedding is going to be absolutely incredible, all because of you, Faith. You are amazing and I'm so lucky I will get to call you my wife in two hundred eighty eight days."

Faith smiles so big she feels like her cheeks are going to burst. "You figured that out?"

"There's a countdown app that made it really easy." He shrugs.

"Two hundred eighty eight days seems like a lot of time, but it's going to fly by."

Jonathan gets up and walks into the large kitchen. He grabs two glasses from the cupboard and then a bottle of cabernet sauvignon, Faith's favorite. He pours them each a glass and brings them into the living room, handing one to Faith he sits back down beside her.

"Thank you." Faith says smiling at him.

"You're welcome. This all deserves a celebration!"

"We're not even half way there."

"We got our venue! And on our date at that! We've got to be the luckiest couple ever!"

"I'm happy to see you're so excited!"

"I'm excited for us! This is a huge deal! Plus, seeing you figuring all of this out and being excited about it makes me feel good."

"Thank you. I'm happy to do it. Besides, I wouldn't want anyone else to be doing it."

"I know. How was the café today?"

"It was OK. Jackie came to see me actually. She had a pretty good idea, I think."

"What was that?"

"What do you think about having Andy as your best person? I know you just met them and everything, but you've got time to get to know them better. It doesn't have to be something you decide on now."

"It's not a bad idea at all. I'm sure Jackie liked that better than the idea of Tom."

"Yeah, she pretty much said that."

"I don't have a problem with him, but I could see how having him as my best man could make the day a little more awkward and that's not what we want."

"No, it isn't."

"How do you think Andy will feel about it?"

"I brought it up to Hope. She thought it was a good idea too, but we also both thought it'd be best to wait until you two got a chance to get to know each other a bit better."

"I'd like to do that. We should invite them both over for a fire and some drinks one of these nights."

"That's a great idea. We can ask them at Sunday dinner."

"That'll work. What else happened at work?"

"Nothing really. Just got people their food and drinks. I told both Jackie and Hope the wedding date."

"They're not busy right?"

Faith chuckles. "I don't think so."

"Good. That's the last thing we need." Jonathan laughs barely able to hold it in.

Faith laughs harder then says, "My parents may declare it a holiday and close the café for the day."

"I could totally see Frank and Diane doing that!"

"I think they'll be in tomorrow. I'll have to let them know what day we chose."

"Why weren't they in today?"

"I'm not entirely sure. I think it had something to do with taking Orpheus to the vet. I've started noticing them backing away from the café a bit more this year. Well, ever since Hope got back after her car accident."

"I can't blame them. The whole point of them having Hope take over for them is so they can retire at some point right?"

"I don't think they're retiring any time soon."

"No, but slowing down probably sounds pretty good to them. They've put a lot into the café over the years."

"They definitely have."

"I'm going to start on dinner. Would you like to come into the kitchen with me?"

"I sure do!" She smiles up at him.

Jonathan grabs their wine glasses and carries them to the kitchen leaving hers on the table in the booth style seating area. Faith follows him with her laptop.

She ends up watching him cook more than getting anything else done in her workbook.

After dinner they take Zeke outside for a walk. They walk down the path they originally found him on, but this time it's not dark at all and there are no weird noises as they meander. The birds are chirping in the trees surrounding them and the blue sky is as clear as can be.

"This is the best. The house is incredible, but having this five acres is like having our very own park." Faith says as she looks at the row of pine trees casting shadows across their path.

"We always said the property was the best part, but now that the house is finished it would be hard to choose which one is better."

"Good thing we don't have to." Faith says. "It's a package deal now. They both make up our perfect home."

Jonathan stops and takes Faith's hand in his. He pulls it up to his lips kissing it. Faith smiles at him with a twinge of pink in her cheeks.

"We're all a package deal. Me, you, Zeke," He looks at their surroundings, "This property and the house. This is our home now, it's where we belong."

"I completely agree." She goes up on her tip toes and kisses him.

He pulls her into him kissing her fiercely.

As she pulls away he pulls her back in to him. "I'm not done with you yet." He says against her lips right before he kisses her harder. She feels herself give into him, pushing her body against his.

Her breath picks up as her head starts swimming feeling Jonathan's passion. Suddenly, he pulls back. "Our walk is done."

Faith can't find her voice so she simply shakes her head in agreement. They quickly walk back to the house with Zeke leading the way.

Jonathan pulls Faith into the bedroom taking his shirt off in between kisses. Faith starts pulling at the button on his pants. Faith feels him pulling at the buttons on her shirt exposing her breasts. He takes his lips from hers kissing her collar bone and moving down to her cleavage.

Faith inhales sharply feeling Jonathan's lips against her skin. He picks her up and carries her to their bed, placing her gently down. He stands in front of her and removes his dress pants and boxer briefs. Then he turns his attention to removing her shirt entirely. He kisses Faith fiercely making her lay down and then pulls her shorts and underwear down. Faith feels his lips follow the trail her shorts and underwear take as he pulls them off, leaving goose bumps.

Faith entwines her fingers in his hair and pulls his face into her. He reaches up and grips her hips. She lets out a soft moan as his mouth finds its way up her thighs.

She moves her fingers to the side of his face, feeling the movement of his jaw as he ignites the pleasure in her. He stops as she starts thrusting against him and pulls himself on top of her. She draws him into her with her arms wrapped around him.

Jonathan thrusts forcing a loud moan from Faith.

"I love you, Faith." He says as he thrusts once again.

"I love you, Jonathan." She says as her breath catches and he thrusts again.

She raises her hips to meet him as their bodies collide with pleasure. Both of them breathing heavily, Jonathan buries his face in Faith's hair which is splayed across her pillow.

Faith feels the edge of ecstasy coming fast and hard when she feels Jonathan's pleasure peak. They ride the waves together, breathing heavily, they collapse into one another.

Chapter 5

Habitude

Noun; habitual disposition or mode of behavior or procedure

The next night, while Faith is working the closing shift at the café, Jonathan finds himself driving the all too familiar highway on his way to Duffy's bar in Caulfield. The urge hit him hard last night after Faith had fallen asleep. He fought it off in the same way he has previously; by looking at pictures he has saved in an encrypted folder in his phone.

He knew if he left it would raise questions and that is the last thing he wants. Since his urges came back following the miscarriage, Jonathan has become even more anxious about Faith finding out. His entire future and five year plan rides on Faith believing he is the person he shows her on the surface.

The lights above the highway cast their glow in rows cast across the concrete followed by shadows which reminds Jonathan of stripes on a zebra. An oncoming car distorts the stripes but only for a moment before it passes.

As he approaches the turn off for Caulfield he begins to feel the queasiness building just like it had the last time. He takes a drink from his water bottle and feels the cold water hit his empty stomach which does nothing for its unsettledness.

By the time he gets to the dilapidated warehouse where he keeps the backup car, there is sweat beading on his forehead.

Jonathan feels the clamminess as he swipes his hand across his forehead wondering why he's suddenly having this re-action. These urges are not new. He's had them for nearly as long as his parents have been gone and he went to live with his Aunt Suz. The uncontrollable urges started from the day that rundown shed became his sacred place after his first kill. There has always been an ebb and flow to them, but that never included this level of anxiety.

He climbs out of his Mercedes and opens the door to the unregistered Lexus he keeps in the open area on the main floor that used to be a warehouse. He starts the car suddenly feeling extremely nauseous. Jonathan quickly opens the door once again and crouches down next to the vehicle. The smell of the exhaust hits him unexpectedly. He begins to retch uncontrollably. The small amount of water he drank on the drive comes back up along with stomach acid which burns his esophagus.

Why is he suddenly having this reaction? The last time he came to Caulfield, before he decided to propose, he had a similar reaction, but once he saw his freshest victim the anxiety went away. It was almost as if someone else entirely took over. He no longer felt the emotions that made him feel nauseous and was completely sure of what he was doing. Once he saw her he simply knew she was the one he came for.

Could that possibly happen again tonight? Jonathan contemplates that as he wipes some spittle from the corner of his mouth and gets back into the driver's seat of the Lexus. Jonathan feels the heat of the day trapped within the car so he turns the air on as well as the seat cooler.

The cool air blowing on his face helps to alleviate his upset stomach. He places the Lexus in reverse and drives straight to Duffy's bar. As he gets closer the nausea returns with a vengeance.

He questions once again if he should be doing this. He takes a deep breath as he pulls into the parking lot in an attempt to clear his mind and ready himself for his hunt. He glances at the clock on the dash. It's nearly ten thirty. Faith is surely home and more than likely in bed. Jonathan had sent her a text before she would have been done at the café explaining that he would be working late followed by an apology.

It still surprises him that she hasn't questioned him which also makes him feel grateful for her trust. Unfortunately, it could be entirely shattered with just one slip up on his part.

Most evenings like this go without a hiccup, there have, however, been a small handful that have required quick thinking by Jonathan which has then caused an increased amount of stress.

Although, thinking back, Erica, his most memorable and favorite kill of them all had nearly been a disaster. Jonathan reveled in the struggle at the time, but afterwards he was able to see all of the ways it could have gone wrong. Which is exactly what lead him to make a few changes to his strategic plan including switching vehicles.

Jonathan steps out of the Lexus and looks up at the few stars in the sky. The view at their house is so much better without the light pollution from the city. He walks across the parking lot just as the door to the bar swings open. The light fills the parking lot, practically blinding Jonathan, the tall gentleman coming through the door recognizes him instantly.

"Jonathan! Jonathan Hall! I can't believe it! How long has it been? Like ten years, at least?"

Taken aback, Jonathan squints at the guy and tries to recognize him since his voice wasn't helpful. As the man turns so the light from the door hits the side of his face Jonathan instantly smiles. "Rowen? How the hell are you, man?"

Rowen grabs Jonathan's hand and pulls him in for a hug. As he pulls back he says, "I've been good! How have you been?"

"I'm great! I'm a general manager at Kansen Corp, and hoping CEO is in the cards for me this year. I'm also engaged!"

"Yeah, I tried the marriage thing. Didn't work well for me, but congrats." Rowen shrugs his broad shoulders.

"What the hell are you doing here? I thought you moved to Illinois or some shit?"

"Yeah, I was living just outside of Chicago working for a law firm, but like I said the marriage thing didn't work out so I decided to come back. Well, come back and live in Caulfield. I don't think I could deal with how small Luna Shores is now. I had a hard time when we were kids. I've opened my own practice here."

"Yeah. I don't blame you for that and that's awesome!"

"Thanks! So, who's the lucky lady?"

"Her name is Faith Brandt. Her parents own Love's Café on Main."

"No fucking way, man!"

Jonathan's eyes fill with surprise that Rowen has any recollection of her.

Rowen continues, "I don't think I ever met Faith, but I do know Love's Café has the best food!"

Jonathan feels himself relax. "No kidding!"

"So, are you heading in to meet someone then? Is she here?"

"Oh, no she was working all day so she's at home." Jonathan says quickly trying to think of why he might be coming to a bar all alone on a Friday night. "I was just coming for a drink. Are you heading out?"

"Yeah." Rowen looks back towards the door expectantly. He leans in close to Jonathan and says, "There's a woman I'm taking home tonight. She should be coming any minute now."

As soon as he finishes the sentence, the door opens, once again flooding the parking lot with the glow from inside. A tall slender brunette walks out dressed in a short skirt and heels. She stumbles a bit as she traverses the threshold. Rowen is quick to put his hand out for her to grab and steady herself.

Giggling she says, "Thanks, Rowen." Her words a bit slurred. She looks at Jonathan and smiles widely. "Well, aren't you handsome." She adjusts her weight more to one side and leans into Jonathan at the same time.

"Well, we should get going, right Delaney?" Rowen says still holding onto her hand.

Delaney looks at Rowen almost as if she had forgotten he even existed. "Oh, right." She leans into Rowen putting her hand on his chest and moving to kiss him.

He pulls her into him and kisses her fiercely.

When she pulls back she clumsily swipes the hair from her face. Wearing a huge smile she says, "Damn. That was one hell of a kiss!"

Rowen flashes Jonathan a smile. "We should catch up soon. Let me get your number." He hands Jonathan his phone to input his number into. Jonathan enters it, hits save, and hands it back to Rowen. "Cool! Thanks, man. I'll hit you up soon." Before Rowen can finish his sentence Delaney is pulling him towards the parking lot.

"Woman, you have no idea which of these is mine." Jonathan hears Rowen tell her as he continues watching to see which vehicle they end up going to. Jonathan sees

Rowen take his keys out, hitting the unlock button which makes lights flash on a dark colored lifted truck in the back of the parking lot.

Jonathan turns to enter the bar, but is suddenly hit with the realization that someone knows he was here tonight. If anything were to go awry there is a way it could come back to him. Maybe he's over thinking it, but he's not willing to take the chance. There's got to be a reason he's been having these feelings, maybe this is it.

He looks up as he turns to leave and sees three cameras pointed towards the parking lot. He decides his hunting days at Duffy's bar are over. He watches as Rowen pulls out of the parking lot feeling grateful for the run-in. Rowen has no idea, but he may have saved Jonathan from a disastrous fate tonight.

He walks to the Lexus trying to think of how he can overcome this. He will need to find new grounds for hunting. He knows he can't hunt solely at the Blue Rooster. He'll surely be recognized which puts him at a higher risk, at the very least, of becoming a suspect if questions are raised about any of his victims' whereabouts.

Climbing into bed with Faith an hour later makes Jonathan feel as though he did the right thing. He tries to hold onto the feeling, to lock it away and save it for when his urge shows it's self again. A tinge of anxiety hits him as he realizes that it probably won't be long before it does. He pulls her sleepy body into him feeling her warmth against his naked torso soothes away some of those fears.

Faith sleepily turns towards him, barely opening her eyes she says with a happy smile, "You're home."

"I am." Jonathan says smiling at how damn cute she is. "How was work?"

"It was work. We were busy and I was exhausted."

"I bet."

Faith's arm wraps around him and she scoots as close to him as she can physically get. He smiles again holding onto the love he feels in this moment, hoping and praying that it will be enough to keep his urges at bay. If it's not enough to keep them away maybe it will be enough to keep him from seeking the relief only killing can provide.

Chapter 6

Verisimilitude

Noun; having the appearance of truth, probable

So many memories are coming up for Faith while sitting in the living room of her parents' nineteen fifties rambler. They've updated the house some since she was little, but not enough that it doesn't still feel like her childhood home. They have dinner every Sunday night as a family, a tradition started when Faith and Hope were in high school and schedules started getting more hectic than ever. It's typically when they all share any big news they have with everyone. This week is no different.

Faith is currently sitting on their couch, daydreaming; thinking about all of the times she played pretend, with Barbies, dolls, or even stuffed animals and would put on a wedding ceremony. She had no idea then how much work they were or how stressful it would actually be, but now she's aware and she wishes she could go back to sitting on the floor in this living room with her parents watching from their seats while she was the officiant. Hope would usually try to ruin the wedding somehow in her own obnoxious little sister way, of course.

As a kid, when Faith thought of her wedding someday she had grand plans and an unlimited budget, which is also something her and Jonathan need to determine yet. With her huge imagination she envisioned a perfectly dreamy day with the man of her dreams, a prince, of course! She would walk down the aisle to him in her huge wedding gown and all of the attendants would be crying because they were so happy for them. There was romance and magic, but most of all love.

For her actual real life wedding, she doesn't need all of the attendants to cry, or even show up. All that matters to her is that her and Jonathan become husband and wife. Obviously she wants her parents, sister and best friend there, but there are no other requirements to make it the most perfect day like there had been when she was just a child playing pretend.

"Are you OK, Faith? It seems like you were somewhere else for a bit." Frank says concerned.

Faith snaps out of the memories and back to reality. "Yeah." She giggles a little. "I was thinking about all those times my stuffed animals or Barbie and Ken got married. Do you guys remember that?"

Hope scoffs. "I never understood how you thought that was fun."

"That was apparent." Faith says as she shoots her sister a steely glance.

"What? It just wasn't my thing."

"I know. That's why you'd have your T-Rex come and destroy everything."

Hope laughs so hard and Andy joins in too. "Did you really do that? A T-Rex?" They say laughing even harder at the mental image.

"I sure did!" She looks at Faith. "Do you remember Tee-Bee?"

"Your giant teddy bear? Yes, of course I do!"

Hope looks at Andy. "Tee-Bee used to stomp all over them because he was so big. Nothing could stop him."

Andy looks at Faith. "I can't believe you put up with that."

"I didn't have a choice. Mom and dad didn't do anything if I complained to them. They'd explain it away saying she's little and she'll grow out of it." Faith rolls her eyes. "Clearly she hasn't."

Everyone laughs including Hope who is practically tearing up, she's laughing so hard.

Jonathan says, "Well Tee-Bee is definitely off the invite list!" He looks at Faith who laughs even harder.

"What invite list?" She couldn't help herself.

Once everyone calms down Faith figures it's a perfect time to tell her parents about when and where the wedding will be.

"We got the Amethyst Hotel for May fourteenth next year!" She announces.

Her mom, Diane, looks splendidly surprised. "I wasn't sure where you guys were going to want to have the wedding. Part of me thought you might want it at your house! It's so beautiful and could work perfectly."

"I hadn't thought of that." Faith says knowing a backyard wedding, even on their beautiful property isn't what Jonathan would have wanted.

"The Amethyst Hotel." Frank repeats. "That place is as old as the town and has some incredibly ornate architectural features."

"That's the biggest reason we chose it, sir. We got lucky that they had our date available even though it's less than year away." Jonathan says smiling.

"That was super lucky." Diane agrees. "I can imagine they're in high demand for weddings around here. It's quite possibly the nicest place without having to go into Caulfield."

"I'm sure they are. I think it helps that the date we chose is early in the wedding season. I think more couples get married in June and beyond." Faith says.

"My sister is a concert pianist. I can see if she is available and would be interested in playing for you guys. Maybe for the ceremony?" Andy offers.

Faith's face lights up. "That's a great idea! Thanks Andy!"

They smile. "You're welcome. If she's available I can send you her contact information."

"I'd appreciate that. I honestly have no idea what we're doing for music for the ceremony or reception, but I think a pianist would be amazing!"

"Yeah, she's really good. She even won first place at the Gina Bauchauer International Piano Competition for her age group."

"That is quite impressive!" Diane says raising her eyebrows. Just then the timer goes off in the kitchen and Diane stands abruptly. "That'll be dinner."

Faith stands as well. "I'll help."

As everyone else files into the dining room, Faith and Diane go into the kitchen to gather the food and bring it to the table.

As Faith carries out the main dish, Jonathan's face lights up like it does every week. She'd love to think it's because of her, but she knows how much he thoroughly enjoys her mother's cooking. It could be a combination of the two, as well.

When they're done eating, Faith helps put away the leftovers while Frank and everyone else goes into the den to watch the Stallions game.

"Frank, you should think about putting a TV out on the patio. We could enjoy the weather, but also watch the game." Jonathan says as he takes a sip from the beer Hope had grabbed for them.

"I think Orpheus would enjoy it too." Hope says as she pets him behind the ears.

Frank nods his head. "I'll discuss it with your mom."

Hope smiles at Jonathan like a silent high five.

When Diane and Faith walk into the den everyone's attention is locked onto the TV. Faith sees that the bases are loaded and Strewn is up to bat. He's already got two balls and the pitcher is getting ready to throw his next pitch.

In an instant both Frank, Jonathan and Hope are standing shouting and giving high fives. "I can't believe he did it again!" Jonathan says a little too loud. "Another grand slam!"

Frank smiles widely. "I think they're going to do it this year, son! I think we'll be going to the World Series."

"If the Stallions are there, we'll be there!"

Diane looks at Faith. "Did you have any idea Frank would rub off on Jonathan in such a way?"

"None at all."

"It's good though. There are worse things. Plus, it's something besides you and work that he can focus on."

"That's true. Except when it interferes with wedding planning." Faith rolls her eyes.

"Well, the season will be done before you know it."

"Yeah, it seems like there are almost always games on or he's working late." She inhales sharply. "It's fine though. For the most part I can plan everything on my own."

"He doesn't want to have a part in it?"

"He does, but he basically said to just do what I want. He said it's like the house. I can pick out whatever I want."

"That works nicely then."

"It does, but it's still our wedding and I want, and sometimes need his input on things."

"We'll need to figure out a good place and date for your bridal shower."

"Yes, we will."

"If there's anything else you need help planning, just let me know. I'm so excited for your wedding and your dad and I want to help anyway we can."

Another shout erupts from the others watching the game so Diane nods towards the living room for the two of them to be able to sit and talk.

"Thanks, Mom. I appreciate that! There's so much to plan it can be hard to know where to start. I've got a workbook started with different sheets for everything, but I've got to look into a lot of different vendors. We have a meeting at the Amethyst Hotel in a couple of weeks which will help me know what all they can take care of."

"I can help. I only need you to tell me what you need. Let me help you cross some things off your list."

"Well, we're going to need a florist. Do you want to get a list of a handful of them and maybe some quotes?" Faith thinks for a moment. "This is where I get stuck. I'm not even sure what questions to ask a florist. I've never worked with one before nor have I planned a wedding."

"Typically, dear, they'll lead the conversation. They'll ask how many bouquets and boutonnieres. I'm sure they'll want to know the venue, if you'll want flowers to help decorate the ceremony, and what kind of center pieces you're think-ing for the reception tables. Do you have any idea of a color scheme or which specific flowers you want?"

Faith sits looking at her mother so thankful to have her help. "You're really good at this."

"You've got this, Faith, I'm just here to help. Plus, it helps that I've assisted in planning a few weddings."

"For colors we're going with black and white, as far as flowers go, I'm not sure, maybe white roses?"

"That will be so pretty!"

"We thought so too. I had to look at pictures to be convinced." Faith laughs a bit.

"Like I said honey, I'm very excited for you two." Diane puts her hand on top of Faith's on her leg. "Your father and I would like to pay for your dress."

"You don't have to do that, Mom."

"We know, but we would really like to. It's something I've always wanted to be able to do for you and your sister ever since you both were little."

Faith's gratitude grows making her heart feel so full. "Thank you, Mom." She smiles at her.

Diane pulls her in for a hug. When they hear another loud celebration come from the den they both start laughing and get up and walk back towards the den.

Jonathan is standing and walking towards the couple of stairs that lead down into the den. "The game is over! They won!" He says with a wide smile and a so much excitement in his voice Faith can't help but be happy for them.

"That's awesome! Are you about ready to go? I'm exhausted and would still like to get a couple of things done for the wedding tonight."

"Yes, of course!"

On the drive home Jonathan asks, "Are you doing OK, Faith? You don't typically want to leave early?"

"I'm fine, like I said, I'm just exhausted. You'd think teaching would take more energy, but waitressing definitely does."

"Maybe because it's more physical, you're on your feet going from table to table taking orders and then taking them from the kitchen to the tables. It's a lot more physically demanding." Jonathan reasons with her.

"You're probably right." She concedes.

The landscape lights guide their way up the hill of their driveway and into the garage. Jonathan parks and they walk in through the service door as Jonathan hits the button to close the garage door behind them.

Faith lets Zeke outside and then goes directly into the office to start looking up bridal shops that carry the designers she's been most drawn to. Jonathan follows, sitting at his desk on the other side of the office.

"Jonathan, I've got an email about a bridal show in Caulfield next weekend. What do you think about going?"

"Isn't that more for brides?"

"They only call it that. It doesn't mean it's only for brides. It's for wedding planning. There will be all different kinds of vendors there."

"OK, Faith. Whatever you want."

"I'll add it to the calendar." She says flatly, not really feeling very good about his answer.

Faith adds six bridal shops to her worksheet with their phone numbers, hours and addresses. She'll have to call to schedule appointments. Hopefully they'll be able to work it out where she can get to most of them in one weekend.

There is only one shop in Luna Shores and one in Sol Port. The rest of them are in Caulfield which Faith had anticipated would be the case. Luckily she has a day off tomorrow so she'll be able to call and figure it all out. She will also need to make sure that her mom, Hope, and Jackie can come as well.

Jonathan closes his laptop, kisses Faith on the top of her head and says, "Maybe we should head to bed soon. You mentioned you were exhausted."

"Yeah. I'll be in there soon."

"OK. I'll take care of Zeke."

"Thanks."

Faith takes a few moments to make sure she's found the best options before washing her face, brushing her teeth, and climbing into bed with Jonathan.

Chapter 7

Promptitude

Noun; the quality or state of being prompt

Faith is looking forward to the bridal show coming up tomorrow and Jonathan seems to be a little more keen on going now as well. She isn't entirely sure what to expect since she's never been to one, but her anticipation is that it will help her find vendors. There is also a runway show of gowns that she is excited to see. She has no idea what Jonathan would like.

Not that she's basing her dress decision off of what he wants, but she does at least want to take it into account. Who wants to walk down the aisle to their soon-to-be husband and he's looking at her like she's got a bird on her head because of what she chose to wear? She hasn't mentioned the fashion show to him yet, but she's sure it'll be fine.

Sitting in her kitchen at the built in banquette she looks over the workbook she's made feeling pretty proud of herself. She worked another long shift at the café and isn't sure if Jonathan will be home on time yet or not.

He has been good during the week about coming home at a decent hour to make dinner together and have a chance for quality time, but Fridays always seem to be a toss-up. Some Friday nights he's home at his normal time, and others he doesn't get home until way after Faith has already fallen asleep.

She taps her finger on the table after she inputs the information her mom gave her about the florists she's called into the sheet labeled Flowers. She has some inspiration photos of what she's looking for both for center pieces and bouquets as reference on there as well.

Her thoughts drift back to Jonathan. If she weren't so secure in their relationship and how well she believes she knows him she would probably be concerned that he's cheating. Why else would it only be on Friday nights? She reasons that the work builds up throughout the week and he's got to get it done so that he isn't behind first thing on Monday mornings. There were times in the past when he was working on Saturdays as well, but he hasn't had to do that in a while, which she's grateful for.

Jonathan and her still haven't discussed a budget, but she plans on bringing that up after dinner. She has a feeling she knows what he's going to say. That the budget doesn't matter and that she should have exactly what she wants.

She puts 'wedding photographer near me' into the search bar on her internet browser and a ton of results fill the page.

She wants to make sure the pictures they have of the day show exactly how magical she wants the entire thing to feel. She clicks on a few of the websites and is blown away at the quality and talent on one especially. When she clicks on pricing, she's blown away by the price. The images do seem worth it and clearly this photographer has that special something she's looking for.

She clicks another, but this one's images are lackluster in comparison. She goes down the line until a few moments later Jonathan walks through the door. She stands as he walks through the service door of the garage. Zeke has beaten her to him and a smile lights up Jonathan's face as he ruffles Zeke's ears.

Faith smiles back and Jonathan wraps his arms around her seeming thankful to be home. "I missed you so much today." He says.

"I missed you too, Jonathan. There's some wedding things I've been wanting to talk to you about." She motions towards her laptop sitting on the table. "It can wait, but I definitely want to discuss them before tomorrow morning."

"OK, Faith. How was your day?"

"Exhausting." She says flatly.

"You know you don't have to work there. You could take the rest of the summer off and use that time to plan the wedding."

"I know, but I feel obligated to my parents and Hope. They expect me to be there every summer. If I'm not going to be working then they'll need to hire and train someone else and that takes time and money. I don't mind, really."

"I'm sure your parents would understand."

"I'm sure they would too, I just don't want to leave them high and dry."

"I'm not saying leave them high and dry. I'm only saying give a notice and give yourself some time before school starts to work on wedding things."

"School is coming up quickly. There'll be things I need to do to get ready for that too." Faith brushes a few strands of hair from her forehead.

"I can see you're getting stressed between working there, planning the wedding, and now with school coming up. I think you need to take something off of your plate and the only thing that can really go is the café."

Faith nods her head. "I'll talk to my parents and Hope about it on Sunday."

Jonathan kisses her forehead. "Thank you."

They head into the kitchen and Jonathan sits down at the table looking as if he's ready to discuss whatever Faith needs. That's a breath of fresh air. She thought she was going to have to pull teeth in order to get him to talk about wedding things.

She sits down beside him with her laptop in front of her, she pulls up the worksheet she has set up for their budget. "We need to discuss a budget. What do you have in mind as a whole for the wedding, but also per vendor?" Before he can answer she puts her finger up and says, "As far as per vendor goes, I'll have to show you some of the pricing I've found because it's quite a bit more than I anticipated."

"It's not a problem Faith. You know tat we have it. Just spend whatever you want and get everything you want exactly how you want it. I simply want you to be happy." Jonathan smiles looking at her with genuine happiness in his eyes. "You're going to be my wife. That is literally all I could ask for." He leans in and kisses her, as he places his hand on the side of her face.

Faith leans her body into his, giving herself over to him. His hand moves to her back, pulling her into him then he pulls his head back slightly.

She opens her eyes and says, "I don't think we should have an unlimited budget. Not that I plan to go overboard on spending, but it can be easy to let it get out of hand, especially when there are so many things we need to pay for. Which reminds me, my parents would like to pay for my wedding dress. I told them that wasn't necessary, but my mom basically insisted."

"I get that. I don't want them paying for anything else though. It's unnecessary."

"I agree. I wasn't expecting them to pay for anything, honestly."

"No, me either, but I also understand why they would want to pay for it. Have you been looking at dresses? Any ideas of what you like or want?"

"Oh, I've got ideas." She says playfully. "I can't share them with you though. There is a fashion show at the bridal show tomorrow that I'd like for us to go to, if that's OK?"

"Whatever you want, Faith. That's an all-day thing right?"

"The bridal show?" she asks and Jonathan nods. "It is, but I doubt it will take us all day to go through."

"OK. Maybe we can grab lunch or dinner or something while we're in Caulfield then."

"That's a great idea."

"Is there anything else we need to discuss?"

"Well, we still haven't settled on a budget."

"I think as a whole, let's try to keep it around fifty thousand." He takes a moment and then says, "It's kind of hard to set a definitive budget when we haven't had the meeting at the Amethyst Hotel to know how much all of that is going to be, or even what all they include in their price. I'd assume they take care of catering and they most likely have a list of vendors they typically work with or who have done well there previously."

"That's true. I guess I hadn't thought of that. I was hoping to have more planned by the meeting, but it kind of makes more sense to just have a very strong vision of what we want, which I think we have, and go from there."

"I completely agree." He smiles and taps his pointer finger on the tip of her nose.

"Thank you for being so willing to talk about this, Jonathan. It's kind of seemed like you haven't really been interested."

"I am not the planner here. The details aren't as important to me as they are to you, but I also want you to know I'm here if you need anything and I'll be happy to give you my opinion on all of it."

"I appreciate that. Thank you." She leans her shoulder into his, nudging him gently.

"OK, I'm going to start making dinner now. We can keep talking about wedding things if you want. Maybe show me what you were talking about as far as the pricing that was higher than you thought it would be."

Faith's face lights up thinking about that first photographer's website she clicked on. First she stands, letting Jonathan get up. Then she brings the website back up. She shows him the incredible images and she can see by the look on his face that he is impressed as well.

Then she goes into the tab for their pricing.

"They want how much?" Jonathan says surprised as he leans over the island counter looking at the laptop screen. "I mean, those pictures are gorgeous, but damn, that's a lot of money."

"That's what I thought too."

"Can you click the most expensive one and see what all it includes, please?"

Faith does and they see a large list of inclusions, which also has videography on it.

"Well, if it includes an edited video of the ceremony and reception I could see it being worth it."

Faith tilts her head to one side then the other. "Yeah, it's still a lot of money, though."

"Maybe look at pricing from other videographers separately and see if we get a deal from combining the two with the same people."

"That's a good idea." Faith opens a new tab and searches for that while Jonathan puts a large pot full of water on the stove top. "Remember, we also have money coming from the sale of the condo, that can always go towards the wedding too."

"We should probably invest that, Jonathan."

"You're right. I know all too well how much money can grow in twenty years when invested properly."

"Exactly." Faith says, thinking of how Jonathan's parents were so smart to do that for him. They were truly looking out for his best interest, which is more than she can say for his Aunt Suz who she hasn't even met yet. Faith also realizes this year will be the twenty year anniversary of his parents' car accident and passing. How he managed to become such an incredible man with so many obstacles in his way still surprises her, but she's so grateful for his determination.

After clicking on three different websites and seeing videographers pricing, plus the pricing of photography would be substantially more than the package price at the place she really likes. She closes that tab and goes back to the first website.

"You were right, Jonathan. Adding the two together through separate vendors' costs quite a bit more."

"Why don't you reach out to them and see if they have our date available."

Faith laughs. "I'm already on it." She says as she begins typing a message into their 'contact us' form. "Could we get this lucky twice?"

"What do you mean?"

"That the Amethyst Hotel, our number one pick for venue and our number one pick for photographer and videographer would both have availability."

"Right. I think we are incredibly lucky, Faith. Everything is going to work out perfectly for our wedding because it is meant to be."

"I couldn't agree with you more." She says smiling at him.

Chapter 8

Splenditude

Noun; the quality or state of being splendid

The next morning, Faith is in the shower, while Jonathan makes them a quick breakfast. Zeke is laying directly outside the bathroom door in their bedroom comfortably sleeping. When Faith gets out of the shower, Jonathan is sitting on the vanity stool waiting patiently.

She jumps at the sight of him and then giggles with embarrassment. "I thought you were in the kitchen."

"Breakfast is done, and besides I wanted to come watch my naked, sexy, beautiful fiancé get out of the shower. Is that OK with you?"

"Of course it is, but you could have announced yourself. Hell, even just a sound would have been better than sitting there silent like a stalker."

"It was more like a ninja, thank you."

"Whatever you say, Jonathan." She laughs as she towels herself dry.

"You are absolutely stunning though, Faith." He says looking at her intently.

She can tell by the look in his eye he's got more than breakfast in mind. "We don't have time, Jonathan."

"We have all the time in the world, Faith." He stands and walks over to her pulling her naked body into his bare chest. Faith drops the towel as he kisses her passionately.

With heavy breaths he leads her into the bedroom.

"I thought breakfast was ready?" She asks in a low voice with her lips so close to his they brush against them with every word.

"Seeing your naked body stepping out of that steaming hot shower made me crave some desert first."

Jonathan warms breakfast up, while Faith gets dressed and finishes getting ready to go. They quickly eat and head out the door after they put Zeke in his crate.

The drive seems to take longer than the typical forty-five minutes, at least to Faith. Once they arrive at the hotel that is hosting the bridal showcase, Faith hops out of the Mercedes feeling so ready to see what this place has to offer.

There are other couples, friend groups, and moms and daughters all walking in at the same time. From what they can see the building is pretty packed with people. The employees working the event are all funneling them to a check-in point with tables lined up.

While standing in line waiting, Faith actually feels like she has more done than most of the brides here, she overhears some of them don't even have their date or venue figured out. Once they reach the table, Faith answers all the questions and gives them the information about their wedding.

The person behind the table inputs the information in a tablet and then takes a large grab bag from behind them and hands it to Faith. As they walk through they see a lot of travel agents, a couple of smaller venues, some caterers, and bakeries. They stop and talk to some of the vendors. Faith is happy to have the large bag because each vendor they talk to hands them a business card or brochure along with some other trinket to remember them by.

Once they move through the initial twenty or so vendors picking and choosing who to see, the crowd seems to lessen which makes navigating the vendors they want to visit easier. Faith watches the time to be sure they aren't late for the fashion show.

With fifteen minutes to spare they head towards the seating area for the fashion show to make certain they can get seats. The line to get in seems a bit long which worries Faith, but they choose to wait. When they start letting people in Faith and Jonathan attempt to get seats towards the front. They see there is another grab bag beneath all of the chairs.

There is music playing softly in the background. The fashion show host steps out onto the runway. "Welcome, brides, grooms, moms, dads, best men, sisters, maids of honor, cousins, aunts, and grandparents. I'm Jasmine. We've got a full house today and an impressive lineup of designers. I can't wait to get this show started! But first! If you could all look under your chairs, you'll find a bag with some goodies. Which in and of itself is awesome, but if your bag has the words "I Do" on it then I will need you to come up here for further direction."

There is some commotion while everyone reaches under their chairs and checks all sides of their bags.

Jonathan looks at his not finding anything, but when Faith checks, she sees her bag does indeed have the words "I Do" on it. She stands as the music gets slightly louder. The host says "It looks like we have a winner! Everyone give her a round of applause!" The entire room begins clapping as Faith climbs the stairs to get onto the runway. She stands beside Jasmine who tells her she'll come back stage and everything will be explained.

"What's your name?" Jasmine says into the microphone.

"Faith Brandt."

"Welcome and congratulations, Faith. Are you here because you're engaged?"

Before Faith can even answer the host's eyes get huge and say, "Never mind." She takes Faith's hand looking at her ring. "I can clearly see you are in fact engaged!" Jasmine smiles at Faith and asks, "So, who is the lucky guy? Is he here with you today?"

Faith shakes her head yes and then she gestures towards Jonathan and says, "This is my fiancé, Jonathan Hall." Jonathan stands and does a quick wave before sitting back down not wanting the attention on him.

Jasmine elbows Faith. "It looks like you both hit the jackpot!"

Faith smiles, feeling her cheeks turning an even brighter shade of red than they already were.

"What is it that you do for a living, Faith?"

"I'm a first grade teacher in Luna Shores."

Everyone applauses and Jasmine says, "OK, we're going to get the show started!"

The music picks up and gets louder as Jasmine leads the way backstage. Faith follows her unsure of what to expect.

"It's so great to meet you, Faith. We've got a couple of choices for you. With your fiancé being here you may not want to participate in the first option. We would like to offer you the opportunity to be a model and wear one of the dresses and walk the runway."

Faith smiles at the thought, but doesn't want Jonathan to see her in any wedding dress besides the one she chooses for their wedding.

"You're right, Jasmine. I don't think I want to do that. It's an amazing opportunity, but I don't want Jonathan to see me in a wedding dress until our wedding day."

"OK. I'll be right back, I have to go announce the next designer."

Jasmine is only gone a few moments. When she comes back she says, "You still have the option to try on some dresses. You don't have to walk out there. Is there a designer you've been eyeing that we might have here?"

Faith thinks for a moment. "Can I look on my phone? I can't think of their name off the top of my head."

"Of course! I'll be right back. Take your time."

While Jasmine is back on the runway announcing the dresses the crowd is going to see, Faith checks the dresses she has saved to see if any of them have the same designers. She finds three of the dresses have the same one. Caltroney.

When Jasmine comes back Faith tells her that most of the dresses she's got saved are all by Caltroney.

"We have a few of theirs here. Would you like to take a look?"

"I'd love to!"

Jasmine takes Faith into the dressing area which is bustling with the activity of the models coming and going and getting changed in between. It's a little bit of chaos and Faith can't help but be happy at the chance to see the behind the scenes. Jasmine walks to one rack that is chock full of wedding dresses.

"These are all Caltroney." Jasmine motions to someone with a headset on. She comes over and Jasmine continues, "This is Joan, she'll help you try some of these on." Jasmine turns to Joan. "This is Faith Brandt, she's the winner of the I Do bag."

"Congratulations!" Joan tells Faith.

"Thank you."

"I've got to get back out there, but Joan, Faith doesn't know everything she's won yet, so don't go giving anything away." Jasmine winks at Joan and then walks away to go back on stage with the models.

Faith realizes she definitely hadn't thought about what undergarments she would wear under a wedding dress yet, so she mentally adds that to the list of things to shop for.

Joan asks, "Did you have any styles in mind to try on?"

Faith pulls her phone out and shows Joan the ones she has saved.

"Those are all gorgeous and I believe we may have all of them except one."

"Really? That's awesome!"

"Follow me to the dressing room!" She says grabbing the two dresses they have available.

Faith laughs and says, "I was afraid there wouldn't be one. All the models are changing out here." She motions to the chaos surrounding them.

"Yeah, they don't have time for a fitting room." Joan laughs as well.

When Faith enters the room she sees a white silk robe hanging up. Joan puts both dresses on hooks and begins unzipping the bags.

"These two aren't in the show?"

"They might be, but you get first pick." Joan smiles at her and Faith wonders what she did to deserve such a VIP experience. "Go ahead and change into the robe. I'll step out and when you're ready, simply crack the door open."

"OK. I am sure I don't have the right undergarments on for these." Faith says a bit embarrassed.

"That's OK. I wouldn't worry. You and I will be the only ones seeing them and we might be able to do a couple of things to hide bra straps and things."

"Perfect." Faith says and Joan walks out, closing the door behind her.

As Faith changes into the robe, she thinks about how much she wishes her mom, Jackie, and Hope could be there with her. She never imagined she would be trying dresses on all alone. Then again, she never imagined she would win anything here especially during the fashion show.

She cracks the door after she's gotten the robe tied around her. Joan must have been waiting close by because she enters fairly quickly.

"Are you ready?" Joan asks excitedly.

Faith takes a deep breath. "I am."

"Is there one you would like to try on first?"

Faith chooses the strapless one that flares at the bottom.

Joan removes it from the hanger and undoes the zipper in the back. She sets it on the floor and makes an opening for Faith to step into. As Joan pulls it up, Faith removes the robe. Joan zips the dress up.

She stands back looking at Faith and says, "It fits like a glove. That never happens. Not even with the models."

Faith turns to look at herself in the mirror. She sees herself looking back in disbelief. The dress is absolutely gorgeous. It has everything Faith is looking for, but even more than that is the fact that she's wearing a wedding dress for the first time ever.

She takes in the sight as a whole, but then narrows her vision on specific areas. The way the top perfectly hugs her cleavage. The way the dress flows perfectly over her hips and then flares out at the knees creating a bit of drama without hiding her body.

She swings her hips from side to side making the subtle sequins shimmer in the light and the fabric at the bottom makes a swooshing noise. Then she turns to see the back. There is a zipper, but there are also fabric covered round buttons.

Joan smiles, "It seems you really like it. I don't think there's anything not to like!"

"It's absolutely gorgeous, Joan. Would you mind taking a picture so that I can remember what it looked like on me?"

"No problem! Then do you want to try the next one on?"

"Of course I do! I'm kind of wishing I had started with that one though." Faith laughs a little. Joan takes a few pictures from different angles and then begins to work on getting the second dress off the hanger and unfastened.

She puts this one in a puddle on the floor as well, opening a space in the middle for Faith to step into. Once she has the second one set up, she begins to unfasten the first dress and help Faith step out of that one. Once she's out, she steps directly into the second one and Joan fastens the hooks in the back and then zips it.

Faith watches as the sides of the dress get pulled in against her silhouette and loves what she sees.

"Have you ever thought of being a model? The way these dresses fit you would make a runway show a breeze!"

Faith smiles and takes it as a compliment. For a moment she wonders what Jonathan is doing sitting out there all by himself. She was hoping to use the examples of the dresses on the models to figure out what he liked, or didn't like.

She again takes in the sight of herself in a wedding gown and feels as if it could all be a dream. This one is extremely similar, but instead of having a sweetheart neckline with no straps it has a square neckline with wide lace straps. There is still a subtle shimmer and this dress also flares at the bottom. Faith found herself drawn most to those kinds of dresses, but also sheath style.

"Do you have any appointments set up at any bridal stores?"

"I actually just set them up this week. I've got appointments at a few places next Sunday."

"I can imagine you'll have as great an experience doing that as you've had here." Joan smiles.

"I'm sure. Plus my best friend, sister, and mom will be there."

"At least this way you know what you like and how this silhouette looks on you. Although, I don't think there's a silhouette out there that wouldn't look amazing on you."

"Thank you." Faith says. Her cheeks turning a shade of pink that compliments the champagne color of the dress.

"What do you think of the color of this one? It's not as bright white as the other one is."

"I think I might prefer this color."

"Do you want me to take pictures of this one too?"

"Yes, please. Thank you, Joan! You've been great!"

"Aww, you're welcome, Faith. It's been fun working with you. I'll help you get out of this one and get these dresses back out on the rack. Jasmine is almost done out there and then she'll come take you from me."

"OK." Faith says a bit confused as to what could possibly be next.

Chapter 9

Pulchritude

Noun; beauty, especially a woman's beauty

Jasmine comes back to get Faith after she's tried the dresses on. "Come, follow me." She says. "How did that go?"

"It was wonderful! It gave me a really good idea of what I'm looking for too, I think."

"It's always good to have an idea of what you like and what looks best on you when you go shopping for wedding gowns. We've got a couple more surprises in store for you."

"OK." Faith says with a bit of trepidation in her voice.

"Don't worry, you'll love them."

"What about my fiancé?"

"He's been shown the way to the bar and given a couple of drinks on the house."

"Seriously?"

"Seriously." Jasmine chuckles.

Just as Faith is trying to wrap her head around that Jasmine motions for her to sit down on a seat in front of a large vanity with a huge lighted mirror. Faith sees a gentleman standing beside the vanity with makeup brushes in hand.

"Trey will take it from here."

Faith sits down and Trey smiles.

"I honestly am not sure what I could possibly improve on, but I'm up for the challenge." He says.

Faith smiles. "What are you going to be doing?"

"Well, we'll start with your makeup and then I'll do your hair. I did everything for the models today as well. I have my own company where we come to your house or your venue and do yours and your bridal party's hair and makeup on the day of your wedding."

"That's awesome!"

"We enjoy it! Since you won today we'll need to set something up to get you on the books."

"What do you mean?"

"You've won our services for your big day!"

"You're kidding me! You can't be serious." Faith shakes her head.

Trey laughs. "I am completely serious and I am not kidding."

Faith still can't believe her ears. "This is incredible! I had no idea!"

"We like to keep the surprises coming!"

"I can see that!"

"Are you ready to get started?"

"Absolutely!" Faith says excitedly.

Trey begins with her makeup. After about twenty minutes he switches to her hair.

"Do you and your fiancé have anything planned tonight? Because after I get done with you, you should really make some plans!" He chuckles.

"We were planning on grabbing some food after the showcase."

"That's a great idea! Are you guys from around here?"

"We live in Luna Shores."

"Oh, so not too far."

"Not at all."

"We're almost finished here and then Jasmine will be back again."

"There can't possibly be more." Faith says in disbelief.

"I cannot confirm nor deny that." Trey says with a smirk which gives it away entirely.

"I can't think of anything else you guys could do for me."

"That is the point."

"How many times have you done this?"

"We choose one person from the crowd every show. So there will be another one tomorrow."

"That's incredible."

"It really is. Some of them are so blown away, they cry. You can't cry now though. Your makeup is absolutely perfect."

When he's finished curling and styling her hair, Jasmine is back in time for the reveal. Faith looks at her hair and makeup in the mirror, it's not what she would want for her wedding, but it's perfect for today!

"Trey, you're so talented. Thank you so much!"

"Of course, Faith! It was great to meet you and I can't wait for your big day."

They exchange the details and Trey tells her he'll be in touch before the big day to confirm there are no changes. Then Jasmine has Faith follow her once again. She leads her into a small conference room where a man is sitting.

"Faith, it is my pleasure to introduce you to Mr. Victor Caltroney."

Faith holds out her hand to shake his. "It is an honor, sir. I was literally just wearing a couple of your dresses."

"I heard! It's great to meet you as well, Faith."

Jasmine motions for Faith to sit down at the table then she gives Mr. Caltroney and Faith each a bottle of water.

"Thank you, Jasmine." Faith says.

Jasmine takes a seat next to Faith and begins to explain. "I'm sure you are probably wondering what you're doing here. Once we approached Mr. Caltroney and explained to him that he is your designer of choice he wanted to do something special for you."

Faith nods, less out of understanding and more because she wants Jasmine to continue.

Mr. Caltroney takes over the explanation. "Faith, I would be honored to create a custom designed wedding gown for you."

Faith feels tears begin to well up in her eyes, but quickly remembers what Trey told her. "I'm sorry. I don't know what to say. Thank you. This is incredible. I can't…there's no way. Thank you isn't even enough."

"It is more than enough. I assure you." Mr. Caltroney says. "My mom was a teacher when she was alive. I'm more than happy to do this for an educator that helps to shape the minds of our future."

"That is so kind of you, Mr. Caltroney. It would be an absolute privilege to wear one of your gowns, sir."

Caltroney brings out a pad of paper and a pencil. "We'll need to get some measurements if that's OK. I'll also be asking you a lot of questions about your preferences."

Faith takes a deep breath trying to wrap her head around what is about to happen. "OK."

A short statured woman with dark hair knocks on the glass conference room door. Mr. Caltroney motions for her to come in.

"This is my assistant Tracy, she'll be the one to take your measurements."

"OK, that sounds good." Faith stands. Tracy motions for her to step up onto the pedestal she placed on the floor along with a step stool for herself. Tracy begins taking measurements and writing them down in her little spiral notebook.

Mr. Caltroney begins asking Faith questions about what she likes. Jasmine informs him of the two dresses she tried on and Mr. Caltroney asks her specifically what she liked or didn't like about those.

The measurements and questions go on for nearly a half an hour. Then Mr. Caltroney begins drawing up a rough rendition of Faith's custom dress. By the time he turns the paper around to show Faith the sketch, her anticipation has built up so much.

When she sees the beautiful drawing signed by Mr. Caltroney himself her breath is taken away. She feels the tears begin to form once again at the thought of walking down the aisle to Jonathan, wearing that dress. She pushes the tears away and says, "It is absolutely perfect Mr. Caltroney. I couldn't possibly have described this, but somehow, from the questions you asked this is exactly what I was envisioning. Thank you so much! I can't wait to see this in person!"

"You're so welcome, Faith. I'm so glad you love it! It's my pleasure to create this for you!"

"I can't believe that is going to be my dress!"

"We'll keep in touch letting you know how the production is going." Tracy tells Faith.

Faith stands, thanking them once again and shakes Mr. Caltroney's hand, thanking him profusely.

Jasmine shows Faith the way to the bar where Jonathan is waiting, watching the baseball game on the TV above the bar.

His face lights up as he sees Faith approach.

"I'm so sorry. I had no idea it was going to take so long."

"You don't have to apologize. Jasmine explained every-thing to me. I'm so happy you got this opportunity, Faith! I bet it was incredible."

"It really was. I missed having my mom, Hope, and Jackie there, but I'm sure they'll understand."

"They will."

"What are you going to do about the appointments you have set up next Sunday?"

Faith thinks for a moment. "I'm not sure. My mom is going to want to see me in dresses and I can try on one of the ones I tried on today for them all to see. I should only keep one of the appointments though."

"That's probably a good idea. Your hair and makeup look beautiful, but it always does."

Jonathan leans in to kiss Faith then she sits down in the bar stool beside him.

"I can order you a drink if you'd like."

"I would like." She smiles at him.

He motions for the bartender and Faith is reminded of the first night they met. It was Jackie's birthday and she went up to the bar to buy drinks for Jackie and herself. Jonathan stopped her and insisted that he buy them their drinks.

"So while you waited here, did you happen to find a restaurant? I'm hungry."

"I did find a place. We can get going right away or we can always eat here too if you're that hungry."

"I think I'll be OK. Is the restaurant close?"

"Less than ten minutes away."

"OK."

The bartender brings Faith's glass of wine.

Jonathan watches Faith as she takes a sip, closing her eyes as she enjoys the red cabernet.

She knows Jonathan wouldn't let anything happen to her, but she keeps her wine glass in her hand anyway. Ever since she was drugged by a couple of truckers at Lee's Pub on a random Friday night, she doesn't feel entirely comfortable in bar settings. Her anxiety has gotten better, but she's not sure if it will ever go away completely.

In some respects she doesn't want it to since it keeps her diligent in protecting herself. Having Jonathan with her does silence those thoughts somewhat. She knows he would do anything to protect her.

Faith takes another drink of her wine.

"I'm glad you had such a fun day, Faith. If anyone deserves to be pampered like that, it's you."

"Thank you, Jonathan. I really couldn't believe it was happening. I'm sorry you had to sit here and wait."

"It was totally worth it."

Chapter 10

Habitude

Noun; habitual disposition or mode of behavior or procedure

The next day at Sunday night dinner, Faith explains to her mom and Hope everything that happened at the bridal show.

"That's incredible that Mr. Caltroney is going to make a custom gown for you!" Hope says.

"I know. I couldn't believe it. I couldn't believe the whole thing. It was as if I stepped into a dream. Lying in bed last night I was replaying the whole thing and kept questioning if it really did happen. It seemed like there's no way that all happened to me."

"I do wish we could have been there." Diane says.

"I know, Mom. I was thinking that the entire time too! I'm going to keep one of the appointments so you guys can still see me in a dress, I'll have to try to find one that's close to what we designed."

"Did they let you take a picture of the sketch?"

"No. I did get pictures of the two dresses I tried on though."

"That's good."

Faith pulls her phone from her pocket and sits down next to Diane and shows her the pictures first, then moves over next to Hope and Andy. She makes sure Jonathan doesn't see them.

"Those are beautiful Faith. I can't imagine what the designer could have drawn up that's better, but I'm excited to see it." Diane says.

"How long did they say it would take?" Andy asks.

"They didn't really say, but I shouldn't need any alterations since they took measurements."

"That's helpful. Alterations can take months. When my cousin got married I think hers took like three months, and that was on top of the amount of time it took to get her dress in."

"I get it, they're all works of art, you can't rush that, but also it makes it harder for people who are planning a wedding on a tight deadline. Ours isn't even a year out and some of the vendors yesterday were a bit taken aback at how quickly we were trying to get married. I didn't feel like it was all that quick when we chose the date."

Jonathan pats her knee. "We'll get it all figured out. I have no doubt."

Faith smiles at him. "We will, but mostly me." She laughs then addresses her parents and Hope. "Speaking of which, I was hoping to take some time off from the café a bit earlier than normal. With planning the wedding and school coming up in just a few weeks I'm starting to feel the pressure."

Frank nods. "If that's what you need, peanut. Take the time. We'll be fine."

Hope raises a finger. "I second that."

Diane nods her head in agreement.

"I feel bad, like I'm leaving you high and dry."

"It's not that big of a deal. Georgina is back from vacation and Valerie has been doing really well. I'm pretty sure she's going to work evenings after school starts back up." Hope says.

"She's a junior this year, right?" Faith asks.

"Yeah, I'm not sure what her plans are for after she graduates, but we've got some time before that happens."

Diane slaps her knees. "Are you all ready for dinner?"

Everyone says 'yes' simultaneously and Frank laughs. "We clearly all love your cooking, my love."

After dinner Jonathan and Frank take Zeke and Orpheus for a walk. While they're gone, Diane, Faith, Hope and Andy talk a little more about the wedding, but then the subject switches to Hope.

"Are you planning anything for your graduation, Despair?" Faith asks.

"A vacation."

"It is well deserved." Diane says.

"Where are you planning on going?"

"Anywhere warm, hopefully with a beach!"

"I think I'm going to plan it and surprise her." Andy says.

"That's an awesome idea! That's actually what Jonathan is doing for our honeymoon."

"Seriously?" Hope asks.

"Yup. But back to you. You're not planning a party or anything?"

"No, I don't need a party."

"What if your dad and I want to throw you one?" Diane asks.

"I'll show up if you want to have a party for me. I'm just not going to plan it for myself."

"That's fair." Faith says.

Jonathan and Frank walk through the door with Zeke and Orpheus leading the way and nearly tangling their leashes together.

Faith starts laughing and everyone joins in. Frank quickly unhooks Orpheus' leash untangling them instantly. Zeke tries to run over to Faith, but the leash stops him in his tracks and yanks Jonathan's arm.

Faith laughs again as Jonathan leans down to unhook the leash from Zeke, making him sit first. As soon as he feels the clip release, Zeke takes off across the living room and runs straight to Faith with his tail wagging wildly behind him.

"I missed you too, Zekie." Faith says as she scratches under his chin.

"What about me?" Jonathan asks trying to keep the corners of his mouth from turning up.

"Of course I missed you too."

Jonathan leans down and gives her a quick kiss.

"What were you guys talking about before we walked in?"

"We were talking about Hope's graduation coming up."

"Yeah, Jonomeister, you guys are lucky you didn't choose the weekend after the date you did. I definitely wouldn't be making it."

"It's a good thing then." Jonathan says laughing. "Seriously though, congratulations."

"Well, I'm not done yet."

"You're really close." Jonathan offers. "We would be happy to host a party at our house. Right, Faith?"

"Yeah, we won't be able to go on our honeymoon for a few weeks after the wedding anyways."

"Really?" Hope asks in disbelief.

"Of course! You deserve a party." Faith looks at her mom. "You and dad can help. We don't want to take it away from you guys."

"That works. Your house is probably a better place to have it anyway."

"It's definitely big enough." Faith elbows Jonathan jokingly.

"That was the point." Jonathan chuckles.

"Once it gets a little closer we'll decide on a day and start planning." Diane says.

Faith gets up to go to the bathroom and Diane steps out of the room with her.

"You're sure it'll be OK to have the party at your house so soon after the wedding? It'll be like planning two parties at once."

"It'll be OK, Mom. You'll be able to help and it'll be similar to the party we just had for the fourth of July except we'll actually have the house set up with our new furniture."

"OK."

Diane walks back into the living room. When Faith comes back in Hope and Andy stand and announce they will be heading out. They hug everyone, including the dogs and Frank and Diane walk them to the door.

As Frank is sitting back down in his arm chair he says, "I like them together. Hope seems happier."

"She does." Faith agrees. "Andy has been good for her."

Diane smiles. "Maybe this time next year we'll be planning their wedding."

"It could happen." Jonathan says.

"You know I don't understand exactly why Andy wants their pronouns to be they/them, but it doesn't really matter to me." Frank says with a shrug.

"It's not about you understanding why, Dad. It's about you being understanding of it and respectful."

"I think I have been." He says introspectively.

"You have and I'm sure they appreciate it very much."

"It doesn't matter to me what someone wants to be called, if that's what they want." Diane says matter of factly. "Who am I to tell them otherwise? It's their choice, right?"

"Exactly, ma'am." Jonathan agrees.

Diane looks at Faith with a look of realization. "Not to change the subject, but if the designer is creating you a custom gown, then we won't be able to buy you your dress."

"No, I know. I thought of that too. You guys don't have to pay for anything at all."

Diane looks at Frank and he nods. "We would like to pay for something. We budgeted a little over two thousand for your dress, if there's something else around that amount that we could cover, we would like to do that."

"Maybe the florist." Faith offers. "Those quotes were around that amount, right?"

Jonathan looks surprised. "For flowers?"

"I told you things are more expensive than you think. It's like if you put the label 'wedding' on something it gives the company a reason to charge well over twice the normal price." Faith explains.

"That's just wrong." Jonathan says.

"That's capitalism, son." Frank says simply.

"We'll get the flowers then." Diane says.

"I know this isn't how we imagined going wedding dress shopping or anything, but it's too amazing of an opportunity to pass up."

"I completely agree, honey. I wouldn't expect you to tell a wedding gown designer that you don't want them to create a custom gown for you for free. That would simply be rude."

"I enjoyed the surprise, of course, but I also missed having you guys there with me."

"I can imagine, sweetheart. But we'll still get to go see you try on dresses, so it isn't an issue. We just won't get to see your dress until it's finished."

Faith and Jonathan stay for a little while longer with Frank and Jonathan talking baseball and Diane and Faith talking wedding plans while Zeke and Orpheus sleep nestled together on the floor.

Chapter 11

Incertitude

Noun; absence of assurance or confidence, doubt

The next morning Faith wakes up bright and early then quickly gets ready for her shift at the café. They hadn't talked about when her last shift would actually be so she keeps that in the front of her mind as she gets ready to be sure she talks to Hope about it when she gets there.

Once she gets to the café, she walks past the outdoor seating area where Georgina is sitting smoking a cigarette.

"Good morning, Georgina."

"Good morning, Miss Faith. How are you doing today?"

"I'm doing alright. Slept pretty good. I'm not sure exactly when, but I wanted to give you a heads up that my last day of the summer is going to be coming up a little quicker. I'm planning my wedding and I have to prep for the school year."

"That's understandable. Thanks for letting me know. You know how much I love waitressing with you! You help make the day go by quicker, I never have to tell you what to do and you help cover my tables when I need you to. I'll miss you being here, like I always do, but you know we'll be fine."

"I do, and thanks Georgina."

"You're welcome, sweetie."

"I'll see you inside when you're ready."

Georgina takes another hit of her cigarette as she nods her head. Faith walks through the door and goes right into the office where Hope is sitting at her desk laser focused on her laptop screen.

"Hey, Hope."

Without looking up from the screen Hope says, "Hey, Doubt. I'm surprised you're here. I thought we all agreed you were done for the summer."

A bit taken aback Faith says, "Oh, I didn't know when that started and figured I was on the schedule for today so I should be here."

"That's fine then. You can be done tomorrow if you want. Whatever works."

"OK." Faith says thinking for a moment. "That will work. I also let Georgina know."

"That was nice of you. I'm sure she appreciates that."

"What are you so diligently looking for?"

"There's something not quite right with this invoice from the company we get our fries from."

"Do you want me to take a look? Maybe a fresh set of eyes will help."

"Sure."

Faith is a little surprised her sister gave up so easily. Part of her wants to ask if Hope is feeling OK this morning, but instead she lets it go and walks over to look at Hope's screen.

She looks at the top of the invoice and then scrolls down to the bottom. "Could it be that there's two delivery fees listed on here?"

Hope looks at her with wide eyes. "You're kidding me!"

"Nope. Look." Faith gestures towards the screen for Hope to see for herself.

"Holy shit. You're right, Doubt."

"So the question is why are they trying to double charge us for delivery."

"I am going to call them as soon as they open to find that out! Thanks for looking. I woke up with a headache and this screen is only making it worse."

"Happy to help! I'm going to see what Mom needs out front."

"OK."

Faith heads to the front of the café. She sees her mom putting the till into the register. Faith begins taking the chairs down from the tables and wiping them all down.

"Good morning, Faith." Diane says.

"Good morning, Mom."

"I didn't think you were going to be here."

"That's what Hope said too." Faith chuckles. "She basically told me today is my last day."

"Well good. You've got other things to do besides be here. We'll be fine."

"That's what Georgina said when I told her too."

The kitchen staff is working hard getting everything prepared for the breakfast rush. The doors of the café will open soon. Faith takes the stools down from the front counter and sets them carefully on the floor as Diane follows behind her with a rag.

"I am going to miss seeing you guys so much, but I'm not going to miss going home exhausted every night."

"I can't say I blame you for that. You worked so hard going to school to be a teacher and yet you still help out during the summers here. We appreciate it, of course, but if at some point you change your mind about working here we'll understand."

"Thank you, Mom."

Diane smiles at her. "It's time, Faith. Do you want to unlock the doors?"

Faith unlocks the doors and within less than a minute there are five customers taking their seats.

Georgina and Faith both begin taking orders and gives them to the kitchen staff. Waitressing isn't something Faith enjoys, but it's been a part of her life for as long as she can remember. Her parents opened the café when she was ten and it's been a staple in their lives ever since.

She's not sure if she'd know what to do with herself if she wasn't doing this in the summers, especially when she doesn't have any little ones to take care of at home. She could probably spend a little more time in her garden then.

The café feels like something that has always tied them together as a family and it feels as if not having any part of it at all would lessen Faith's connection to her family somehow. She isn't sure she's willing to give up that connection, not yet anyway.

Jonathan stops in the café for his lunch so Faith takes her break at the same time.

She tells him about what her mom said earlier.

"I think it's something we should think about. You don't need to waitress in the summers, Faith."

"It's not as much about the need to do it, Jonathan."

"I get that, but think of all the other things you could do in your spare time."

"I have been thinking about that. There's just something about this place." She looks around. "It's kind of like a childhood home in a way."

"I can understand how that would be the case."

When they finish eating their lunch, Faith walks Jonathan out the door. He pulls her in for a quick kiss and then she heads back into the café.

About an hour before her shift ends a tall broad shouldered man dressed in an expensive suit sits down at one of her tables.

"Good afternoon, I'm Faith and I'll be your waitress. What can I start you off with?" She asks him.

A smile slowly spreads across his face. "Hi, Faith. It's great to meet you. I'll start off with a water."

"Perfect. I'll be right back with that." As she turns to walk away the man reaches for her hand, stopping her.

He pulls his hand away quickly as he says, "I'm so sorry. I have to ask. Is your fiancé Jonathan Hall?"

Faith is quite confused at his question, but with it being such a small town she assumes maybe he works with Jonathan at Kansen Corp. "Yes, as a matter of fact, he is."

"I thought so! It's so great to meet you!" He says excitedly reaching to shake her hand. She swears she can see his eyes go big at the sight of her engagement ring.

"How do you know Jonathan?"

"We went to high school together actually. I just moved back. I was living in Illinois, but a divorce gave me the excuse I needed to move closer to home."

"That's nice." Faith says, unsure of what to say.

"I actually ran into Jonathan in Caulfield not too long ago. I told him I would reach out to him, but then I found myself driving into Luna Shores and figured I'd stop for a bite to eat at Love's café."

"Well, we're happy you did."

"I'm glad to hear you say that."

Faith smiles and says, "I'll go get your water for you now."

"OK. I'm going to look at the menu."

"Sounds good."

As she walks away she can feel his eyes on her, but tries to ignore the feeling. She fills the cup with some ice hearing it clink against the plastic as it falls in. She recalls that he said he saw Jonathan in Caulfield. It could have been while they were at the bridal show, but why wouldn't Jonathan have mentioned anything?

Before she knows it the cold water is running over the edge of the cup and spilling onto her hand. Instinctively she pulls her hand out of the stream, stopping the flow of water. She grabs a towel and dries the cup before taking it to the man's table.

"Did you have a chance to figure out what you want to order?" She asks suddenly realizing he hadn't told her his name.

"I did. I'll take the double cheese burger with a side of fries and a root beer float." The man smiles and Faith smiles back politely.

If it didn't seem like he was up to something Faith would think he's a pretty good guy.

"I'll get that order put in. What did you say your name was?"

"Oh, I'm sorry! It's Rowen. Rowen Mitchell."

"It's nice to meet you, Rowen. Your food should be up shortly."

"Great! Thank you, Faith."

She walks away, again feeling his gaze on her. She puts the order in and walks back to the office.

With her head and her voice low she says, "Hope, I need your help!"

Hope's head picks up. "I'm game. What can I help with?"

"There's this guy."

"You're engaged. Just walk away and forget about him."

"No. It's not like that. He says he knows Jonathan from high school. It seems like he's trying to do something, I can't figure out what."

Hope looks at Faith with slight annoyance. "He's a guy. You're a beautiful woman. What do you think he's trying to do, Doubt?"

Faith rolls her eyes at her sister. "No, I mean, yeah probably, but I mean I think it's something else."

"What is it that you need me to do?"

"Can you go out there and gauge him for me? Use your magical powers to figure this guy out."

"Sure." Hope says as she stands up from her desk.

Hope walks out into the café and instantly knows which guy Faith is referencing. She walks over to him and confidently introduces herself. "Hi, I'm Hope, Faith's sister. She said you knew Jonathan?"

"Yeah." Rowen says with a confused look on his face.

"So what else brings you in today?" She says pulling the chair out that sits directly next to Rowen.

His voice stammers a bit when he says, "I'm not sure I know what you mean. Like I told Faith, I'm only here for the food. When Jonathan mentioned that your parents owned Love's Café it reminded me of how amazing the food was and then I started craving a good burger so I drove to Luna Shores for some high school nostalgia. I had no idea Faith was even going to be my waitress." He puts his hands up in an effort to show that he has nothing to hide.

"So, you don't live in Luna Shores anymore?"

"No, I lived in the Chicago area, but when I moved back I decided Caulfield would be a better fit for me now. I have a practice there."

"Oh, you're a lawyer."

"I am."

Hope simply nods her head, stands, and walks away. Faith ducks her head back from the corner she was peeking around and walks back to the office with Hope following behind her.

"So…what did you think?"

"He's a lawyer so that explains it. Honestly, and I can't believe I'm about to say this, I think he's being honest. I don't think he came here with any ill intentions."

Faith lets out a heavy breath. "OK. Thanks, Hope. You know how much I value your opinion. It doesn't hurt that your intuition is usually spot on."

Hope smiles proudly. "I'm glad my trauma has given me a gift I can use to help others." She says sarcastically.

Faith laughs dryly and then heads back to the kitchen to grab Rowen's lunch.

She sees him watching her as she brings his plate to his table so she smiles politely.

As she sets his plate down in front of him she says, "You actually missed Jonathan by a couple of hours. He was here for his lunch."

"I wish I would have come earlier then. I was happy to run into him and it's really cool to have met you today."

"I'll let him know you stopped by." Faith turns to walk away, but Rowen stops her again, reaching for her hand.

"Wait, Faith?"

She turns back towards him confusion on her face and feeling a mild uncomfortable feeling creep up, but she doesn't pull her hand away.

"Could you not tell him? I'm afraid he might think I was up to something nefarious." He shrugs his shoulders. "I'd hate to have him think I was trying to hit on you behind his back or something."

"Well, I'm glad to know that's not your purpose here." Faith pulls her hand away slowly. "Enjoy your meal Rowen. I'll be back in a bit to check and make sure you're still set."

"Thank you, Faith."

She walks away calmly, but as soon as she gets around the corner she hustles into the office and closes the door leaning up against it.

Hope looks up at her. Half laughing she asks, "What happened?"

"I gave him his food and told him he'd missed Jonathan by a few hours and that I'd tell him he stopped in. Then he asked me not to tell him because he didn't want Jonathan to think he was here hitting on me and I said I was glad to know that isn't why he's here and to enjoy his food. Then I walked away."

"So you never agreed not to tell Jonathan?"

"No! Of course I didn't agree to that! I'm not going to lie to my fiancé!"

"Well, technically it isn't lying when you don't say anything, but I agree it's a slippery slope."

"I don't see the difference."

"Jonathan better know how lucky he is."

"I'm pretty sure he does."

"Maybe telling him Rowen was here will help to remind him." Hope says in a half serious tone.

"I'm not going to tell him as a way of playing games either, Despair."

"I didn't say you should play games just that a reminder never hurts." She shrugs.

Faith stands reaching for the door knob. "I'm so glad my shift is almost done."

"Not only your shift today. You're done for the rest of the year!"

"I nearly forgot!"

"I don't want to see you here tomorrow."

"Don't worry. I'm going to sleep in!" Faith says as she heads back out into the café to check in with her other tables.

As she makes her rounds she still feels Rowen watching her. A part of her wants to confront him, the other part chalks it up to curiosity. She accidentally glances his way while handing a customer their check. He doesn't look away and instead holds her gaze for what feels like a moment too long before Faith breaks the eye contact by looking back to her customer, smiling at them.

When she's done taking care of that customer's payment she walks back over to Rowen's table and asks, "How are you doing? Can I get you anything else?"

"No, thank you though, Faith. I'm fine. I'll take the check, please."

"I'll be right back."

She is only gone for a moment, but feels his eyes follow her the entire time. She can't quite place the look on his face as she's walking back towards him, but chooses to ignore it knowing that he'll be leaving after he'd paid.

Faith sets the slip of paper down on the table and Rowen sets a one-hundred dollar bill down on top of it.

She takes it and makes change for him then brings it back to the table.

"Thank you, Faith. It really was great to meet you!"

"Thanks, Rowen. It was great to meet you too."

"I'm sure I'll see you again soon."

Faith isn't sure how to take that so she simply smiles as kindly as she can muster and walks back to the counter to cover Georgina for her break.

Rowen catches her eye as he walks out the door and nods in her direction. Faith feels her cheeks turn pink unsure of why she's having that involuntary reaction.

Chapter 12

Vicissitude

Noun; the quality or state of being changeable, mutability

Faith's attempt to stay busy until Jonathan gets home is proving futile. She's sitting in their office, staring at the workbook on the too bright laptop screen, completely unable to concentrate. She keeps going back over the encounter with Rowen and how she's going to tell Jonathan.

When she hears the sound of the service door open and Zeke's paws running across the travertine floor, she feels the anxiety that's been building ever since Rowen walked through Love's Café's doors overflow. Faith knows she won't be able to wait to have this conversation.

She stands, determined to talk to him as soon the opportunity presents itself. Jonathan's face lights up at the sight of her. He wraps his arms around her, placing one under her ass, he picks her up. She instinctively wraps her legs around him as he leans in to kiss her.

As he sets her down she says, "You seem to be in a good mood."

"I am!"

"Is there a reason?"

"Can't I sinmply be happy to come home to my beautiful fiancé?"

"Of course you can and you should be."

"How was your day?"

This is it. The opportunity has presented itself. Faith takes a deep breath trying to calm herself and shove the anxiety back down out of her throat so she can speak. "Do you know a guy named Rowen?"

She watches Jonathan's face for any sign of a reaction to the name, but doesn't see one.

"Yeah, I actually ran into him in Caulfield. We went to high school together."

"That's what he said. He stopped in today, he said he just had a craving for our food."

Jonathan narrows his eyes. "When I saw him I mentioned that I was engaged to you and your parents own Love's Café. It was more for reference than anything, but apparently he felt the need to come see you."

"He asked me not to say anything. He thought you would think he came in to hit on me."

"Did he?"

"Not directly." Faith can see anger just below the surface on Jonathan's face. She doesn't want to say anything that will make his anger worse, but she also needs to be honest.

"What exactly does that mean?"

"Overall he seemed polite, it just seemed like he enjoyed watching me a bit too much. His attention made me uncomfortable."

"Did you tell him that?"

"Well, no, it wasn't exactly obvious, if that makes sense. Plus, I was working and didn't want to be outwardly rude when he technically wasn't doing anything wrong."

"Faith, if he was making you uncomfortable then he was doing something wrong."

"I understand that, but it's not always easy in the moment." Faith looks down at the floor.

Jonathan places a finger under her chin and gently lifts so she's looking him in the eyes. "I'm glad you told me. If he reaches out to me I'll talk to him about it." Jonathan brushes a piece of hair from Faith's face.

"OK. I didn't agree to not tell you." Faith shakes her head.

"I didn't think you did."

"Hope talked to him because I wasn't sure what he was after."

"Well, knowing Rowen he was after you."

"What makes you say that?" Faith's eyebrows tense.

"He's always been like that. In high school any girl I dated he made every attempt to mess around with after we broke up."

"That's messed up."

"Yeah. He's not a bad guy, just competitive like that and a bit of a womanizer."

"I did get that feeling."

"What did Hope say about him?"

"She said she didn't think he was lying about his reason for being there and that him being a lawyer basically explains everything."

Jonathan laughs loudly. "Hope is hilarious and is at least partially right."

"You didn't get his number when you saw him?" Faith questions.

"No, he was leaving with a woman and I didn't want to interrupt that."

Faith rolls her eyes and decides to change the subject. "How was your day?"

"It was really good! I got some news this afternoon."

"Really? Care to share?"

"I'm on the short list of candidates for CEO." Jonathan smiles widely.

"Jonathan, that is incredible!"

"I know, right! I'm so happy! A little nervous, but my plan is unfolding pretty perfectly!"

"I guess it is! I'm so happy for you! You deserve this so much!" Faith walks into the kitchen and removes two wine glasses from the cabinet, then grabs a bottle of wine and uncorks it. "We need to celebrate!"

Jonathan laughs. "I haven't gotten the job yet."

"You will! They'd be stupid not to give it to you!"

"Yeah. Get this, I'm going up against Vern."

Faith makes a sour face and then says, "Eww, now there's a complete creep!"

Jonathan laughs harder. "Such a creep."

"He's definitely not getting that job!"

"No, I'll make sure that doesn't happen. He wouldn't bring anything good to the company."

"So when do you find out for sure?"

"They're going to hold interviews next week on Tuesday and we should be notified by Friday. The position would start next month then."

"That's amazing, Jonathan!" Faith says as she hands him the glass of wine.

"Thank you, Faith. I honestly couldn't wait to get home and tell you about it!"

"I'm sorry I made you wait so long."

"It's OK. I'm glad you told me about Rowen." His eyes searching hers.

"Me too. It was bothering me from the moment he walked through the doors."

"You don't have to worry about him, Faith."

"Thank you, Jonathan." Faith smiles knowing Jonathan would do anything for her.

As they finish their glasses of wine, they discuss a little about what changes will happen when Jonathan gets the promotion while they make dinner together.

After dinner, they head out to the fire pit. Jonathan lights a fire and they sit watching the sun go down over Amethyst Bay. The sky's colors change from warm to cool. Before too long they see the first twinkles of stars against the inky blue night sky.

Faith is thinking about everything she will be able to accomplish now that she won't be working at the café. Jonathan thinks of how the CEO promotion will change their lives.

Chapter 13

Crassitude

Noun; the quality or state of being crass, grossness

Jonathan had made the decision the moment Faith told him about Rowen coming into the café on Monday that he would spend tonight hunting Rowen down in Caulfield. He wouldn't go home until he had a chance to confront him. There's no way he can let him get away with showing up at his fiancé's work, out of the blue, acting like he wasn't doing anything wrong.

No, Jonathan couldn't allow that kind of behavior, especially from someone who claims to be a friend, even if he did recently come back into his life. He's not planning on hurting him, Jonathan simply wants to remind Rowen of his place and to make it clear if he steps out of that place again there will be grave consequences.

First, Jonathan drives to Duffy's bar since that's where he'd seen him the first time. When he sees Rowen isn't there, he checks the Blue Rooster. Again, Rowen is nowhere in sight.

Jonathan sits down to enjoy a drink for a moment thinking maybe he should have swapped cars. He forces the thought away remembering what it felt like to climb into bed with Faith after not acting on his urge.

Just as he swallows down the cold brown liquid he swears he hears Rowen's voice. He glances around the room then staring at the door. The music is quite loud, could he have been imagining it?

Before he can answer that question he sees Rowen by the pool table with his arm hanging on a different woman than from a couple weekends ago. He sets the sweaty highball glass down on the bar top and the ice cubes shift. He watches Rowen a few moments before deciding he can't sit there any longer.

As Jonathan walks over to him, he puts a fake smile on in an attempt to make it seem like everything is fine. It's not a total lie, Jonathan is happy to see him, only not for the reason Rowen will think.

Rowen turns just enough to see Jonathan striding over and his face lights up. If he were concerned about why Jonathan were here he wasn't showing it.

"Hey, man!" Rowen greets him with a handshake and a one arm hug.

"It's good to see you again!" Jonathan says as he takes a step back from the short embrace.

"How are things going? Sorry I haven't gotten in touch yet, things have been crazy at the practice and my free time has been taken up with this." He nods his head in the direction of the woman he had his arm around.

Jonathan smiles. "No big deal, man. I totally get it, my job is demanding too, plus planning a wedding. I don't have much free time." He shrugs his shoulders.

Rowen looks around. "Is Faith here with you?"

"Not tonight. I actually wanted to talk to you about that." As the words come out of Jonathan's mouth he watches the color drain out of Rowen's face as the realization sets in.

"I wasn't hitting on her, honest. I wanted some food nostalgia. It tasted just like it did in high school! It was incredible!"

"I get it, and I'd even understand if you were hitting on her. She's a gorgeous woman, but she's MY woman and it's my understanding you knew that as soon as you saw her."

Rowen looks down at his cognac colored oxfords. "I did." He looks back up at Jonathan with indignation in his eyes. "I'm not sure what she told you, but I didn't say a single thing that was inappropriate. Her sister even came over to question me and my intentions. I was polite. I wouldn't do something to disrespect you like that, Jonathan."

"See, Rowen, here's the thing. I'm not nearly as worried about you disrespecting me, as I am about you disrespecting my future wife." He takes a step forward, closing the space between them. Rowen fidgets, but doesn't take a step back. Jonathan lowers his voice and says, "You don't want to know what I'd do to you if you disrespect her again."

Rowen could barely hear him over the music. "Woah, Jonathan. I didn't disrespect her. You've got it all wrong."

"Denying it isn't going to do you any favors, Rowen."

"I'm not sure what I did that was disrespectful. I went, I introduced myself, I had lunch and I left."

"And you watched her like a stalker the entire time."

"I'd have to pluck my eyes out to not notice how sexy she is."

"If it happens again you won't have to worry about doing it yourself because I'll take care of it for you."

"You're serious? I am an officer of the court. You don't want to threaten me."

"It's not a threat Rowen, it's a promise. You've been like this for as long as I can remember. I cannot allow you to treat my fiancé like every other woman you take home from the bar."

"That was high school, Jonathan. I've grown and matured since then. And this?" He nods to the woman behind him at the pool table. "This is because I'm divorced and I can. I wouldn't go after your fiancé." He shakes his head as if the thought is incomprehensible to him.

"You went after every ex I had in high school as if you couldn't get enough of my sloppy seconds."

"That was just coincidence." He nudges Jonathan with his elbow. "High school was slim pickings and those girls were easy targets, they were getting over you by getting under me." He laughs at his own joke.

Jonathan doesn't find that nearly as amusing as Rowen does. He stands there looking at him expressionless.

Rowen can't handle the awkwardness so he says, "Loosen up man, it was only a joke."

"I need you to take this seriously because I am not joking."

"Alright, alright. I get it. Message received loud and clear, man. I won't go into Love's Café again and I won't talk to Faith ever again."

"Oh, you'll talk to her again."

Rowen shoots Jonathan a thoroughly confused look. "What do you mean? I thought you wanted me to leave her alone?"

"Oh, I do, but first I need you to apologize to her."

"How am I supposed to do that if you don't want me near her?"

"We'll all go out to dinner, your treat."

Rowen blinks his eyes trying to make sense of what Jonathan is saying. "You want me to take you both to dinner to apologize to Faith?"

"Exactly. And this." Jonathan gestures to himself and then to Rowen. "This never happened."

"Understood."

"So, when do you want to do dinner? Jonathan asks as he pulls his phone from his pocket.

Rowen brushes the few strands of his dark hair that are tickling his forehead back in place. "Umm, next weekend?"

"Perfect. Let's do Saturday since I'm getting a promotion on Friday and would like to celebrate with Faith alone."

"Congratulations, man."

"Thanks." Jonathan begins to walk away, he waves and says, "See you Saturday. Text me the restaurant and time."

Jonathan feels Rowen stare behind him as he walks outside feeling like he made his point and from here on out Rowen will not overstep, especially when it comes to Faith.

Chapter 14

Amplitude

Noun; extent of dignity, excellence, or splendor

Faith is already in the shower when she hears Jonathan walk into the bathroom. She figured she would let him sleep since he had a late night at work last night and it takes her longer to get ready.

The door to the shower cracks open and Faith sees Jonathan's head peak in.

"Hey there, beautiful. Mind if I join you?"

"I don't mind one bit. I am almost done, though."

"I'll enjoy whatever time I have with you then." Jonathan says as he steps in the steamed shower.

Faith begins rinsing her long brown hair as she says, "I'm excited for our meeting today."

"I am too. I think it will help us get a better idea of what all we need to arrange as far as planning goes."

Faith lets the hot water run down her back rinsing any residual conditioner off. She leans in and kisses Jonathan before opening the door to get ready.

"I'll get breakfast going when I'm done."

"Thank you, Jonathan." She says smiling at his thoughtfulness.

After she dries herself off she wraps the cozy towel around her, tucking in the top corner to hold it in place as she picks out her outfit. Faith walks into the closet and stares at her clothes. She has her closet set up with her teacher clothes on one side and her normal everyday clothes on the other, with some dresses and a shoe rack on the back wall.

She doesn't want to wear her work clothes, they are mostly business casual in appearance, but nothing is jumping out at her as something she is excited to wear for wedding planning. She decides a semi-casual dress will work well.

She walks to the back wall and slides a couple of hangers over to reveal a white dress she'd forgotten she had. She's never worn it, but found it on clearance over a year ago and thought she could possibly have a place to wear it someday so she bought it. The dress is white with thick straps, it hugs her curves, but isn't skin tight. It has a 'v' neck and is knee length. She pulls it from the hanger and looks down at her shoes, a simple nude sandal with a small heel will work well.

She removes her towel and gets dressed. Then goes to look at the jewelry she keeps in a simple clear acrylic box on a shelf below the rack of dresses, she selects some simple white gold earrings with sapphire accents and the matching necklace for a pop of color.

She goes back into the bathroom where Jonathan is getting out of the shower and sits at the vanity to do her hair and makeup.

"Is that a new dress?"

"Yes and no. I've had it, but never worn it. I thought this was the perfect opportunity."

"It looks stunning on you. And you're right, it's absolutely perfect." Jonathan says and he bends down to kiss her on the top of her head.

She smiles at him and his half naked body. "I am one lucky woman." She say almost to herself.

"I'm the lucky one, Faith." He says still bent over inhaling the scent of her conditioner.

"Thank you." She says smiling.

"No, thank you." He says as he stands up to go get dressed.

Faith pulls her hair back in a ponytail to begin doing her makeup. Before she knows it Jonathan has already headed into the kitchen to make breakfast. Zeke has padded into the bathroom to check on Faith. Once he sees she is sitting at the vanity he curls up directly outside the door.

When they've finished breakfast they take the short drive to Amethyst Hotel. As they walk in Faith notices the openness of the two story lobby. There is a wall of windows above the door that allow the sunlight to bathe through cascading across the expansive room. They walk directly to the large dark wood and metal desk. The receptionist greets them and Faith explains they have a meeting with Brenda scheduled for ten a.m. The older gentleman behind the counter smiles knowingly at them, says "Congratulations", then dials Brenda's extension letting her know they've arrived. Then he instructs them to take a seat wherever they'd like.

Faith and Jonathan look around and see a large two seat sofa against the far wall under a very large painting of a ship in the middle of a violent storm. Faith gestures to the use of different mediums in the architecture from the warmth of the woodwork to the cold iron railings to the texture of the stone on the oversized fireplace. It all creates such a beautiful atmosphere. She can only imagine the ambiance that will be created with candlelight in their reception space.

Before they know it, a woman is walking towards them. She outstretches her hand and says, "Welcome to the Amethyst Hotel! I'm Brenda and you two must be Faith and Jonathan?"

Faith takes Brenda's hand and gently shakes it. "Yes. It's great to meet you!"

"It's great to meet the two of you! So we'll start in the grand ballroom, if you'd like to follow me."

Faith's eyes light up and she gives Jonathan a look of pure happiness.

Brenda takes them through the large dark ornate wood double doors and into the ballroom. This room is even bigger than the lobby. The ceiling is domed and has a beautiful hand painted mural that gives the appearance of stained glass.

Brenda speaks a little of the architecture before gesturing for them to sit down at the table nearest them.

"This is absolutely beautiful." Faith says with wonder filling her voice.

"It truly is." Brenda agrees as she looks around the room. "I feel so fortunate to be able to work here." She looks back to Faith and Jonathan. "And to work with couples, such as yourselves, and help to bring one of the most important days of your life into reality and to try to make it just how you envision it."

"I can't wait." Faith says smiling from ear to ear.

On the table in front of them are a series of binders with different color tabs creating sections. Brenda reaches for the top one and opens it, then turns it towards Jonathan and Faith. She points at the heading of the first section.

"We'll begin with the ceremony. With your wedding being in May the weather should be pretty nice. It can still be unpredictable, however. Were you two thinking of having the ceremony on the roof top terrace?" She pauses for a moment to gauge Faith and Jonathan's reaction to the suggestion and then continues, "If you choose to do that then I suggest we have a backup plan in case of inclement weather. I know the old adage is April showers bring May flowers, but sometimes May showers also bring June flowers."

The three of them chuckle. Faith explains, "I think the rooftop terrace would be wonderful. I bet it has a gorgeous view of the bay."

"I can take you up there. Let me just grab my key card." Brenda walks to her office and back into the ballroom much faster than Faith thought she would. She's grateful she fought the impulse to thumb through the binders while she was gone.

Faith and Jonathan stand and follow Brenda through the hotel to the elevator. She swipes her keycard and hits the button for the twenty fifth floor. Brenda explains while they wait for the elevator to reach the top, "You'll have the honeymoon suite for the night of the wedding. If you would like to have additional rooms you would need to book those soon to make sure they are available. You can also reserve a block of rooms for any out of town guests. Faith, once we get into the space, I'll take you to the bridal suite first so that you can see where you'll get ready."

"Perfect." Faith says as she squeezes Jonathan's hand excitedly.

The elevator doors open and before them sits a beautiful area with tables, a large grand piano and a huge wall of glass.

"This entire wall will open up to the terrace. If there is inclement weather we can either set up the ceremony in here or in the ballroom." Brenda leads them down a hall where they pass a set of bathrooms and a couple of other doors marked with employees only signs. Brenda swipes her keycard once again on a door marked 'Bridal Suite'. The light from the tall windows spills out the door as Brenda opens it.

The room is filled with pink and cream colored frilly things. "We really need to think about redecorating this room, but it has such ornate details in the plaster and wallpaper that it's difficult to keep original and decorate around."

Faith smiles. "It's very girly, so it works." She looks around the room and sees a soft pink velvet sofa and large white marble fireplace with a baroque style mantle. The wood floors reflect the sunlight. There is an area rug in the center of the room adorned with flowers and foliage.

There is an en suite restroom with marble tiles that match the fireplace and a pink sink and toilet.

"This will be perfect, Brenda. Thank you."

"You're welcome." She looks at Jonathan. "Would you like to see the Groom's Suite?"

"Is it also pink?"

Brenda laughs. "No, thank goodness it isn't."

Jonathan chuckles and nods his head. "I would, yes."

They follow Brenda the opposite way down the hallway, they pass the area where the elevators open to then down the hallway further they pass another set of bathrooms before they reach the door that is labeled "Groom's Suite."

Brenda swipes her keycard and opens the door. This room has a very different feel to it. The walls are covered in a rich dark hunter green. The curtains are navy blue and fall from the height of the ceiling all the way down to pool on the hardwood floor. There is a brown leather sofa and a couple of leather wing back chairs. It reminds Faith of a smoking room.

Whereas in the bridal suite all of the woodwork was painted cream, this woodwork is untouched and still in its stained deep tone. Which gives the room a more masculine esthetic.

Jonathan smiles at Brenda. "This is an incredible room."

"It is pretty perfect, isn't it? Most of the grooms love this room, and the photographs prior to the ceremony always turn out stunning."

Faith looks around and finds this room also has an en suite bathroom. Jonathan pokes his head in there and says, "This will work."

Faith smiles at the thought of him getting ready standing in front of the mirror and how handsome he'll look in his tuxedo.

"OK, let's go look at the terrace, shall we?" Brenda suggests.

"Great idea. I think we're both loving all of this so far."

As they walk through the open area before going out onto the terrace Brenda mentions, "We can have hors d'oeuvres and cocktail hour up here while you and the wedding party take pictures. Then we'll head downstairs to the grand ballroom.

Faith notices the piano sitting in the corner of the room and makes a mental note to remember to ask Andy if they've asked their sister about availability for the wedding yet.

Brenda demonstrates how the wall of windows folds open and says, "This obviously isn't original to the hotel. Before the renovations this was a wall of French doors and windows alternating, which worked fine, but this makes the room and the terrace feel more cohesive."

"It was a great upgrade." Jonathan comments.

"We have something very similar in our walkout basement, actually." Faith adds surprised Jonathan hadn't said it first.

They walk outside feeling the slight humidity in the August air. The sun is shining high in the sky over Amethyst Bay making the water look more like millions of diamonds sparkling below.

Faith breathes in deeply and imagines what the weather will be like for their wedding in May. It should be slightly less humid and a bit less warm as well. She hopes the sun is shining exactly like this and the wind isn't too strong.

Jonathan squeezes her hand bringing her back to the present. He points out a sailboat in the distance.

Brenda begins explaining how the space will be set up depending on the number of guests they're planning on having. She points out a wooden arch that is leaned up against the side of the building. "That can be decorated with flowers, ribbons, or really anything you can think of and used as the arch you'll stand under as you say your vows. Do you already have an officiant?"

"No. We've done very little planning up to this point. We were kind of hoping you might have some vendor suggestions." Faith says.

"We definitely have preferred vendors we work with. We'll go over all of that when we get back to the grand ballroom. The decoration of the archway can either be taken care of by us or by your florist if you prefer."

"That's wonderful."

"We do our best to make your day as stress free as we possibly can."

"That sounds absolutely perfect." Faith smiles at Brenda.

Jonathan leads Faith around the terrace taking in the view of the bay.

"This is almost as beautiful as the view from our yard." Jonathan says.

Brenda's eyebrows shoot up. "Where do you live?"

"We recently built a house between Luna Shores and Sol Port. We're still in Luna Shores, just on the outskirts."

"That is a gorgeous drive, I've always loved it."

"We got so lucky with the way everything worked out, like it was meant to be." Faith says.

Jonathan gently nudges her with his elbow and says, "That's because it is."

Faith and Brenda smile.

"Well, if you guys have seen enough up here we can head back down to the grand ballroom and go through the binders."

"That would be great!" Faith says enthusiastically.

Back in the grand ballroom, Brenda pages through the binders, going over all of the details just like Faith was hoping she would.

Brenda reaches beside her and grabs a bag with the Amethyst Hotel's logo on it, then sets it on the table in front of Faith. "This is for you to take with you. It has a binder with copies of preferred vendor information, pricing and course options. You can take this and make some decisions and then when you're ready, I'd suggest approximately

four months prior to your wedding date, we meet again and finalize everything. Once you choose three course options we can do a food tasting if you'd like."

"Is there a deposit due today?"

"Yes, we will collect that at the end."

"OK, that's no problem." Faith says unsurprised.

"Is there anything you two had any questions on?"

Faith looks at the bag. "I think if we do we'll probably be able to find the answer in here."

Brenda chuckles. "That is true. You can follow me and we'll go into my office. I can process your payment there."

Jonathan and Faith follow Brenda into her office. The room is covered in rich woodwork and deep muted tones.

"Please, sit." Brenda motions for them to take a seat in the two tall leatherback chairs across the desk from her own chair.

Jonathan pulls the chair out first for Faith to sit and then sits beside her.

Brenda continues, "There is a minimum cost of twenty thousand dollars for the grand ballroom on a Saturday night. We require fifty percent down up front to hold your date."

Jonathan has a curious look on his face when he asks, "What do you mean by minimum cost."

"There are various charges for the rental space, the linens, tables, chairs, dinner and drinks. You'll need to reach at least twenty thousand for all of those things."

"Oh, that won't be a problem."

"No, it usually isn't."

Jonathan begins removing his wallet from his back pocket. Brenda wakes her computer up and signs in. She inputs the information for their wedding and saves it in their file.

She brings up the program to charge them for the deposit and takes Jonathan's card. After she swipes it she prints them a receipt and hands it to Faith, who puts it in the bag with the binder.

Brenda then reaches behind her and grabs a white box and hands it to Faith. "This is our gift to you for choosing Amethyst Hotel as your wedding venue."

Faith smiles and opens the box revealing beautiful champagne flutes.

Brenda continues, "You can bring them back to our next meeting and we'll have them engraved with 'Mr. and Mrs. Hall' and your wedding date."

"That is so perfect! Thank you so much!" Faith holds the glass up for Jonathan to see.

He smiles and says, "Thank you. That's such a kind thing for you to do."

"We pride ourselves on taking care of our brides and grooms."

"That has been apparent through the entire tour." Faith says feeling very confident in their decision of venue.

Chapter 15

Attitude

Noun; a negative or hostile state of mind

Faith walks out of the dressing room at the bridal store in Luna Shores with her mom, Jackie, and Hope all waiting and watching patiently. They know the dress she's wearing isn't going to be the one she wears down the aisle, but Faith did her best to find one that had the most similarities.

Diane audibly inhales as she sees her daughter in a wedding dress for the very first time. The way Faith's dark hair contrasts the champagne colored fabric is so stunning. "You look absolutely beautiful, Faith." Diane says with tears forming in her eyes.

"Thank you, Mom." Faith smiles at her mom so incredibly happy to be able to share this with her.

Jackie asks, "I think it's gorgeous on you, but what is similar and what is different from the one you'll actually be wearing?"

"Well, the color is the same, I believe. The neckline is as well." Faith points at the neckline. "This one has a bit more lace than the one Mr. Caltroney custom designed for me." Faith tries to remember the rendering. "It's hard to remember everything specifically, especially since I only saw it drawn on paper. It's not like he had it there for me to try on."

"It was still an incredibly kind gesture." Diane says.

"I can't believe he wanted to do it. All because I had something under my chair."

"That's incredibly lucky of you." Hope says.

"It is!" Faith agrees.

Prior to the appointment, Faith had explained to the sales woman over the phone what the circumstances were and she agreed to keep Faith's appointment for her. She did shorten it, but Faith completely understood that since she would only be trying on one dress and the saleswoman wouldn't be getting a sale from Faith.

"Have you found a veil yet?" Sandy, the saleswoman, asks.

"I haven't even looked. I'm not sure if I want to wear one."

"Most brides wear them more as hair accessories than anything. It doesn't actually have to cover your face. I'll bring some over for you to look at."

"That would be great, Sandy. Thank you!"

She brings a few options over and begins affixing the first one in Faith's hair. Faith watches Sandy's movements in the mirror and suddenly feels overwhelmed with emotion.

Diane stands, walks over to Faith who is standing on a pedestal and hands her a tissue. Faith blots the corners of her eyes.

"Are you OK?" Diane asks concerned.

"Yes, it just feels so entirely real and I'm so grateful to feel such joy."

"After the year you've had, I can imagine how amazing this feels right now. I'm proud of you for everything you've brought yourself through. It's a true testament to how strong you are, Faith. I wish you didn't have to go through any of it, but I'm proud of the way you've handled yourself through it all."

"Mom, you're making me cry more." Faith says as she blots the tears from her cheeks.

Sandy takes a step back and lets them have a moment. Diane wraps her arms around her daughter and says, "I'm sure I'll do it again on your wedding day too. Then again, I'm sure I'll be crying too."

They all laugh. Faith stands straighter and adjusts the dress slightly. She takes a look in the mirror and turns to be able to see the veil. Sandy places the edge of the veil over Faith's shoulder so she can see the details.

Faith doesn't want to allow her emotions to skew her decision making in the moment. She runs her fingers over the mesh taking note of the sequins along the edge.

Sandy grabs the next one and holds it up, then asks Faith, "Would you like to try this one now?"

"Yes, I would." Faith smiles at her.

Sandy removes the first veil and replaces it with the second.

Faith looks in the mirror for a few more moments before asking for the third and final veil that Sandy brought.

"We do have more, these were just the ones I grabbed. So, if you're not happy with any of these we can go look at others if you'd like."

"I'll try this one and then we'll see. It might be good to see everything available."

"OK." Sandy says as she affixes the third veil in Faith's hair. Jackie stands and walks over to take a closer look.

"What are your thoughts, Jackie?" Faith asks as she looks in the mirror at her best friend.

"I think they are all beautiful and it doesn't matter what I think. All that matters is if you like it."

"I'm having a hard time choosing, but I am sure I want one."

"Then I think you're right, you should go with Sandy to look at them all."

Sandy overhears the conversation and asks Faith to follow her. She leads Faith to a different section of the store where there are even more bridal gowns lining the walls with one section in the center reserved for the veils.

Faith is impressed with the number they have on display. Sandy gestures towards the rack of them on the wall. "Go ahead. We can take as many as you'd like to try."

So Faith begins combing through them one by one. She ends up finding half a dozen to take back to try on in front of her mom, Hope, and Jackie.

Faith tries to picture each one of the veils with what will be her dress, but only having seen the drawing makes it a bit more difficult than she anticipated. She apologizes profusely to Sandy and assures her that after she has her dress she will be back in to shop for veils.

Sandy helps her change out of the gown she tried on and makes sure Faith knows that she understands entirely.

As they leave the bridal shop, Diane suggests they go have lunch.

"How about Tollero's?" Hope recommends.

Diane wears an expression of shock. "Why don't you want to eat at the café, Hope?"

"Well, because I don't want to feel like I'm at work, Mummy."

Diane laughs and says, "I don't either."

Faith drives them all to Tollero's in her red Range Rover Evoque. When they arrive at the restaurant they're seated right away and the waitress brings them all waters and utensils.

After she walks away, Hope looks around, leans in towards everyone sitting at the table and says, "I bet the café is busier than this right now."

Faith laughs at her. "I'm sure it is." She nods her head in agreement.

Diane gives Hope a sideways glance and says, "I thought you didn't want to think about work."

"I said I didn't want to feel like I was at work. Work is almost always on my mind in some shape or form. Hazards of running the place."

"Don't I know it." Diane retorts.

Jackie adds, "I think that's a pretty common problem to have."

"Luckily for us it's still the summer, but we are going to have to start thinking about it all very soon." Faith says.

Jackie asks, "Did you see the email they sent about the meetings the week prior to school starting?"

"I did."

"So now we'll have to do our room set up and any prep two weeks before unless we feel like working a sixty five hour week, the week before the first day. I honestly can't wait until I'm in charge and I can be the one making these decisions. I promise you it'll be better."

Faith smiles. "Everyone would be better off with you running things. I don't think anyone could deny that. Not even old Mr. Halvors."

"I hope he retires within the next couple of years. It would honestly be perfect timing since I'll be finishing school next year."

"When was the last time we had a different principal?" Faith asks trying hard to remember.

Diane interjects. "I think it was a few years before you two were born."

"Mr. Halvers has been in that position for over twenty years?"

"He has been, yes." Diane nods.

"He really needs to retire then." Jackie says with a slight annoyed tone.

"How old is he now?" Diane asks.

"He's got to be over sixty. I'm not saying he's a bad principal, it's more that he's out of touch with things going on in kids' lives today." Jackie explains.

"I can see how that would happen." Diane looks at Hope and then Faith. "You know you're Dad and I are not too far from that age, right?"

"You've still got like six more years before you're sixty, Mummy." Hope says.

"Dear, six years flies by in the blink of an eye. The older you get the faster the years seem to go."

"Why do you think that is, Mom?" Faith asks curiously.

"I think it may simply be because life can get monotonous. Especially as you age, when you no longer have little kids to keep you on your toes."

"Hence why you got a dog now, even though you refused to when we were little." Hope says giving her mom a sideways glance.

"Something like that." Diane smirks at her.

The waitress comes to take their orders, luckily everyone has a good idea of what's on the menu already since they were all so caught up in conversation to even glance at it.

Faith sits back and takes a sip of her water. She looks at the women sitting around the table and feels so grateful for each of their presences in her life.

"I'm so glad you could all make it today."

"I wouldn't have missed it, honey."

"I know mom, and I'm sorry it wasn't everything I'm sure you thought it would be."

"You've got nothing to apologize for, Faith. You have a wonderful opportunity, I wouldn't expect you to pass that up. Plus, we made the absolute best of the situation anyway. That's what truly matters."

"That's true."

"I just can't wait to see the actual dress." Hope says.

"I know, me either!" Faith says with a chuckle. "I wish they would have let me keep the drawing Mr. Caltroney did, but I suppose they need that and they wouldn't want some random person to have it."

"You're hardly a random person. You're the one their custom making the gown for!" Diane says defiantly.

"It's OK. I get it." Faith says trying to reassure her mom she is in fact understanding of why it needed to be done the way it has been.

"It still would have been good to see it at least."

"I didn't even think to ask if I could take a picture of it. They probably would have told me 'no'."

The waitress brings their dishes. Faith ordered the same as she did on her and Jonathan's first date. She smiles to herself when she sees the plate and the memory of that night appears almost as if a movie is playing in her head. The conversations they had and the walk right after dinner were all so perfect. Now she's marrying him and she couldn't be happier.

All the ladies begin eating and the conversation dies down as a result. When they finish they sit and talk for a bit longer before heading back out to Faith's SUV.

"This is a really nice car." Hope says as she gets in the back seat. "It was super sweet of Jonathan to buy it for you."

"It really was. I still can't wrap my head around the fact that it's mine, but it was lucky for us both that he had already decided to get it for me for Christmas."

"Yeah, we're both lucky. Not that I don't like you're old car, but I really want my Blue Baby back."

Jackie looks at Hope slightly confused. "What do you mean 'Blue Baby'?"

"That's what I called my Honda Civic Type R. She was a sporty girl and I miss her. Some asshole driving a semi just had to run a stop sign on Christmas. Who does that?"

"Speaking of that." Faith begins. "What has come of working with the lawyer to sue Dalton Freight?"

"The lawyer says it can take up to a year to reach a settlement."

"Is that why you're waiting to get a car?"

"Part of the reason. I'm also working on saving money and paying down student loans now so that I'm not hit with them so hard after graduation."

"All very fiscally responsible things, dear." Diane says proudly.

"Thanks, Mummy. Andy and I have been talking about buying a house together. They're not quite ready yet since they've got a bit more schooling left. They're worried that both of our student loans, plus a house payment could be too much, then if anything goes wrong with either of our cars or the house we'd be in trouble."

"Why don't you move in together into an apartment?" Faith asks.

"We've talked about that too. We're not rushing anything. It's only been five months."

"Jonathan and I were only together for four when we first decided to move in together. I don't think the amount of time matters. It's more about how the relationship feels to you. Obviously this one feels pretty right."

"It does." Hope smiles and Faith can't help but be so happy for her sister.

"I love seeing you like this!"

"Like what?" Hope questions.

"Happy. In love. Damn near swooning."

Hope smacks Faith in the arm from the back seat. "OK, Doubt. We can't all be happy-go-lucky all the time."

Faith acts as if that hurt her feelings, putting her hand on her chest in a gesture of pain. "I am not happy-go-lucky all the time."

"Only since Jonathan came into your life."

"Well, who can blame me? He's amazing!"

"And he spoils you." Hope says with an almost accusing tone.

"I don't ask for that. He just does it. Even when I try to tell him not to, he does. Plus, who wants to argue with someone that wants to do something so nice for you."

"Some of the things he's done have been a bit over the top." Diane says.

"Whoa. Now I do feel attacked." Faith says with a hint of a laugh.

"It's OK." Jackie says. "I wouldn't have told him he couldn't buy me a car, or build me a house, or take me on a fancy vacation to Napa Valley." She gestures towards Faith's left hand on the steering wheel and says, "And I certainly would have said yes to a man asking me to marry him with a ring like that."

Faith's cheeks are starting to turn pink. "You guys are making it out to seem like I'm only with him for the money."

"No, honey. We completely understand you didn't even know about the money at first and at that point it was more of a perk." Diane says matter-of-factly.

"Yeah, a very nice perk that makes life so much easier." Hope adds just as Faith pulls up to the curb outside of her apartment.

"Bye, Despair, I'd say it was good having you with, but after these comments I'm rethinking how nice it really is." Faith laughs she knows her sister is only trying to get under her skin. She does have to admit that it does happen from time to time.

Hope waves and shouts, "See you later for dinner!" as she walks down the sidewalk towards the entryway door.

Chapter 16

Magnitude

Noun; the importance, quality, or caliber of something

When Faith gets home Jonathan has nearly finished her surprise. From an upstairs bedroom he hears the garage door open and then close. He shoves what he's working on in the closet and closes the door before going downstairs in time to sit down on the couch and put the game on.

"Hey." Faith says from the kitchen.

Jonathan stands and walks over to her taking her in his arms. He kisses her then barely backs up when he says, "Hey, how was your day?"

"It went well. That was until I was driving everyone home and they all decided to give me shit about how much money you have and how much of a spoiled brat I am."

"None of them actually used those words…did they?"

"Not exactly those words, no. They might as well have though."

Jonathan pulls her in for a tight hug and kisses the top of her head. "Let me guess, Hope started that whole thing?"

"Yes, she did."

"Did the conversation start in the car on the way home?" Faith nods and Jonathan continues. "Maybe it was just because she was feeling badly about not having a new car yet."

"Maybe. That doesn't explain why my own mother and best friend jumped in on it too."

"Because it was easy. People do what's easier sometimes."

"We'd had such a great day together too."

"Why don't we go sit down and you can tell me all about it."

Jonathan leads the way over to the couch. Faith looks at the TV and says, "Isn't this last night's game?"

"Yeah." Jonathan says as he hits the power button on the remote turning the TV off.

Faith tells him about how wonderful the day had been which seems to help her forget about feeling offended by their joking.

When she finishes Jonathan says, "It sounds like it was a really good day otherwise."

"It was." Faith says as she snuggles into the crook of his arm.

"Did you want to go through everything we got from Brenda yesterday and see about making some decisions?"

"That sounds like a productive use of the rest of our Sunday."

Jonathan sits down at the banquet style seating below the island after he poured each of them a glass of wine. Then he waits for Faith to come back with the bag they received from the Amethyst Hotel.

Faith walks into the kitchen beaming.

"What's got you smiling?" Jonathan asks.

"I'm happy that you suggested this." She slides into the booth seating beside him and sets the bag on the floor.

She reaches in the bag, taking the binder out. Jonathan watches as she leafs through the pages and pages of information.

Once she gets to the menu options Jonathan says, "This is what I'm most looking forward to making decisions on."

Faith giggles. "Do you remember if she mentioned when we would do the tasting?"

"I don't think she did. I remember her saying that we'll finalize everything four months before our wedding."

"I'm glad you were listening."

"I definitely was. Even though it was difficult to concentrate with you looking so damn sexy in that white dress sitting right next to me."

Faith smiles seductively and Jonathan continues, "I couldn't take my eyes off of you." He leans in to kiss her. Faith kisses him back, but then places her hand on his chest and says, "We're not going to get anything done if we start that. Besides, we need to leave in about an hour to go to dinner."

"Yes, we do." Jonathan says backing away slightly. "Let's look at the menus." He points towards the page then adds. "I think it would be a good idea to have almost a second dinner like finger foods such as pizza or something towards the end of the night."

"That's a great idea!"

As they look through the menu, Faith takes notes and marks down the options they both like most and creates a ranking system to help narrow them down to three.

"I'm so excited to taste these!" Jonathan says.

"I bet you are." Faith laughs. "It's a good thing we're going to my parent's for dinner soon!"

"I do love your mom's cooking."

"With good reason, it's delicious."

Jonathan kisses Faith's forehead. "Have I told you how grateful I am that your family has taken me in the way they have? It had been years since I'd felt any sense of family. That is, until I was at your family's Sunday dinner that first time when your foot was hurt."

"That seems like it was so long ago now." Faith says as she remembers how Hope gave both her and Jonathan so much crap that night.

"It really does." Jonathan puts his arm around Faith. "You know after my parents died my Aunt Suz wasn't the best to me." Faith nods and Jonathan continues. "I honestly had no hope of ever having the feeling of a family again." Jonathan looks down at his glass of wine.

"You never thought you'd get married and have your own kids?"

"It was something I wanted, but never thought was meant for me. It was easier to bury myself in work and ignore that aspect of life entirely."

"You still dated though."

"I did, but I never felt like it was going to end in marriage."

"Then what made you know you were going to marry me?"

Jonathan pauses for a moment thinking. "It was the first thought I had when I saw you dancing. Then when I bought you that drink I knew there was nothing I wouldn't do to make it happen."

"I'm glad you didn't. When I was at Tollero's this afternoon with them I ordered what I always do and it brought me back to our first date."

"It's funny how foods and smells can do that."

"Right. I can't wait to create all the memories with you, Jonathan." Faith says as she lays her head against his shoulder.

"We'll make memories in every part of the world. May can't come soon enough. I want to be able to call you my wife now."

"Well, there's too much to do between now and May for it to come any sooner." Faith laughs. "For now you'll have to settle with me being your fiancé, but I can't wait to be able to call you my husband either."

"Being able to call you my fiancé isn't settling, Faith. It's nearly the best thing ever." Jonathan kisses the top of her head and pulls her body into him.

She snuggles closer and awkwardly attempts to reach her arm around his side to squeeze him back which makes them both laugh.

At Sunday dinner, Faith announces to everyone in the middle of the meal that Jonathan has an interview for CEO on Tuesday. It wasn't until right after the words came out of her mouth that she realized maybe Jonathan didn't want anyone to know yet.

"Congratulations Jonathan, getting the interview is a huge step. When will you find out?" Frank asks.

"Well the initial interviews are on Tuesday, I believe there is only one other person going for it so I'm pretty sure they won't require more than one interview. Plus, we've both worked for the company for quite some time so they know us and our work ethic. We should find out on Friday."

"That's fantastic." Diane says. "I'm sure you'll get it." She smiles at him, a motherly smile.

"Thanks Mrs. Brandt. I'm fairly certain as well. I feel like I'm a better fit for the direction the company has been heading in the past couple of years."

Frank says, "I'm sure that's a question they'll ask; why you feel like you're a good fit."

"Oh, I have a much more in depth answer ready for them, sir."

"Good." Frank nods.

After they finish eating dinner, Frank turns the TV on in the den. Faith has been trying to forget this afternoon in her car.

She asks Andy, "Were you able to ask your sister about playing for our wedding? I only ask because we had the meeting at Amethyst Hotel yesterday and I noticed a beautiful grand piano near the terrace where we'll have the ceremony."

"Oh, that sounds lovely." Diane says.

Andy answers, "I spoke to her yesterday, in fact. She has that day free and said she would be honored to play for your wedding. She would like you to give her a list of songs and a schedule as to when you'd like them played."

Faith breathes a sigh of relief. "That's amazing! Thank you so much for suggesting her and talking to her."

"It's no problem. I'll give you her contact information so you guys can work out the details."

"That would be great!" Faith smiles widely as she hands her phone to Andy feeling like something major has been accomplished. Now though, she begins wondering about the logistics and feels like she should have cleared hiring someone to play the piano with Brenda.

After the Stallions win again, Frank, Andy, Jonathan, and Hope are all showing their excitement boisterously. Faith and Diane can't help but laugh.

"In less than a month we'll be there." Faith says as she gestures towards the images of the now nearly empty stadium on the TV.

This statement makes them all cheer even louder and Faith and Diane laugh even more.

Faith looks at Jonathan thinking of what he shared with her earlier about how grateful he was for her family and can see how important this time spent with her parents and siblings is to him.

There's no way to know if Jonathan's parents would have had more kids, at eight years old that would have been a pretty big age gap between the two. There have been larger gaps though. Faith wonders if her and Jonathan would even have found each other and be together now if his childhood had been different.

The way she sees it, she was lucky he even came out that night and wasn't working late. Tom was either really convincing or Jonathan had a slow week.

Her heart fills as she watches her dad and Jonathan high-five. These moments make her feel grateful for her parents too. The way they've accepted Jonathan, and Andy too. There's no doubt that Hope is grateful for how amazing their parents are too.

Chapter 17

Solicitude

Noun; attentive care and protectiveness

Jonathan smells the food as soon as he walks in through the service door of the attached garage. It's Tuesday night and Faith has dinner ready when he gets home. She is definitely more than he deserves. It was a long day especially with the interview process being more grueling than Jonathan anticipated and it sucked a lot of energy out of him. He's grateful not to have to cook tonight.

He greets her as happily as he does every time he gets home, after all coming home to her is the best part of his day. Tonight, however, she greets him with a glass of wine which he's also very thankful for.

"You're so thoughtful, Faith. Thank you." He gives her a strong kiss.

"You're welcome, Jonathan. I figured we needed to celebrate! You're one step closer to being CEO!"

"That is definitely worth celebrating!"

They walk into the kitchen. As Faith plates their food she says, "I want to hear all about the interview! How did it go? What kinds of questions did they ask?"

The amount of energy she's exuding is giving him a second wind. She's clearly very excited for him and he can't help but smile because of it.

"Well, it was a very long interview. I didn't get much actual work done today, but since they passed that onto someone else it helped free me up, so that was good."

Faith nods her head. "That is nice of them, good forethought."

"Yeah, it really was. There were a ton of questions; deep, multi-layered questions. It all took a lot of brain power." He says and then takes a long pull from the wine glass.

"That sounds stressful." Faith says as she brings their plates to the table.

"That's exactly what it was." Jonathan agrees.

"Did they say there would be another interview?"

"I hardly see how there could be. They asked everything they could possibly want to know today."

"Well, that's good then, right?"

"It is. I only hope my answers were better than Vern's."

"I'm sure they were. How are you feeling about it overall?"

"I feel really good. I left the conference room feeling exhausted, but confident."

"That's awesome!" Faith smiles.

Jonathan picks up his fork and leans over to Faith to give her another quick kiss before they dig in to the ziti she made. "This smells delicious, by the way. I smelled it the moment I walked in."

"Thanks! You know I don't mind cooking for you. You hardly ever let me." She gently elbows him in jest.

"I like cooking for you. It was never meant to make you feel like I didn't think your cooking was good. It's probably better than mine."

"I think you've had more practice as of late."

"That may be true." He says as he looks at her from the corner of his eye and puts the fork full of sauce and cheese covered pasta in his mouth.

"So, what you're saying is, I'm right." She smiles and takes a bite of her cheesy garlic bread.

"You could say that."

They both laugh and continue eating their dinner with Zeke curled up on the floor between their feet.

Once they've finished dinner, Faith gets everything put away and they decide to take Zeke for a walk around the property. The sun is still high in the sky and the heat has barely started to die down from the hot August afternoon.

They walk into the woods following the same trail that lead them to Zeke. Jonathan takes Faith's hand and asks, "How has the wedding planning been going?"

"I called a couple of the vendors that were on the list Brenda gave us and set up appointments. I've got one this week and a couple next week."

"Is that something I need to take off of work for?"

"I don't think so. I will need you to pick out yours and the other's suits, help me make a play list for the DJ for the reception, and do a cake tasting with me."

"Cake tasting? That sounds like the perfect job for me!" Jonathan says with a playful grin.

"I didn't think you'd complain about that one."

"I'm still not sure who I want to have stand up with me."

"I know, and that's fine. We're not in a hurry yet. I'm sure it'll get figured out."

Jonathan looks around at the trees surrounding them. The green leaves are illuminated by the sun. He takes a deep breath and says, "I'm not against having Andy as my best person, it's just that I kind of always thought it would be someone I've known and have been close with for a longer period of time."

"I completely get it." Faith says as she rubs his arm. Then continues, "I'd also like to schedule engagement photos soon so that I can use them on our invitations."

"That's a wonderful idea, Faith."

"One of the meetings I have is with the photographer we both really liked. I'm hoping to get a package deal with the engagement and wedding photography and videography."

"A deal would be great! Are you sure you don't want me to come with?"

"I'm sure. You don't need to miss work for that, especially not right now."

"No, I suppose I don't. Plus, I trust your judgment."

"Thank you." Faith squeezes his hand.

They walk on with Zeke leading the way.

"I don't think we've been this far in before." Faith says with a hint of hesitation in her voice.

"No, I don't think we have either. We should really explore our land a bit more though."

"I agree, but maybe we should have brought a gun with."

"We don't own a gun, Faith."

"Maybe we should get one. We could get attacked by a mountain lion out here."

"You do have a point, but I'm pretty sure Zeke will keep us safe."

"I'd hate to see him go up against a mountain lion."

"Or a skunk for that matter." Jonathan laughs, but quickly notices the serious look on Faith's face and gets quiet. He stops walking and turns to her and says, "How about this, we'll go to the shooting range and try out different handguns. That way we'll know which kind we like best and we'll each get one for protection."

"I should have gotten one years ago after I'd taken the class."

"I'd forgotten you told me you did that. Wasn't it your dad's idea?"

"Yeah. I took it and then that was it. I looked at guns, but wasn't sure what I wanted so I never got one."

"We'll take care of that." Jonathan says smiling at her.

They begin walking again until Zeke stops in his tracks.

"What is it boy?" Faith asks in a half whisper.

They both stop as well when they hear a low growl coming from deep in Zeke's throat.

"I think we should go back." Faith says with fear in her voice.

"You're right again." Jonathan says whispering.

Faith crouches down near Zeke and attempts to see what he's seeing then says, "It's OK Zekie, we're going back home now."

The low growl has stopped and Zeke looks at her with his big brown eyes and licks her face.

As they make their way back down the trail to the yard Zeke keeps watching behind them which makes Jonathan and Faith look back now and then as well. Zeke finally relaxes when they reach the yard.

"We're definitely getting ourselves some protection before we go that far in again."

"I agree." Jonathan nods. "Maybe we should go this weekend? Oh, I almost forgot to tell you, Rowen invited us to dinner on Saturday night. I hope you're OK with that, I told him we'd be happy to go."

"Yeah, it will be nice to meet him when you're there and see if he acts differently."

They sit down in the reclining pool chairs on the patio and Zeke lays down behind them keeping his eyes on the woods they just came out of.

"Something tells me you don't have anything to worry about."

"Jonathan, did you say something to him?"

"I told you I would if he reached out to me. He said dinner would be a good way to make it up to us and I agreed."

"OK. You said that's Saturday?"

"Yes, and then on Sunday I have a surprise for us."

Faith's face lights up. "A surprise? Now I'm looking forward to this weekend! So, shooting & gun shopping on Saturday, then dinner with Rowen and a surprise on Sunday?"

"That sounds about right!"

"OK! What do you want to do on Friday when you find out you're the newest CEO of Kansen Corp?"

"I just want to come home to my beautiful fiancé."

"We need to celebrate your accomplishment though!"

"Maybe I'll grab some food from Tollero's on my way home."

"You don't want to go out to dinner?"

"No. I'd like to stay home with you." Jonathan says as he reaches for her. Faith stands and walks over to stand beside the chair Jonathan is laying on. He places his fingers just inside the waist band of her jean shorts, grips them tight, and pulls her to come closer. Instead, she swings her leg over him to straddle him.

"Did you have something like this in mind?" Faith asks with her voice low.

"I've always got something like this in mind, Faith." He smiles and puts his hand on the back of her head and pulls her face to his.

He kisses her forcefully as he entangles his fingers in her dark brown hair. His tongue slips in between her lips to find hers. He hears her breathing pick up and knows she is enjoying the way he makes her feel.

Faith tries to pull her head back, but Jonathan isn't done. He pulls her back into him not letting her go.

With his other hand he pulls her shirt and bra up revealing her breasts. He cups one and then the other still kissing her fiercely.

Again she attempts to pull back, but his hand on the back of her head is unrelenting. Instead she unclasps her bra and pulls her arms out of her tank top straps then removes her bra entirely.

Jonathan lets her pull back only enough to take her tank top off and then pulls her back in to kiss him. Both of them now breathing very heavily.

Faith's hands are pulling and tugging to untuck his shirts. Then she runs them under Jonathan's button down and undershirt sending an electric wave through his skin with every touch.

Jonathan unbuttons Faith's shorts easily and she stands over him removing them. She focuses her attention on unlatching his belt and unfastening his dress pants while Jonathan kicks his shoes off. He lifts his hips up to make it easier for Faith to remove them and she pulls them off. Getting back on top of him, Jonathan once again places his hand on the back of her head pulling her lips into his.

He kisses her deeply, not wanting the splendor of this moment to pass. The humidity in the air is causing sweat to bead on both of them. Faith easily slides him inside of her making Jonathan let out an audible exhale.

Jonathan's hands move to Faith's hips as she rocks back and forth on him. He pulls her body into him making her fight against his force. They're both teetering on the precipice of ecstasy. Faith lets out a loud moan when she cannot fight it any longer pulling Jonathan over the edge with her into joyful oblivion.

She collapses against him as her wave of splendor ends. Jonathan kisses her neck as she nuzzles into him. She sits up abruptly and says, "I can't believe we just did that outside."

"Our backyard is private enough. No one could have seen us."

Faith looks around realizing he's right.

Jonathan asks, "We had sex outside in Napa Valley. What makes this any different?"

"That was inside a pool. It's kind of like being under a blanket."

Jonathan swoops her up in his arms and carries her to the steps going into their pool. He slowly and carefully descends them with her in his arms and her legs wrapped around his waist. "Is this better?" He asks as he laughs at the shocked look on her face.

Zeke comes to the edge of the pool looking at them with his head cocked to one side seemingly confused with their antics.

Faith laughs and tries to swim away from Jonathan, but his hold is too tight, proving her attempt futile. "I know you're stronger than me, you don't have to keep proving it."

Jonathan feigns surprise, "Whatever do you mean, Faith?"

Faith laughs louder. "You've had a tight grip on me since the moment I got out of that chair and came over to yours."

"Is there a problem with me wanting a tight grip on my fiancé? Also, I think that goes both ways." He flashes her a playful, knowing smile.

Another shocked look flashes on Faith's face followed by a laugh. Her hand hits the water making it splash between them. They both laugh and kiss.

Zeke decides to lay back down where he had been keeping his eye on the woods again.

Chapter 18

Certitude

Noun; the state of being or feeling certain

On Friday afternoon, Faith meets the photographer in the lobby of the Amethyst Hotel. When she set up the meeting she asked if they have worked at the hotel before and they had, which made her feel that much more confident in her selection.

"It's so great to meet you, Faith." Carmine says as they outstretch their hand to her.

"It's great to meet you as well, Carmine!" Faith smiles feeling like she is a little too excited to meet them.

"So, you saw the website, you fell in love and you wanted to meet. What kinds of questions do you have for me?"

"Well, I think the biggest one is do you have availability on my wedding day, and then the next biggest one is about scheduling engagement photos."

"Ah, yes." Carmine says as they pull their phone from the soft brown leather satchel. They wake it up and go to the calendar app. "We definitely have your day available or we wouldn't have set up the meeting." They say and smile at her with a slight tilt to their head. "As far as setting up engagement photos, when were you thinking of doing that?"

"I'd say within the next month or so if possible. I want to be able to use them in our invitations."

"Right, makes sense. And where would you like them done at?"

"I was actually thinking, we have a beautiful new home we recently finished building and I'd love to have pictures of us there. We have a gorgeous yard, some woods, a pool and an insane lookout over the bay. I think we could get some really good shots there."

"That sounds incredible! We can schedule that today, but I'd also love to come look at it before hand, either the day of or a week or two ahead of time simply to get an idea of backdrop and what equipment I'd need for lighting. You're thinking some indoor and some outdoor photos?"

"Yes."

"Great! I can do Saturday September twenty-fifth, if that works for you guys."

Faith checks her calendar and says, "That will be perfect!" She can already feel the excitement for the day building and begins wondering what she'll wear.

"I did bring my portfolio in case you wanted to see it." Carmine says as they pull a large leather bound book from the satchel.

"I'm not going to turn down looking at your amazing work." She says with a wide smile.

Carmine opens the book and turns to the first page. "As I said on the phone I've done work here before. The rich colors are a favorite, they add so much depth and dimension to the photographs." They gesture towards the photos and Faith recognizes the room as the Groom's suite.

"We had our meeting here and saw this room last week. I knew the photos in that room would be gorgeous."

Next, Carmine shows her some photos they'd taken outside at a different venue and explains, "This way you can see a bit of the difference. If you'd like to leave the hotel on your wedding day and have a second location for photos, we can do that. I'll also want a list of shots you'd like, if there are certain family members and group shots you need me to make sure I get, let me know."

"I'll have to think about that a bit more and also talk to my fiancé. I'm sorry he couldn't make it, by the way. It's easier for me to do these things since school hasn't started back up yet."

"It's not a problem. I would have loved to meet him, but it's not necessary. Are you a teacher?"

"Yeah! I teach first grade at Hilltop Elementary."

"No kidding. I have a niece that goes there! She'll be in first grade next year."

"That's great! Maybe I'll have her! That age is so fun, I can't imagine teaching older kids."

"Right! I love going to my partner's sister's house. They've got three kids and it's the best kind of chaos there is!"

Faith laughs. "Chaos is the only word for it."

Carmine looks back at the portfolio and pages through a bit more then asks, "Was it only the photography package that you were going to go with?"

"No, we were actually looking to have the videography added on as well."

"That's perfect! My husband, Jackson, is actually the videographer."

"That's great you guys get to work together too!"

"It's the best. I especially love doing weddings with him! They're such an amazing reminder of love. We always leave them feeling grateful to have been allowed into such an intimate day for the couple and to be able to capture that for them…" They let out a sigh, "It's simply the best."

Faith smiles widely. "I'm so happy to have you two for our day!"

"It's going to be beautiful and I can't wait! Jackson will be so excited when I tell him!"

They discuss cost, payment, and the best methods of communication before hugging goodbye and heading to their cars. Faith is so happy to have found them! Even though they just met, Faith feels like she's known them for years. Sometimes when you meet someone it's more than a good first impression, it's almost as if your souls have known each other in another time. That's what Faith feels with Carmine, as if they were meant to be at Faith's wedding in this aspect.

Chapter 19

Definitude

Noun; precision, definiteness

Faith is trying to wait patiently for Jonathan to get home, she's buzzing with anticipation for them to celebrate him getting the job. She doesn't know for sure, because he hasn't text her at all yet today, but she is confident that he deserves the promotion. He most definitely deserves it over Vern. The thought of him makes her skin crawl and takes her back to that day at Ironshore Park. He just rubbed Faith the wrong way and she knows better than to ignore her intuition.

She didn't make dinner tonight since Jonathan mentioned bringing something home from Tollero's. If that's what he wants to eat tonight she wasn't going to argue, after all, they are celebrating him.

Faith is sitting at her desk looking at various wedding invitation options on her laptop screen. She knows she can't start designing anything yet since they don't have their engagement pictures, but it'll be good to look and get an idea of what she likes. She is leaning towards using black and white photos to go with the black and white theme. She sees the website offers a sample kit that they'll send so she begins filling in the information for that.

The screen on her phone lights up distracting her from the invitations. She checks and sees a text message from Jonathan.

Jonathan: I'll be home in ten. At Tollero's waiting on the food.

Faith: OK. I'm home...working on wedding things.

Jonathan: I want to hear all about your meeting with the photographer today.

Faith: I want to hear all about how they told you you're CEO now.

Jonathan: I guess we have a lot to talk about when I get home. Our food is going to get cold.

Faith: It always does. LOL!

Jonathan: I love you, Faith!

Faith: I love you, Jonathan!

She finishes filling out the form to receive the free samples and then begins searching the numerous options of invitations once again. She finds a few she likes and saves them in a projects folder so she can find them easier when she's ready.

Before she knows it Jonathan is walking into the house with a bag of hot food and a not so happy look on his face.

Faith's stomach drops. "What's wrong?" She asks concerned and thinking something is wrong with their order. She starts peeking in the bag he's holding.

"It's not the food, Faith." Jonathan says with a hint of dejection.

"What is it then?" She asks, genuinely confused.

"I didn't get it. Vern did." Jonathan says flatly.

"You're kidding me." Faith practically spits the words out.

"I'm not." Jonathan lowers his head.

Faith's stomach drops. "What do you want me to do? I can call Mr. Kansen! I can storm up there tomorrow and let him know exactly what a huge mistake he made by giving it to that snake." She visibly shudders at the thought of him.

When she looks in Jonathan's eyes she sees a certain twinkle and something tells her he is trying to trick her. His eyes give him away first and then a smile spreads across his face.

"You're so damn cute, Faith. I'm glad to know you would want to defend my honor like that."

She smacks him playfully on the chest. "That's not funny, Jonathan. I would have gone up there and made a fool of myself!"

Jonathan sets the bag of food down on the island counter and scoops Faith up in his arms.

He says, "You're going to marry the newest CEO of Kansen Corp." Then he kisses her and she lets out a squeal of excitement.

Jonathan begins heading for the bedroom when Faith says, "The food is going to get cold if we celebrate like that first!"

"Food is reheat-able."

"Yeah, but sometimes it's just not the same."

"And sometimes it's better." Jonathan stops and sets Faith down on the travertine floor. "But if you really want, we'll eat first." He kneels down and pulls her torso into him burying his face between her legs.

"Jonathan! That's not the eat I had in mind!"

He stands laughing. "I know, it was too perfect to pass up."

Faith laughs and says, "What I'd like to do is hear about how they told you."

"OK, let's talk and eat then."

They walk back into the kitchen. Faith takes two glasses and plates from the cabinet, she grabs utensils and a bottle of wine from the wine fridge while Jonathan plates their food. Then she uncorks the bottle and pours some in each glass.

Jonathan takes the plates with utensils and Faith grabs the glasses and a couple of napkins and brings them over to the booth-style seating in front of the island.

Faith can hardly contain herself. She sits and scoots in letting Jonathan sit down next to her. Then she turns towards him and excitedly says, "OK, tell me now."

Jonathan chuckles and says, "Well, I was the first one in the office so when Mr. Kansen walked past my door I was thinking he might tell me first thing. He didn't though. Around lunch time he sent a meeting request for two o'clock. I was starting to get concerned, but I hadn't heard anything about Vern getting it, so I wasn't too worried. The when I walked in to Mr. Kansen's office for the meeting he was pouring a fifty year old single-malt scotch, so I had a pretty good feeling. He asked me to sit down and so I did, then he passed me a glass. He raised his and said a toast 'to the newest CEO of Kansen Corp'. The scotch was one of the smoothest things I've ever drank, Faith. It's no wonder it's so damn expensive."

"So what happened next?"

"He told me how impressed he was with my answers in the interview and how he's known for a long time that I was meant for this promotion. It was all good stuff. I sincerely thanked him, finished my drink, and then got back to work."

"I'm not sure I would have been able to just go back to work like that. I would have been too giddy!"

He looks at her from the corner of his eye. "I don't get giddy, Faith." He chuckles. "So, tell me about your meeting with the photographer."

Faith takes a bite of her dinner first, chews a bit, and then starts. "It was fantastic, Jonathan! I scheduled our engagement photos, we're going to have them done here! Oh, and the videographer is actually Carmine's husband, which I thought was so awesome! I can't even tell you how excited I am!"

"I'm glad it went so well!" Jonathan raises his glass and says, "I guess we've got two things to celebrate. Here's to progress in all aspects!"

They clink their glasses together and each take a drink. Faith is still feeling invigorated from the meeting with Carmine and the news of Jonathan's promotion.

"I'm so happy for you, Jonathan. It's a well-deserved and a long awaited promotion."

"Thank you, Faith. I knew it was going to happen someday. I just had to keep putting in the work and have the determination to see it through."

"You managed to cut down your five-year plan, damn near in half." Faith says. "So, what's next?"

"I can't go any higher than CEO. I'm going to keep doing what I can to keep this company relevant and successful and make a lot of money doing it, that's professionally speaking. Personally speaking, I have you to focus on, a wedding to help plan, and this house to help you take care of. We've got a lot of truly amazing things in store for us, Faith and I can't wait."

Faith noticed he didn't directly mention them having a family eventually. She understands why he would avoid bringing the subject up, but by not even mentioning it there seems to be a spot light shone on it instead.

Chapter 20

Aptitude

Noun; a natural ability, talent

"This is so much fun!" Faith practically shouts to Jonathan who can't help but laugh at her. She's holding a lightweight handgun tightly in both hands pointing it down the lane while wearing ear and eye protection. Which explains one reason why she's yelling, the other would be the loud bangs from the others shooting in the range.

"I'm glad you're enjoying yourself!" Jonathan says smiling.

They've been at the range in Caulfield for nearly an hour, each of them has tried three different guns to see what they prefer. The range doesn't sell them, but this way they'll be able to go to a dealer or store who does and purchase what they're most comfortable with.

"We'll have to come back after we buy them to get used to ours. Even same models of guns can feel slightly different when shooting them." Jonathan says.

"I'll be more than happy to come back!" Faith says smiling from ear to ear. She reloads and takes aim unloading her clip on the fresh target she had placed and sent back down the line. The paper is entirely missing it's bullseye by the time she's done.

Jonathan laughs to himself again, finding her enjoyment amusing.

"I think I like this one the most." Faith calls.

"OK, if you think that's the one we can look it up."

"Have you found one that you like?"

"Yeah, I think of the three the second one was my favorite."

"It's settled then. Let's go shopping!"

"You sure you're done trying them out?"

"Certain! I'm ready to buy."

Jonathan laughs and Faith can't help but join him. She woke up this morning very much looking forward to this weekend. Plus, she and Jonathan had an amazing night breaking in a couple of different rooms in the house including the kitchenette in the basement. The counter was the perfect height.

Faith is also strangely looking forward to dinner with Rowen. She isn't quite sure why she is, especially because of the way he acted at the café. It could be the fact that Rowen is a person that has known Jonathan so long that intrigues her. She hasn't met anyone who has known him from high school, let alone childhood. She's not exactly sure when they became friends, but either way he's the only person she's met that has known him the longest.

They turn the unloaded guns and remnant ammo in at the counter and Jonathan pays the rental fees before they head to the sporting goods store not too far from the range.

They both pass the background check with no issue and within a few hours they are walking out with their new hand guns, cases, ammunition, and locks.

Jonathan drives them home to get changed and ready for dinner.

"Rowen text me while we were at the store. He got a reservation for us at The Farmhouse."

"Really? That's where Hope and Andy went for their first date."

"I've heard it's very good."

"I have too. I'm excited." Faith says as she applies her mascara. "I'm glad you told me. I'll have a slightly easier time picking out something to wear."

"Will you though?" Jonathan questions with a chuckle.

"Ha-ha, you're hilarious." Faith says facetiously while rolling her eyes for emphasis.

"Would you like my help?"

"Sure." Faith smiles.

Jonathan goes into her closet and picks out three options for her to choose from. When Faith emerges from their bathroom she finds some of her clothes laid out on their bed. None of which would be appropriate for her to wear to school.

"Are you trying to show me off or something?"

"I always want to show you off, Faith. You are beautiful, smart, sexy, and incredibly amazing. I know exactly how lucky I am to have you. I like others to see how lucky I am too."

Faith picks up a short jean skirt and a white cropped tank top. Under those she sees a little black dress that is more casual and sexy than it is fancy. Under that one she finds a pair of jean shorts and a black cropped tank top.

"I can't pick anything else from my closet?"

"We didn't exactly make rules for this whole thing, but I'm going to say no. I'd like you to wear one of these."

She looks at her choices again and decides the dress would be the best option. She can dress it down with some black strappy sandals.

Faith slips the dress on over her head, pulling it down over her hips. Jonathan watches her with a smile on his face.

"Good choice, Faith. You look sexy as hell."

"Thank you." She says feeling her cheeks turning red. "I definitely wouldn't have picked this."

"What would you have chosen?"

"Something that doesn't show off every curve of my body, especially given the way he was looking at me at the café. I'm not sure how comfortable I'm going to be wearing this."

"He won't look at you like that with me right there, Faith."

"How could you know that?"

"I'm sure of it. Unless of course he has a death wish, which I'm pretty sure he doesn't."

"I sure hope not."

Jonathan wraps his arms around Faith from behind. She catches a glimpse of them in the floor to ceiling mirror she has in her closet. Jonathan is only wearing his boxer briefs and for a brief moment she thinks about skipping dinner. She turns in his arms and kisses him then puts her hands on his bare chest and gently pushes back.

"We need to get ready or we'll be late."

He closes his eyes and slumps his shoulders. "You're right." He releases her.

Faith grabs her shoes and Jonathan goes to his closet to get dressed.

She slips her sandals on and picks out a pair of earrings. She's putting them on when Jonathan walks out of his closet. Once again, Faith finds herself contemplating skipping dinner and spending the rest of the evening wrapped up in one another, but she reminds herself that she wants to give Rowen a chance to redeem himself.

Faith watches as Jonathan sits on the bench at the foot of their bed and puts his matte black dress shoes on.

Jonathan looks up from tying his shoe. Smiling he says, "What are you thinking?"

"I'm thinking that I am so incredibly happy that I get to marry you."

"You're incredibly happy about that? Why?"

Faith laughs and says, "Really Jonathan? Do I need to spell it out for you? Or are you fishing for compliments?"

"A little from column A, a little from column B."

They both laugh and Jonathan stands, walks over to Faith, and kisses her fiercely.

Faith takes a small step back and says, "We need to get going."

"Alright, fine, but we can continue this later, right?"

"Absolutely. I'd be disappointed if we didn't."

"You're the best." Jonathan says emphatically.

Chapter 21

Rectitude

Noun; moral integrity, righteousness, being correct in judgment or procedure

Faith walks into The Farmhouse with Jonathan's hand on the small of her back. She takes a look around. The walls are light brick with black iron fixtures and burned wood tabletops. The dimmed lighting and stone work accents the space beautifully. They approach the counter where the hostess waits.

"Welcome to The Farmhouse. Do you have a reservation?"

"We're meeting a friend who has a reservation. His name is Rowen Mitchell."

"Ah yes, he's already here. I'll take you to your table."

Jonathan and Faith follow her through the restaurant. The ceiling is at least twenty feet high with the mechanicals and structure exposed and painted black.

Rowen stands when they get to the table. First, he shakes Jonathan's hand and then Faith's. Before he sits down he says, "Faith, I'd like to apologize for the way I made you feel at the café last week. It was never my intention to make you feel uncomfortable. You're a very beautiful woman, but I realize now my behavior was uncalled for, especially knowing that you're marrying my friend here." Rowen looks at Jonathan who nods.

"Thank you for the apology, Rowen. It means a lot."

Rowen sits, pulling his chair in under him. "You're welcome, Faith. This dinner is the least I can do. I honestly had no idea you worked there. Having dinner together sooner would have been better than showing up there, but hind sight is twenty-twenty and the food at the café is delicious."

"This was a great idea, man. It would have been better to do it this way in the first place, but its fine now." Jonathan says as he takes a sip of his ice water.

The waiter comes and takes their drink orders. After he walks away Faith asks Rowen, "So, tell me a little about yourself."

Rowen adjusts in his chair. "Well, I'm kind of freshly divorced. I was living just outside of Chicago until that happened. I decided I didn't want to stay in the Midwest anymore, so I came back here. I opened my own practice and everything is going well so far."

"That's great to hear! I'm sorry about the divorce though."

"It is definitely for the best."

"Did you two have kids?"

"No, I wouldn't have left if we did."

"Right. I have a confession, I am kind of hoping to hear some slightly embarrassing stories of Jonathan's from when you guys were younger." Faith says as she tucks a strand of hair behind her ear.

Rowen's face goes from being serious to lighthearted in an instant. "OH, I've got some stories for you."

"I was hoping you might." She laughs.

"I don't know that we need to share embarrassing ones." Jonathan says sounding a bit nervous about what might come out of Rowen's mouth.

Rowen looks at Jonathan. "Man, do you remember that time we were at Joe's for that house party and his older sister came home?" Rowen looks at Faith. "We were all ready to run, we thought we were going to get in so much trouble. Turns out Joe's sister…What was her name?"

"Laura." Jonathan says flatly.

"Yeah, Laura. Joe's sister, Laura, was the one that bought the alcohol. She knew all about it. And this dude," Rowen hooks his thumb to Jonathan. "He was trying to be slick and was like sweet talking her to try to make sure she wasn't going to tell on us. It was hilarious because she just let him go on and on making a complete fool of himself. We were juniors and she was graduating college that year. She must have thought we were so dumb and immature."

Faith laughs with Rowen while Jonathan says, "Yeah, well I wasn't the one who snuck into the girls locker room multiple times senior year."

"That was epic! Honestly, it was the best reason to get suspended ever!"

"You're lucky you weren't expelled." Faith says.

"It wasn't luck. My dad, who was also a lawyer, met with the principle and demanded I only get suspended. They did only catch me the one time." He shrugs his shoulders.

The waiter brings their drinks and asks about taking their order. "It's all farm to table, if you have any questions about what is in season now I can let you know, or maybe you like surprises."

Faith smiles. "I do like surprises." She gives Jonathan a sideways glance and a smirk.

Faith orders first and then Jonathan, and Rowen. The waiter collects the menus and walks away again.

"It sounds like you guys have a ton of stories." Faith says then looks at Jonathan. "Now I know how you feel when Jackie and I get together."

"It happens with Hope, too." He says.

"Yeah, I suppose it would."

"That's your sister, right?" Rowen asks. "I met her at the café. She was the inquisitive one."

"Yeah, she was checking to see if you were up to no good." Faith says in a slightly playful tone even though she isn't joking.

"And what was her analysis."

"Basically that you're a lawyer."

Rowen laughs heartily.

Jonathan laughs too and then says, "Hope is pretty good at pegging people correctly when she first meets them."

"It's why I trust her judgement so much." Faith says laughing with the guys.

"Is she single?" Rowen asks.

Jonathan stops laughing. "No fucking way, man. She isn't single, but even if she were do you really think if she can see right through you in the less than five minute interaction you had that she would even be interested?"

"They're all interested on some level."

"You're so fucking full of yourself."

"Always have been, always will be."

Faith takes a sip of her vodka and fresh squeezed lemonade and sees the waiter coming with their food.

"Thank you." She tells him as he sets the plate down in front of her first.

The waiter asks, "Is there anything else I can get you?"

Both Rowen and Jonathan hold up their empty beer glasses.

"I'll be right back with your refills."

Faith takes the first bite of her dinner and smiles at Jonathan. He nods his head and puts his fork in his mouth.

"Hope was right, this place is really good."

"She's been here before?" Rowen asks.

"Yeah, her and her partner came here for their first date actually."

"He must have been trying to impress her."

"I don't think they needed to." Faith smirks as she shakes her head.

"Why do you say that?"

"Hope isn't easily impressed, for one thing. Plus, she already
liked them."

"OK." Rowen says. Then asks, "How did you two meet? Wait let me guess, it was at the café?"

"Actually, no." Jonathan says. "Faith is a teacher, she only helps out at the café during the summer."

"Sometimes on breaks too." Faith offers.

"Yeah, sometimes then too. We met at Lee's pub. They were out for Jackie's birthday. Tom who I work with and was Jackie's boyfriend at the time invited me out and as soon as I saw Faith out on the dancefloor I knew I couldn't let her leave without getting her number."

"I could see why that would be."

"It was more than that." Jonathan says in a slightly defensive tone.

"So, Jackie is single now?"

Faith laughs. "She is."

"Maybe you'll have to introduce me."

"Maybe." Faith chuckles even more as she notices Jonathan shaking his head and looking down at his plate.

Rowen smiles seemingly knowing he's gotten under Jonathan's skin. To take it one step further he says, "Maybe a blind double date!"

"I'm not so sure Jackie is even looking for anything right now."

"She doesn't have to be looking for anything. I actually prefer it that way."

"I see." Faith says smiling politely.

Jonathan looks slightly uncomfortable when he says, "Maybe I'm wrong, but I don't think Jackie would be interested in that, Rowen."

"You never know though." Rowen offers. "Right, Faith? There's no way to know what Jackie would be game for."

"I've known her for a very long time, and I still couldn't say for sure."

"See, Jonathan? Not even Faith knows for sure." Rowen says gesturing to Faith to prove his point.

As they finish their meal, the waiter comes back and asks if they'd like to have desert. All of them shake their heads and Jonathan says, "I think we have all had our fill, thank you though."

Rowen reaches for the waiter and quietly says, "I'll take the check."

"Will do, captain." The waiter replies.

When the waiter comes back, Rowen already has his card ready.

"Thank you for dinner, Rowen."

"It was my pleasure, Faith. I'm so glad to officially meet you and get to spend this time with you and Jonathan."

"This was a great idea." Jonathan says smiling at Rowen.

"Did you guys want to go out for drinks now? We can head back to my place and have drinks there too, if you'd rather."

The waiter brings Rowen's card and receipt. Faith waits for Jonathan to answer.

"Continuing to catch up at your place sounds good." A wave a relief washes over Faith knowing that she would be more comfortable at Rowen's home.

"Awesome! I've got a fridge full of beer and another full of wine."

Faith smiles and they all stand up to walk out.

"We'll follow you." Jonathan says.

"I'm not far from here."

They reach the parking lot and Rowen heads to his lifted pickup truck parked in the back corner of the lot. Faith and Jonathan get in his Mercedes and follow Rowen down Main Street to a high-rise building.

Rowen parks and gestures towards a guest parking spot for Jonathan to take. When they get out of their car, Rowen is already waiting for them.

"Welcome to my home." He says as he leads them to the front door. He greats the gentleman sitting at the front desk and he heads to the elevator.

When the elevator doors close Rowen scans a key card and pushes the button for the 68th floor. Faith notices it's also the top floor.

As the doors open, they see a vast room with expansive views of the city lights illuminating the space. Rowen leads the way, flicking on the lights as he walks through. To the left is the kitchen which appears to be fairly simple with two banks of glossy black cabinets mirroring each other with high end appliances.

They walk further into the living room to find a large black leather sectional and gleaming white marble floors with grey veining running throughout.

"I can give you guys a tour if you'd like." Rowen offers.

"Sure." Faith concedes.

They walk through the penthouse apartment and see that no expense was spared in making this place feel grand, it doesn't, however, feel homey or welcoming. Everything is glossy black, white and grey. All the appliances are black stainless steel. Faith decides it's pretty fitting for what she knows of Rowen so far.

He leads them back into the living room and they take a seat on the white leather sectional sofa. Rowen heads into the kitchen to get them all drinks. He pours a large glass of red wine for Faith.

Jonathan and Faith are holding hands and enjoying the skyline view when Rowen places their drinks down on the table in front of them.

"This is beautiful, Rowen."

"Thanks. I can't take any of the credit. The place was pretty much exactly like this when I bought it. I didn't have to do a thing besides move my clothes and a small handful of belongings in."

"Wow. That's nice. Jonathan and I recently built a house and we combined both of our things. It was a lot. We're still figuring out what we need and what we can donate."

"Have you always lived in Luna Shores, Faith?" Rowen asks as he takes a drink from his bottle.

"Yeah, I bought a house there a couple of years ago now. I put it on the market and moved in with Jonathan at his condo until our house was done. I'm not sure if I can see myself living anywhere else. My family and my history is there."

"I can see that. My parents still live there, but I don't have any siblings. Living in Chicago was hard and they're only getting older. When the divorce was finalized I knew I wanted to be closer, but not so close. Caulfield was a good compromise." Rowen looks at Jonathan and asks, "What kept you in Luna Shores? You could have literally gone anywhere."

"Well, I started at Kansen Corp right out of college and it seemed like a great place for me to work my way up. I've done that relatively quickly."

"CEO, right?" Rowen asks trying to remember the confrontation at the Blue Rooster that night.

"Yup, I just got the promotion yesterday."

"Congrats, man. That's awesome!"

"It is, but it's not without its sacrifices."

"No, I'm sure it's not." Rowen says as he looks at Faith across the coffee table.

"What made you get into teaching, Faith?"

"I have always enjoyed teaching young minds. I love the way kids see the magic in this world, I feel like they keep me young." She takes a sip of her wine.

Rowen looks over to Jonathan and says, "You've got yourself a good woman, Jonathan."

Looking proudly at Faith he says, "Don't I know it."

"You guys must be busy planning the wedding and everything."

Faith nods her head. "Yeah, I feel like we've got a good start on it."

"So when is it?"

"May fourteenth at the Amethyst Hotel in Luna Shores."

"Yeah, I've been there. That's going to be beautiful."

Suddenly Faith realizes Rowen could be the answer her and Jonathan have been searching for. He could stand up as Jonathan's best man and walk Jackie down the aisle, then Hope and Andy can walk down together. She doesn't want to bring it up in front of Rowen since she's not sure how Jonathan will feel about it so she'll wait until the drive home.

"We're excited! I met with the photographer and the hotel's events manager has been really helpful with the other vendors."

"I know we just met, Faith, but if there's anything I can do to help let me know."

"Thanks, Rowen. We appreciate that." Jonathan smiles genuinely.

"Yeah, no problem. I'm truly happy for you guys and I know I apologized at the restaurant, but I want to reiterate that I am sorry. Sometimes I don't even realize when I'm acting like that. It's clearly something I need to work on."

"I appreciate the apology, Rowen." Faith says.

"I'm sure you didn't mean anything by it, but you've got to understand that it leaves a bad taste in my mouth." Jonathan tells him.

"I totally see that, Jonathan. Plus, I don't want to make anyone feel uncomfortable." Rowen reaches his hand across the coffee table. "Are we cool, man?"

Jonathan shakes Rowen's hand and says, "Yeah, no harm no foul."

Faith smiles seeing Jonathan with his friend makes her so happy they came tonight. The only other time she's seen him interact in a similar way was with Tom, but even then it was clear that they didn't have the history Jonathan and Rowen do.

On the drive home, Faith mentions her idea to Jonathan. "I just thought it might work well. I didn't want to say anything in front of Rowen in case you didn't like the idea."

"It's not a bad idea. I'd like to hang out with him a bit more before asking him just to be sure."

"He seems like he'd be willing to help with wedding stuff which also makes him good best man material."

"Yeah, I was kind of surprised when he offered."

"Me too."

"Like I said I'll spend a bit more time with him. I feel like we got off on the wrong foot with him going into the café, I need to put that behind us entirely if I'm going to ask him to be my best man and that's going to take a bit more time."

"That's understandable."

"I could still have Andy stand up as a groom's person. That way you could have both Hope and Jackie and not feel like you're leaving anyone out."

"It would work quite perfectly I think."

"Do you trust him?" Jonathan asks sounding contemplative.

"Not entirely. He did apologize though, twice. My perception of him is better now than it was. I think that's where the time comes in. Give him a chance to prove to us that he can be a good friend."

"He was a relatively good friend in high school." Jonathan muses.

"Right, so he could be now too."

"People change though, Faith."

"They do, sometimes they even change for the better." Faith gently nudges his arm over the center console.

Chapter 22

Solicitude

Noun; attentive care and protectiveness

The next morning Jonathan is already up making breakfast before Faith even wakes up. The weather will be perfect for what Jonathan has planned. He's gone back and forth a couple of times about taking her today since they have a pool after all. They don't need to go to the beach, but there's a different feeling when you spend the day relaxing at the beach than there is spending it at home beside the pool you're responsible for.

Dinner and then drinks last night went better than Jonathan could have hoped for. Rowen didn't seem phased one bit by his threats which did seem odd, but if Rowen had acted offended in anyway Faith definitely would have picked up on it.

He is going to need more time to figure out if having Rowen as his best man is a good idea. He's slightly concerned about if Rowen will accidentally tell Faith something Jonathan doesn't want her to know. The smart thing to do would be to keep him as far away from her as he can, but she seems to really like the idea of him having a friend. Rowen hasn't given away anything yet, and the fact that he doesn't know Jonathan wouldn't want Faith to know he was at Duffy's bar that night they first ran into each other is best too. Rowen doesn't even realize he has any leverage.

Faith walks into the kitchen a couple minutes before breakfast is finished wearing only an oversized white t-shirt. Jonathan instantly rethinks getting out of bed early.

"You weren't in bed. I wasn't sure where you went."

"I decided to get a start on breakfast." He pulls her into him and says, "Although, I am thinking maybe that wasn't the best idea." He kisses her forehead.

Faith smiles and says, "If I remember correctly there is a surprise today."

Jonathan taps her on the nose and says, "You do remember correctly."

"Do I get any hints?" She asks curiously.

"You need to wear a swim suit."

Faith's face lights up. "A swim suit! I was excited before, but I'm even more excited now." She smiles.

"Surprises are exciting." He kisses her quickly before he says, "Are you ready for breakfast? It should be about done." Jonathan spins around and opens the oven door to see the cinnamon roll bake is perfect. He puts an oven mitt on and takes it out.

"That smells absolutely divine, Jonathan."

"Thanks." He smiles as he starts cutting the breakfast casserole into pieces.

Faith grabs a plate and a fork and Jonathan serves her. She pours them both some orange juice and they sit down to eat at the banquette.

With the sun high in the cloudless blue sky above them they lay on their blanket on the beach feeling the heat radiating from the sand below. The water is gently washing ashore. Jonathan packed a picnic lunch for them to enjoy.

"This was a splendid idea, Jonathan. Thank you for bringing me here."

"You're welcome, Faith. I saw how stressful the wedding planning has been and I know with school starting in a week we could use the time together."

"This is a beautiful beach." Faith says looking around. Jonathan took her to Carlisle Beach in Sol Port.

"Have you been here before?"

"No." Faith says. "If we ever went to the beach when I was a kid it was in Luna Shores."

"My parents brought me here a few times. I'd come here in high school too. We're lucky to live so close to such a beautiful body of water."

"We really are."

The beach only has a handful of other people enjoying it which helps the day feel even more intimate. The birds are chirping happily. Jonathan watches as a couple of cardinals swoop into the pine trees at the far end of the beach they're sitting on.

Jonathan stands and asks Faith, "Do you want to come enjoy the water with me?"

"Of course I do!" She says grabbing his hand. Jonathan helps pull her up to stand.

Faith takes her sandals and shorts off and follows Jonathan into the warm, sparkling water.

He leads her to a deeper area and pulls her into him. Faith wraps her legs around him as he kisses her fiercely.

"Faith, there is plenty of time for planning the wedding. We need to make sure we still take the time to connect and do things together."

"I know that. I'm doing OK, Jonathan. I feel like once I get stuff going it'll be like a ball rolling downhill."

"It probably will, plus, we can contact Brenda if we need a little more help with things."

"That's true."

Jonathan pulls Faith into him and says, "OK. Enough wedding talk." Then he drops down going entirely under the water.

When he comes back up Faith is laughing so hard.

"Aren't you going to go under too?" Jonathan asks.

"OK." She says quickly as she drops down and disappears beneath the water.

For a moment Jonathan doesn't know where she is. She isn't right by him anymore. He turns around searching the water, but doesn't see anything except ripples from the waves. Suddenly, Faith pops up about twenty yards away from him, but still within the buoyed swimming area.

The sun is glistening on her wet skin as she stands up a bit further out of the water. Jonathan watches as the water droplets fall from her dark brown hair, flow onto her olive skin and drop back into the water. If he could save this it would be the perfect memory for him to keep forever. If only memories worked that way.

He quickly swims over to her and says, "That was fast! I had no idea where you went!"

"I thought I'd trick you." She smiles slyly.

"You definitely did."

They play around in the water swimming and cuddling one another for a while longer before Jonathan asks, "Are you ready for some lunch?"

"Sure."

They head back to their blankets and grab their towels to dry off. Then Jonathan starts getting the food out of the cooler.

"Thank you for thinking of this."

"I love to spoil you, Faith. You know that."

"I do, and I love it." She says as she squeezes some of the excess water from her hair.

"Damn. You are gorgeous."

Faith smiles instantly feeling her cheeks get warm at his compliment. "Thank you, Jonathan."

"No, Faith. Thank you." He says as he takes her by the hand and pulls her down onto the blanket with him. "You are by far the best thing that has ever happened to me." He holds her hand up bringing it to him. He looks at the diamond ring on her left ring finger and smiles. "I'm so grateful you said yes."

"I'm so grateful you asked me." Faith says and she leans in to kiss him.

He kisses her back fiercely pulling her into him feeling their still wet skin against each other. Jonathan pulls back slightly and says, "Are we ready to eat?"

"Sure. What did you bring for us?"

"I made us some turkey club wraps with some fruit."

"That sounds delicious, Jonathan. You're so thoughtful."

Jonathan smiles and hands her the wrap and places the bowl of fruit in front of them. Then he takes out a couple of single serve plastic wine bottles.

"No glass allowed on the beach." He says as he hands it to her.

"These are a great compromise then." Faith says as she untwists the cap.

After lunch Faith asks Jonathan to reapply her sunscreen. Then they enjoy the sun and quiet while laying back down on the blanket.

"As relaxing as this is, Jonathan, I can't help but think about all of the stuff we need to do for the wedding still."

"Thinking about it is fine, as long as you can still relax while thinking."

Her eyes still closed she smiles and says, "I'm definitely relaxed. The sound of the water helps."

"It is really calming isn't it?"

"I'm not sure there is anything more calming. Maybe next time we can find a beach we can bring Zeke to. I think he might enjoy swimming."

"Maybe that's something we can invite your parents and Orpheus to as well."

"They'd love that!"

"I think Orpheus and Zeke would love it even more." Jonathan chuckles.

"You're probably right." Faith opens her eyes, blinking them to help them adjust to the bright sun, then she rolls over onto her side to face Jonathan. "Today has been just what I needed, Jonathan. Thank you."

"You're welcome, Faith. We both needed it."

"That's true."

Jonathan thinks about the surprise he's working on for her for the wedding. He doesn't get much time when she isn't home to make it and he doesn't want to take any more time away from them than he already does. He'll have to make time before the wedding to finish it, he wants it to be perfect.

Aside from his parents he's never made anything as a gift for anyone before. He took various classes in high school, but most of those projects ended up in the trash. He didn't want Aunt Suz to have them and he found after some time of seeing them on his own shelf, they were stark reminders that he didn't have his parents.

"Jonathan?" Faith asks.

Coming out of his thoughts he says, "Yeah?"

"I asked when you wanted to get going so we can get ready for dinner at my parents', but you were somewhere else."

"Sorry, umm whenever you're ready is fine. What are your thoughts?"

"Well, now I'd like to know what you were thinking about that had you so engrossed that you tuned me out completely." She says as she reaches up to run her hand along his face.

"I was thinking of my parents and trying to remember the last time we were here as a family."

"Does going to the same places you went to with them help you to remember more?"

"I think it does. I think part of me not remembering my childhood so much is because it's not something I think about. I don't recall the memories because I don't want to relive the worst one of them all."

"It makes sense. I'm sorry I suggested you go to therapy when we were hiking in Napa. You have adjusted well considering everything life threw at you so early on."

"Thank you, Faith. I appreciate the apology, but it's unnecessary. I know you were coming from a place of love when you mentioned that. It's just a sensitive subject."

"Of course it is! I should have chosen my words better, and maybe my timing."

"It's OK, really. Plus, that was months ago now."

"I know, but it seemed like we just went on hiking and then never addressed it again. I don't want either of us holding onto feelings of resentment from past arguments that were never concluded."

"Well, you can consider this one concluded." Jonathan chuckles.

"I'm serious!"

"I know you are, and I agree and appreciate it! I don't want any negative feelings between us either. That's part of the reason I let it go and moved past it. I didn't feel like it needed more of a discussion."

Faith smiles faintly. "I get that, but I needed to be sure."

"I understand that too, Faith." Jonathan smiles at her reassuringly. "What else would you like to do today?"

"We should probably head home soon to let Zeke out."

"That's true." Jonathan checks his phone to see it's nearly three thirty. "You're probably going to want to shower before we go to your parents' right?"

"Definitely."

"We should probably get going then."

They begin cleaning up to head home. The drive back to Luna Shores is gorgeous and doesn't take too long. They pass Catch of the Bay and Jonathan smiles to himself thinking of the day she agreed to be his wife and they went there to celebrate and have dinner. It was all part of him recreating the date he first asked her to be his girlfriend.

Faith takes Zeke outside when they get home and then she and Jonathan quickly shower together. While Faith is getting ready, Jonathan turns the TV on in the living room and then sneaks upstairs to work on her surprise.

He is very careful not to still be up there when Faith is finished. He doesn't want her to get suspicious. So, after about twenty minutes of working he goes back downstairs and sits in the living room as if he'd been there the entire time watching TV.

When Faith emerges from their bedroom she looks slightly sun kissed and refreshed. Jonathan is happy to see the day had its intended effect.

"Ready?" Faith asks.

Jonathan takes a moment, looks at her, and then says, "Yes, my love, I am."

Chapter 23

Plentitude

Noun; the quality or state of being full, completeness

Diane is busy in the kitchen when they first get to Faith's parents' for Sunday dinner. As soon as Zeke gets in the house, Orpheus immediately greets them excitedly at the door. Zeke and Orpheus go into the living room where Orpheus grabs a rope toy and they promptly have a game of tug of war. Andy and Hope aren't there yet. Frank is sitting in his recliner watching the silly dogs play.

After they greet Frank, Faith excuses herself to help her mom in the kitchen.

"She looks less stressed somehow." Frank mentions to Jonathan after Faith is out of ear shot.

"I took her to the beach today."

"That was a great idea."

"I thought so. It seems to have helped." Jonathan shrugs.

"I know we've thanked you for this before, but I can't tell you enough how grateful we are for how well you take care of our girl."

"She deserves it, sir."

"She most definitely does."

Just then Hope and Andy come through the door and are immediately greeted by both dogs wagging their tails quickly back and forth practically tripping over the rope neither of them wants to let go of.

"Hi guys!" Hope says excitedly as she scratches both of them behind the ears simultaneously.

Andy pats each of the dogs on the head and then follows Hope into the living room.

"Hi, daddy." Hope says then she leans down to kiss her dad on the cheek. Turning to Jonathan she says, "Jonameister, how are you?"

"I'm good. How are you two?"

"We're good too." Hope says simply. "Where's Mom and Faith?"

"They're in the kitchen." Frank replies.

"Better them than me."

"We'd agree." Jonathan says with a chuckle.

For a moment Hope's face is stoic, until she can no longer hold it and starts laughing right along with Jonathan. Andy and Frank join them.

Diane and Faith come into the living room and Diane tells everyone dinner is ready.

The dogs are tuckered out from playing and stay in the living room sleeping while everyone gets up and heads into the dining room.

"My dearest, this looks phenomenal. Thank you for making dinner." Frank says with a sincere smile.

"You're welcome." Diane blushes a little.

Jonathan pats Faith's knee as a way to give her acknowledgment as well. He loves seeing Frank and Diane's relationship first hand in this way. It makes him think of his parents and the love they had for one another. He wants to curate a similar relationship that is rooted in love, understanding, and trust.

He also realizes the last quality is one that could be shattered in an instant. He would never cheat on Faith, nor would he ever do anything to disrespect her or their relationship. It's the hold his urges have over him that he cannot control. They come and go like the tide, but never far away for too long. The longer he tries to keep them at bay the worse they become.

He's often thought of the future and how it'll be possible to sustain both his life with Faith and keeping the secret from her. He has no answers for the questions that plague him and figures only time will truly tell.

"Jonathan, can you please pass the green beans?" Frank asks pulling Jonathan from his thoughts.

Jonathan passes the green beans to Frank and then looks at Faith. His eyes move from her to all of the other faces around the oval shaped dining room table where they gather every week.

These people have become his family. A sudden feeling of dread makes his stomach churn. What would they think of him if they found out? How would Faith handle something like that?

The desire to keep them all in the dark has always been there, but now it has grown into desperation. Jonathan doesn't like the urges, he just can't help how he feels once he's killed someone. Even when he was kicking the shit out of those truckers who drugged Faith, that didn't satisfy him in the same way. If he was honest with himself it didn't even come close to making him feel as good as killing does.

Hurting those men only satisfied his desire to get back at them for hurting Faith. Now Faith awaits the trial and can only hope those guys don't get off with a slap on the wrist. Their lawyer has a good feeling the judge will want to make an example of them to send the message that there is no tolerance for such things in Luna Shores.

If they were to get too light of a sentence that Jonathan didn't agree with he has vowed to himself that he will finish what he started that night in the sleazy motel. He feels his fist tense under the table at the thought of how badly he wanted to finish the job that night, but he needed to give Faith a chance at justice. She should be able to see them go through the process she's most familiar with when someone does something unlawful and get the closure she deserves.

Faith takes his hand under the table and gently squeezes. He smiles to himself thinking, *how the fuck did I get so lucky?*

"Jonathan got the promotion!" Faith practically blurts out.

Jonathan smiles and everyone congratulates him and tells him how happy they are for him.

"That is so exciting! I know how much it means to you, Jonathan." Diane smiles gently at him.

She has become the best mother figure he's known aside from his own.

Diane looks at Faith. "I wish you would have told me, I would have had a special desert to celebrate."

"It's OK, Mrs. Brandt."

Hope excuses herself from the table as soon as everyone is done eating. Andy stays while Hope claims she forgot something that she has to run out for. Jonathan is pretty sure she's going to get something for desert, a covert mission sanctioned by the matriarch herself.

Jonathan's suspicions are confirmed when Hope comes back carrying a couple of paper bags and takes them directly into the kitchen. Diane and Faith are already in there while he, Frank, and Andy are watching the game in the den.

"The weather is so nice, Frank. Don't you think it would be better to sit outside?" Diane says as she walks to the top of the steps leading into the sunken in den.

"The game isn't outside." Frank says not taking his eyes off of the TV.

"Correction." Hope says holding one finger up. "The game is outside, it's just not our outside."

Frank gives Hope a look as if to say 'you're not helping the cause, kid.'

Hope shrugs her shoulders and says, "I think sitting outside is a great idea. I'm sure Jonomeister can bring the game up on his phone or something. OR we can listen to it on the radio like they used to do in the olden days!"

Faith can't help but laugh at her sisters antics, especially when they're not aimed at her.

Frank grabs the remote reluctantly. "Fine." He says as he hits the button to power the TV off. "We'll go outside."

"Did you ever talk to mom about getting a TV for the patio?" Hope asks Frank leaning in.

"We talked about it, but didn't really come to a decision."

"Tonight might be a good time to revisit that talk."

"You're probably right, kiddo." He says as he leads the way out of the house. Faith and Diane take a detour into the kitchen before coming out onto the patio. Diane is carrying a cake, some forks, napkins, and paper plates. Faith has drinks for everyone. She hands them all out while Diane starts.

"To Jonathan, our soon to be son-in-law. Congratulations on your promotion. It's so well deserved and a huge accomplishment." Diane nods to Frank who takes over.

"I speak for all of us when I say we are so proud of you, son. You have overcome and accomplished so much and we're proud that you're a part of this family now. You have clearly proven that nothing can hold you down and the sky is the limit. Here's to your future, it is so bright. We love you, son." Frank's voice catches as he finishes.

They all take a drink and Jonathan says, "Thank you both. That was incredibly heartwarming. I can't tell you how much this means to me." He feels tears forming, but he won't let them fall. He blinks quickly until the sensation has subsided.

Diane begins cutting the cake with the word "Congratulations" sprawled in blue script across the center. She plates pieces for each of them as Faith hands them out with forks and napkins.

"How did you get this so fast?" Jonathan asks Hope.

"I know a guy." She says with a simple smirk and a shoulder shrug.

"I'm sure with running the café you know lots of them."

"Sure do!" She says proudly. "It only took a text message and a smile." Hope displays her smile as evidence.

Jonathan looks around to everyone and says, "I am so grateful for you guys. Thank you for allowing me into your family like this. It means so much."

Jonathan takes a drink from his beer and then takes a bite of the cake. "This is delicious!"

"Best in town." Hope says.

"Best in the county." Faith corrects.

"Yeah, that too." Hope concedes.

"So when does the position officially start?" Frank asks.

"Just over two weeks." Jonathan says. "Mr. Kansen did mention I'll sit in on some meetings before then, but the title becomes official in two weeks."

"That's exciting."

"It is! I feel very fortunate to have the opportunity."

"And at such a young age." Diane says then continues, "Most people don't get promoted to CEO until they're in their forties and have been with the company for nearly twenty years."

"Some days I feel like I've been there for that long." Jonathan chuckles.

Hope rolls her eyes. "I definitely feel like I've been working at the café that long. Oh, wait. That's because I have been."

Diane gives her a shocked expression, but she fails at holding it longer than a few short moments before laughter erupts from her.

Everyone joins in. Jonathan laughs with them and is filled with an immense amount of gratefulness.

He drives them home along the road that leads to Sol Port. They'll turn into their driveway before they get that far though.

"Faith?"

"Yes, Jonathan?" She asks, looking at him expectantly if a bit confused.

"I love you." He says as he places his free hand on her knee.

"I love you too." She says, unsure if he's finished. "Are you doing OK?"

"I am fantastic." He says enthusiastically. "Absolutely fantastic. I have the woman of my dreams, the house of my dreams, and now I have the job of my dreams. I don't know how I could possibly be better."

"I'm glad you feel that way." She says as she squeezes his hand. "I do too. This life of ours is what dreams are made of."

Zeke peaks his head in between them from the backseat making Faith giggle. She pats his head with her free hand and says, "Yes, you're included in that too, Zekie." He gives her a quick lick and then sits back down nicely on the seat.

"We're going to have to look into getting him fixed soon." Jonathan says.

"Yeah, I can call the veterinarian and see if they can get him in sometime this week so I can be home with him."

Jonathan pulls into the drive way and then into the garage and parks. He leaves his hand on Faith's knee and she doesn't attempt to get out of the Mercedes. "That's a great idea. I feel like you have a lot on your shoulders right now, Faith. The trip to the beach was hopefully one way to help alleviate some of the stress, but I want you to know I see everything you're doing. I appreciate all that you're taking care of, and

I hope if you need anything from me you know you can ask."

"I do know that. Sometimes I simply don't want to bother you with it. You've got so much going on with work, especially with this promotion now." She offers.

"I do, yes, but you've got practically all the wedding planning, plus taking care of Zeke, and now you have the rest of this week and then you've got stuff for school starting up, so you'll be setting up your classroom and going to meetings for all of that."

"It's the same stuff every year. It's not that big of a deal. And Zeke? He's easy."

Zeke perks his head up and cocks it to one side. Faith looks at him and says in a high pitched voice, "Did you hear your name?"

He licks her face again and then stands, ready to get out of the SUV.

Faith continues, "It's OK, Jonathan. Everything will get done and you will contribute how and when you can." She smiles at him and he moves his hand back and forth on her leg before giving it a quick squeeze and releasing it entirely.

Chapter 24

Quietude

Noun; a quiet state, repose

One of the perks of living in a small town is that the veterinarian isn't so busy that they're booking out weeks or months in advance. Faith was relieved when she called on Monday to find out that they would be able to get Zeke in on Wednesday.

She sits in the quaint waiting room reading a book while Zeke is under anesthesia in the back with the doctor and a handful of techs catering to him. The waiting room is quiet. No one is coming and going which makes getting into her book that much easier. This one was suggested to her by Jackie.

For the most part, they have similar taste in books. They agree that every book should have romance and some spice, but Jackie prefers fantasy or paranormal whereas Faith is indifferent to either. For her, as long as it's well written and she can immerse herself in the story easily, she'll be happy with it.

When the veterinarian, Dr. Fordham, comes out in his scrubs, Faith's stomach drops for a moment until she sees the smile on his face. She knows there is nothing to worry about and this procedure is simply routine for them, but for a moment she was definitely concerned.

"Everything went swell! He's in recovery right now. We'll be able to bring him out to you in about an hour. He'll be groggy still, and we'll give you pain meds and something to help with the healing. He did great, though. No concerns."

"OK. Thank you Dr." Faith smiles as Dr. Fordham turns and heads back through the heavy double doors down the hallway on the left.

Faith thought about bringing her laptop so she could get some stuff done with the wedding, but she decided it could wait and that a good book was exactly what she needed.

She looks back down at the open pages and begins reading again. A few moments later, she barely notices Jonathan walk through the door.

"How's he doing?"

She lifts her gaze to him coming out of the vision in her mind. "He's out of surgery and in recovery. Dr. Fordham said he did wonderfully."

"Good."

"I wasn't expecting you to be here." She smiles at him.

"I figured I'd stop by during lunch."

"That works."

"I can grab us something to eat if you want." Jonathan offers just as they both hear Faith's stomach grumble.

"That would be great. I don't want to leave him here by himself."

"You don't have to." He says as he stands and kisses her on the top of the head.

Jonathan walks a few doors down to the café and orders them some sandwiches while Faith sits and reads a bit more.

When he comes back, he grabs an end table and moves it in front of them. The older lady sitting behind the counter gives him a wry look over the top of her glasses.

"I'll put this back when I leave." He says. She simply nods her head and goes back to whatever she was working on.

"Thank you, Jonathan."

"You're welcome, Faith."

"That was faster than I thought it would be."

"The café hasn't fallen apart without you." He says chuckling.

"I didn't mean that."

"No, I know. Georgina took care of me."

"She's the best! No wonder she got it so fast for us."

"And here I thought she was so quick because it was me."

"I am sure you worked your charm on her like you do all the ladies."

"Not all the ladies. Just you."

"Really?" Faith asks raising her eyebrows in disbelief.

"Really. I'd never use this magic on anyone else. Only you."

"Oh. Now its magic is it?" She giggles and Jonathan wraps his arms around her pulling her into him sideways.

"Of course it's magic, what do you think got you? It wasn't my looks, or my money. You didn't even know about that when you agreed to go out on a date with me."

"You're looks most definitely had something to do with it, Jonathan. You're the most handsome man I've ever seen."

"Thank you, Faith. You're the most beautiful woman I've ever laid eyes on. That's why I had to have you all to myself."

Jonathan releases her and takes his sandwich in his hands instead then takes a bite.

"I'm glad you felt that way."

"I still do." He says through his half-filled mouth.

"So romantic." She says and giggles again.

Jonathan wipes his mouth with a napkin and says, "You know I didn't have the best childhood after the age of eight. Sometimes I forget my manners." He gives her a look letting her know he's joking.

"I'd say you can't use that as an excuse because it isn't fair, but you can because it isn't fair."

"No it isn't." Jonathan says taking another bite of his sandwich and seemingly looking across the room at nothing.

Faith takes a bite of her sandwich and then takes a sip of her frozen lemonade he got her. She feels the tiny little ice pieces melt as they go down her throat. "This was a great idea, Jonathan. Thank you." She says with the cup in her hand.

"It's so good, and on a hot day like today it's that much more refreshing."

Just as they finish eating one of the techs comes out to update them on Zeke's progress.

"We'll help you get him out to the vehicle shortly. Danielle can get you guys checked out and fill Zeke's meds."

"Thank you so much." Faith says with a smile. Then she and Jonathan walk up to the counter.

"I'm going to have to get going after this." He tells her as they walk.

"I know." She says and she squeezes his hand. "I'm just glad you could be here at all." She smiles.

Danielle greets them, then gives them a brief breakdown of the prescriptions Dr. Fordham has ordered and goes over how and when to administer them. She explains the time frame of healing and that they should keep him calm and as still as possible for the next couple of days.

Faith agrees and Danielle tells them the total due. Jonathan pulls out his wallet and pays her.

Then Danielle goes over the paperwork with Faith, highlighting and circling important things. Jonathan kisses Faith on the cheek and says, "I've got to get going. I'll see you and Zeke at home later." He quickly moves the table back to where he originally got it from and heads out into the bright sunlight.

"Thank you for coming, Jonathan." Faith calls after him as he's walking out the door.

"Well he left abruptly." Danielle says.

Faith tries hard to sound polite. "He was only here on his lunch."

"Makes sense, I guess." She shrugs.

Danielle finishes the paperwork and hands Faith a bag with Zeke's prescriptions.

"Thank you."

"You're welcome. They should be out with him soon."

Faith is excited and a bit anxious. She isn't sure what to expect. She's never taken care of a dog that has had surgery before. What happens if he gets too excited and rips something open? She tries to shake the thoughts from her mind and reminds herself that she is a capable woman and everything will be fine.

She loves Zeke and that love will help her to know what to do to help him. At least she's always assumed that's how mothers know what to do to help their babies. She breathes in sharply as her heart sinks when she thinks of the miscarriage she endured just two and a half months earlier. How has time gone so quickly since then?

She isn't able to allow herself to fall into those thoughts because as soon as it hit her she sees the tech bring Zeke through the double doors which drives the thought of her angel baby from her mind. Zeke looks so sleepy and not at all like himself.

"Zeke did manage to go to the bathroom. Remember though a bowel movement might take a bit longer. The meds can sometimes affect that as well. He'll be out of it for the next few hours. You'll want to give him the Rimadyl starting at ten o'clock tomorrow morning. We injected him with a long lasting pain medicine right after surgery."

"Great. Thank you." She says as she takes the leash from the tech.

"Call us if you notice anything out of the ordinary. Otherwise it was a routine procedure and we expect him to be back to his old self in a couple of days.

"That's wonderful!' Faith says as she starts for the door.

Getting Zeke into the car was easier than she anticipated. She has to lift him and he's getting quite heavy, but unlike normal he isn't flailing around trying to right himself.

He sleeps the whole way home. After they park in the garage his eyes open slightly, but then softly close again.

Faith rouses him as she gets him out of her Range Rover. He doesn't seem interested in walking into the house at all, especially since he has a donut around his neck to keep him from licking or chewing on any stitches. Faith and Jonathan agreed that was a little more humane way than the cone of shame.

Feeling the weight of him in her arms, she carefully steps up into the house from the garage and slowly walks over the travertine tile into the living room where she finds one of his beds and gingerly lays him down.

Zeke picks his head up to look at her with sleepy eyes. Faith sits down on the cool tile floor beside him and gently pets him. He closes his eyes once again. She stays there with him until Jonathan gets home an hour and a half later to find her sitting on the floor.

"Hey, how is our guy doing?"

"He's been sleeping since I brought him home. I can't bring myself to stop petting him and giving him whatever comfort I can."

"He's lucky to have you, Faith. Is there anything I can get for you?"

"No, but I do need to use the bathroom."

"I can sit with him if you'd like."

"That would be great. Thank you, Jonathan."

They switch places and Faith quickly walks to the bathroom. When she's finished she walks into the kitchen and takes a couple of glasses and a bottle of wine down.

"Did you want some?" She calls to Jonathan.

"I think I'll have a beer."

"OK." She says as she puts one glass back and takes a beer bottle from the fridge instead. She watches Jonathan as he gently pets Zeke's head.

"Has he woken up at all since you got him home?"

"He walked down the hall to me at the vet's office. He was pretty groggy though and fell asleep in the car on the way home. I carried him in here and laid him down."

"Should we try to wake him?"

"Probably. It wouldn't be a bad idea to try to get him to go potty outside. The tech said he went before he came out to me."

Jonathan looks at Zeke and starts petting him slightly harder. "Zeke, it's time to wake up. Do you want to go outside?" He says excitedly.

At the sound of Jonathan's voice, Zeke opens his eyes and slowly picks his head up. Jonathan keeps petting him. And then repeats, "Do you want to go outside?"

Zeke starts to move as if he's going to stand, so Jonathan moves back a little to give him space. Faith stands beside him and says, "Zekie, are you ready to go outside?"

Faith thinks she sees the slightest tail wag and then he trepidatiously rises to his paws. Gingerly he steps toward Faith. A smile spreads across her face as she starts for the sliding glass doors which lead to the back patio and the yard.

Zeke slowly follows her as she coaxes him to keep coming with her. Jonathan follows behind. The three of them walk around the patio in the grass. Zeke glances up at them every few steps.

Once he's relieved himself, Faith slowly walks him into the house. Zeke heads straight for his bed and lays back down.

"I'm going to start getting dinner going." Jonathan says as he takes a swig from his beer.

"Thank you, Jonathan."

"No problem, Faith. You know I'm happy to do it and Zeke needs you right now."

Faith sits back down on the floor beside the already sleeping dog and goes back to petting him.

After dinner, Faith and Jonathan curl up on the couch and watch a movie while Zeke sleeps in his bed. When the movie finishes, Jonathan picks Zeke up and brings him outside first and then into their room.

Snuggled in bed Jonathan says, "You were really great with Zeke today. Like I said earlier, he's lucky to have you. We both are."

"Thank you, Jonathan."

"I'm serious."

"I know you are."

"You're going to make an amazing mother someday, Faith."

"I appreciate you saying that." A pang suddenly in her gut.

"I wasn't sure if I should."

"The miscarriage still upsets me, but I am starting to think of it a little less. I was reminded of it today, though."

"When was that?"

"When I was at the vet's office. I was thinking about how love guides mothers to know what their babies need. I was hoping it would be the same with Zeke."

"It seemed to be."

"It was and it will be when we have children, eventually. I'm not sure when I'll be ready to try again. I'm afraid of having to go through a miscarriage all over again."

"We'll take as long as you need, Faith."

'Thank you."

Jonathan wraps his arms around her tightly, pulling her into him and he kisses the top of her head.

Chapter 25

Lassitude

Noun; a condition of weariness or debility, fatigue

First days of school never get easier for Faith. She is always equally excited and nervous no matter how many years she's a teacher. She understands there's no reason to feel nervous, the kids are always fun and excited too. She simply has such high hopes for the year.

She met her new students at open house on Thursday night. Zeke was doing better than she could have imagined and Jonathan even came home a little earlier so Zeke wasn't alone. The open house is always somewhat overwhelming with meeting the kids and their parents, plus her nicely refreshed room gets filled to the brim with supplies.

She appreciates everything the parents bring in, of course, but she still has to find a place for it all. This set of students seem entirely as fun as last years, and she even has some siblings from previous years which is always fun for her.

This first day of school is no different than most others. It's warm and humid, even with the air conditioning running in the room it can't cut the humidity down enough to make it comfortable. The kids are all excited to be there, but are also still energetic from the summer and not having the same kind of structure that the school day provides.

Lots of breaks and recess time is key. She also doesn't fool herself into thinking they'll be able to get to anything more important than getting to know each other.

By the end of the day, Faith is exhausted. So when Kay Obrecht walks into her room she has to try really hard to be nice to her.

"How was your first day, Faith?" Kay asks.

Wondering where this conversation is going Faith says, "It was good, as far as first days go. How was yours, Kay?"

"It was good. I love first days. The kids are probably the best behaved they're going to be all year. They haven't figured out how to push your buttons yet."

Faith doesn't agree with her statement so she simply stares at her leaving the silence between them linger.

Kay continues as she walks around Faith's classroom looking around in an almost snooping way. "I heard you had an eventful summer." She turns on her heals to look at Faith.

Faith unsure of what she's getting at exactly simply replies. "Yup."

"Well, I sincerely hope that planning a wedding doesn't get in the way of you doing your job." Kay says as she eyes Faith's engagement ring.

"Kay, what I have going on in my personal life is none of your business."

"It is my business when it affects your work."

"Which it isn't. Besides, you're neither principal nor superintendent, which is to say, you're not my boss, so it isn't your place."

"It hasn't affected it yet." Kay says with emphasis.

Faith rolls her eyes. "You can leave my classroom now. Thanks." She says as she sits down at her desk and moves around some papers. She's done giving Kay any of her attention.

Kay audibly gasps. "You're rude."

"No, I'm busy." She says not looking up from the stack of papers she has in front of her.

It takes Kay a few more moments to realize Faith isn't going to look up and address her anymore before she walks out the door.

A few moments later Faith sees a woman coming to her door. She doesn't want to look up from her papers in case Kay has decided to come back again.

"A-hem. Are you too busy to even notice your best friend has come to see you?" Jackie says joking.

Faith looks up with a wide grin on her face. "Sorry, Kay was just in here. I was afraid she didn't take the hint the first time and came back for more."

"What did you say to her?" Jackie asks, her eyes wide.

"I simply told her she could leave my classroom."

Jackie laughs and then says, "Wait. Why was she in here in the first place?"

"She apparently heard about my engagement and was concerned that wedding planning would keep me from doing a good job."

"What the hell?"

"No kidding."

"I can't believe her sometimes. Where does she get off even coming in here with an accusation like that? I swear once I'm superintendent she's getting canned."

"I'm pretty sure you can't fire someone without probable cause, Jackie. Although I do love the thought and the gesture." Faith nods.

"It's not just for you. I'm certain there are things she's done that would be cause for termination."

"We can only hope. You know you're going to have to build quite the case. It's got to hold buckets of water because she's going to fight like hell, especially if it comes from you."

"What's that supposed to mean?"

"She's going to think you did it to get back at her for me."

"Let her think that. It's only partly true." Jackie laughs then continues, "No, seriously though, she isn't a good teacher. I'm not sure why she even chose to become one."

"I'm not either. You should have heard the way she was talking about the students."

"That's exactly what I mean! And that's exactly what's going to put her ass out on the street."

Faith smiles at the image Jackie has painted on her brain. "Sounds good to me, but you have to become superintendent first."

"In due time, Faith."

"It's kind of crazy, you and Hope are both graduating this year."

"Not so crazy. I'm getting my Masters, that's a bit more involved and obviously takes longer."

"I'm proud of you." Faith gives Jackie an endearing smile.

"Thank you, Faith. That means a lot." She pauses for a moment and then continues, "I don't think anyone has told me that when it comes to school."

"I'm sorry I haven't said it before now. I guess I thought you knew."

"With the parents I grew up with, I don't need the external reassurance. I do appreciate it immensely though, Faith."

"You're welcome, Jackie. Considering your childhood and upbringing you've done extremely well for yourself."

"I did it in spite of them. They will take credit for my success all day, every day, but it doesn't belong to them."

"No, it doesn't. It doesn't belong to anyone but you."

"I think that's why it was more of a breaking point when Tom wasn't supportive. I don't need more unsupportive people in my life. I've had that my whole childhood. I didn't have a choice in that. I do have a choice in who I spend my life with as an adult, though."

"Have you heard anything from him?"

"No. I'm glad I haven't. It makes things easier; cleaner cut."

"Right. I'm glad you did what you needed to do for yourself. It can be hard to put your needs and desires above others. I feel like we're raised, as women, to be nice to everyone, to never want to hurt anyone's feelings, and to put ourselves on the backburner if it makes someone else feel better. It's a pretty shitty thing to have to work through after years of it being expected."

"It's not only parents forcing that down our throats either; teachers, doctors, bus drivers, grandparents, just adults in general. It's terrible. That is going to be something I miss about being a teacher. Having such an influential relationship with the kids. I hope that I can still be a positive example to them when I'm promoted."

"I'm certain you will be. You're an incredible woman, Jackie."

"Thank you, Faith. We both are."

"Yeah, we are." Faith says smiling at her. "How did your first day go?"

"You know, as good as first days can go. The worst part is trying to remember all of their names. I feel like every year it takes me too long to memorize them all."

"Same here." Faith giggles to herself at the similarity between her answer to Kay and Jackie's answer to her.

"What's so funny?"

"That's nearly the same answer I gave Kay. Well, minus the part about the kids' names. I do agree with that though."

"That is funny. We need to plan something soon, dinner or something."

"Yeah, I know we're both busy with school starting back up, you have classes starting back up and I've got wedding planning stuff. All of that makes it harder."

"It's a good thing we work together, we might not see each other otherwise."

"The realities of being adults. As kids we wanted to be adults so bad, now look at us, not doing any of the cool things we thought we would."

"So true." Jackie laughs. "We'll figure something out, and you know I'm always here to help with wedding planning stuff if you need it."

"Thanks hun." Faith says as Jackie turns to walk out her classroom door.

As Faith finishes up for the day she decides to text Jonathan.

> Faith: I was thinking, we should go out to dinner with Jackie and Rowen sometime. If they're going to be in the wedding together, it might be good for them to meet.

Jonathan: That's not a bad idea, but I haven't decided if Rowen should be my best man yet.

Faith: Right, I thought dinner and drinks went well and you've known each other a long time...

Jonathan: I'm still thinking about it. How did your first day go?

Faith: It was good, but I can't wait to go home. I'm finishing up a couple of things and then I'm going to head home.

Jonathan: Sounds good. I shouldn't be late tonight.

Faith: OK, see you in a little while.

Faith looks back down at the stack of workbooks on her desk. She grabs them and walks around the room placing one on each of her students' desks. Hopefully this will help them understand tomorrow will be the start of getting back into learning. The structure of the day is a bit different when they go from kindergarten to first grade so it's important to introduce that to them, along with the expectations early on in the school year.

The sun is pouring in through the large windows casting a yellow glow across the room. As she sets the last workbook down on the desk, she looks around the class and takes a moment to appreciate the end of the first day of the school year. She has a good feeling about all of it.

Last year was special because she had a lot of the same students as the year before since she moved from kindergarten to first grade. She feels much more settled in this year, though, which is giving her much more confidence and reassurance.

Chapter 26

Altitude

Noun; a high level

The Stallions stadium is packed. There isn't an empty seat in the place! The sun is high in the afternoon sky on a beautiful Sunday. Jonathan, Faith, Diane, Frank, Hope and Andy are sitting together in a row enjoying the game.

"They've been playing so well lately. This is bound to be a great game!" Frank says excitedly. "Thank you guys so much for getting these tickets for us all."

"We thought what better way to celebrate Father's day than to go to a baseball game as a family in September?" Jonathan chuckles.

Frank pats Jonathan on the shoulder and says, "It's the perfect way! Especially when we might make it to the World Series!"

"If we win this one we're one game closer!" Jonathan finishes and takes a swig of his beer.

Sitting behind home plate gives them one of the best vantage points in the game. It can be somewhat hard to see the outfield plays, but they usually run the replay on the jumbotron anyway. Frank at least seems very pleased with everything about today. Including the fact that their team is winning.

Jonathan is even more pleased with being able to order food and drinks from their seats and have it delivered. They only miss a part of the game if they have to use the restroom!

He thinks back to Father's day. It was filled with a mix of feelings. He and Faith had lost the baby a few weeks before and the fact that no one brought it up was almost worst. But then again, would he even be considered a father if the baby was never born?

Faith was extremely thoughtful, though. She understood better than anyone how tough that day was going to be. She had gotten him a small picture frame with the words "Angel Baby" inscribed and one of the pictures from the ultrasound inside. She cried as he opened it. He still isn't sure what to do with it. Putting it on his desk doesn't seem right, so for now it's displayed in his closet.

Jonathan figured with it being in there it also isn't a constant reminder for Faith.

Just then Strewn hits a homerun and the stadium erupts in cheers all around him, pulling Jonathan back to the present.

"Yes! Way to go Strewn! Way to go!" Frank yells in excitement next to Jonathan. Then he looks at him and continues, "That was an awesome hit!"

Jonathan nods his head as he watches Strewn round the bases. Faith reaches for Jonathan's hand squeezing it. She leans in to him. "I love seeing you two like this. It makes me happy."

Jonathan kisses the top of her head. "That is all I want to do in this life, Faith, simply make you the happiest I possibly can."

"You do, Jonathan."

Next up is the Stallion's second baseman, Trenton, who is also a great hitter. Frank says, "They should have spaced these two out more. Let more guys get on base in between them!"

"Maybe we should go tell the Stallion's manager that." Jonathan laughs.

Frank puts his hands up. "I don't mean to tell the man how to do his job. If this is what has been working for them, then so be it. It makes more sense to me to have your big hitters up when there's a better chance of having guys on bases."

"I hear you." Jonathan says in agreement.

Trenton swings and hits a strong foul ball down the third baseline. The pitcher winds up again, sending a fastball towards Trenton. Trenton swings and the ball explodes from his bat flying out over center field into the stands. The cheers from the crowd surrounding them are deafening. Trenton trots around the bases easily and celebrates with his teammates as he approaches the dugout.

"I love watching them celebrate like that! That's what the game should be about, just having fun playing!" Diane shouts above the hoots and hollers from the crowd.

Faith looks at her mom around Jonathan and her dad and nods her head in agreement with a huge smile on her face. Hope and Andy are sitting on the other side of Faith.

Jonathan has a thought that maybe they should split the seats up between two rows next time to help keep all of them within talking distance at least. If the Stallions make it to the World Series he'll have to make sure he buys the tickets in that way.

"How is the new position going?" Diane asks Jonathan.

"It's been great! Not too different from what I expected it to be."

"Well that's good." Diane says.

"It is, plus, I'm able to work the same amount of hours which is nice!"

"That is great! I'm sure Faith appreciates that!"

Poking her head out around Jonathan she says loudly, "I do!" And then lets out a giggle.

In the last inning of the game, the score is too tight for comfort. The Crows have bases loaded. If their player that's up to bat hits a grand slam, the Stallions will lose. This game is the last in the series which is currently tied.

Everyone in the stadium is collectively holding their breath as the Stallion's pitcher delivers a curve ball to the Crows' batter who swings and narrowly misses. The stadium is as silent as it's been all day as the pitcher winds up to send another ball over home plate.

The umpire calls a strike and the batter gives him a look of disbelief. Then he steadies himself back into the now barely visible batter's box. The pitcher sends another baseball in the batter's direction, but a bit on the inside this time. The batter jumps back in an exaggerated manner.

Frank shakes his head. "They need to end it. Stop messing with him, and strike him out already!"

"You tell him, Daddy." Hope shouts down the row.

As Jonathan looks around the stands he sees that there are some people who are too on edge to sit in their seats. The pitcher is getting ready to throw again as the batter steps back into the box. He does his wind up and delivers a perfect changeup. The umpire calls a strike. The batter throws his bat in frustration. The umpire then ejects him from the game.

Again, the stadium is filled with deafening cheers! The Stallions have won the game and the series! They are one step closer to going to the playoffs!

Jonathan feels both proud of the team and excited to see them continue on! Faith looks at him and begins laughing.

"What's so funny?" He asks.

"I find it hilarious that a year ago you could have cared less about all of this, and now you're entirely wrapped up in how this team is doing."

"I blame your dad, but I also blame Aunt Suz."

"How so?" Faith asks with a confused look on her face.

"Aunt Suz had zero interest in any sports and she certainly wasn't going to cover the cost for me to play any."

"I'm sorry she was so horrible to you."

"It's absolutely not your fault, Faith. She should have never been the one to take me in after my parents passed, but there was no one else."

Jonathan feels Faith reach for his hand, takes it in hers and gives it a quick squeeze. He smiles at her and takes his attention back to the players celebrating with one another on the field.

Frank pats him on the back. "I can feel it, son. We're going to the playoffs and then we're going to the World Series!"

"I think you're right!" Jonathan puts his arm around Frank and says, "Thank you for fostering this new interest and being the one to introduce me to it!"

"You're very welcome, son. I'm glad it's something we can share!" Frank says enthusiastically.

"I am too, Frank."

Everyone slowly begins to file out of the packed stadium. The line of cars leaving the parking lot is so long that it wraps around the stadium in multiple lanes.

Jonathan drove his Mercedes to the stadium which fits all of them fairly comfortably. The drive home takes quite a bit longer than the typical forty-five minutes due to traffic and the stadium being on the far west side of Caulfield.

By the time Jonathan has dropped everyone off at their homes he and Faith are both entirely exhausted. Between the excitement of the win and the downtime in the car after, it has taken its toll on their energy. It's barely even eight and they're ready for bed.

Chapter 27

Pulchritude

Noun; beauty, especially a woman's beauty

On the Saturday following the Stallions' game, Carmine rings the doorbell to Jonathan and Faith's opulent home. They rest their hand atop the handle of the large hard covered rolling case which contains all of their photography equipment. Faith promptly opens the double doors welcoming them inside with a huge smile. Zeke comes over to sniff both them and their case of things.

"I've so been looking forward to this since we set it up over a month ago!"

Carmine takes both her hands in theirs and says, "I have too! You look so gorgeous." Then they spin her to have a full look at her. "Oh yeah, you're going to photograph so beautifully! Where's the husband to be?" They ask.

Jonathan clears his throat as he stands in the living room leaning against the massive fireplace mantle. "That would be me."

Carmine releases Faith's hand and moves to take Jonathan's in theirs instead. "Faith wasn't kidding when she said you were easy on the eyes. It's great to finally meet you, Jonathan. I'm Carmine Williams."

Jonathan shakes Carmine's hand and says, "It's great to meet you too. Faith had so many wonderful things to say about you as well."

Carmine fans themself and says, "Stop! You're going to make me blush!" They all laugh and Carmine asks, "Would you like to give me a tour and show me any rooms or spaces you'd like photos taken in?" Just then their eyes move through the space to the sliding glass doors which lead to the back yard. "This is going to be gorgeous! I can't wait. I do apologize that we weren't able to set up a time for me to come look at the space before now. Things have been extremely busy with the end of wedding season approaching and now parents are booking their kid's senior portraits."

"It's no problem at all, Carmine. We're happy to have you today." Faith says smiling as she walks towards them and Jonathan.

Jonathan outstretches his arms to show off the place. "As you can see we have many magnificent backdrops to work with. Follow me and we'll show you the place." As he finishes he takes Faith's hand in his.

They walk with Carmine through the house, including the space in the walkout basement and outside to the pool.

"I've got a few ideas, but I'm not sure of your comfort level."

Intrigued, Faith asks, "What do you mean?"

"Well, I'd like to get some shots in your bedroom with the two of you comfortable on your bed. I was also thinking a few in your swim suits by the pool. Of course we have to use that amazing scenic view you guys have over there." They gesture to the area overlooking Amethyst Bay. "We have as long as you need today. I'm free all day, so as many clothing changes and scenery changes as you'd like. I've got a huge memory card and the time."

Faith's face lights up! "I'm fine with all of those ideas!"

Jonathan gives Faith a look. "I don't think we need to use pictures of us by the pool for the invites."

"No, but we'll have others to use for those and we will at least still have the pictures of us by the pool."

"That's true." Jonathan concedes.

They are both dressed in business casual attire so Carmine decides to start with those pictures first.

"I think what we'll end up doing is running around your house all day. We'll base it off of outfits. When you change then we'll go to each of the areas that work with that outfit."

"That works!" Faith says excitedly.

They begin sitting in front of the fireplace and include Zeke in some of the shots. Then they go outside and walk around the property a bit taking photos both candid and posed. Zeke follows them unsure of what is going on, but not wanting to miss out on anything.

When they've visited all of the places Carmine had in mind for that outfit Jonathan and Faith change into a new one and they begin all over again. They repeat this a few more times.

"You should stay for dinner." Faith suggests. She quickly continues with, "Invite Jackson over! We can all go swimming! Jonathan is a great cook!"

"That's a wonderful offer."

Jonathan steps up and says, "We insist."

"Well, in that case, I'll give Jackson a call."

For the shots in the bedroom, Carmine suggests they have on more comfortable clothes. They save the photographs by the pool for last. When they've finished taking photos Faith and Jonathan jump in as Carmine shoots a couple more action shots.

They put their equipment away just as Jackson pulls into the driveway.

"Perfect timing! They've just jumped into the pool."

"I'm surprised you didn't jump right on in there with them!"

"I would have if I wasn't worried about my camera and their pictures."

"Do you know where we can change?"

Carmine loads the rolling case into their car and says, "Yup! There's a half bath off of the kitchen. Follow me, I'll show you where. The house is absolutely gorgeous!"

After the two change, they go out to the backyard to find Jonathan and Faith playing in the pool. Jackson nudges Carmine, "Their wedding is going to be a blast to shoot."

"I know right!"

Both of them go to opposite sides of the pool. Jackson yells, "Cannonball!" and they both run and jump into the pool simultaneously splashing Jonathan and Faith.

The four of them are laughing and Carmine introduces them to Jackson saying, "In case you didn't realize, this is Jackson, my amazing husband." They glance at Jackson with such a loving look in their eyes. Faith is sure their love will surpass lifetimes.

"It's so great to finally meet you Jackson! Carmine has told us so much about you!"

"It's great to meet you as well, Faith! After you two had your meeting they couldn't stop talking about how incredible you were."

"That is so kind!"

"No, really. I was starting to worry they were second guessing their sexuality."

Carmine's mouth opens wide. "I would never!"

"It was a joke, Carmine. I know you would never. You're my husband and I am entirely infatuated with you."

"As I am with you."

"You two are adorable!" Faith says.

Jackson's smile spreads wide. "Thank you." He says graciously.

Jonathan says, "Those were some badass cannonballs! You two got us good!"

"A friend of ours has pool parties all summer. It's our favorite way to get into the pool." Carmine says.

"I can see why it would be." Jonathan chuckles.

"We were just talking about how fun your wedding is going to be."

"We're so excited for it!" Jonathan says.

"And it's at the Amethyst hotel, right?" Jackson asks.

"Yes."

"That place is gorgeous! It's honestly one of my favorite places to do weddings. They get some wonderful sunlight coming through making the videography easy with a dramatic edge to it. I fucking love it."

Carmine looks at Jackson again with that same loving gaze and says, "I fucking love how excited you get when you talk about the things that you love."

Jackson kisses Carmine on the nose and says. "Thank you, baby."

Faith feels as if her heart is going to explode with how absolutely sweet these two are. Jonathan places his arms around her and pulls her in for a kiss.

After a few more minutes, Jonathan gets out of the pool to go start on dinner, leaving Faith, Carmine, and Jackson to keep swimming.

"Your home is gorgeous by the way." Jackson tells Faith.

"Thank you! We recently finished building it in July."

"You two have been quite busy then!" Carmine says.

"We have, it wasn't even stressful though. We had Amethyst Bay Construction build it and everything went so incredibly smooth, like a dream really. I strongly suggest them if you two or anyone else you know might be interested in building."

"Thanks! We actually bought a house in Break Water Hills a couple of years ago."

"Jonathan and I were looking there, but at that time there wasn't much available at all. Which is why we shifted and started looking for land to buy and build on."

"We were lucky to get in there while the houses were being built still!" Carmine says.

"Yeah, it seems like it! We were pretty happy when we found this property. It's gorgeous and the lookout over the bay is so spectacular! We had to have it."

They all look towards the bay. Faith continues, "If you want, we can have a fire over there after dinner."

"That's a wonderful idea. Thank you, Faith." Carmine smiles.

"I'm glad you decided to stay and that Jackson joined us!"

"Me too, we don't get out too much, so this is perfect!" Carmine says.

"Especially if Jonathan's cooking is as good as you say it is." Jackson adds.

"Oh, it is!" Faith assures them.

A little while later, Jonathan comes back out fully clothed. He runs his fingers through his still damp hair and says,

"Dinner will be done in ten minutes or so, if you guys want to get out, dry off and change before we eat."

"That sounds great!" Carmine says.

Faith adds, "There are bedrooms and bathrooms upstairs you can use if you'd like."

"That's a brilliant idea! Thank you, Faith." Jackson says.

Jonathan turns to go back in the house while one by one they all get out of the pool. The sun is beginning to go down, but it hasn't hit the precipice of color yet. Even still, the air is definitely cooling off already.

Once everyone is sitting in the dining room Carmine says, "Thank you for making dinner, Jonathan."

Jackson continues, "And for opening your house and your pool to us. It made for a wonderful day."

Faith and Jonathan say, "You're welcome." Simultaneously and everyone laughs.

Faith looks at Jonathan as she fills her fork with food and says, "I suggested we have a fire out by the overlook after dinner."

"That sounds great!" Jonathan says.

Throughout dinner Carmine asks them a few questions about the wedding, the wedding party, and how much planning Faith has been able to get done since they first met.

The conversation flows and before they know it everyone has finished eating and are heading out to the Adirondack chairs on the far patio. Jonathan turns the string lights on and begins building the fire as Zeke lays down next to

Faith who's sitting comfortably in her chair with jeans and a hoodie on.

The colors in the sky are nearly done. Their vibrancy a shadow of what they had been just moments before. Faith looks out over the water as the colors ripple with the wind. She's thankful for the new friends they've made and the day they've been able to spend with them.

Chapter 28

Incertitude

Noun; absence of assurance or confidence, doubt

As summer turns to autumn Jonathan's hours get longer once again. Faith is actually surprised his nights didn't start getting later the moment the CEO position started. The colors of the leaves haven't begun changing yet, but the temperature is beginning it's descent for the year.

Carmine sent the photos over a week and a half after they had them taken and Faith is absolutely enthralled by them. With so many options, she's having a hard time deciding which ones to include on their invitation. Luckily, though, they can include more on the wedding website that will give guests any additional information and links they need as well as collect their RSVPs.

They sit comfortably on the couch in the living room while her and Jonathan go through the pictures together the following Sunday. He gives her his input on which ones will be best for the invites. She makes note of them, then goes to the website she intends to order them from. She pulls up their invitation options.

"We need to get this done today so that I can order them and we can send them out." Faith tells him.

"I'm right here, Faith. I can help you with whatever you need." He says assuringly.

"I just need your input right now."

"You got it."

As she pages through all of the options she looks back at Jonathan who is staring at the screen blankly.

"Did you see any you liked?"

"Well, there is a ton to choose from. I think we can narrow it down to white and black ones, though."

Faith goes to the filter and chooses those colors which only takes away about a quarter of the options.

"How many pictures do we want to include?"

"I think three would be a good start. We can't forget there's a back. There's also some that are either bi-fold or accordion style."

"What would we need that for?"

"Well, it's helpful if there's a lot of information to include on there."

"I don't think we need to include that much. I mean, the ceremony and reception are at the same venue."

"That's true."

Faith scrolls through and clicks on one and begins inputting information and pictures just to get a sense of what they may look like. She saves that version and then picks a different one from the numerous options and does the same. She does this with four more, not entirely satisfied with any of them.

"I liked the third one out of all of those the best." Jonathan offers. "But I also don't think any of them are quite hitting the mark."

"There are things we can add like foiling and raised lettering. We can also get lined envelopes. I think all of those things will help make our invitations feel more like what we're going for."

"I agree."

Faith inputs those filters as well narrowing down their selection by over half now.

The next two invitations she makes up are harder to choose between so she adds a third in for good measure.

Jonathan laughs at her. "You're only making it harder to make a decision."

"No. I'm giving us more options to choose from!" She insists.

"That too." Jonathan laughs some more.

Faith finishes the third one and sits back to take it in. She clicks to view the backside and sits back once again.

Jonathan chimes in, "This one is by far my favorite."

"What do you like about it?" Faith asks curiously.

"This one has great contrast with the black, white and different shades of grey. The silver foiling adds a cool pop and decorations on the edges also have that foiling so it is all cohesive and looks really nice."

"I like all of those things too." Faith says.

"So, what makes you unsure?"

"I'm not entirely certain. I think it's because once we make a decision and order them then it's final. We can't return them. They're going to be the first thing people see about our wedding. It's a big deal!"

"I agree it's a big deal. I just think if we choose the one we like now we probably won't have regrets when they come in the mail."

"But what if we do?"

"Then we make different ones and recycle these."

Faith laughs. "What?"

"I'm serious! If there's something you're not happy with, Faith, anything at all we'll keep trying until we find whatever it is that you will be happy with. The cost doesn't matter, you should know that."

"Thank you, Jonathan."

"Does that help you make a decision?"

"Only because it makes it feel a bit less final."

"Good. I'm glad I can help."

Faith leans into Jonathan as he puts his arm around her and pulls her into him. He places his lips on the top of her head and kisses her gently.

"You're the best, Jonathan."

"I want to give you everything you've ever wanted, Faith. You deserve that."

"Thank you."

"You're so very welcome, Faith. It is entirely my pleasure."

Faith finishes with the design and looks at Jonathan.

"I know we're going to want extra, but how many should we order?"

"Can you go to the guest list tab in your super neat workbook?"

Faith smiles from ear to ear as she minimizes the webpage and opens her wedding planning workbook, then she navigates to the tab labeled guest list. Opening it, she shows Jonathan the number of people they previously listed, in no particular order. The rows count up to three hundred-thirty-six which includes guests who are likely to bring a plus one.

"I didn't even think we knew three hundred people." Jonathan says flatly.

"No, not individually, but collectively. I'm not sure what the final numbers will be as far as RSVPs and who actually shows up."

"I'm sure there's an average percentage wedding planners figure on."

"I'm sure there is." Faith opens a new browser window and does a search for 'percentage of wedding guests that decline.'

"Twenty percent?! That seems high!" Jonathan says in surprise.

"It does, but it's probably right."

"That would be like seventy people declining. That seems like a lot."

"I'd rather them decline so we aren't paying for dinners no one is eating."

"That's true." Jonathan nods.

"We don't need to order three hundred and fifty invites since most of these cover at least two people." Faith does some quick calculations and then continues, "Two hundred should suffice and give us some extras to save."

"Perfect!"

Faith goes through the order process and closes the webpage after she receives the order confirmation.

"So what else needs to get done?" Jonathan asks eagerly.

"I don't think there's much more we can do today. There aren't many places open on Sundays." Faith notices the light dim in Jonathan's eyes so she opens the tab for the dinner options they had attempted to narrow down the day after their meeting with Brenda at the Amethyst Hotel. "We can try to pin this down a bit more. Then I'll call Brenda tomorrow and see when we can set up a time for a tasting."

"That's a great idea."

For the next hour they go back and forth pouring over the menu and discussing all of the incredibly delicious sounding options listed. Faith refers to the ranking system they used previous and double checks that they are still in agreement with what they'd decided previously.

"Picking options for other people to eat isn't easy." Jonathan says.

"No, it's not. Remember, though, they'll get to tell us what they want to order. Or well, they'll mark it on the website when they RSVP."

"That makes this all so much easier."

"It really does. We do need to register for gifts as well. We can include links for the stores we register at on the website as well."

"It's a one stop shop for our guests."

"Sure is!"

"I can't imagine what it would have been like planning a wedding before the internet." Jonathan muses.

"You have no idea how much of a nightmare that sounds like." Faith says with a chuckle.

Faith opens their wedding website and navigates to the registry page. Jonathan watches her add a way for their guests to give them monetary gifts to go specifically towards their honeymoon.

"Faith, I told you I was paying for the honeymoon."

"I know, but this way if they want to they can send us money to have an adventure or for a fancy dinner or something."

"I guess." He concedes.

"I'm sure most people prefer to put money in a card still." She shrugs.

"That's true."

Faith navigates to a couple of stores where they browse the inventory and add a couple of things from each to the registry.

"We don't need anything." Jonathan says in an almost frustrated tone.

"You do realize that's a good problem to have, right."

"Of course I do. It just makes me not want our guests to spend money on us."

Faith scrolls down on their wedding website and notices something that may help Jonathan feel better. "The wedding website will donate to a non-profit of our choice for every gift purchased through their website."

"That's really nice they do that!"

"It is! We can also include a note saying something about not expecting gifts that their presence at the wedding is gift enough."

"That sounds good, I guess."

Faith does a search through all of the organizations they can have donated to on their behalf. Jonathan and Faith agree on a local children's hospital who do a lot in Caulfield for families of children with cancer and other diseases that typically require long treatments.

"This makes me feel better about accepting gifts."

"Good. You know there are going to be many guests who still insist on buying a gift."

"I'm sure."

Faith looks at her wedding workbook and tabs through each page to see the progress they've made. She goes back to the very first tab and checks off some of the things they just finished. She smiles to herself.

"Are you feeling accomplished?" Jonathan asks already knowing the answer.

"Maybe." Faith teases. "I appreciate your eagerness with helping today."

"You're welcome, Faith. It's not that I wasn't eager before, it's just that sometimes other things, like the Stallions, take my attention. I realize that isn't fair and I'm sorry."

"Thank you. That apology means a lot."

"You're welcome, but it probably should have come sooner."

"Probably?"

"Definitely."

Faith checks the time in the lower right corner of her laptop's screen. "We should probably get ready for Sunday dinner soon."

"Probably?" Jonathan asks jokingly.

"Definitely." Faith replies with a sly smile.

Chapter 29

Solitude

Noun; the quality or state of being alone, or remote from society, seclusion

Autumn turns to winter as the days pass seemingly slower than ever. Faith has gotten more wedding planning done and even a couple of exciting updates from Mr. Caltroney about her wedding dress.

As Christmas approaches, Faith can't help but think of her sister's accident last year on that day. She and Jonathan have again agreed not to buy each other gifts for this holiday since they have the wedding and honeymoon to pay for. Faith likes this agreement for a couple of reasons; they're not spending money needlessly when there are other expenses, and more selfishly she doesn't have to try to come up with ideas of things to get Jonathan.

He's really good at picking out gifts for her, especially extravagant ones and she knows it isn't a competition, but she still can't help but feel like what she receives both in thoughtfulness and expense is greater than what Jonathan receives.

Over a month ago, they met with Brenda at Amethyst Hotel and had the tasting which helped to solidify their menu significantly. They also sampled cake, which Jonathan was extremely fond of. Brenda was then able to give them a quote for price per plate. During this meeting Faith also asked Brenda's opinion on a couple of the vendors she was leaning towards for music and flowers. Brenda was extremely happy to find out that Carmine and Jackson were doing their photographs and videography. "You won't be disappointed." She assured Faith.

Now, its five days prior to Christmas and this is the first day of Christmas break for Faith. She has decided to use this time to get more wedding planning done. Jackie and her mom have agreed to visit a couple of flower shops with her.

Rowen and Jonathan have gotten closer over the past couple of months, as well and he has decided to ask Rowen to be his best man. Faith and Jonathan are planning a New Year's Eve party with everyone which will help them all get to know one another better.

Faith is especially looking forward to the party. Their house looks so much better now than it did in July, mostly because they have all of their new furniture and have since been able to unpack and organize their things.

Faith is sitting on the couch when Zeke nuzzles up against her leaning all of his weight into her leg. Faith reaches down to absentmindedly pet him while she scrolls through her idea board for the wedding. Then she makes a couple of phone calls to florists to set up appointments. Similarly to how she had planned on dress shopping, she schedules them staggered throughout the day on Wednesday.

She sends both Jackie and her mom texts to tell them the times and explains that she will drive them all. There is one florist in Luna Shores, one in Sol Port, and the other in Caulfield. She wasn't sure about choosing one that was further away, but the shop owner assured her they've done many weddings at the Amethyst Hotel and the distance has never been an issue. They were all shops that came highly recommended by Brenda.

She and Jonathan discussed it and decided they would formally ask Rowen, Andy, Jackie, and Hope to stand up in their wedding at the New Year's party so, Faith begins to search for cute ways to do that.

Andy and Jonathan have since gotten closer as well, especially when the Stallions lost the last playoff game that would have gotten them into the World Series. Jonathan was really bummed, but Andy assured him there is always next year. They've been talking and getting to know one another even more at Sunday dinners ever since. Faith is loving being able to watch their friendship grow.

She has even added a countdown to their wedding day on the refrigerator. It is both exciting to see it change every day and daunting to know there is still so much to do.

With one hundred-forty-four days left to go Faith is starting to feel as if she has fallen behind. Because of the holidays though, it can be hard to plan meetings with vendors, she reasons.

As she scrolls through a couple more ideas she decides to begin ordering gifts to make them each special, personalized boxes. She'll need a little help from Jonathan for Rowen and Andy's, but she can order a couple of things now she knows they'll both appreciate.

Faith is still petting Zeke absentmindedly when she feels him tense up and then the doorbell rings. Zeke begins barking as Faith brings up the doorbell app to see who's at the door. She isn't expecting anyone. When her phone screen loads she sees Jackie standing on the porch waiting patiently.

She opens the door and says, "Hi! I wasn't sure who the hell was here." Jackie stands there smiling.

"Sorry, I probably could have text and let you know I was heading over, but figured I'd surprise you with my presence." She frames her large grin with her hands.

"I'm happy you're here."

"Oh, really? Why is that?"

"Because Zekie and I were just thinking it would be nice if it weren't only the two of us. Jonathan has been working a lot lately." Faith reaches down and pats Zeke's head.

"Well, I'm glad I showed up when you needed me."

Faith lights the fireplace and the two friends sit down on the couch in the living room.

"You never text me back about the florists."

"I'll be there." She grins at Faith.

"Good. I figured."

"Did your mom get back to you?"

"Yeah, she'll be there too."

"Do you have an idea of what you want yet?"

"That's the thing, with the wedding colors being black and white it kind of limits what colors I can have for flowers." Faith pulls up pictures of flowers from the inspiration black and white weddings she found before. "Most of these pictures are either in black and white or they have dark red, white, and then there's some that even have black flowers."

"Do you want to have red as a pop of color?"

"I don't think it looks bad…I'm just not certain about it."

"Maybe once we visit the florists you'll have a better idea of what you want."

"I'm hoping."

"I'm sure they'll have plenty of flowers and arrangements for inspiration."

Faith pulls up photos of black and white flower bouquets on her laptop screen.

"Or we can look online." Jackie laughs.

"Sometimes I don't want to wait for other people. I'd like to go into the meeting with the florists with an idea of what I want. Otherwise, I'm afraid I'll be convinced to do something they suggest even if it isn't exactly what I want simply because I don't know what I want. You know?"

Jackie stares at Faith for a moment and then says, "It makes perfect sense and I love that about you."

Faith laughs uncomfortably then says, "Thank you, Jackie. That means a lot."

"You're welcome, but I'm serious. When school first started we were talking about doing what I needed to when it came to ending things with Tom. This is so similar." Jackie motions towards Faith's research.

"I guess it is. Both instances are about not settling."

"Never settle. It's a waste of perfectly good time."

"And we both know how finite time is."

"Exactly. We can't go wasting it. Totally random question, but do you feel like you're settling when it comes to anything in your life?"

"Right now? No, not at all. This house is not even remotely close to settling. Marrying Jonathan definitely isn't me settling. He's amazing and treats me so well. Work is work, but I'm happy there and the kids have been great this year so far! I'm not planning on settling for anything with our wedding either. I think that about covers it, so no."

"Good. I'm glad to hear that. You deserve the best, Faith."

"Do you feel like you're settling with anything in your life, Jackie?" Faith asks curiously.

"Yes, and no. I feel like my apartment is settling. It's nice and works well for me, but I'd love to be able to buy a house someday, I just don't want to buy now when I owe so much on student loans that the mortgage is impossible. I'd rather wait a couple of years and buy when I'm making more money. And with that too, I feel like I'm currently settling with work because it's ultimately not where I want to be, but knowing that I'll get there eventually helps. I know I'm obviously not settling in a relationship so that's where the 'no' comes in."

Faith thinks about that for a moment and then responds. "It seems like all of the things you mentioned that you're settling for, you have either a plan or things in place to help you get to where you would rather be. That has to make it all feel better."

"It does in some ways."

"Do you want to stay for dinner? It'll probably be just us." Faith says and motions to herself, Jackie, and Zeke.

"That sounds great! You two are the best company in like three counties."

"Only three?" Faith asks raising an eyebrow.

"I was being conservative."

"Clearly." Faith says flatly until she can't hold her laughter back any longer.

Both she and Jackie erupt into a fit of giggles simultaneously.

Between laughs Jackie says, "You are the best company in every county in all the states!"

"Thank you, Jackie." Faith takes a deep breath trying to calm herself. Then asks, "Would you like some wine while I make dinner?"

"I can help." Jackie offers.

"If you want to, I won't turn down the assistance."

They both stand and go into the kitchen with Zeke in tow. Faith gives Jackie a couple of options to pick from. She decides on a pink moscato that Faith opens and pours into their wine glasses.

When they've finished eating dinner Faith leads the way into the great room in the basement where she puts on a movie. She grabs a couple of blankets and she and Jackie snuggle in on either end of the couch with Zeke just below them lying on the floor.

Towards the end of the second movie with both of them nearly asleep, Faith hears the familiar sound of Jonathan come in from the garage. She calls up from the basement, but Jonathan must not have heard her because there's no answer.

Faith sits up and tops off both of their glasses of wine.

"Thank you, Faith."

"You're welcome. I'm going to run upstairs and see Jonathan."

"You can pause the movie if you want."

"No, it's OK. I've seen this one before."

"It seems good!"

"Just wait, it gets better!" Faith smiles and then she turns to walk up the stairs. Zeke looks up at her and then promptly lays his head back down on his paws.

Jonathan is in the kitchen heating up some dinner when Faith walks in.

"Was someone else here for dinner?"

"It's nice to see you too… and yes, Jackie is still here. We're in the basement watching movies with Zeke."

"I didn't mean anything by that."

"Your tone was a bit accusatory."

"More curious than anything." Jonathan shrugs while giving her an innocent look. "I know you'd never cheat on me, Faith. I honestly thought you were already in bed."

"If Jackie weren't here, I probably would be."

"Come here." Jonathan moves closer to Faith. Reaching for her he takes her by the hips and pulls her into him.

He presses his lips against hers putting pressure on the small of her back while he pulls her body closer to his. As he pulls back slightly he says, "I've been waiting for that all day. I was afraid I wasn't going to get it."

"I'm glad I can give you what you want."

Jonathan's hands are under her ass before she knows what's happening. He picks her up and she quickly wraps her legs around him mid squeal. "What are you doing?"

"I was going to take you into the bedroom."

"Jonathan, I just told you Jackie is downstairs. Plus, you've got dinner waiting for you."

"Dinner can wait. I'd like desert first, please."

"Not when Jackie is here. I'm being a bad friend."

"OK." He says dejectedly as he places her back down on the travertine tile floor.

She feels the solidness of the floor beneath her and she lets out a giggle. "I'm going back downstairs now. You're welcome to join us if you'd like."

"I think I'm going to eat quick and then shower. How much time is left on the movie?"

Faith glances at the clock on the range and says "Probably about fifteen minutes."

"OK, I'll see you when the movie is done then. I'm sorry, I'm beat."

"It's understandable. You've had a long day. I've been meaning to ask, is any of this stuff you could be bringing home? We have the double office and all." She says glancing in the direction of the room that was intended to be used by both of them.

"I know, I wish it was."

"OK." Faith says simply as she heads back down into the basement.

Jackie smiles at her as she sits back down on the couch. "Seems like a long day. I bet he's tired."

"Yeah, he's eating and getting in the shower."

"It must be hard being home alone so much. Especially when we're on break from school."

"I keep thinking at least I have the wedding planning to keep me occupied."

"It'll be here before you know it."

The movie finishes and Jackie stands, gently folds her blanket placing it on the back of the couch, and then takes her wine glass and tips the remnants of it into her mouth.

"This was a good pink moscato."

They both start up the stairs with Zeke lazily following behind.

"It is! Hey, I was thinking, we're going to have to start planning the trip for your graduation soon!"

"I think figuring out when to go would be good for now. Obviously during the school year doesn't work and I'm not sure when you're planning on going on your honeymoon."

"Actually, I'm not either."

Both women laugh and Jackie says, "What do you mean? Haven't you and Jonathan talked about it at all?"

"We've talked about it, but he's planning it. Basically all we've discussed is that we'll be going when school gets out."

"So probably June."

"Probably."

They stop in the kitchen, setting their wine glasses down in the sink.

"We can shoot for the end of July into August." Jackie offers.

"Do you want it to be just us? Or should we also invite Hope? Come to think of it I think Andy mentioned something about planning a graduation vacation for her."

"Awww! That's so sweet. They're such a good couple! Hope seems happy."

"She does, I think Andy has been really good for her."

"I agree. As far as the trip goes we can do whatever works. It doesn't matter to me as long as it's warm and we can relax in the sun."

"That leaves a ton of options!"

Jackie starts for the door. "Thanks for asking me to stay for dinner. The movies were good too! We need more nights like this!"

"We do! They're always so fun!"

"I'll see you on Wednesday!"

"Yup, I'll pick you up. Don't forget."

"I couldn't possibly."

After Faith closes the door behind her she heads into the bedroom to find Jonathan fast asleep in bed. She walks carefully into her closet trying to avoid any stubbed toes and changes into her pajamas then climbs into the nice warm bed.

Jonathan sleepily wraps his arms around her and mumbles, "I love you, Faith."

She whispers back, "I love you, Jonathan." Then softly kisses his forehead.

Chapter 30

Splenditude

Noun; the quality or state of being splendid

All of the appointments with the florists went well. Faith had a very difficult time deciding who to go with since all of their ideas were great. She especially felt comfortable with Tutti though, who owns Tutti's Whimsical Florals in Luna Shores. She went above and beyond to calm any fears or misgivings Faith had. She was very impressed with her, which definitely helped in making the decision.

"Does this look OK?" Faith asks with her eyebrows pinched together.

"You look fabulous. Besides we're only going to your parents', it doesn't matter that much."

"I just want this Christmas to go better than the last one."

"We all do, Faith." Jonathan says as he places a hand on her shoulder.

They're standing in Faith's closet. Jonathan is standing behind her and they're both looking into the mirror. Faith has a navy blue long sleeved sweater dress on. The dark color complimenting her olive skin tone well.

Jonathan takes her silky long hair in his hands and moves it to one side, then he leans down and kisses her neck. Faith allows her head to fall back and be supported by his shoulder.

He lifts his head, just barely, leaving his lips close enough to brush her skin as he speaks. "Merry Christmas, Faith."

"Merry Christmas, Jonathan."

He kisses her neck again and then releases her. "I need to stop or we'll be late. You look amazing and this year will be better than last year. There's no way it couldn't be."

"Thank you." She says as she purses her lips.

"What? Don't you believe me?"

"I want to, I really do."

"You just gotta have faith." Jonathan practically sings.

Faith swiftly turns around and swats playfully at him. "You don't think I've heard that a thousand times?"

"Well, a thousand and one isn't overkill at all." He laughs.

"Yes, it definitely is."

"I'm surprised it hasn't come out before now."

"I was hoping that you would have thought better of it."

"Nope. It just now came to me. It's making me think I'm not as sharp as I used to be."

"You're getting old. It's to be expected."

"Hold on! I make a joke about your name, and you're going to make a joke about my age? Those are not even close to the same!"

"Sure they are."

"How so?"

"Both of which were chosen for us."

Jonathan takes a deep breath in knowing he's been outsmarted. "Alright, fine. You're right, Faith Brandt. Faith Hall in one hundred thirty nine days!"

"That's going to take some getting used to."

"What's that? Me telling you you're right or the last name change."

"Definitely the last name change. I do revel in you admitting when I'm right."

Jonathan smiles looking at her from the corner of his eye. "I know you do." He kisses the top of her head and says, "Finish getting ready now my love."

Faith smiles as he walks out of her closet and into his own. Zeke is laying in his bed in between the two doorways. He's always close, especially when it's only him and Faith at home.

"I'm excited to have our first Christmas with Zekie!" Faith shouts through the wall in between them.

"It'll be interesting to see him try to open his gifts."

Faith slips her heels on and walks to the doorway of Jonathan's closet, leaning up against the doorway.

Jonathan buttons his shirt and notices Faith in the mirror. "Don't you look sexy?"

"Thank you! You look pretty damn good yourself."

Jonathan flattens the shirt with his hands. "Thank you." He smiles at her.

"Are we almost ready?"

"I am, if you are." He says as he tucks his shirt in and then zips and buttons his pants and fastens his belt.

A wave of relief washes over Faith when they arrive at her parents' house, once she sees Andy and Hope are already there. The decorations and lights are creating the most magical Christmas ambiance. Frank has a Frank Sinatra Christmas song playing softly in the background.

"Good to see you made it in one piece this year, Despair." Faith says.

"Andy drove us. I thought it was probably the safest idea since my track record for driving on Christmas isn't all that great."

"Technically, your driving was fine. It was the truck driver's that wasn't good; mostly the fact that he ignored the stop sign." Faith walks over to the couch and pats her sister on the shoulder. "Seriously though, I'm glad you're here. I've been thinking about the accident a lot."

"Me too. And me too." Hope says with a shrug.

"I'm sure." Faith looks at Andy. "Thank you for getting her here safely."

"I wouldn't have it any other way." They say as they look at Hope with a smile.

Diane comes into the living room and asks Faith for help in the kitchen. Hope stands as well and follows them.

The three women work on dishing up the sides Diane has already made. Diane takes the ham out of the oven and replaces it with the pan of biscuits.

Hope starts taking the side dishes out to the already set table and lets everyone know dinner will be served soon.

After dinner everyone sits back down in the living room while Hope hands out gifts from under the large Christmas tree. Zeke and Orpheus even have some to open. They go around the room taking turns watching one another and simply being happy to be able to spend Christmas together this way. Last year's trip to the hospital and Hope's emergency surgery seems more on everyone's minds than it has been in months.

Diane seems especially grateful to have all of the people she loves most in the world sitting in her living room with their bellies full and joy written on their faces. Faith smiles at her mother.

Hope hands out another round of gifts and the whole thing starts all over again.

"Thank you for having us all over for Christmas." Andy tells Frank and Diane.

"Oh, you are all so welcome! I'm just glad everyone could make it!" Diane beams at them.

"Yeah, me too." Hope says flatly.

"Last year's Christmas wasn't all bad." Frank offers.

"What do you mean? I literally had a hole internally that needed to be fixed with surgery!"

"I meant that it's kind of what brought you and Andy together." He says gesturing to the two of them, then shrugs and continues, "Maybe not exactly, but it was the start. It's how you two met."

Hope looks at Andy. "That is true." She concedes.

"And we did eventually celebrate Christmas." Faith offers. "It was a little later than we would have liked."

"But the meal was still just as delicious and we spent time together as a family. That's what holidays are about, right?"

"Yes! That's exactly right." Diane says exuberantly.

Hope looks off into the distance for a moment and then says, "I don't actually recall much when it comes to our Christmas celebration last year."

"It was probably the pain meds." Andy offers.

Hope places her hand on their knee. "You're most likely right." She says as she leans into them.

Faith smiles, "We're looking forward to the New Year's Eve party. Are you all able to make it?"

"We'll be there!" Diane says.

"We will too." Adds Hope.

"Great! We might have a few surprises in store." Jonathan says.

"Would it be alright if we bring Orpheus with us?"

"Of course!" Faith says as she looks at the two dogs laying on the floor surrounded by new toys and wrapping paper. "They'll have a blast and Zeke can show Orpheus his yard for a change."

"I'm sure he'll be so happy to explore it!" Frank says.

Jonathan laughs. "There's plenty for him to explore. I spent a weekend building Faith some garden beds a month or more ago." He looks at Faith smiling. "Now they'll be ready for spring planting when the weather is better."

"I can't wait." She smiles back at him.

"What are you planning on planting?" Diane asks.

"I haven't thought too much about it, but definitely tomatoes and peppers, maybe some green beans or broccoli. I need to look into it more to know for sure."

"That all sounds good." Diane smiles.

"We'll be sure to share!"

"We would love that!"

"There's nothing like home grown tomatoes." Andy says.

"No there isn't." Diane agrees.

"We used to have a garden, right Mummy?" Hope asks. "How come you don't anymore?"

"It's a lot of work, and with the café I kind of gave it up one year and never got back into it." Diane looks at Frank. "Maybe we'll take it back up when we retire."

Frank starts laughing. "Right. When we retire."

"Hold up." Hope says, "Retirement when? I figure you two have at least ten more years before that happens."

"Yeah, ten more, probably." Frank says with a smile.

Hope sits up on the edge of the couch. "I'm not kidding. If you two are planning on retiring, I should be the first to know about it."

"We're not planning on it anytime soon, Hope. If we begin to, we'll let you know."

She visibly relaxes and simply says, "OK."

"You know, I know someone that might be helpful for retirement planning." Jonathan says. Then he adds, "It's not ever too early to start."

"I'll take their name and number." Frank says. "We've discussed things with our banker, but someone specifically for retirement planning would be ideal."

"Great!"

Faith thinks about how much closer Jonathan and her dad are now, even just since last Christmas. It makes her feel so grateful for finding Jonathan and for her family being so accepting of him.

Jonathan begins loading the gifts into his Mercedes shortly before midnight in preparation to head home. Andy follows him out to do the same.

"How was your first Christmas with the Brandt's?" Jonathan asks half-jokingly.

"I think it's better than last year." Andy chuckles. "It was actually Christmas when we all met last year."

"At least you didn't have to work this Christmas."

"That's true! See? So it is infinitely better than last year."

They both laugh as they walk back into the house. All of them go around giving hugs and saying goodbye and merry Christmas to one another.

Chapter 31

Latitude

Noun; freedom of action or choice

Faith has spent the last week preparing for this party; putting together the gift boxes for the wedding party and cleaning the entire house. Everyone will be showing up in an hour or so. Diane and Jonathan are getting everything prepped in the kitchen. Frank and Diane both came over early to help get everything ready.

Jonathan has put music on that's playing throughout the house. He's also built a fire in the fireplace.

Rowen arrives before all the others. The island is lined with plates full of hors d'oeuvres and the house has mixed aromas of various delicious food. Jonathan twists the cap off a beer bottle and hands it to Rowen.

"Thanks, man." Rowen says as he tips the bottle slightly in Jonathan's direction.

"No problem." Jonathan says as he starts up the stairs to give Rowen the tour.

"This place is incredible." Rowen says as he looks around taking it all in.

"Thanks, Faith picked most of the décor, but we both worked with the architect to plan the layout."

"You two make a good team."

"We think so too."

As they get to the top of the stairs, Jonathan shows him the bedrooms and bathrooms. Rowen says, "I've been thinking a lot about how everything went down when we first ran back into each other and I wanted to apologize for it getting off on the wrong foot. I'm glad we've been able to move past that. I'm happy to have you as a friend, Jonathan."

"I appreciate that, man. It's been great having you back in town. I should probably apologize for my response to your behavior as well. I'm sorry for threatening you the way I did."

"Water under the bridge." Rowen swats at the air. "Honestly, I would have reacted the same way. It was completely warranted. I'm starting to think the divorce gave me an excuse to act like a man whore. Not that I wasn't already acting like that in some ways before the divorce, but it definitely got worse after."

Jonathan looks at Rowen with a bit of sympathy in his eyes. It takes a lot to admit when you're wrong and to do the work to recognize what may be causing your behavior.

"We all have our moments, Rowen. It's good that you see it now."

"It's something that has been so engrained in me for so long, I'm not sure if it will ever be gone."

"Why did you get married then?"

"I thought she could save me from myself. She was incredible, Jonathan. So truly gorgeous and sweet, she was everything a man wants. Deep down I knew I would fuck it up." Rowen's voice trails off as his gaze lowers. When he picks it back up he's wearing a forced smile. "This place is really nice and you and Faith seem perfect for each other. Don't be like me, don't fuck up a perfectly good thing."

"I'm definitely doing everything I can to keep that from happening."

"Good." He stops and grabs Jonathan's arm before they continue walking. "This is the lawyer in me talking more than anything, but have you thought about a prenup? You know, just in case?"

"I know that won't be necessary."

"People can get very nasty during a divorce. They can become unrecognizable. I've seen in first hand."

"Rowen, I understand you're trying to help, and in that capacity, I appreciate this. However, I know a prenup is not something that I want to start my married life with Faith. Not that I need to explain my relationship to you, but she has never been about the money."

Rowen holds his hands up in surrender and then says. "I won't bring it up again."

With Jonathan so clearly putting an end to the conversation they descend the grand staircase back towards the entryway. They find the rest of the guests milling around the island. Most of them are snacking on food.

"It's nearly time to eat." Jonathan says loudly enough for everyone to hear over their conversations.

Rowen follows Jonathan into the kitchen where he's introduced to everyone who has since arrived while Jonathan gave him the tour.

Jonathan begins to introduce him to Hope when Rowen interrupts him by saying, "No introduction needed. We met at the café." He outstretches his hand. "It is great to meet you officially, Hope."

"It's great to meet you as well."

Faith introduces him to Jackie, next, who seems a little more smiley than normal. Rowen also seems to hold her hand and gaze slightly longer than he held Hope's or Andy's. Carmine gives Faith a look as if they noticed it as well.

When Rowen's eyes finally come away from being locked on Jackie's, Faith continues introducing him to her parents.

Once introductions are finished, Jonathan takes dinner out of the oven, and everyone makes their plates. Then they all head into the dining room to eat.

After they're finished eating, Faith and her mom work on getting everything put away while Jonathan leads everyone into the great room in the basement.

Lined up on the counter in the kitchenette are four large black boxes each wrapped with a white satin bow. Before handing them to their recipients he fills champagne glasses for everyone and hands one to each person. Faith and Diane come downstairs just in time to receive the last two glasses.

"A toast," Jonathan raises his glass then continues, "to all of the most important people in our lives. This past year wouldn't have been the same without you all." He walks over and puts his arm around Faith. "We both agree that our wedding wouldn't be the same if you all weren't a part of it."

Faith moves to grab the two boxes for Hope and Jackie. She hands the boxes to them as Jonathan hands the other two boxes to Rowen and Andy.

Faith begins, "Jackie, you can open your box first." Faith continues speaking as Jackie pulls the ribbon of her box and opens the lid. "You have been my best friend for as long as I can remember and I couldn't imagine my wedding without you standing by my side. Will you be my maid of honor?"

"I'd love to!" She smiles looking into the box. On the inside of the lid is the same question. In the box she finds a stemless wine glass that says 'I might be the maid of honor, but I'm not made of honor'. Jackie laughs. "This is so true." She holds up the glass.

As Jackie is going through all of her gifts, Faith turns to Hope. "Hope," She smiles at her sister. "You can go ahead and open your box. I know as kids we didn't always see eye to eye. Even now sometimes we don't, but I need my sister by my side on my wedding day. Would you be my bride's maid?"

"Of course." Hope says with what looks like tears forming in her eyes.

Faith holds up her finger. "Just so you know, Tee-Bee isn't getting an invite, though."

Hope laughs at the memory. "No, he couldn't possibly stomp all over everything now. And besides, I wouldn't allow it." She shakes her head.

"Thank you." Faith smiles then she turns to Jonathan.

"Rowen, go ahead and open yours next. It's been great having you back in my life these past few months. It may have gotten off to a rocky start, but we're definitely in a better place now. I'd really appreciate it if you'd agree to be my best man."

"I'd be honored, man. Thank you." Rowen looks in his box and pulls out a Movado box.

Hope and Jackie look at each other, smile, and then pull their boxes out too. Jonathan goes into the kitchenette and grabs Frank and Diane Movado boxes as well while Faith grabs Carmine and Jackson theirs. Then Jonathan says, "Andy, you can start opening your box. I couldn't have known when Hope first brought you around to meet everyone that we would have gotten so close. It's been great getting to know you and I would be honored if you'd stand up in the wedding as my groom's person."

"I'm grateful you've even thought of me. I would love to!" Andy opens their box and pulls out the box with Movado on it as well.

All of their guests open the watch boxes simultaneously followed by various different reactions. Faith hears her mom say "Oh my! That's a beautiful watch!" Frank agrees and begins taking it from the box to put his on right away.

Hope and Andy hold them up next to each other smiling.

"They're all matching. Since the wedding colors are black and white we went with a black face with a silver band. If you need them sized just take them into Riteger's Jewelry shop on Main and they will take care of you."

Carmine looks at Faith and says, "This is too much."

"No. It's just enough. The pictures you took of us for our engagement were incredible. I can't wait to see what you capture for us of the wedding. Plus, I am so grateful that on top of working together for the wedding we've all become friends. Our friendship means so much."

"Thank you." Carmine says and pulls Faith in for a hug.

"You're welcome!"

The four of them all have other things in their boxes that are more personalized to each of them. The ladies also have jewelry to wear for the wedding. The watches were Jonathan's idea. He came up with it when he was trying to think of something to get Rowen then suggested they get them all matching ones.

That day when they walked into Riteger's, Faith had no idea they would also pick out their wedding bands. It was quite an expensive day, but they did find exactly what they were looking for and Faith can't wait to place the wedding band on Jonathan's finger.

Hope stands and walks over to Faith embracing her quickly and powerfully. "Thank you, Doubt. I'm so happy for you guys and I can't wait for the wedding!"

"You're so welcome, Despair. I wouldn't be able to do it without you! You're not upset Jackie is my maid of honor, are you?"

"No, not at all. I've seen everything Jackie has done for you and how your friendship has grown and evolved over the years. I wouldn't want you to choose me over her. Plus, I'll have less stuff to do this way."

They both laugh and take drinks of their champagne. Jackie joins them. "Those boxes were such a great idea. Thank you guys."

"You're welcome! I'm glad you liked it."

"All the personal touches were perfect!"

"Well, I didn't want to do anything generic. You both deserve better than that."

"You didn't do Andy's?" Hope asks.

"No. That was all Jonathan. He did both Rowen's and Andy's and the watches were all his idea."

"Seriously? He did awesome!"

"He's pretty thoughtful."

"That's very apparent." Hope says with a sincere smile.

Faith smiles back feeling proud of Jonathan and even more grateful that he's going to be her husband. She looks across the room to find him and Rowen laughing about something. She's happy to see him having a good time with a good friend.

"Does it feel like the wedding is five months away?" Hope asks.

"Not at all. I feel like I have so much left to do and the time is going by so quickly."

"Have you gotten to see your dress yet?"

"No, and that's causing me even more anxiety. I mean I trust Mr. Caltroney and all, but what if I end up not liking it?"

"You can't think like that." Jackie says. "You're going to love it! You need to keep thinking about how you felt after that initial meeting with him. You were so excited!"

"It would have helped if I could have taken a picture of the drawing he did for me that day."

"I'm sure it would." Jackie agrees. "I think you'd still be a little worried at least until you see it in person."

"That's true. We need to pick out your dresses next!"

"What do you have in mind?" Hope asks.

"Something long and black."

"Any specific material or cut?"

"I think we need to go look before any decisions are made. Plus, I want you guys to be comfortable."

Jackie gives Hope a sideways glance with a smile. She chuckles and says, "We appreciate that."

"Speaking of comfort" Hope begins, "What about shoes?"

"Well, you both have black heels, right?"

"Yeah." Jackie and Hope respond simultaneously.

"Then those should be fine."

"That's great!" Hope says.

Just then Jonathan turns the TV on and switches the channel to the New Year's Eve ball drop in New York City. The lull from all the different conversations dies down as everyone's attention switches to the screen.

Faith walks over to Jonathan. "Do you remember this time last year?"

Jonathan smiles. "We were on our way here."

"The house wasn't even close to being done and I was hoping for a ring." Faith laughs a little embarrassed at the admission.

Jonathan wraps his arms around her. "And now you have one."

"We've been through so much in the last year. It's kind of mind boggling to think about."

Jonathan takes a moment to think back over the past three-hundred-sixty-five days. He breathes in deeply thinking about the bad things first, then he shifts his mind to some of the most beautiful moments like finding Zeke, the vacation to Napa Valley for their anniversary, and their engagement. "It sure has been a wild year. All that matters though is we're both still here. We've navigated it all together and I'm so grateful for that. I love you Faith Brandt, soon to be Hall."

"I love you Jonathan Hall, soon to be my husband." She smiles as he leans in for a kiss. Putting her finger up she says, "It's not midnight yet."

"I don't think there's anything saying you can't kiss before midnight, Faith."

"No, you're probably right."

"I know I am."

Faith beams at him as he kisses her fiercely.

As the clock strikes midnight a little over an hour later, the ball drops. There are kisses and cheering. When Faith and Jonathan pull away after their kiss, they notice there are two people still kissing quite passionately.

They look at one another, Faith is trying to hold back a laugh. Jonathan clears his throat and Jackie opens one eye recognizing that everyone is watching them. She taps Rowen on the shoulder letting him know to stop.

Rowen sheepishly pulls away and smiles, then says, "Happy New Year, everyone!"

Faith cannot contain her laughter any longer and bursts out in a fit of giggles. Jonathan rolls his eyes and says, "Happy New Year, Rowen."

Carmine, Jackson, and Hope all join Faith in laughter.

A few moments after the commotion, Frank and Diane announce that they're going home. "Thank you so much for inviting us, and for the watches! They're absolutely beautiful. Exactly like our little girl will be on her wedding day!" Frank says.

"Thank you, Dad. It's got to be a better year than the last one."

"It sure does!" Diane agrees.

"I'll walk you both out." Jonathan says.

"We both will." Faith says and she follows their lead up the stairs.

Jackie and Rowen are getting comfortable on the couch when they come back down the stairs into the great room. The two are sitting so close to each other that Jackie might as well be sitting on his lap.

Jonathan goes to the refrigerator and Faith follows. As he closes the door to the fridge he says, "What are your thoughts on that?"

"Given what you've told me about him, I'm not sure it's the best thing."

"I agree. Unless of course, Jackie is just using him in the same way, for some fun."

"I've never known her to do that, but it wouldn't surprise me either."

"So, we simply let it be then?"

"I think so."

"OK." Jonathan exhales sharply.

"You never know how these things could end up." Faith offers.

"No, we don't."

Carmine and Jackson say their goodbyes followed closely by Jackie and Rowen. Hope and Andy aren't too far behind them and Jonathan and Faith soon find themselves alone.

"Do you want to go for a walk?" Jonathan asks.

"Not in the woods." Faith shakes her head adamantly.

Jonathan chuckles. "No, just out to the lookout."

"Yes, in that case, I'd love to."

They head out the sliding door in the great room with Zeke following. When they reach the far patio area that overlooks Amethyst Bay, Jonathan turns on the string lights and pulls Faith into him, gently placing his lips on hers.

He pulls away and fishes his phone from his pocket. He starts his music app and pulls her back into him. "Will you dance with me?"

"Our first dance of the year." She says as she nods her head.

He wraps his arms around her tightly as they spin around the patio. "I know I said this last year, and in some ways it didn't live up to it, but this year is definitely going to be the best year yet!"

"Last year wasn't all bad." Faith says with a slight shrug.

"No, definitely not all bad. We made some incredibly beautiful memories that I'll cherish for a lifetime."

They end their evening dancing in the moonlight in one another's arms feeling the deep love between them and knowing that soon enough they'll be husband and wife. Finishing the evening in this way echoes their first New Year's Eve. Faith thinks back to the uncertainty she felt that night and feels grateful for the credence she feels now.

Chapter 32

Lippitude

Noun; soreness or bleary eyed

A mix of sadness and gratefulness washes over Faith as she wakes up in the late morning of January fifth. Today would have been their angel baby's due date. She hasn't told Jonathan, but she has been having dreams of the baby for the past week. She's sure it's because this day has been approaching. Now that it's here she is wishing she'd done more to plan to keep herself busy.

She's grateful she has the day off, but is wishing Jonathan did too. He gave her a kiss before he left early this morning to head into the office. Zeke comes over to her side of the bed and sniffs near her face giving her a quick lick.

"Good morning, buddy. I bet you have to go outside." She is also happy to have Zeke here with her.

Faith gets out of bed and lets him outside then heads into the kitchen to make a smoothie for breakfast. She rubs the tears from her eyes that seemingly formed out of nowhere. She clears her throat and peels her banana then drops it into the blender cup. As she adds the rest of the ingredients she replays all of the mixed emotions she first felt when she thought she might be pregnant. Then she thinks of how excited everyone was when they told all of them. When her thoughts move through to the early morning she woke up with such horrible cramps Faith feels the hot tears run down her cheeks again.

She grabs a tissue from the box on the credenza in the dining room and goes back to making her smoothie. In all these months she still hasn't been able to figure out why she had to go through that. She's wanted a large family for as long as she can remember. She's never even had a pregnancy scare before, but the first time she gets pregnant it's not viable? Why? It's a question that haunts her and even though she knows asking it is futile, she still finds herself doing it.

As she sits in the office staring blankly at the computer screen sipping her smoothie, Faith decides she should text Jackie. They haven't spoken much about what happened with Rowen on New Year's Eve and that could be just the thing to distract her.

> **Faith: Good Morning! What are your plans for today? I think I need to get out of the house.**

> **Jackie: I'm your girl! I can be there in twenty.**

> **Faith: I'll be ready.**

After she lets Zeke in the house, Faith goes into her closet, with her smoothie in hand, to begin getting herself dressed and ready. Before she knows it, Zeke is barking to alert her someone is there and then she hears the doorbell and his barking gets even louder.

Faith opens one of the double doors to let Jackie inside. "Thanks for coming over."

"No problem, I was thinking it would be nice to hang out before we have to go back to school tomorrow."

"Yeah. I agree. I'm glad to have today off." Her voice trails off as she continues, "It would have been my due date."

"Oh my! Hun, I'm so sorry. I forgot!"

"It's OK. I wouldn't expect anyone else to remember, and besides even if they did what would they say? Sorry your baby died inside of you? No thanks."

"No, I would say that I'm sorry you had to go through that. Are you still blaming yourself? Faith, it wasn't your fault." Jackie places a hand on Faith's arm

"I know that." Faith notices the disbelieving look that Jackie flashes her. "I do! I have a hard time accepting it some days. Today is one of those days."

"Understandably so. What would you like to do?"

"Anything. Just get me out of the house."

"Well, we can start with some lunch."

"Sounds like a plan."

Jackie pulls into the parking lot of Mama Garcia's and Faith feels some of her anxiety lift.

"Mexican works, right?" Jackie looks over at her with a smile on her face.

"Always!" She smiles back.

They head into the restaurant and are seated at a booth they've been seated in a handful of times before.

Faith decides to steer the conversation to Jackie and Rowen. "So, what exactly happened between you and Rowen on New Year's Eve?"

"We kissed when the ball dropped." Jackie says nonchalantly.

"Yeah, we all saw that." Faith chuckles.

"We saw literally everyone else in the room kissing and Rowen suggested we try it." Jackie smiles slyly. "It was really nice."

"Nice?...Nice!? It looked like you two were getting ready to tear each other's clothes off."

"It was not that bad."

"You didn't see it."

"No, I did experience it though." She flashes Faith that sly smile once again.

"You guys left at the same time, did you two continue the evening elsewhere?"

"No. There was definitely a part of me that wanted to though." Jackie says as she mindlessly flips through the menu she's seen a thousand times.

"It definitely looked that way."

"We exchanged numbers and haven't seen each other since."

"Maybe I should have forewarned you about him. I honestly didn't think you'd be interested. Your radar is usually spot on."

"Yeah, I definitely know he's not a man to commit. He's still relatively recently divorced and I get the feeling that it was all caused by him cheating."

"I'd guess the same. If all you're doing is having fun, then there's nothing wrong with that."

"Fun sounds good right now." A smile spreads across Jackie's face just as the waitress approaches the table.

They place their usual order and continue the conversation once the waitress has walked away.

"He has text me a few times, but it's all super casual."

"Casual would be best when all you're doing is having some fun."

"Agreed. What are Jonathan's thoughts on the matter? I'm sure you two have talked about it."

"Oh, we did." Faith laughs. "He agreed that the two of you having a good time wouldn't be a bad thing. Rowen isn't serious dating material."

"I get the idea that he doesn't want to be any kind of dating material."

"Right."

Their margaritas are delivered and both women take sips from their glasses. A few moments later the guac shows up and they begin snacking on that until their food arrives.

"Have you mentioned anything to Jonathan about how you're feeling today?" Jackie asks gently.

"He knows what today is. He actually left me a cute note and a fancy chocolate bar."

"Fancy chocolate? He's so sweet! You were definitely lucky finding him."

"I was. It's all because of you, well, and Tom."

"Yeah. It was good of him to invite Jonathan out that night. It was only because he knew he'd be sitting at the table by himself otherwise." Jackie half rolls her eyes.

"Well, either way it worked out well for me." Faith laughs as she glances at the large diamond ring on her finger. "My life has changed so drastically since that night. It's kind of crazy to think about."

"You deserve the best. It seems like he gives you that."

"He really does." Faith agrees. "Are you ready to go back to school tomorrow?"

"Yes and no. The kids are usually pretty unruly the week after Christmas break, but it's nice to get back into the daily schedule of it all."

"I feel the same way." Faith says.

The waitress brings their plates and asks if there is anything else they need. Both women shake their heads and thank her.

"We need to find a day to go brides maid dress shopping with Hope." Jackie says taking a bite of her chicken tamale.

"I think a weekend will work best for her, but either way she will need to make sure everything is covered at the café. I've also got an appointment with Brenda at the Amethyst Hotel, not this weekend, but next weekend to go over and hopefully finalize everything." Faith holds up her hand with two fingers crossed.

"That's exciting!"

"It is, it's also a lot, but I'm glad for the distraction. Between the house and wedding planning it's been very helpful in keeping my mind occupied. Sometimes I think it's the only reason I've managed to make it through losing the baby."

"There will be other chances, you know."

"I do. Knowing that doesn't make it easier though. In some ways it almost makes me more concerned for next time."

"Have you and Jonathan talked about when you might want to start trying again?"

"He's said whenever I'm ready. The problem is I have no idea when that will be. At this point, I'm afraid I'll never be."

"You've wanted a ton of kids since forever, Faith. There's no way you won't be ready at some point."

"That's true, I guess."

Feeling like she should change the subject Jackie asks, "What do you want to do after this?"

"I'm not sure. I hadn't thought about it, I just knew I needed to get out of the house."

"How about a movie? That new one came out at Christmas. The romantic comedy with what's his name?"

Faith stares blankly at her friend. No actor's names are coming to mind. She can't even think of the movie Jackie is referencing. "I'm not sure which one you're talking about, but if it seemed good, I'm game. Maybe a romantic comedy is just what I need."

"Perfect." Jackie checks show times at the closest couple of theaters and then orders tickets.

When they've finished eating, Jackie drives them into Caulfield to the nicest of the movie theaters in the area. Her phone vibrates as she pulls into the parking lot. After she parks she sees that Rowen has text her. A smile spreads across her face.

Faith watches her slightly concerned at the amount of swooning that appears to be happening. "It's just fun, right?"

"Yes. Just fun."

"It looks like you might be crushing a bit." Faith says in the most playful tone she can find.

"I'm not, but he is hot and he is handsome as hell. This could be a lot of fun and I rather like the prospects of that!" Jackie says in defense.

"OK." Faith says simply as she opens her car door and steps out into the cold dry January air.

Jackie's focus is stuck on her phone for the first few moments they're walking. Faith has to grab her by the arm and pull Jackie towards her to keep her from getting hit by a car that came around the corner too fast.

Jackie laughs nervously as she looks up from her phone at Faith. "Thanks." She says sheepishly.

"You're welcome. I guess we can say we're even now."

Jackie looks at her with total confusion on her face. "What do you mean?"

"The whole being drugged thing at Lee's Pub and almost dying…"

"Oh, yeah, right. I kind of think of it like this; there have been a ton of times in our lives that we have done things to 'save' the other. There is and never will be a tally sheet keeping track of whose turn it is to save the other."

"That sounds good to me!" Faith says as she opens the heavy door to the theater's vestibule.

Jackie's phone vibrates again and Faith laughs.

"It's nothing I'm sure." Jackie says as she glances at her phone screen. "Definitely nothing." She laughs.

"It's him again, isn't it?" Faith says.

"Yup. Which means it's nothing." Jackie smiles as she shoves her phone back in her pocket.

"OK." Faith shrugs.

After the movie is over Jackie drops Faith off at home. "Thank you for today, Jackie. I'm lucky to have you as a friend."

"We're both lucky to have each other, Faith."

"Especially for as long as we have."

"That's true."

Faith gives her a hug and goes into the house to find Jonathan standing at the island preparing dinner. Zeke excitedly greets her as she walks in the door.

"Hi there, beautiful. How was your day?" He asks as he walks towards her to embrace her.

His arms wrap around Faith and every worry that was in the back of her mind all day magically subsides. "It was surprisingly pretty good."

"That's good."

"How was your day?"

"It was busy, but I was able to get out at a decent time so that's always nice."

"Yes, I tend to agree." She smiles.

"I'm sorry I couldn't stay home with you today." Jonathan says as he lowers his forehead to hers.

"It's OK, I get it. It just happened that I was still on break today, it won't be like that next year."

"Right, but still. This year is the first major date when it comes to all of that. It would have been nice if I was here for you."

"Thank you, Jonathan. I did manage OK on my own. Luckily, Jackie also had off so we hung out."

"That's nice of her." Jonathan moves his head back as a smile spreads. "Did you talk to her about Rowen?"

"I did. Nothing has really happened yet."

"That kiss didn't look like nothing."

"That's exactly what I said! Well, almost exactly. She said if something does it's nothing serious."

"Well, I guess that makes me feel a little better about the whole thing."

"Me too."

Jonathan turns back to the range to finish making dinner. "Thank you for cooking, Jonathan."

"You know how much I love taking care of you. Speaking of which, would you like some wine?"

"That sounds splendid."

Jonathan grabs two glasses from the cabinet and then reaches for a bottle of Cabernet Sauvignon. After opening it he pours some in each glass and slides one to Faith across the counter.

"Thank you, Jonathan."

"You're welcome, Faith." He smiles at her. "I can't tell you how much I love coming home to you."

"I wasn't even here when you got home." She says half laughing.

"That's what made it that much more apparent."

"You realize what you would be missing?"

"Faith," He looks her directly in her eyes over the island counter. "I have always known exactly what I would be missing without you. I would never jeopardize what we have to go back to a life without you in it."

She lowers her eyes to her wine glass and then looks up at him through her lashes. "You're being awfully sweet tonight."

"You deserve it every night."

"Are you handling today OK?" Faith asks curiously.

"I think so. With being so busy at work I was preoccupied with that and worrying about you."

"You don't need to worry about me."

"I care about you though, Faith. Which means when something has upset you I get to worry about how that's affecting you."

"You know, I was talking to Jackie today about how amazing you are. Now I'm thinking I may not have been giving you enough credit." Faith reaches across the island and takes Jonathan by his tie pulling him in to kiss her over the countertop.

Jonathan pulls back, walks around the counter and pulls Faith in for a proper kiss. With her body pressed against his she feels his excitement grow. She runs her fingers through his hair, grasping it tightly. He kisses her fiercely before pulling back once again.

Without a word he walks over to the range, turns off all the knobs and then he walks back over to Faith and scoops her up into his arms. She wraps her arms around his neck and kisses him hard. He carries her to the bedroom kicking the door closed behind him.

As he lays her down gently on the bed, he lowers his head to kiss her neck, then moves his lips lower to her chest. Raising her shirt up he kisses her torso, completely worshiping the gift that is her body.

Faith's head is swimming as Jonathan removes her clothing. She starts pulling at the buttons on his shirt. He loosens his tie and slips his arms out of the sleeves. Then he lifts his arms up so Faith can remove his undershirt easily.

She looks down at his amazing body and watches as Jonathan unlatches his belt. She reaches for the button on his pants and pulls hard to release it. Jonathan lowers the zipper and then pulls his pants down and they fall to his ankles.

Faith follows Jonathan's eyes as they wander over her body while he takes in the naked sight of her. He pulls his boxer briefs down and removes his socks in one motion. His excitement is extremely clear to Faith.

Jonathan lowers himself on top of her kissing her neck as he parts her legs with his own. He kisses her lips passionately as she welcomes him inside her.

Suddenly, Faith is overcome with emotion. With confusion, Jonathan stops. "What's wrong, Faith? Did I hurt you?"

"No." She says softly. "I'm sorry. It was wonderful and then I just…I don't know. I don't think I can do this right now."

"OK." Jonathan says as he moves to lay down beside her. He wraps his arms around her, pulling her into him as tightly as he can. "I'm sorry. I thought you wanted to."

The tears are streaming down Faith's face pooling into the pillow case as she nods her head. "I did." She inhales and exhales quickly trying to calm herself. "Then I don't know what happened. I suddenly felt all of the emotions, all at once."

"I only wanted to make you feel good." Jonathan says in a nearly desperate tone.

"You did." She rolls over to face him. "You made me feel amazing, and loved, and desired." She reaches up and brushes her hand against his cheek. "You always do."

"Don't cry. Please." Jonathan says as he wipes away her tears.

"I'm sorry, Jonathan. I didn't mean for it to be like this."

"It's OK, Faith. We can't control our feelings sometimes."

"No, we definitely can't." She says and takes a deep breath.

Jonathan kisses her forehead. "Should we go finish making dinner?"

Faith simply nods her head. Jonathan promptly gets out of bed and grabs their robes. "Who needs clothes, right?"

"Right." She half smiles grateful for his attempt to cheer her up.

Chapter 33

Gratitude

Noun; the state of being grateful, thankfulness

By early April the days are getting longer and the salty air off the bay is warmer. Faith has been dually busy with wedding planning and planting. Jonathan built her raised garden beds to help keep Zeke from messing with any of the plants while they're first growing. She has also been adding some perennials around the yard.

The landscapers did a wonderful job after the house was finished, especially with the landscaping around the pool to make it blend in and look more like part of its surroundings. Faith found herself wanting to add some more color throughout the yard including by the patio which overlooks the bay. She has added some shorter shrubs and flowers that will add color and dimension without blocking their view.

Faith is finally feeling like she's made progress with the wedding planning. Once she met with Brenda and was able to solidify the plans with her it felt like a huge weight lifted.

The men have been fitted for their suits and the ladies all have their dresses picked out and ordered. They should be in by the end of the month.

Today is not a day for planning though. Today is Faith's bridal shower. Jackie, Hope and her mom, Diane, all pitched in to plan this special day for Faith.

Diane decided to close the café for the afternoon and throw the shower there. They had an hour to clean up from the morning rush and decorate. Hope picked up the cake from the same bakery that the café gets their pies from, and also the cake they got last minute to celebrate Jonathan's promotion.

Faith arrives fifteen minutes early to find the café transformed. There are black and white streamers and balloons as well as red roses and baby's breath for centerpieces on each of the tables, which are now covered in white and black table cloths. Diane embraces her.

Faith gestures to the space. "Thank you for doing all of this."

"You're welcome, my dear. It's my pleasure!"

As the guests begin to arrive, Faith stands near the door to greet them. Once they have all found their chairs, Faith takes a seat at the curved counter facing everyone. The cake and gifts are lined up down the counter from where she sits.

The food is, of course, provided by the café's kitchen staff, made to order. Diane decided they might as well use the café to their advantage for something like this.

"You look beautiful." Hope says as she walks up to Faith to place one of the guests cards in the card box. "How are you feeling?"

Faith is wearing a white flowy lace dress with strappy white sandals. She smiles at her sister. "Thanks for the compliment! I'm doing pretty well." She gestures to the decorations. "This place looks awesome."

"That was all Mom and Jackie. I was in charge of putting the vases on the tables and bringing the cake."

"Well, you did a good job, too. The flowers are very well centered." Faith laughs. "The cake also looks delicious. I'm surprised Carlos couldn't get Juan to deliver it."

"I offered to pick it up."

"That explains it."

Jackie slides up next to Faith. "Good turn out so far." She nudges her with her elbow.

"Yeah. I'm somewhat surprised by the number of other teachers here."

"Don't worry. I didn't invite your arch nemesis."

"Faith has an arch nemesis? How come I didn't know about this?" Hope asks.

Faith rolls her eyes. "It's Kay Obrecht. She's not my arch nemesis per se. She just has an issue with me, a completely unwarranted issue."

Hope rests her chin on her hands. "You have my full attention."

Faith chuckles. "It's really not that good of a story and I don't think right now is the time to tell it."

"OK."

Diane stands in front of the three of them facing the guests and clears her throat. "I'm so glad you all could make it today to celebrate Faith's upcoming wedding! We're going to get started soon. You'll all notice there are rings around the base of the flowers on your table. Each person gets one ring to start, but if you say 'bride' someone can take your ring! The person with the most rings at the end will win a gift. For now, while you wait for the other games to begin, please take a look at the menu and someone will be around to take your lunch order soon."

"Wait," Faith says softly. "Who's waitressing the party?"

"Valerie volunteered so that Georgina could be here and enjoy the party without having to waitress."

"Seriously? She shouldn't be taking everyone's orders. There's at least thirty-five, maybe even forty people here!"

"She's good."

"I think it's a lot."

"She'll be OK, Faith."

"I feel like I should help her take orders."

"Don't you dare even think about it." Hope says threateningly. "This is your party, you are the guest of honor. You cannot, I repeat cannot, waitress at your own party."

Faith holds up her hands. "OK, OK."

"I'm serious."

"Trust me you've made that very clear."

Jackie butts in, "I don't think I should waitress. I'd mess up more orders than I get right. This brain of mine only holds so much information and right now it's chock full of school stuff and work stuff."

"We can't let Mom do it." Faith insists.

"Well, I don't want to do it." Hope complains.

"No, but you know either Mom or Georgina are going to jump in if Valerie even begins to look overwhelmed."

Hope's head drops in defeat. "I know. Fine, I'll do it."

"I'm sorry, Despair. I wish there was someone else, there just isn't." Faith offers sincerely.

Valerie comes by to take Faith, Hope, and Jackie's orders. After she's written everything down Hope asks, "Are you sure you're OK handling everyone's orders?"

"Yeah! Diane assured me that all I needed to do was take my time. She said we're not in a hurry."

Hope shrugs. "If you're sure…but if you change your mind and need some help, let me know."

"I think I'll be fine, but thanks!" Valerie says as she briskly walks off to turn their orders into the kitchen.

Hope looks at Faith. "She has done a great job at handling everything so far. Plus, it's been nearly a year since she started, even if it's mostly been part-time while she's in school."

"Will she be full time in the summer then?" Faith asks thinking of the conversation her and Jonathan had when she stepped back to plan the wedding at the end of last summer.

"It seems that way. Are you planning on working here this summer?" Hope gives Faith a sideways glance.

"I was thinking about that. With the honeymoon and us all possibly going on a vacation that leaves maybe a month and half I'd be able to help out."

"You know, Faith, at some point you're not going to want to do that anymore. Hell, if I had a job where I had off in the summers I wouldn't want to."

"It gives me something to do."

"With how creative you are, I'm sure you could find more fun ways to fill your time." Hope looks at Jackie. "Jackie, what do you do in the summer to help fill the time?"

"Mostly day drink." The three women laugh and Jackie continues with laughter still filling her voice, "No, seriously though, I try to have something to look forward to every week." She nudges Faith. "We could hang out more if you were working here less in the summers. Maybe go shopping, go for walks, or whatever."

"That would be nice."

"Then I'm not going to plan on having you back this summer, Doubt."

"Sounds good, Despair." Faith says feeling a slight sense of relief. It's not that she doesn't want to help out, it's more that waitressing isn't what she enjoys doing. Helping her family was the only reason she was doing it in the first place. Besides, Jonathan will be happy to hear she won't be working at the café this summer.

The three women sit at the counter they've all grown up around, watching Valerie busily take everyone's orders.

Hope was right, she can handle herself. By the time most of the orders are in, the first orders are ready.

When Valerie delivers Faith, Hope, and Jackie's food the women turn around in their seats to utilize the counter.

In between bites, Faith says, "The café actually works really well for this. Doubt, you could have a lucrative idea on your hands."

"Do you realize how pissed our regulars would be if we were randomly closed when they're used to us being open? We've had this posted for a couple of months and we still had people belly aching. When we explained it was for your bridal shower they lightened up, though."

"Well, that makes me feel special!"

"It should. I'd guess the next time something like this happens it'll be my wedding."

Faith looks at Jackie and they share the same look of surprise. "Wait, has Andy asked you?"

"Not yet, but we've had discussions. How could we not with all the wedding talk surrounding yours."

"True." Faith shrugs and takes another bite of her club sandwich. After chewing she says, "The only problem with your shower being here is that you'll be the one dealing with the invoices and upset customers."

"You're right. I'll have to tell mom we can't do it here."

Faith laughs and takes another bite of her sandwich.

Diane sits down beside Hope. "How's everything going?"

"You're the one doing everything." Hope says. "Is there anything I can help with?"

"Not right now, dear. Thank you though. It seems everyone is content to eat their food for now."

When Diane finishes her lunch she stands again, addressing all of the guests. "I hope you all enjoyed your lunch! Now it's time to play some games! Then Faith will open gifts and we'll have some cake!"

The numerous tables filled with women are all smiling back at her. Hope and Jackie begin handing out sheets of paper and pens. While Diane continues.

"On the sheets of paper you'll find questions and the option of whether or not it applies to Faith or Jonathan. Make the best selection and whoever has the most correct answers will win a prize!"

Once everyone has finished filling in their answers Faith and Diane both stand in the front. Diane reads the question and Faith answers which one is correct.

Some of the questions pertain to childhood things, but most focus on the wedding planning. The winner of this game is Sylvia, a dear friend of Diane's who has known Faith her entire life. She picks her prize from the numerous gift bags lined up on the table nearest the door and goes back to her seat.

"OK, up next we're going to play 'What's in your purse'. For every item listed that you have in your purse you receive the corresponding points! The person with the most points wins a gift!"

Jackie hands out the 'What's in your purse' paper while Hope hands out small cards with prompts for each guest to write something to Faith and Jonathan.

"You'll see that Hope is giving you each a card. These are for any messages you'd like to give the bride and groom either for their wedding day or their marriage."

Hope stops in her tracks, turns and walks straight to her mom, and holds out her hand. Diane is confused and stares at her for a moment before Hope says, "Your ring, Mummy."

Diane's cheeks turn a fun shade of pink as she hands the ring over to Hope.

"Thank you." Hope says as she smiles and walks back to the table where she was handing out the cards.

Once everyone has tallied up their scores for the 'What's in your purse' game Diane has them raise their hands to find out who has the most points. A teacher named Brianna wins that one!

Everyone is filling out their message cards while Faith begins opening her gifts. Faith starts with the numerous cards which have cash or checks, some with extremely sweet and heartfelt messages. The gifts she opens are mostly things they registered for.

Diane hands the last gift to Faith with a sly smile on her face. From the corner of her eye she sees Jonathan walk in from the back door and come down the hallway. Her face lights up at the sight of him. He looks so handsome with the light coming from behind him it showcases his height and strong figure.

"Looks like you've got one present left to open. I guess I missed the fun part!"

"You're here just in time." Diane says with a smirk.

Faith has a feeling something is up, but cannot figure out what it is.

"Go ahead, open it up." Jonathan says as he takes a seat next to her.

Faith does exactly that, unwrapping the beautiful silver wrapping paper only to reveal a black box. She throws the paper aside and lifts the lid of the box seeing dark stained wood and metal. As she opens the box further she sees a beautiful plaque with their last name 'Hall' and an established date of their wedding.

Jonathan leans into her. "It's for the house. I made it."

Her eyes open wider. "You made this? Jonathan it's absolutely beautiful."

"Thanks!" He smiles at her as if the compliment means everything to him. Faith stands and pulls him in for a kiss.

"Seriously, Jonathan. This is amazing! Thank you! When have you had time to work on it?"

"It's been hard to find time, but a little here and a little there. The worst part was hiding it from you."

"It was a surprise, sometimes that's what you have to do to keep it that way."

"That's true. I'm going to start taking some of this stuff to my car." Jonathan motions towards the pile of gifts sitting next to Faith.

As he starts bringing everything out the back door, Diane addresses the rest of the guests. "Who's ready for cake? We'll get these served up for you all shortly." She smiles and walks over to the cake where Hope is already putting slices on small plates. Valerie takes the plates from the counter and delivers them to the waiting guests.

After cake, Faith thanks everyone for coming. She is surprised by the number of women who have showed up for her today. The gathering has made her even more excited for the wedding.

Diane asks each of the women to count their rings. Theresa, one of Faith's friend's from high school, wins the most rings with fifteen. She selects her gift and then Diane instructs everyone to take a bag on their way out.

On her way out, Diane's friend, Sylvia, gives Faith a long hug. "I'm so happy for you, sweetie! And your fiancé is really good looking!" She says with wide eyes.

Faith giggles and says as if it's a secret, "I know, right!"

"And he looks at you in a way that I've never seen a man look at a woman before."

Faith smiles. "I am an extremely lucky lady. I'm so glad you could come today!"

"I wouldn't have missed it!" She turns to Diane, takes both of her hands, and says, "Thank you so much for inviting me."

"Of course! It's been great spending time with you, we need to plan something soon when I'm not the hostess with the mostest." Diane laughs at her own joke as Sylvia nods her head in agreement before giving her a hug and heading out the door.

With just Faith, Jackie, Hope, Diane, and Jonathan left they begin cleaning and undecorating so they can open for the dinner rush.

"Honey, you don't need to help clean up after your own party!" Diane says adamantly.

"It's OK, Mom. We need to get this done so that you can open back up. I don't mind helping." She sets down the table cloth she was folding and turns to her mom. "I want to thank you for working so hard to throw this shower for me. It was great and I think everyone had a good time."

"I hope so. I'm really glad you enjoyed it. That's all that matters to me." Diane smiles and touches Faith's face gently.

Faith nuzzles her cheek in her mom's hand as a smiles spreads across her face. "You're the best mother I could have ever asked for."

"Thank you, dear. Now, you and Jonathan need to get going. We'll get all of this taken care of."

Faith looks around to see Jonathan sweeping under the tables. She hooks her thumb in his direction. "I don't think I'm going to be able to tear him away from his work."

"No, maybe not." Diane laughs. "OK, I guess you can have five more minutes."

"That's fair." Faith says picking up the folded table cloth and placing it on top of the pile of the others.

Once she has folded the last couple she takes them into the storage room. She finds Hope in there wiping tears from her face.

"Hope, what's wrong?"

"It's nothing." Hope says as she turns away.

"It's obviously something." Faith says gently and places her hand on Hope's shoulder. Leaning to try to see her face she says, "Tell me who I need to beat up!"

Hope chuckles half-heartedly. "You would have to beat me up. I'm the one not being nice to myself."

"Why would you do such a thing?"

"Because intrusive thoughts just happen."

"That is true. Care to share your intrusive thought that brought tears to your eyes?"

"Everything is going so good with Andy now. I'm happier than I've ever been." Her voice trails off. She takes a deep breath and continues, "It's just, I don't know, there's so much going on in here right now." She gestures to her head and then despairingly places it in her hands.

Faith sees a couple of five gallon buckets full of pickles she pulls over for her and Hope to sit down on.

"I get it." Faith says softly. "Sometimes being happy is scarier than the alternative. The fact that at any given moment you can lose the person who means the most to you. That is some scary shit. But do you know what else is scary?"

Hope looks up at her expectantly with blood shot eyes and Faith continues, "It's even scarier to push people away who love us like this. It's even scarier to imagine if we'd never met those people. So we have to cherish them and the time we have with them.”

Hope's tears are still streaming down her face, but Faith thinks she sees a light in them. “Thank you, Faith. Have I ever told you that you're a good big sister?”

“I actually don't think you have, no.”

A small smile forms and Hope says, “Well, you are. Thank you for putting up with me. Ugh, I don't know how Andy does it?”

“Does what?”

“Put up with me! You have to because you're family, but they don't. They choose to.”

“That's the beauty of it, Hope. We get to feel loved just as much as we make them feel loved.”

“I was jealous of that at first with you and Jonathan.” Hope admits softly.

“I know and it's OK. I understood where it was coming from. I'm glad you have Andy now and can see how amazing all of this feels when you let your walls down a bit.”

Just then Diane opens the door to the storage room. “Oh, I'm sorry. Am I interrupting?”

Hope looks up at her mom. “It's OK, I think we were just finishing up.” She stands and wipes her hands on her pants. “What's left to clean up out there?”

“Nothing. Jonathan and Jackie have been extremely helpful.”

Hope checks the time on her watch. “And with time to spare. Awesome.”

Standing, Faith says, "Well, Jonathan and I should get going. We've got a lot of things to find places for at home. Thank you both for everything you did to make this happen."

"You're welcome, Faith." Hope says. "I do expect you to return the favor when it's my turn."

Faith holds up a finger. "Yes, but not here."

"No, not here." Hope laughs a little.

Faith gives them both hugs before she heads out to say goodbye to Jackie and let Jonathan know it's time to go.

When she gets into the dining area, Jonathan and Jackie are joking around and laughing. She smiles to herself grateful that the two of them get along. Jackie has never liked any of her boyfriends before. She had hoped one day that Jackie would put aside any misgivings for the man she chose to marry.

Jonathan looks up and smiles at Faith. "Ready?" She asks.

"Definitely." He replies.

Faith says goodbye to Jackie thanks her and gives her a hug. "I'll see you at school on Monday!" She says as they walk down the hallway to the back door.

Chapter 34

Attitude

Noun; a negative or hostile state of mind

The next few weeks fly by in a blur of school, last minute wedding things, and various get-togethers. Jonathan and Faith celebrated their two year anniversary and Jackie's birthday. Everyone's dresses came in, even Faith's! Which fits her like a glove! She's so happy with the magic Mr. Caltroney seemed to conjure in order to design this dress to be exactly what Faith wanted.

It's exactly one week before their wedding day and Jonathan and Faith are having separate bachelor and bachelorette parties. Jackie was in charge of planning Faith's and Rowen was in charge of planning Jonathan's, which did concern Faith a little bit. She trusts Jonathan though and hopes that he laid some ground rules for Rowen to abide by.

In the past week, Faith has found herself a little anxious about going out. It's been over a year since she was drugged, but she still finds herself worrying that it could happen again.

"Hey!" Jackie says when Faith opens the door to let her inside. "I've got a couple things for you!"

Faith smiles seeing the bag in her hands. "What's that?"

"Bachelorette gifts of course!" She shoves a large gift bag in Faith's direction.

The bag is heavier than Faith anticipated, she sits down on the couch and sets it on the floor. Then she begins removing the black and white tissue paper. She finds a tiara and sashes for herself and the small group of women who are coming with as well.

Jackie is watching her intently as she rummages through the bag pulling each gift out one by one. Some are more obscene than others. "Am I supposed to bring this with?" Faith asks while holding up a penis shaped water gun. She aims it at Jackie and pulls the trigger shooting a puff of air in her face.

"That's not the type of facial I prefer." Jackie says laughing. "And to answer your question, yes, all of this is coming with us!"

"I'm going to need a different bag." Faith says laughing.

When Faith finally grabs the small package Jackie is waiting for she scoots closer to her on the couch and says, "Normally, I wouldn't buy something like this," referring to the 'as seen on TV' sticker on the package, "but after what happened last year, I figure we can't be too careful."

Faith flips the package over to see that it is a set of covers for their drinks while they're out.

Jackie shrugs her shoulders and says, "I thought it might give us some peace of mind."

"This is an awesome idea! Thank you, Jackie!"

"You're welcome!"

Faith hugs her tightly, grateful for her thoughtfulness.

"What time did Jonathan say the limo would be here?"

Faith checks the time on her phone. "About a half hour, I think."

Jonathan had insisted on renting them a limo for the night so no one would have to be designated driver. He also damn near insisted on hiring a body guard to keep watch over Faith. Faith put her foot down, refusing to even go if he did that.

Faith stands and walks over to a mirror. She places the tiara on her head and slips the white sash over her shoulder. Across the front it says 'bride to be', the others have all different cute and funny names for each person in her entourage. Jackie's says 'Maid of dishonor'. She follows Faith and puts her sash on as well. "I thought this one was super fitting."

They both laugh. Faith asks through giggles, "Did you pick one out for Hope?"

"I thought about giving her either 'Miss Behaving' or 'Wild Child'." Jackie says.

"Either of them would be perfect, honestly!"

"I know right! I thought the same thing!"

The sun is set, and the air has cooled down by the time the limo gets to Faith's house to pick up her and Jackie. Jackie brings the gift bag full of goodies with them. First, they drive around Luna Shores picking everyone up. Then, they start out at Lee's Pub. Jackie figured starting there would be best to get the night started. She believes it's good to face your fears.

Neither of them have stepped foot in Lee's Pub since Faith was drugged. It wasn't the bar's fault, or even the bartender, Tracy's, fault. It was something that just happened. Tracy and the bar handled everything as well as they could, considering it was foreign territory for them.

Faith fidgets in her seat and Jackie reaches for her hand. She smiles at her and reassuringly says, "It's going to be OK. We can't avoid our favorite bar in town forever! Besides, if there's ever a time to go to Lee's Pub, its tonight!"

Faith squeezes Jackie's hand. "We've got this, especially with your drink covers!"

"I'm glad you like the idea!"

"I love it!"

The Limo driver opens the car door and the five women exit the vehicle as lady like as they can. Once they get inside, Jackie hands each of them their sashes. Brianna and Theresa both laugh at the sashes Jackie gave them. They slip them on and then take a selfie together wearing them.

Hope looks at the one Jackie chose for her, "Miss Behaving. Huh, that's actually quite fitting."

"We thought so too." Faith says laughing.

"You were in on this?"

"No, I only just found out about it right before we came to pick you up!"

Tracy is behind the bar when Faith, Jackie, and Hope approach to order drinks.

Her face both softens and lights up when she realizes Faith is standing in front of her. "It's so great to see you two out again! How are you doing, Faith? I've been wanting to tell you how sorry I am for what happened."

"You don't need to apologize Tracy. You didn't do anything wrong. I've been doing really well!" She gestures to her sash. "We're here to kick off my bachelorette party!"

"You chose the best place." Tracy smiles and says, "Your drinks are on the house!"

"Seriously?"

"Seriously." Tracy says with no trace of uncertainty. "We hired a security guard after what happened. Mostly he just gets rid of the people who've had too much to drink and refuse to leave of their own volition."

Faith looks and finds the man with his large muscular arms folded across his chest and white letters across the pocket which reads security on his tight black T-shirt. "I think that was a good call."

"He's been great! He helped the cops and your boyfriend get the footage they were looking for."

The room starts spinning and Faith grabs the bar stool to sit down. She feels as though she's just been punched in the chest. Her ears are ringing and for a split second she questions if she heard Tracy correctly.

Before she has a chance to ask a question, Hope and Jackie simultaneously ask, "Did you say her boyfriend?"

Tracy nearly flinches at the accusatory tone. "Yeah. He came in a day or two after it all happened, if I remember correctly. We hired Hector like literally the next day. I told Trevor, the owner, there was no way around it."

Finding her voice Faith asks, "What was it that Jonathan was looking for when he came here?"

Both Jackie and Hope look at Faith astonished she hadn't known he'd done that. Tracy's eyes dart back and forth to each of their faces and then back to Faith's.

"He seemed really calm, he asked to see the footage to help you remember things from that night. He didn't mention it to you at all?"

"No. Not at all." Faith says flatly looking down at her hands. Suddenly she's got so many questions.

"Hmmm, that's strange." Tracy says. "I'm sorry, I thought for sure he would have. He seemed like he genuinely want-ed to help you. Since the cops had already been here to see the footage, I didn't see the harm in having Hector show it to him too.

"Thank you for letting me know." Faith says simply. She takes a deep breath realizing there's nothing that she can do about it right now. She also doesn't want to let it ruin her night. "I think we'll order some drinks now, if that's alright with you guys?" She asks Jackie and Hope.

"We would love drinks." Hope says nodding her head.

Theresa and Brianna come to the bar from the bathroom and order as well. Then all of the ladies grab a table in the corner of the room nearest the windows.

Faith's glass is empty before any of the other's drinks are even half gone.

"I'm going to go grab another. Does anyone else need anything?"

Jackie and Hope both look at one another, but they shake their heads.

"OK. I'll be right back."

Faith is sitting back down a moment later with the straw in her mouth. Jackie can see the level of the liquid go down with every passing moment.

A few moments later, Faith suddenly stands with an empty glass and says, "We should go dance."

The other women stand as well and follow Faith. They all place their empty glasses on the bar and then walk out to the dance floor. The music is loud, but dancing feels good. Faith can't help herself, she keeps looking around the bar for anyone who seems even the slightest bit suspicious.

Jackie watches her as her sways become more off tempo. "How are you feeling, Faith?" She shouts.

"Drunk!!" Faith says with a huge smile.

"OK! So you want to keep dancing?"

"Of course I do!" Faith shouts back.

Hope leans into Jackie and says, "At least if she's dancing, she's not downing drinks."

"That's true." Jackie replies.

"Maybe we should get her some water."

"We will when we go sit back down."

"Good plan."

Faith leans in to both of them. "What are you two talking about?" She shouts.

"Just some plans for your bachelorette party." Hope says.

"But we're here! This is the bachelorette party!"

"Yes, it is, Faith." Jackie reassures her.

Chapter 35

Disquietude

Noun; anxiety, agitation

Meanwhile in Caulfield, Jonathan, Rowen, Tom, and Andy are pre-gaming at Rowen's penthouse before they head out to a comedy show. Jonathan keeps checking his phone.

"What's going on, man? We're all here to drink and have a good time." Rowen says gesturing towards the living room where Andy and Tom are sitting.

"I know, but I'm worried about Faith. I just want to make sure if she texts I don't miss it."

"Why are you worried about her? What was Jackie planning?"

"She didn't tell you?"

"No. Why would she tell me?"

"I don't know, I just assumed since you guys are" Jonathan pauses searching for the words. "Well you know…that you may have discussed the plan for tonight."

"We don't talk like that, man. We're just fucking."

"I don't know how you do it."

"What? Fuck? I'd hope you know how to do that…" Rowen chuckles.

"Not what I meant and you know it." Jonathan says looking at him from the corner of his eye.

"I'm giving you shit. Seriously though, why are you worried about Faith?"

"About a year ago she was drugged when she and Jackie went out one night."

"Like roofied? That's fucked up."

"Yes, exactly. Thankfully Jackie got her to the hospital, but it was a really fucked up night."

Tom walks up to the two of them and hands them each drinks. "You guys looked like you needed a refill."

"Thanks, Tom. I was just telling Rowen about when Faith was drugged."

"Yeah, that was a bad night."

Rowen takes a swig of his drink. "I know you're worried, but you need to trust that she's in good hands. This is your bachelor party, so let's party."

"You're right." Jonathan says as he slips his phone into his pocket and takes a drink from the glass Tom handed him. The sip leaves a burning sensation as it goes down, but it's still good.

Rowen turns the music up and the three of them go back into the living room to sit with Andy.

An hour later, their ride shows up and takes them to the comedy show at Jester's Jovial Junction. Rowen didn't tell

Jonathan, but he's made sure that Jonathan will be front and center during the comedian's crowd work part of the show. When they're seated in the front row, Jonathan gives Rowen a look.

"What? I wanted to make sure we wouldn't miss a thing, plus they've got servers that come right to the table for us to order!"

"Thanks, Rowen." Jonathan says clapping his hand on Rowen's shoulder.

Rowen shrugs. "No big deal."

"I think Faith was worried we'd be going to a bunch of strip clubs."

"I knew that wouldn't be your scene. After seeing the way you look at Faith, there's no way any other woman could grab your attention like that. Besides, you can't compete with perfection."

Jonathan feels a twinge of anger bubble up at that comment. He fully knows Faith is perfection, but he doesn't like hearing it come out of another man's mouth, especially Rowen's.

Feeling the intensity in his eyes, he looks down at his drink and reminds himself that Rowen has apologized for everything that happened at the end of last summer. There's no reason to think he wants anything with Faith now. Besides, he's got Jackie and who knows how many other women to keep him occupied.

Andy is sitting in between Tom and Jonathan with Rowen on Jonathan's other side at the half-circle table.

There is a small flickering battery-powered candle in the center which will give just enough light after the lights go down when the show starts, which should be shortly.

Andy nudges Jonathan. "Thanks for inviting me. Between work and school I've been so busy that I don't get out much. It's been nice."

"You're welcome! I'm glad you could make it." Jonathan glances down and sees they're wearing the Movado watch he and Faith picked out for them all and smiles to himself. It's nice to be able to see a gift being appreciated.

The lights begin to go down and a man walks out onto the brightly lit stage. There is a wooden stool with a small table next to it that has a bottle of water sitting on top. A few feet in front of those sits a mic stand and mic with the comedian's name in bold black letters as the backdrop.

"Thank you all for coming out tonight! There's nowhere better to be! Michael Trandelle is here! He's got an amazing show for you all here at Jester's Jovial Junction. Because his show is…"

The crowd says in unison with the man on stage, "Laugh 'til you cry funny!"

"Exactly! So let's give him a warm welcome and get ready to laugh 'til we cry!"

Jonathan leans into Andy, "I don't think I want to laugh 'til I cry." He shrugs his shoulders.

"No, I don't want to cry either."

Both of them laugh.

Michael Trandelle walks out on stage and thanks the guy who did his introduction then grabs the microphone and says, "Hey everybody! It's great to be here! I heard Chad say there's nowhere better to be, but I'm sure some of you had better places to be than here. I hope no one is missing the birth of their child or like a wedding or something."

Michael scans the crowd and sees a handful of people laughing.

"Well it seems like there aren't very many of you missing those important events. So that's good! Do we have anyone here that is celebrating a bachelor or bachelorette party?"

He looks around the room again seeing a few hands in the air. Rowen shouts out, "Bachelor party!"

In the middle of his shout another one comes from the middle of the room. A female voice yells, "Bachelorette party!" in a high pitched tone.

Michael looks to the women sitting at that table and says with laughter filling his voice, "I was about to ask who the bachelorette was, but then looking at your table I realized that would be a really dumb question." He looks out at the crowd and says, "There are no dumb questions, though." Then looks at the table Jonathan and his group are sitting at and says, "It's much more difficult to make out which one of you is the bachelor."

Rowen points to Jonathan and says, "It's him!"

Michael points towards the women's table and asks Jonathan, "Is that your fiancé up there?"

Jonathan checks curiously and then says, "Nope, not mine."

"I was going to say, if it was you could have sprung for better seats for the ladies!"

The room laughs, especially the bachelorette's table. "You could give us better seats!" One of the women shouts.

Michael looks around the room and says, "I'm sorry, but it seems this is a full house tonight. Let me know where you'll be after the show and I'll see if I have a better seat for you there." The woman laughs and a handful of others in the crowd do as well.

He addresses both tables. "So when are you each getting married?"

The bachelorette shouts, "Tomorrow!"

Michael laughs. "You're going to be quite hung over then."

He looks at Jonathan and Jonathan answers, "Next Saturday."

"See that's the way to do it! Then you've got all week to recover! Tell me, who's idea was it to have your bachelor party the week before?"

"My fiancé's."

"She is a smart woman! What's her name?"

"Faith."

"And how long have the two of you been together?"

"Two years now."

"That's a sufficient amount of time to know if you want to spend the next fifty plus years with someone, right?"

The crowd laughs.

"You know, that's what I don't understand. We spend all this time with someone and fall madly, deeply in love with them and 'just know' then it's like I like you so much I need you ALL OF THE TIME! Like, I'm sorry, I don't see how we think that's going to last in the long term."

Again, the crowd laughs. Michael looks up at the Bachelorette table.

"How long have you and your fiancé been together?"

"Six months!" she shouts.

Michael's head drops, when he picks it back up again he's holding a finger up. "Did you know, that when they did a poll of, I don't know the number of men, just pick a big number. But when they did a poll of men who had recently bought engagement rings and asked them how long it took them to know if their fiancé was 'the one', most of them answered six months. It takes me longer than six months to buy a new car, and that's only a five, maybe six, year commitment!"

The crowd laughs and Michael continues. "Can you tell I'm divorced?" He holds up three fingers. "Three times over. And every single time I thought I'd found 'the one'. Now, I'm convinced there never was 'the one' there's always only been 'the for now'." He looks out over the crowd then at Jonathan's table. He moves his gaze to the bachelorette's table and says, "But I'm sure you're marriages will be just fine!" He addresses the entire crowd again. "Are there any married couples in the crowd?"

A few hands go up in the air. Michael chooses one couple and asks them, "How long have you two been married?"

The woman answers, "Going on twenty years."

"Seriously? Neither of you look old enough!"

The man shouts, "We got married young!"

"How young? Were you ten? Because she doesn't look a day over thirty-two." Michael laughs.

The woman beams at him and her husband says, "She was eighteen. I was twenty-two."

"At least you waited until she was legal, I guess."

"Barely." The man shouts in a proud voice. "We got married two days after her birthday."

"How long did you date before getting married?"

The woman answers this time simply saying, "Four years."

Jonathan rolls his eyes as soon as he does the quick math. Rowen laughs along with a few more people in the audience.

Michael seems stunned for a moment, but then says, "OK. Who else here is married? Is there anyone that's been married more than twenty years? This time I'd like to stay away from men who are proud to be pedophiles."

Jonathan laughs at that and is grateful the comedian had the balls to call the guy out like that, even if it was slightly indirectly.

Two hands in the audience raise and Michael looks in their direction and sees that it's two gray haired men sitting next to one another holding hands.

He questions, "You two have been married for over twenty years?"

The man sitting on the left answers, "Well, technically not legally, but we had our commitment ceremony nearly forty-years ago."

"Holy shit. Forty years is a long time! How long were you two together before deciding to have a commitment ceremony?"

The man on the left looks at the man on the right shrugs and says, "I think it was about a year and a half. We weathered the aids epidemic and marched on Washington with a million other LGBTQ+ members of the community in nineteen ninety-three together."

In awe, Michael says, "It sounds like you two have lead epic lives."

The man on the right looks lovingly at his partner and says, "We definitely have."

"Would you mind sharing with the two people here that'll be getting married soon, what your secret is?"

"I'd say, the two biggest things are," The man on the left starts, "accept your partner for who they are in every different time of your lives, and never keep secrets. If you have to keep secrets you're either doing things you shouldn't be or you're with someone you shouldn't be with."

The man's partner says, "I'd add to that, no one is perfect and you can't expect perfection from your partner. The love has to outweigh any imperfections. I'd even say that you should love their imperfections. Also, you have to be able to admit when you're wrong." He looks at his partner. "We have been through so much together, some years were better than others, but ultimately sticking it out with this guy has been the best thing I've done in my life. So, don't give up when you're going through something. I'd bet that you haven't even seen the best years you're going to yet."

"Wow, that is amazing advice." Michael looks over at Jonathan and asks, "Are you taking notes?"

"I probably should have been." He takes a drink from the glass the waitress set in front of him only a few moments before.

The comedian waves it off and says, "I'm sure you'll remember." Then Michael looks back to the two men. "What are your names?"

"I'm Daniel and this is Wayne."

"It's great to meet you two, thank you for coming to my show and being willing to share your story."

"We're happy to be here."

Michael nods his head and starts into a funny story about him and his dad's strained relationship.

Jonathan checks his phone to see a text message, but it's not from Faith.

Heading to the Stellar Amphitheatre.

Jonathan: Thanks for the heads up.

No Problem. I'll keep you posted if they go somewhere after the concert.

Jonathan: Sounds good.

He slides the phone back into his pocket when Rowen looks at him sideways.

"What? I didn't say I wouldn't check my phone at all."

"And everything is OK?" Rowen asks.

"Yes, everything is fine."

"See. Nothing to worry about." Rowen takes a swig from his beer bottle.

"I wouldn't say nothing. It's just that everything is fine for right now." Jonathan says. He may have put things in place to help assure Faith's safety, and give him peace of mind, but knowing that she's out drinking and he isn't there doesn't help put his mind at ease.

Chapter 36

Inquietude

Noun; disturbed state

The limo feels as though it is barely moving down the highway, but Faith can feel every time the driver steps on the accelerator. It's a constant back and forth of inertia pulling on her body making her feel slightly nauseous. The nausea may also be caused by the number of drinks she consumed in the hour they were at Lee's Pub.

"I can't wait to see Sisterhood of Delirium. I've heard they put on a hell of a show." Hope says with excitement in her voice.

Jackie looks at Faith and asks, "Are you doing OK?" Concern on her face.

Faith takes a deep breath trying to get some cool air in hopes to clear her head. "I'm OK. I don't feel so great, but I'll be fine." Her words are slow and slurred.

Jackie gives Hope a look and then says, "Are you sure you don't want to go home?"

"I am certain that I don't want to go home." Faith says adamantly.

Hope grabs a bottle of water from the limo's mini bar, twists off the cap, and hands the bottle to Faith. "Drink this slowly. It should help."

"Who's the big sister here?" Faith asks in a mean tone.

"I'm only trying to help, Faith. You would do the same for me." Hope says holding her hands up.

Suddenly Faith has tears streaming down her cheeks. "You're such a good little sister. I'm sorry I got mad. I didn't mean it. I'm just angry with Jonathan."

"I get it. You have every right to be, but we don't want to ruin tonight, and we definitely don't want you to feel sick. No one likes that."

"No, they don't."

Jackie puts her arm around Faith. "It's OK, Faith. We can end the night now if you want to."

Faith shakes her head no. She takes a deep breath and then sips from the full bottle of water Hope had given her. "I don't want to end our night early. I want to see the concert and I want to have fun."

"OK then. Let's get you cleaned up." Jackie says as she takes some tissues from the gift bag and hands them to Faith.

Faith wipes the tears away and blots the mascara that has run down her face. "I've ruined my makeup!" She complains.

"It's OK, Faith. I've got some you can use." Faith smiles at Theresa.

"I'd say you could use mine, but the complexion would be way too dark." Brianna says.

Faith half laughs, it's all she can muster in the moment. "The thought is still sweet, thank you, Brianna. I'm glad you were able to come tonight."

"Me too, Hun! It's been so much fun already! I can't wait to see the concert!"

"Me either." Faith says as she takes the makeup bag from Theresa and rummages through it to find anything to help her look as if she hadn't been crying.

The limo driver pulls up to the Stellar Amphitheatre in Caulfield and opens the door for the ladies to exit.

Faith thanks him and they go inside. The women walk up the steps of the hundred and fifty year old building. Faith stumbles, but manages to catch herself with the metal railing. The person at the door scans their tickets and the women walk into the entryway.

Past the entry they see the numerous windows that sprawl up the height of the wall with stairs on either side of the entrance that take you up to the balcony seats. The walls are a cream color with some exposed brick accents.

Faith asks if they could go to the bathroom before finding their seats and everyone agrees that's a good plan. They all use the facilities and then spend some time freshening up before heading back out into the hallway. They stop to order something to drink. Faith gets both a bottle of water and a sweet cocktail.

"Have you eaten anything, Faith?" Jackie asks wondering if that might be playing a part in Faith's drunkenness.

"I ate around three this afternoon."

Jackie gives her a look. "You definitely should have eaten before we came out." She looks at the attendant at the stand and asks for a large pretzel and some popcorn. Then she looks at Faith and says, "We can share both."

Faith drunkenly smiles back at her friend. "Thank you, Jackie. You're the best!"

They walk to their seats, finding them easily even with how dark the amphitheatre is already. Thankfully they have the aisles lit pretty well, illuminating the row and seat numbers.

The opener is a relatively new singer with only one semi-big hit. She will be coming on in fifteen minutes and then the Sisterhood of Delirium will take the stage. Faith loves their music, but also their values and beliefs in general. They're feminists through and through wanting equality for everyone. Many of their songs deal with how difficult it can be to be a woman in a patriarchal society and the dream of how that could all change some day.

Their music is mostly punk rock, but with more singing than screaming. They've been together since they were young teens and found popularity five years after their first indie album released. They've since been signed to a record deal and are doing pretty well for themselves.

Faith sits in her cushioned chair and sips on her bottle of water, she feels the soothing cool liquid go down her throat.

Jackie hands her the tray with the pretzel and cheese on it and says, "Eat."

"Yes, mother." Faith says facetiously, but rips a piece off and takes a bite anyway. The salt hits her tongue first, then the warmth of the pretzel dough and the gooeyness of the cheese ignites the rest of her taste buds. "This is really good!" She tells Jackie mid chew.

"Good, I'm glad. So eat it up!"

They watch as a few people walk out onto the stage to test microphones and lighting. Faith smiles at Jackie. With a giggle she says, "They're testers."

Jackie looks at Faith confused. "What?"

"They're testers." Faith laughs even harder.

Jackie looks at Hope sitting on the other side of Faith and says, "She isn't making any sense."

Hope sees Faith take another bite of the pretzel. "She's drunk. Hopefully the pretzel helps." She shrugs.

Jackie rolls her eyes. "I guess it's all we've got." She says as she grabs a handful of popcorn and puts it in her mouth.

Faith's eyes get wide and she reaches across into the bucket of popcorn Jackie is holding. She fills her hand and shoves the entire handful into her mouth.

"You should probably slow down a bit, you don't want to upset your stomach more."

"My stomach feels fine now!" Faith says with a mouthful of popcorn and pretzel.

Faith sets the tray down then sits up in her seat crossing her legs crisscross underneath her. As she reaches forward for the pretzel she leans too far and nearly falls out of the chair. Both Jackie and Hope catch her before she tips right over.

Faith just laughs. "That was fun! We should do it again!"

Both women whisper "No!" sternly.

Faith stops laughing and begins pouting. "It's my bachelorette party and you two don't want me to have any fun!"

"Yes, we do, we just don't want anyone to get hurt." Jackie says.

"Yeah." Hope agrees. "What would happen if you fell and got a black eye before your wedding? Or worse, you broke an arm?"

Faith audibly sucks in air. "That would be so bad!"

Hope nods her head. "So bad." She repeats.

"I wonder what the boys are doing." Faith says out of nowhere in a slightly forlorn tone.

"Andy told me they were going to a comedy club. Whether they're still there, I'm not sure."

The lights come down, then the music starts as colorful lights and a spot light illuminate the stage as the opener comes out. She grabs the microphone and says, "How are we tonight, Caulfield?"

The crowd cheers and the band starts playing a song Faith has never heard before.

"This sounds good, I don't know it, but I like it!" Faith shouts above the music.

All of the women nod in agreement.

"It does sound good!" Brianna agrees leaning forward to see past Theresa and Hope.

The opener plays three more songs before the testers, as Faith calls them, come back out to get everything set up for the Sisterhood of Delirium. Faith's bottle of water is empty now. She's eaten the pretzel and has taken her fair share of handfuls of popcorn. She takes a couple drinks of her cocktail feeling pretty good about it.

She tries to take her time drinking it, but it is quite delicious, and with all the salt she's consumed, she's really thirsty. Hope and Jackie both notice and exchange another glance.

"I'm going to grab some waters for us all before the Sisterhood of Delirium gets on." Hope announces.

"Thank you, Hope." Jackie says.

When Hope comes back, she hands each of them bottles of water.

Brianna says, "Those must have cost you like forty bucks."

"They weren't cheap, but it's fine. Faith definitely needs to rehydrate."

"It's a good idea for us all to." Jackie agrees.

A few moments later Sisterhood of Delirium steps on stage. Faith hoots and hollers, then, when the music starts, she stands up and starts dancing wildly. Jackie and Hope let her go because at least she's having fun.

When the band has finished their first song everyone is cheering loudly. Just as the crowd begins to die down Faith screams, "Down with the patriarchy!"

The lead singer laughs and looks in Faith's direction and says "Hell yeah!" Then the music starts up for the second song. Faith is both embarrassed and exhilarated!

Her face is a violent shade of pink, but she's wearing the biggest smile! Hope stands up and starts dancing with Faith, followed by Jackie and then Brianna and Theresa.

Faith has finished her water by the middle of the show. They're all still dancing and having a blast. The lead singer, Freya, even makes eye contact with their group multiple times, smiling. She is clearly happy they're having such a good time.

After the next song, Freya looks at them and asks, "Are you guys here for a bachelorette party?"

All the women, with the exception of Faith, look around trying to figure out if she's actually talking to them.

Faith shouts, "I'm the bachelorette!"

"I could kind of tell, but it's hard to read your sash from here! I'm glad you chose our show for your bachelorette party! I feel like it's kind of an ironic thing though, considering the patriarchy, government, and religion are the reasons we have the institution of marriage." Freya surveys the crowd. "I digress… Is anyone else in the audience celebrating anything?"

There are a few loud cheers from different sections in response.

"What are you celebrating?" Freya asks one of the groups.

"My twenty-first birthday!"

"Now that's something to celebrate at a feminist punk rock concert!" Freya looks at the other side of the audience and asks the same question of them.

"My fortieth birthday!"

"Right on! I've heard forty is when you feel most like you've come into your power as a woman. Is that how you feel?"

"Hell yeah I do!" The brown haired woman shouts with confidence.

Freya signals for the drummer to begin the next song. As soon as the band plays the first few chords the amphitheatre erupts in cheers. This song is by far their most popular. It's also one of their oldest.

In the chaos of the crowd, Faith looks around and notices a man that had also been at Lee's Pub. He stands out like a sore thumb because he's one of very few men in the entire building. What are the odds that he would have been at both locations at the same time they were there? It seems too unlikely to be a coincidence.

Faith nudges Jackie and says, "See that guy over there?" She nods her head in his direction. Just then her eyes are met with the man's who looks away immediately.

His quick movement to avoid being seen is what catches Jackie's attention. "Yeah. What about him?" She asks, clearly not concerned or finding anything odd about him being here.

"He was at Lee's Pub too."

"Are you sure?"

"Absolutely certain."

"I wish I would have seen him there. He's pretty hot!"

"Not the point!" Faith says.

"OK. What is the point, then?"

"He's clearly following us."

"I think that's kind of a leap, Faith."

Hope overhears their discussion and begins listening in.

"I don't. Think about it Jackie, why would he have been there and now here at the same time we were? You're telling me he also drove the forty-five minutes here? Wouldn't most people have just gone out to a bar in Caulfield before heading to the concert? It doesn't make sense."

"I don't recognize him. Do you?" Hope asks curiously.

"Nope. Not at all." Faith says.

"I don't either." Jackie agrees.

Faith stands and both Jackie and Hope try to grab a hold of her arms to make her sit down, but she moves too quickly. She's already beelining for the guy.

The two women hurry after her. By the time they reach her she has already gotten to him.

"What are you doing here?" Faith demands.

The man's face is completely shocked at the question. "What are you asking me that for?"

Faith repeats, "What are you doing here?" in the same demanding tone.

The man takes a step back from her and looks around to see if anyone else is seeing this. Faith stands there unwavering in her scrutiny.

"I…I…" The man stammers, looking for the proper explanation.

"You what?"

Jackie and Hope both move to pull Faith away from the confrontation, but she isn't budging.

"You what?" She asks again."

"I don't know what to do."

"What the hell do you mean you don't know what to do?"

Jackie blurts out, "That doesn't answer the question she asked you."

The man's eyes dart to Jackie, then to Hope, and back to Faith again. He takes another step back, prompting the three women to step toward him again.

"Tell me why you're here or I'll get security involved." Faith says adamantly.

"No. Please. You don't have to do that." He says holding his hands up.

"Then tell me why you're here. I'm not going to ask again."

"Jonathan."

For a split second Faith isn't sure she heard the man correctly. When her brain finally does register the name he said she has to ask him to repeat himself.

"Excuse me, what?"

"Jonathan. He hired me."

"For what?" She commands.

"To make sure you're OK."

Faith looks at him sternly and says, "I am fine. You won't be if you don't leave right now though."

"I won't get paid if I leave."

"That man shouldn't have hired you."

"He's only trying to keep you safe, Faith." The man reasons.

"I can keep myself safe." She turns, her hair whipping around with her and she quickly walks away.

Jackie looks at the man and asks, "What was he paying you?"

"Two grand for the night."

"Seriously?" Hope blurts out.

"What's your experience? Because clearly you weren't very good at not being seen." Jackie says.

"I was in the Army."

"The Army?" Hope asks.

"Well, the reserves." He looks down at the ground.

"What's your name, soldier?" Jackie asks.

"Jayce."

"Well Jayce, it would seem that you have failed at your mission tonight, luckily it wasn't to the detriment of Faith. It was however enough to piss her off and ruin her night. Do you think you should get paid for that?"

Jayce shakes his head. "You don't understand though. I really need that money."

"Where did Jonathan find you?" Hope asks curiously.

"I work security at Kansen Corp."

"We will keep Faith safe. You're going to have to figure out what you're going to tell Jonathan." Jackie holds up her hands. "That's not on us. We need to go back to our friend now and make sure she's doing OK after finding out her soon to be husband went behind her back, after she told him, in no uncertain terms, that he better not hire a body guard for her. You understand."

Jayce nods his head and turns to start walking towards the entryway. Jackie quickly walks after him, taking his arm to stop him and pulls him into her placing her lips on his.

When she pulls back she says, "I just had to do that."

Jayce's cheeks turn a deep shade of pink before he turns to walk away.

As Hope and Jackie head back to their seats Hope asks, "What was that about?"

Jackie smiles. "I'm not sure what came over me. I simply felt the urge to kiss him, so I did."

"He didn't seem to hate it."

"No, he definitely didn't."

"What happened to you and Rowen?"

She pinches her eyebrows together for a moment. "Oh, nothing. We're only sleeping together. It's not serious."

"Right on! He's really good looking. I don't think he's boyfriend material, let alone husband material, but he is most definitely friends with benefits material."

"Yes, he is." Jackie smiles slyly.

They sit back down on either side of Faith. She has another drink in her hand, obviously she made a stop at the concessions before coming back to her seat.

"Faith, I don't think you should be drinking more right now." Jackie says in a concerned tone.

"I'm sure you don't, but I am." She says matter-of-factly.

Jackie sits forward and leans in to Faith. "What do you want to do?"

"I want to tear his head off. I want to call the wedding off. I want to scream and cry and punch something."

"Those are all valid." Jackie assures her.

"I'd even go so far as to add kick him in the nuts." Hope says with a chuckle.

Tears start to form in Faith's eyes. She wipes them away annoyed with their presence. "I shouldn't be crying at my bachelorette party. I shouldn't be this mad, or upset, or hurt. What the hell was he thinking?"

"Faith, he was going to pay that guy two thousand dollars. He obviously did it because he cares about you very much." Hope says. "I'm not trying to defend him, but I think calling off the wedding would be a bit drastic."

"Yeah, but he went behind my back after I told him I didn't want him to do that. Hell, I thought he was kidding at first. The moment I realized he wasn't I put my foot down and told him no. He obviously doesn't care about my feelings. He totally disrespected me."

"While it was disrespectful, I want to say, his heart was in the right place." Jackie says.

The Sisterhood of Delirium plays one more song before exiting the stage. The lights in the amphitheatre come back up and the women have a decision to make about where they're going next.

"I don't want to go home. I don't want my bachelorette party to end like this."

"Then it won't." Brianna says. "We can go out where ever you want, Faith. It's your night."

"Thank you, Brianna."

"So where do you want to go?" Jackie asks.

Faith looks down at her phone screen to check the time. "It's still early!"

Hope looks at her phone as well and sees that it's eleven. As far as bachelorette parties go, that is relatively early.

"So where are we going?" Jackie asks as they descend the steps to go to the limo.

Just before they reach the limo, Jayce comes out of nowhere and stops them.

"Please, you've got to let me know where you're going. Just let me follow you. I won't get in your way. You won't even know I'm there. I need that money."

Jackie holds her hand up. "What do you need that money for, Jayce?"

Faith looks at Jackie incredulously.

"My kid is sick, like really sick. Her name is Gracie and she has a brain tumor. I need that money to help pay for some of her doctor bills." There are tears forming in his eyes.

Faith's face drops and her whole demeanor changes. She can be mad at Jonathan, but it isn't OK to be mad at this guy. He was only doing what he was getting paid to do. "You can follow us. We're not sure where we're going yet. Do you have any good suggestions? I want it to be fun!"

The four woman all smile at Faith, they're happy to see that she's moved past her anger, at least for the moment.

"I've got the perfect place! It's called Jack's in the Box. They've got an awesome DJ and a good crowd on Saturday nights. You'll definitely have fun there."

"Jack's in the Box it is." Faith says.

"Perfect! Thank you so much, Faith! You have no idea how much I appreciate this!"

"I'm a teacher, which isn't the same as a parent, but I care deeply for all of my students and if one of them was sick like that it would be heart breaking. I can't even imagine what you're going through. I hope everything turns out OK for Gracie. I'll be thinking about her."

"Thank you." Jayce smiles at her then pulls out his phone and texts Jonathan.

Chapter 37

Habitude

Noun; habitual disposition or mode of behavior or procedure

"R owen!" Jonathan shouts over the loud music. Rowen turns in Jonathan's direction. "Where's Jack's in the Box? I've never heard of it."

"It's in Caulfield, south of downtown. Why? Do you want to go there? We just got here."

Jonathan thinks for a moment, but knows that would be asking for trouble if he just happened to show up at the same place Faith is. "No, I was looking up bars." He holds up his phone.

"If you were looking them up, you should have seen where it was." Rowen says flatly.

Jonathan rolls his eyes as he takes a drink from his glass. Tom and Andy seem deep in conversation while Rowen doesn't seem like he wants to take his eyes off of the bottle service hostesses.

The two women start dancing on each other in their short skirts. Rowen gives each of them a hundred dollar bill.

"Keep that up and there's more where that came from." The women laugh and keep dancing seductively.

Jonathan scoots his chair closer to Tom. "What are you two talking about?"

Andy looks up. "The difference between my job and his."

"I'm sure there's a vast difference."

"We both have our plights."

"As everyone does with their jobs. Even Faith does, and she's a first grade teacher."

"The problem comes when we're no longer doing what we enjoy about the job and we get stuck doing what we have to. All the extra admin or bureaucratic bullshit that we have to do as added work." Andy says.

"There's a lot of that in any field." Jonathan reasons.

"True, but not when you're the boss." Andy says.

Tom laughs sitting between the two. Andy asks, "What? What did I say that was funny?"

"You do know Jonathan is a CEO, right?"

"I do. I simply wasn't thinking about how much of a boss he is in that position. I don't see him at work." Andy explains shrugging their shoulders.

"No, I do though."

Jonathan looks at Tom. "Do you think I don't have to deal with similar bureaucratic bullshit I did when I was a sales manager?"

"I'm not sure, man. I mean it's not like there's any transparency with what it is you all work on."

Jonathan takes a drink trying to think of how he should respond. He hadn't thought being CEO would change his relationship with Tom, but it seems that it has. "There is even more of that to deal with, except it's not coming down from a boss, its coming from a client and if we don't make it happen, they walk. It's a shit ton of pressure that gets passed down the line, but only because of its dire nature."

Andy nods in understanding, but Tom sits stoic. When he finally says something, he tells Jonathan, "That sounds exactly like what a boss would say." There is no chuckle in his voice. He is completely serious.

"Well it's the truth." Jonathan tells him. He's starting to get frustrated with this conversation, but he doesn't want Tom to know he's gotten under his skin. "If you plan on moving up, like you've expressed to me, these negative feelings toward higher ups isn't going to serve you."

Andy nods again. "I've seen that, even in hospitals. The CNAs who are most negative about the APRNs get transferred to departments they don't want and get most of the scut work. You have to be willing to play the game in order to get ahead." They shrug and continue as they look at Tom. "I'm not saying it's fair, it's simply how this corporate minded world works."

"They're right, you have to be willing to play the game, Tom. It's exactly what I did, well that and pour myself into the job. You might not want to do that part of it and that's fine. I do feel like it sped things up for me. Not everyone can be as understanding as Faith is, though."

"Yeah, well I don't have anyone else that I need to consider at the moment." Tom says in a slightly melancholy tone.

"Finding the right one takes time." Jonathan says reassuringly.

"Yeah, and a bit of luck. You could try a dating app, otherwise, just see what life throws at you. That's what I did. I met Hope when she was in the hospital, we flirted a bit, but I wasn't wanting to be inappropriate with a patient, obviously. Then I couldn't stop thinking about her and all I could do was stay optimistic that somehow, someway we would run into each other again. And it happened, unfortunately it was when Faith was drugged, but it's what brought us together. Life can be super coincidental like that sometimes. It's kismet."

"I agree with all of that." Jonathan smiles at Andy. "I'm also really happy you were the one there taking care of Faith that night, and that we're such good friends now. Kismet is definitely the word for it."

Tom is stuck in his wallowing and makes no comment other than to take a drink from his nearly empty glass.

The three of them look over to Rowen who has the two women's undivided attention, if only for his tips. Jonathan speaks up. "Can we get refills over here please, ladies?"

The brunette looks surprised that he even asked, then jumps right to making their drinks. "Thank you." Jonathan says.

"You're welcome." She leans over the table, getting close to Jonathan, she whispers to him. "Hey, is your friend here single?" She nods her head in Rowen's direction.

"As single as he can be."

She smiles broadly and saunters over and sits down next to Rowen who places his arm around her as if he's been doing it his whole life, smooth and natural.

"Maybe I should be taking notes from him." Tom says gesturing to Rowen.

"No, you definitely shouldn't. Besides, I don't think you're the type to date women the way Rowen does. If you can even call it that."

"No, you're probably right. I'd get attached or friend zoned. Probably both."

"You need a bit more confidence." Andy offers gently.

Jonathan's mind wanders to Faith and he reaches for his phone to check and see if Jayce has sent him any more messages.

Nothing. At least he knows where they are, even if it is a club he's never been to before, or even heard of for that matter.

"You OK, Jonathan?" Andy asks.

"Yeah. Why?"

"The way you were looking at your phone." They smile understandingly.

"It's like we were talking about earlier. I worry about Faith when she goes out."

"What are the odds that she would be targeted again?" Tom asks.

"I'm not sure, but I don't really want to find out either."

Tom takes a drink from his glass. "No I suppose you don't. Hey, where were you that night when it all happened? Everyone was trying to get ahold of you and you were nowhere to be found."

Jonathan thinks for a moment. "I worked late, but then after that I drove to the cemetery. Usually when I do that I don't have my phone on."

"Why didn't you tell anyone where you were going?"

"It's a pretty private thing. I found when I let people know where I was going it would bring them down. So I stopped mentioning it."

Andy nods. "I could see how that would be the case. Let's change the subject." They suggest.

"Good call." Jonathan says as he looks at his phone again, just in case. There's still no new messages.

Part of him wants to text her, but he knows that he shouldn't. It's the one night they should be out with their friends separately celebrating the marriage to come.

This tradition never made sense to Jonathan, especially the ones who use it as an excuse to cheat on their fiancés. Those are the same guys, like Rowen, who then go on to cheat on their wives with no excuses needed what so ever. Jonathan wonders if they even have a conscious.

There's no way he could cheat on Faith, it would destroy him knowing he did something so hurtful to her. Whether she found out or not. It wouldn't matter. He would know and that is enough for him to never want to do it.

The irony of these thoughts aren't lost on him. Maybe, he supposes, these men's urges simply differ from his own. Because in a similar way, Jonathan knows if Faith found out about his time in Caulfield, the building and Lexus she would be incredibly hurt. It would be enough for her to leave him. He's sure of that.

Rowen turns his head away from the bottle hostess sitting next to him long enough to see Jonathan lost in thought.

"Hey, why aren't you enjoying yourself?" He shouts over the music.

Snapping out of it he says, "I am. Clearly you are too!" He raises an eyebrow.

"What can I say, they're hot."

"And you don't feel any type of way about the fact that you're flirting with them when you're sleeping with Jackie?" Jonathan asks in a slightly accusatory tone.

"Nope. It's like I said. We're only fucking. She's free to flirt and do whatever she wants with whoever she wants, just like I am. The arrangement we have is that simple."

"I don't find it simple. I don't think I could do it."

"We're just built differently."

"Let me ask you something." Jonathan says curiously.

"Shoot."

"Did your dad also cheat on your mom?" Judging by the instant reaction on Rowen's face he doesn't like the question, and his dad did in fact cheat on his mom. Jonathan holds his hands up. "I'm not judging, it just jumped into my head. Like maybe that was the behavior your dad modeled at home and that's why you're so OK with it."

Rowen sits silent for a few moments and then says, "I'm not one to psychoanalyze myself or anything, but that would make sense."

"I thought it would." Jonathan says.

"That's enough of that, though. This is a fucking party. YOUR fucking bachelor party at that! What do you want to do?"

Jonathan can't tell Rowen what his first thought was when the question came out of his mouth. If it were up to him he'd be hunting right now. If he weren't so worried about Faith being out, he would have been scanning the bar for someone simply to tease his urges.

Realizing he's been too quiet for too long he simply says, "Drink some more."

"Hell yeah!" Rowen says. "Ladies! Refills please!"

Both girls stand quickly and make new drinks for the four of them.

Chapter 38

Latitude

Noun; freedom of action or choice

Meanwhile at Jack's in the Box, Faith is out on the dance floor with Brianna and Theresa. Jackie and Hope are at the bar getting them all drinks. They've been using the drink covers and it's given Faith such peace of mind. She still hasn't left a drink unattended, though.

In a way, her knowing Jonathan was so worried about her that he was willing to pay such a large amount of money, plus risk pissing her off just to protect her is sweet. It doesn't negate the fact that when they had that conversation Faith made it very clear her wishes were to not have a body guard of any kind.

She's also still upset about finding out that he visited Lee's Pub right after that horrible night and never told her. She's wondering if there's anything else he might be hiding from her. Clearly he doesn't have a problem with keeping secrets from her. Knowing this now, how is she supposed to marry him in a week?

Faith sees Hope trying to get her attention and motioning towards the table they've been using.

"They got the drinks! Are we ready for a break?" Faith asks over the music.

"I am!" Brianna shouts.

"Me too! I'm getting warm!" Theresa says fanning herself.

The women walk off the dance floor and over to the table where Jackie and Hope wait with the drinks. "Where's Jayce?" Faith asks.

"I think he went to the bathroom." Hope says.

When they first got to Jack's in the Box, they got their drinks and sat at the table initially, Jayce kept his distance. Faith didn't think he wanted to intrude more than he already had. She took the initiative to go invite him to hang out if he wanted to. She assured him there was no pressure and her feelings would be just fine if he decided to do his own thing, but the option is open. It only took a little while for him to take her up on the offer.

Faith takes a drink of her fruity cocktail. "This is really fucking good!"

"I'm glad you like it!" Hope says. "I almost didn't get you one!"

"It's my bachelorette party! Alcohol must be involved!"

"It already has been! That's why I almost didn't get you a drink. Could've just as well have gotten you water."

"You could have." Faith says looking at her with an eyebrow raised. "But you didn't!" Faith wraps her arms around Hope. "Thank you, sister!"

"You're welcome." Hope says laughing at Faith's goofiness. "I'm glad you're having fun!"

"That's what today was supposed to be all about!" Faith says feeling somewhat cheated by the anger that is still eating away at her having a good time. She takes a big gulp from the straw. Then she stands and says, "Who wants to go back out on the dance floor?"

Jackie says, "I'll go with you!"

Faith takes another drink emptying her glass. "Let's go!"

Jayce comes to the table and says, "Where are we going?"

"The dance floor! Come on!" Jackie grabs him by the hand and pulls him with her.

Faith spins around to see him following Jackie and smiles to herself. Jackie and she start dancing, holding hands, the moment they reach the floor. Jayce starts dancing behind Jackie placing his hand on her hip. Jackie grinds up against him in response.

They dance to a couple of songs before going back to the table. Jayce detours and goes to the bar to get them all refills.

The later it gets the more Faith worries about going home. How is she going to handle seeing Jonathan? She's not even sure she can sleep in the same bed as him, but not going home isn't an option. Maybe she could sleep in one of the guest bedrooms. It's not fair that she should have to be the one sleeping elsewhere, though. She might be able to lock the bedroom door.

Faith's mind flashes back to their first big fight outside Jonathan's condo. They were supposed to have dinner, but he was extremely late. He'd told her that it was because he realized it was the anniversary of his parent's death, but not until after he wouldn't let her leave.

There was a desperation in his eyes that surprised and scared her that night. Especially as he held on tight to her car door even though she asked him multiple times to let her leave. She didn't want to hear him out. She was too angry. Maybe it was all supposed to end that night. How different would everything be now if she left and never looked back?

Jackie pulls her from her thoughts abruptly by saying, "Penny for your thoughts?"

"Hmmm?"

"It's an old saying."

"I know what it is." She laughs and takes a long pull from her straw. These drinks are really good and are going down a little too well!

"Are you feeling OK?"

"Just drink!" Faith says.

"I think you mean drunk!" Jackie laughs.

"Yeah, that too!" Faith laughs with her. "Definitely that too." She says between giggles.

A half an hour later the bartender calls last call. Faith gets one more drink and Jayce orders them all a round of shots.

After they finish their drinks, Faith stands to leave. The floor suddenly seems uneven and her legs don't want to move properly. Once they get out the door there is a couple of steps down to the sidewalk.

They all walk out together towards the limo which is parked down the street. Jayce walks with them to ensure they get to the limo safely. He'll update Jonathan once Faith is in the car.

Faith is being cautious as she walks, watching the ground with every step. She looks up to see how far the limo is and a crack in the sidewalk trips her. She falls hard against the concrete, skinning both of her knees.

"Oh man, Faith! Are you OK?" Jayce asks as he reaches to help her up.

She begins to reach for his hand, but when she does, her stomach lurches. She's feeling queasy and embarrassed. She holds up one finger to let him know she can't get up quite yet.

Faith adjusts herself to a sitting position instead of on her knees which are stinging so incredibly much. Blood begins to come to the surface and she starts to laugh and cry at the same time.

Jackie rushes to her side, crouching down as she puts a hand on Faith's shoulder. "It's OK Faith. I'm right here. We're going to get you home and get your knees cleaned up."

"I guess it's a good thing my wedding dress is long." She wails in a drunken crying slur. "And we aren't going on our honeymoon for a couple of months."

Hope and the other women circle around her as well. "Yes it is!" Hope says. "That looks like it hurts!"

Faith looks around to see that the other patrons of Jack's in the Box are standing around looking at her as they also make their way out of the club.

Brianna and Theresa move in closer to Jayce to make it more difficult for the onlookers to see Faith sitting on the ground essentially having a drunken breakdown.

"Thank you guys." She says looking up with black mascara filled tears streaming down her face.

"You'd do it for any one of us." Brianna says.

Her stomach starts feeling slightly better so she says, "I think I can get up now."

The women take a step back except for Jackie who moves behind her to help while Jayce reaches his hand out once again. This time Faith takes it and she finds the ground beneath her feet.

"Are you OK to walk?" Jayce asks her concerned. A bit of blood has started running down her shin.

"I can walk."

They all help in their own way to get Faith to the limo. Jayce and Jackie linger outside for a bit longer once everyone else has gotten in.

Faith looks at Hope. "Can I get one of those bottles of water please, Despair?"

"No problem, Doubt." She says as she twists the top off and hands it to her. "Go slow." She reminds her.

Faith takes a couple of big gulps before she says, "Yup. Slow. We should probably tell the driver that."

Hope rolls her eyes and then knocks on the divider. It slowly rolls down. "Hey, unless you want my sister blowing chunks back here, I'd take it pretty easy on the accelerator."

"Thanks for the heads up." He says as the divider begins its ascent back up.

"You're so ellloqu-e-nnnt." Faith says drawing out the word.

"I simply wanted to be as straight forward as I can be. It's better that, than to mislead him into thinking you only have a little tummy ache." She says the last part as if she's talking to a little girl. "And besides, I'm sure he deals with this sort of thing all the time."

Faith looks out the open door, but doesn't see Jackie. "Jaaaackie! Jaaaackie? Where are yoooou?" She says loudly in a sing song voice.

Jackie pops her head in right away, "Hold on silly! I'll be right in!" She says in a hushed yell.

Faith holds her finger up to her mouth. "Shhh. The adults are talking." She says and then starts laughing loudly.

A few moments pass before Jackie climbs into the seat next to Faith in the limo.

Once the door closes the car lurches forward and with it Faith's stomach. She tries to ignore it and asks Jackie, "Sooo, what happened?"

"What do you mean what happened? Jayce and I were talking."

Faith does air quotes and says "Just talking." Then she points her finger at Jackie and says, "I know exactly what the two of you were doing out there! Don't you lie to me." Then Faith gets quiet and the tears begin to fall again. "There's been too much of that tonight."

Confused Jackie asks, "Too much of what?"

"Lying! Too many lies and too much lying." She looks at her best friend. "What am I going to dooo?"

Jackie pulls Faith in for a hug and says, "I'm not sure hun, but I'm sure this is all simply a misunderstanding. He was only trying to protect you. Besides, Jayce seemed like a good guy, right? And he clearly needed the money. So Jonathan was trying to do something good either way."

"But I still told him not to."

"You did. And you're going to have to decide if you can get past that or not."

"I'm going to have to decide." Faith says thoughtfully.

As the limo comes to a stop at the stop light before getting on the highway to head in the direction of Luna Shores, Faith's stomach churns again. She decides to roll the window down and get some fresh air. Then she takes a drink of her water feeling the cool liquid flow down her throat. It sends a sense of relief through her for only a moment. Then the nausea is back and she's trying to take deep breaths of the cool night air.

The moon is high in the sky as they drive along the highway. They come to the exit for Mama Garcia's and Hope says, "I wish they were open, I could really go for some guac and margaritas!"

"Don't forget about the tamales and tacos!" Jackie says.

At the thought of food, Faith's nausea builds and she feels her mouth salivating more than it should be. She breathes deeply trying to fight what's inevitably coming. The thought of taking another drink of water crosses her mind, but as soon as it does she instantly feels worse and decides that wouldn't be a good idea.

At this point her head is practically out the window. Hope has taken notice and asks the driver to pull over, but they're going too fast and Faith's stomach contents won't wait.

She begins throwing up uncontrollably, all over the driver's side of the limo. She has no control over it and cannot stop it now if she tried. Jackie pulls Faith's hair back from her face and the wind trying to whip it right into the stream of vomit. Faith feels horrible as she heaves once again.

They make it back to Luna Shores, and the driver drops Brianna off and then Theresa. He drops Hope off last and Jackie goes back to Faith's house with her since her car is there from when the limo initially picked them up. When they get inside she runs a bath for Faith and helps her get undressed and cleaned up.

Initially, the steaming water stings Faith's knees, but once that subsides the water feels so comforting. She sinks down in it for a bit letting it hold her like a warm blanket.

Jackie comes back with an electrolyte drink and two ibuprofen. "You need to finish this bottle entirely and take both of these. Your future self, the one who's going to be waking up tomorrow, will thank you."

"I thank you now." Faith says warily. Throwing up and being this intoxicated has taken its toll on her, not to mention the mental and emotional anguish she's been fighting to stuff down all night.

"You're welcome, Faith."

Just then Faith sits up as straight as she can in the bathtub. "Shit!"

"What?"

"Jonathan is going to be home soon." She sinks down in the tub again, she closes her eyes, and repeats, "Jonathan is going to be home soon." Slower and in a more melancholy tone.

"Yes, he is. How would you like me to handle that?"

"What do you mean?" Faith asks opening one eye to look at Jackie.

"I can stay until he gets home and let him know what you found out tonight. If you want me to, that is. Or I can leave and not mention anything."

"You shouldn't have to be the go between."

"I know, but if it helps you, I'll do it in a heartbeat."

"I don't even know what to say to him."

"No, I suppose you don't. That's a big reason I'm offering."

Faith holds her breath and goes under the water for a moment, she blows air through her nose, making bubbles float up to the surface of the water. Then she pops her head back up. She opens her eyes and wipes the water from them. "I was thinking of locking the bedroom door."

"What? So he can't come in here?"

"Exactly, yes."

"Do you think that would go over well?"

"No, probably not. I don't think he would try the knob, find it doesn't work, and go sleep elsewhere. Hell, he would probably break the door down."

"Right." Jackie says. "You need to drink more of that." She nods to the bottle sitting beside the tub.

Faith reaches down and pets Zeke, who's lying by the side of the tub, then grabs the bottle nestled in next to him and takes a drink.

"Are you feeling OK?" Jackie asks.

"I feel better now. There's not really anything left in my stomach."

"Are you hungry?"

"Not really."

"What about some crackers? You probably shouldn't have an entirely empty stomach. Having something in there can help settle it a bit."

"OK. Whatever you think is best. It's been a REALLY long time since I drank that much." Faith nods.

"Yeah, I think the last time was probably after your college graduation when we went out partying to celebrate."

"That was a crazy night."

"Sure was. A little crazier than tonight." Jackie says with a smile.

"We were younger."

"Just a few years." She shrugs

"A few years can feel like a lifetime sometimes."

Jackie looks at her best friend soaking in the large tub still drunk, but at least the color is back in her cheeks. "I'd have to say you're right."

A tear runs down Faith's cheek. "I don't know what to do about Jonathan, Jackie."

"You don't have to figure it out tonight. In fact, I strongly discourage you to even try to figure that out tonight. Both of you have been drinking and that's not going to be a good combination with the amount of emotions you have coursing through you right now."

"No. You have a point."

"I know. So, when he gets here, I will talk to him and let him know you don't want to talk about it tonight."

Faith sees the desperation in Jonathan's eyes from their first argument. "I'm not sure he's going to leave it at that."

Curious and a bit concerned, Jackie furrows her brow and gently asks, "What do you mean, Faith?"

"There was a fight we had once, it was only about six months into our relationship, he was late for dinner and so I was going to leave. I got in my car and everything, but he got there before I could go and he wouldn't let me leave."

"What do you mean? Like he held you against your will? Did he hurt you?"

"NO! Nothing like that at all! He was just holding onto my car door, but he was so desperate for me to listen to him, but I was so angry I didn't want to."

"No, I suppose you didn't."

"I ended up listening though, and his reason was really sad." Faith says letting the sadness come through in her tone.

Jackie thinks for a moment. "Did it have something to do with his parents?"

"It did! How did you know?"

"Call it a hunch." Jackie says flatly.

Just then both women hear the garage door open. Zeke sits up with his ears perked.

Faith's eyes get huge and she looks at Jackie.

"Stay in here. I'll go talk to him."

"I don't feel so good, Jackie."

"I know, Hun. It's just anxiety. It'll be OK. I'll be right back." With that, Jackie slips out of the bathroom and closes the door behind her.

Zeke stays with Faith, which she is so entirely grateful for. She scratches behind his ears and tells him how much of a good boy he is to help distract her from what's happening in another part of the house.

Faith hears the bedroom door open and she freezes. She's still holding her breath when Jackie walks in. She feels herself instantly relax.

"He's going to sleep in the basement guest bedroom. You don't have anything to worry about."

Faith exhales hard. "Thank you, Jackie. I don't know what I'd do without you!" Tears begin streaming down her face.

"I'll always be here for you, Faith. No matter what."

"You're the best friend I could ever ask for."

"And you're the best friend I could ever ask for too, Faith."

"He's really going to go downstairs and sleep?"

"He already went down there."

"Good."

"Do you want me to stay? I will."

"No. It's OK, you can go home. I'll be OK. Thank you for helping me and taking care of me tonight."

Jackie crouches down next to the tub and says, "I know tonight didn't turn out the way that you wanted it to, we can't go back and change the way everything happened. We also can't let the things that came out tonight change everything. Wait until your head is clear and you've had some time to think about all of this when alcohol isn't clouding your judgement. Then, you and Jonathan need to have a talk."

"You're right and so smart."

"Thank you, Faith. I might not have had any successful relationships to date, but I know a thing or two about how to make the right one work when I find them."

"I'm sure you will someday."

"I'm going to head home if you're sure that you'll be OK."

"I'll be fine. Promise."

"OK. I'll text you tomorrow."

"Thank you, for everything!"

Jackie closes the bathroom door on her way out then Faith hears the bedroom door close as well.

The water in the tub is beginning to cool, but Faith isn't ready to get out just yet. She lets some water out and then refills the tub with hot water and sinks down in it letting the warmth envelop her.

With the water filling her ears the sound of a muffled knock startles her making her sit up quickly. The knock comes again, but this time it's louder.

Faith freezes, unsure of what to do, then she hears, "Faith? I know you're in there. I only want to see you. We don't have to talk if you don't want to."

Faith isn't sure what to say, but the sound of his voice makes all of the anger that has been building all evening come back with full force.

"I don't want to see you right now, Jonathan. Please. Leave me alone tonight."

He doesn't say anything else. The silence coming from the bedroom door is making Faith more anxious than his knocking did. Suddenly she hears the lock click.

"Faith, I'm coming in."

"Jonathan, I asked you not to." Faith says in a warning tone.

"This is my house too, Faith and you're going to be my wife."

"Don't do this, Jonathan. I don't need yet another thing to be pissed off at you for and to feel even more disrespected by you." She hears a couple of footsteps and then they stop, turn around, and go in the other direction. When she hears the door shut once again, she exhales a sigh of relief.

She quickly rinses off and gets out of the tub, dries off, and puts pajamas on. Before she climbs into bed she locks the door again.

Chapter 39

Aptitude

Noun; a natural ability, talent

Jonathan is already up making breakfast in the morning when Faith finally makes it out of bed. Her hair is still slightly damp from the bath and is matted down on one side and sticking up on the other. To Jonathan she's still the most beautiful woman he's ever seen.

"Good morning, beautiful." He says enthusiastically.

She won't even look at him. She silently walks over to the fridge takes out an electrolyte drink and twists the cap off then takes a drink. She turns around and goes with Zeke out the sliding glass door to the back yard.

Jonathan's heart sinks. Jackie didn't tell him much beyond that Faith found out he hired Jayce to follow them and keep an eye on her. He knew if she found out she'd be pissed, but he hadn't prepared himself for the silent treatment.

Throughout the rest of the day, Jonathan tries to make positive, upbeat, comments to Faith to try to entice her into talking to him. Every single time he's met with silence.

They've got a half an hour before it's time to go to Faith's parents' house for Sunday night dinner and Jonathan asks, "Are you not going to talk to me at all? You know we have dinner at your parent's tonight." He tries to limit the accusatory tone, but feels like he failed miserably.

Faith is sitting in the office working on her laptop and Jonathan is leaning against the door frame. She still doesn't say a word. She doesn't look at him. She simply shrugs her shoulders in response.

When they get into the car to head over to her parents', Faith doesn't even acknowledge that he opened her door for her or anything. Her face is stoic and she still hasn't made eye contact with him.

Jonathan isn't sure how to go about fixing this. They've had a small handful of arguments before, but never anything like this. Faith has never given him the silent treatment. He knows she must really be upset and hurt.

As he drives the familiar route to Frank and Diane's he thinks about what it'll be like while they're there. Surely she can't keep giving him the silent treatment. There's less than a week before their wedding, how long is this going to go on? What happens if when they go home tonight she locks him out of their bedroom? He's going to need to get into his closet since he goes into work before she does. Not to mention that he wants to sleep in his bed with his fiancé.

"Faith, I know you don't want to talk to me. That's OK. I can do all of the talking right now. I need you to listen to me. I love you. The thought of you going out drinking with a bunch of women without me or someone I trust there to protect you scared the shit out of me. I couldn't live with myself if something happened to you again. I know you said you didn't want me to get you a body guard, but I needed to do it for my own peace of mind. Even with having Jayce following you guys I was anxious as hell. You can ask Rowen, I was checking my phone every five seconds."

Faith scoffs, but no words come out and the only difference in her facial expression is her eye brows being pursed.

"I know that isn't the best reason to have gone behind your back like that, but it really felt like the only way. I felt like I was keeping you safe and giving myself peace of mind. I swear my heart was in the right place. I understand you're mad at me. I can't even blame you, but can you be mad and still at least talk to me? I can't deal with you not talking to me."

He can tell Faith is thinking and he can only hope that what he's said to her has made enough of a difference to make her want to speak. He takes his eyes off of the road to look at her. She looks so unhappy, this isn't the Faith he knows, but this is the Faith he's caused.

They pull up to park outside her parents' nineteen fifties light blue rambler. Jonathan isn't quick enough to get to the car door before Faith opens it for herself. She doesn't say a word, simply gets out of the car, opens the back door to get Zeke and walks up the walkway to the front door.

Once inside everyone asks about their nights and Faith talks to them as if nothing is wrong. He does catch Hope giving him the death stare a couple of times so when he gets the chance he pulls Andy aside and asks, "What's going on? Why does it seem like Hope is mad at me too?"

"I'm thinking its sister solidarity. If Faith is mad about something then Hope is going to be too."

"Did she tell you anything about why?"

"Yeah, she said something about some guy named Jayce. You hired him? Something like that."

"Yeah, I hired him. It was against Faith's wishes, but I was worried." He gestures towards Andy. "You saw how worried I was. I only wanted to keep her safe." He lowers his head to look down at his hands.

"I understand why you did it and I'm sure a part of Faith does as well. She's a smart woman. I'd think it was the way you did it rather than what you actually did that's bothering her."

"That makes sense." Jonathan nods his head. "I don't know how to fix it."

"Well, start by giving her time and maybe even a little space."

"That's as good a place to start as any."

Just then Diane announces dinner is ready and Jonathan follows Andy down the hallway and to the dining room. He sits beside Faith like always. She doesn't acknowledge his presence at all. Jonathan is sure every-one else in the room notices her behavior towards him as well which makes him feel self-conscious.

Suddenly he's worried they're all upset with him. Surely Frank and Diane will side with Faith just like Hope did. He takes a deep breath feeling pressure in his chest then he takes a sip from the glass of water sitting in front of him.

"Did you want a beer instead, son?" Frank asks.

"No, I had enough last night." Jonathan forces a chuckle. "Thank you though." He smiles slightly.

"I bet you did." Frank laughs. "My bachelor party was quite a drunken disaster." He looks at Diane. "Do you remember?"

Diane's knowing smile clearly says she does. "It was a complete disaster."

Jonathan is really curious. "What happened?"

"Well, my best man, Bruce, decided we'd have a party out in the woods of old man Turner's property. We knew we weren't supposed to be there, we'd done it so many times in high school and had gotten away with it that we thought it'd be no big deal. What we didn't know was that Farmer Turner had gotten a couple of dogs. Big guard dogs at that. They chased us through the property and their barking alerted old man Turner of course who then called the cops. So the group of about ten of us guys were all arrested."

Diane finishes the story with, "The night before our wedding I had to go bail him out of jail."

"I was lucky you still wanted to marry me after that."

"Yes, you were. I can honestly say my parents were trying to talk me out of it."

Frank's mouth drops open. "They were?"

"They were. Obviously I didn't listen, and I'm glad I didn't." She smiles conveying all the love she has for her husband in her eyes.

Frank smiles back and says, "I'm glad you didn't, too. And I'm glad I was able to eventually get back in their good graces."

Jonathan wonders for a moment, as he chews the delicious chicken Diane made, if Frank brought that story up because of the slight similarities in his current circumstances. In a way, it brings him some peace of mind knowing that in Frank and Diane's story, even though Diane's parents were against her marrying him, she's still glad she did. Maybe the message of the story was just as equally for Faith.

Once they're all finished eating dinner Frank, Andy, and Jonathan go into the den to watch the Stallions' game. Faith and Hope stay in the kitchen to help Diane get dinner put away.

Jonathan doesn't even realize he's fallen asleep until he's woken up by Diane nudging him. Jonathan opens his eyes to see that it's already dark outside.

"How long was I asleep?"

Diane nods to Faith who's sleeping in the arm chair next to Frank. "You've both been out for an hour and a half. I didn't want to wake you guys up. It seemed like you both needed the sleep."

"Thanks, Diane."

She begins to rouse Faith as well. "I'm not saying you have to go home, but you can't stay here." She laughs at her own joke.

Faith yawns and says, "I can't believe I fell asleep."

Diane looks at Jonathan and then back to Faith. "You both did. That's what happens when you go out drinking all night." She places her hands on her hips and then laughs again. "I'm kidding. I'm glad you all had a good time."

Faith stretches and stands up. Jonathan follows her lead. "We should probably get going." He tells Frank and Diane.

"Let us know if you two need us to do anything for the wedding."

Jonathan's stomach drops at the mention of the wedding. He feels like so much is up in the air now with how angry Faith is.

The silence on the drive home is broken by Jonathan, "I'm going to need to get into my closet and the bathroom for a few things when we get home. Then I'll go sleep back down in the guest bedroom."

His statement is met with more silence. For a moment though, he senses her anger may have softened some. For the rest of the drive home he wonders if it was only his imagination.

When he pulls into the garage, Faith once again opens her own door and gets Zeke out of the Mercedes. She walks into the house and goes into the office and closes the door.

Jonathan hangs his head as he walks into their bedroom to grab his things from the bathroom and closet. He solemnly packs a suitcase full so he doesn't have to keep doing this. As he walks past the office door he reaches for the knob. He feels the cold metal in his grip, but as he attempts to turn it, the knob only turns partway before stopping abruptly.

She locked the door.

"I'm going downstairs now, Faith. I'm sorry and I love you. Good night."

Jonathan lays in that basement bedroom staring up at the ceiling wishing sleep would come. He heard Faith's little footsteps followed closely by Zeke's walk in the direction of their bedroom over an hour ago. He can't stop thinking about how upset she is with him and wonder how he's ever going to be able to fix this in time for their wedding next Saturday.

Last night while he was in Caulfield with Rowen, Andy, and Tom, it wasn't difficult to not want to hunt. He's never gotten the urge when he's out with other people. It's as if that part of him knows it needs to stay hidden or it risks losing everything.

Right now because of everything with Faith, he's feeling out of control which is bringing the urge on in full force. He sits up in bed and opens the encrypted folder he keeps all of his photos of past kills in. It's like his very own trophy room without taking up an entire room in a house. Plus, with the encryption, no one else can see it if they were to get into his phone. They'd have to be seriously tech savvy to even find it and even more so to get it open in order to view its contents.

He scrolls through the photos back to the beginning. The first one he kept record of, there were many before this one, but the thought of keeping something like photos from them scared him. He was twenty-one and not nearly as smart about things as he is now at twenty-nine.

He was so afraid of getting caught, but at that time knowing he had the pictures on his phone that he could look at whenever he wanted was almost as good of a feeling to him as the act of doing it. He figured it was a similar feeling porn addicts have knowing they have access to what they yearn for at all times.

After the first year, and a handful of murders later, the exhilaration of simply having them on his phone, in his pocket, wore off. It did nothing to subdue his urges and may have even made them worse. Jonathan doesn't try to figure this side of him out in fear of what he might find, but it could have just been time that made the desires worse as well.

Tonight though, Jonathan can already tell that these pictures won't be enough to curb his compulsion. Instead of sitting in bed and putting off the inevitable even longer, he gets dressed and begins driving into Caulfield.

He's certain the bars will be fairly empty considering it's a Sunday night, so it could end up being a lost cause, as has happened from time to time.

He contemplates trying Jack's in the Box. From the way Rowen had made it sound it's a pretty popular club. If it's that popular it may be busier than some of his other options.

The drive gives him plenty of time to make a decision. He goes to the run down building and switches vehicles, then drives the Lexus to Jack's in the Box. Part of him wants to check out some new hunting grounds and part of him wants to know where his fiancé was, which makes it an easy decision.

As he walks into the club he's pleasantly surprised to see they are nearly packed. The Blue Rooster would be dead right now if he'd chosen to go there. The music at Jack's in the Box is a little louder and there are no pool tables or dart boards or anything like that. He doubts Jack's in the Box even offers food and if they do it's probably something beyond your typical pub food.

There's a large dance floor with tables lined outside of it. Along the walls there are counter height tables and no matter where you're sitting there's a clear path to the bar and the bathrooms. It's dimly lit like most clubs or bars are, but the dance floor has various colored and flashing lights.

Jonathan isn't sure how he feels about Faith coming here for her bachelorette party, it doesn't seem like a place she would enjoy. Maybe the dancing and the music, but he can imagine the busyness would make her feel uneasy. He has a bit of solace knowing Jayce was keeping watch over her and clearly nothing bad happened.

There are a couple of women that catch his eye right away, but he's starting to wonder if his typical target woman would even come here. The loner types he chooses for obvious reasons aren't coming out to have a good time for the most part. They're out to drink and blend in. There is a good chance though, if they're out to find a man to take them home they could come here. His selection will depend on their motives just as much as his own.

He orders a drink and then sits at the curve of the bar where he can see nearly everything, especially the rest of the bar area and the dance floor. The couple of women he first noticed seem to be alone. One is sitting at a bar height table near the door and the other is sitting at one near the bathroom. Both of them have their faces in their phones and their hands on their drinks.

Jonathan feels the need to be extra careful since he hasn't been here before. One of these women could be a regular, or the DJ's girlfriend or something. He's going to have to sit and observe for some time before he feels comfortable enough to begin his luring tactics on anyone.

He watches as the woman sitting by the door walks past him to the bathroom. He doesn't acknowledge her because in these cases the less a woman thinks you want her the more she wants to be wanted by you.

He takes a sip from his rum and coke, which is now somewhat watered down by the ice, as she walks past him again to go back to her table. Before she does though, she stops at the bar and orders another drink. If this were the Blue Rooster or even Duffy's Bar Jonathan would have ordered her a drink from the bartender, but with her being here before him and this being new grounds for him, he isn't willing to start that quite yet.

She takes her drink and sits back down at a table a couple of rows closer to Jonathan. Had he not noted where she was sitting before he may not have noticed the subtle change. He believes he has her attention which is a promising sign.

An hour and a half later Jonathan is helping her to his car, his adrenaline is pumping and he can hardly wait to get her up to those dank living quarters, if you can even call it that.

Jonathan purposely parked down the road from the club so he wasn't on the main road trying to help a very drunk looking woman to his car where onlookers can easily see and possibly remember. The side street is dark which works perfectly.

"You're taking me back to your place, right?" The woman asks him.

"Only if that's where you want to go, Suzanne." The fact that she has the same name as his aunt only piqued his desire even more.

"It's the only place I want to be tonight."

Jonathan hits the unlock button making the lights on the Lexus flash.

"That's your car?" She asks in a high tone while slurring the words together and pointing as she wears a huge smile.

"That's my car." He nods.

"I hit the fucking jackpot! Like I thought you'd have money, you're dressed like you would and you're clearly hot as hell and take care of yourself, but damn, a Lexus? I've never even sat in one of them before."

"I guess tonight is your lucky night then."

"Tonight is your lucky night." She says with her eyes half closed as she sits down in the passenger seat.

Jack's in the Box is only a ten minute drive from Jonathan's building which hopefully will be enough time for her to get to the point he needs her at for what's to come. He keeps an eye on her while he drives. If it seems like the drugs need a bit more time to work he will drive around a little longer. It shouldn't take too much more time though, she's fighting pretty hard to hold her head up and her one arm is just hanging between the seat and the door.

"Are you feeling OK?" Jonathan asks Suzanne to help figure out her state.

"I'm…" Her voice trails off. She must have fought pretty hard to even get that out.

Suddenly, the sight of Faith lying in the hospital bed fighting to let them know she was OK flashes in his mind's eye. Jonathan's stomach drops and he begins to wrestle with the reality of life as he wants it to be and the double life he's leading.

He resolves to at least get Suzanne up to the living quarters in the building as he parks the Lexus.

Once he sees Suzanne's face as he helps her out of the car, he knows his urge won't allow him to turn back now, no matter how he's feeling about everything else. The look on her face amplifies the adrenaline coursing through his veins ten-fold. The fear in her eyes is what's feeding his urge at the moment, making it grow exponentially. How he ever thought he'd be able to control it, he isn't sure now.

He carries her up the rusted metal stairs. The treads creak with every step. When he gets the door to the living quarters open the smell brings him back to every kill he's ever had here, a very welcome nostalgia. He lays Suzanne down on the couch while he changes into his blood splattered jeans and a dingy old T-shirt.

Suzanne is lying motionless on the couch that has become so stained and matted with various bodily fluids through the years that the original velvety pea green color is barely visible. Jonathan would think she's sleeping, but he knows the truth. The drug is working perfectly. Her eyes are open and moving around frantically trying to see what's going on, which brings a smile to his face. He savors this part almost as much as what's going to happen in the bathroom.

He readies his tools, various blades he'll use to remove parts of Suzanne until all that remains are pieces of flesh and bone, not to mention the blood that will seep from her numerous wounds. Jonathan has always found the sticky copper smelling substance to be one of his favorite things his victims give him.

As he thinks about that, the memory of Faith's injured foot comes to mind. She bled a lot the night she stepped on a glass shard from a broken wine glass, but her blood didn't have the same effect on him. Her blood scared him because he knew all too well if she lost too much it wouldn't be good for her.

He shakes the memory from his mind and turns back to look at Suzanne lying on the couch. He walks over there, leans down and touches her shoulder while smiling. He says, "It's all going to be OK Suzanne. I'm only going to cut you apart, bit by bit."

He wanted to soothe her, but the urge wanted to scare her. The more fear, the better it makes Jonathan feel. Tears start running down Suzanne's face, one rolls right off her cheek and onto the unfinished wood floor beneath. Jonathan strokes her cheek, wiping the rest of her tears away.

"It's OK, Suzanne. I'm going to take good care of you."

Jonathan can only imagine the facial expressions she would make if the drug weren't in full effect.

"I'm going to undress you now and put you in the bathtub."

Again more tears fall and he begins to carefully remove her clothing. They'll end up in the bathtub with her to be eaten away by the acid as well before he leaves tonight.

With Suzanne laying naked in the disgustingly dirty bathtub, Jonathan begins. He starts with pieces of her thigh, then her calf. He decides to remove her toes next. Suzanne's toe nails have a beautiful red paint on them that reminds Jonathan of how bright red blood is when it first begins to flow.

At first he removes both big toes, setting each on the side of the bathtub, purposely putting them where Suzanne can see them. As he works he begins to talk to Suzanne, it's not something he always does, but in this case he can't help it.

"I have an aunt named Suzanne. I simply call her Aunt Suz. She took me in after my parents died in a car accident when I was eight. Aunt Suz never wanted me though. So here I was a poor little eight year old boy with no parents, who was forced to go live with a woman that didn't want me around and who couldn't be bothered to do anything to take care of me. She never loved me. She loved her brother, my dad, and I was the constant reminder that he was gone."

Jonathan looks at Suzanne's face and smiles. "I don't think I've ever told one of you that much about me before. I guess your name is probably the reason." He squints his eyes and then says, "You kind of remind me of her too."

Then again, all of them do in some way or another or he wouldn't have been drawn to them at all. This isn't about attraction, he's never had sex of any type with any of them. This is a different urge entirely, one he feels deep down to his soul. One he's sure he'll never cure.

Suzanne's blood begins to pool in the bottom of the bathtub and the coppery scent fills the air intermingling with her perfume. The smell is intoxicating to Jonathan. It never ceases to amaze him how much blood is contained in the human body and how they all smell so similar.

"I usually enjoy taking my time with this next part, but I'm in kind of a hurry tonight. I need to get to work in the morning and should get some amount of sleep." A fear creeps up that maybe Faith went down to the basement guest bedroom to talk to him only to find out he's not there. Then he reminds himself that the likelihood of her doing that tonight is extremely low. She locked the office door, no doubt she also locked the bedroom door.

He slides the long blade of his knife from Suzanne's belly button to her sternum revealing her intestines and digestive tract. The blood is really beginning to puddle now. He runs his hands through the sticky substance while pulling her insides out and placing them in the tub.

He watches her face as he does this, He can tell the moment is coming soon. Her skin is pale and he sees as he lifts her eye lids there is no life left in them. Her life is literally draining away into Jonathan's putrid bathtub. The rise and fall of her chest is shallow and slowing.

Cleanup doesn't take him long at all, at this point he could practically do it all in his sleep. He's perfected his craft enough that he's become quite efficient at it.

Chapter 40

Fortitude

Noun; strength of mind that enables a person to encounter danger or bear pain or adversity with courage

When Jonathan leaves for work the next morning, Faith is still in bed. She purposely stayed there until he was gone instead of going down into their gym for a run on the treadmill, like she normally does, so she wouldn't have to see him. She's not sure how to approach anything with him right now. The fact that it's so close to the wedding makes it all even worse.

As she gets ready for the day, she keeps trying to remind herself of how great he's been to her and that he's not done anything like this before. *At least not that she knows of.* He's never given her a reason not to trust him and even with her giving him the silent treatment all day yesterday he's respected her and hasn't gotten angry. Not that he has a reason to get angry since he's the cause of all of this, but some men are like that. Even if it's their fault, they still get mad at you.

Jonathan has treated her wonderfully, and not only with material things either. He was incredibly supportive through the miscarriage last year. He doesn't have a temper to speak of, the only time she was slightly scared was when he wouldn't let her leave during that argument. She can explain that away too though since his parents died in a car accident and he was worried about her driving angry and upset.

As she drives to Hilltop Elementary School she tries to prepare herself to focus on the kids. They're getting antsy with it getting so close to the end of the school year. She's also shared some of the wedding details with them and how after the wedding her last name will change. She was sure to explain that it isn't the only way, but it's what she is choosing to do.

When she walks down the silent hallway to her classroom she sees that Jackie is standing by her door waiting for her.

"So…how are things?" She had text Faith yesterday, but it is so much easier to talk in person.

"Things are quiet, I'd say." She walks over to her desk and sets her tote bag down.

"You two haven't talked yet?" Jackie follows her.

"No. I haven't talked to him at all, except to let him know not to come into the bedroom when he tried shortly after you left." Faith rolls her eyes and plops down in her chair.

"You're kidding me! He really tried that?"

"He did that! He unlocked the door and started walking in. I told him it was going to piss me off more and he turned around and walked out before getting to the bathroom, thank goodness."

"When do you think you'll talk to him?"

"I don't know. Honestly, Jackie, I'm not sure how we can fix this."

"You're not going to see how you can fix it when you haven't even talked to him about any of it yet, Faith. You trust him right?"

Faith gives her a discerning look. "It was much easier to answer that question before all of this happened."

"OK, fair point, I'll rephrase. Do you think he would purposely go out of his way to hurt you, or cause you harm in anyway?"

"No! Not at all!"

"Then talk to him. He'll listen to you. I'm sure he wants to get this all fixed just as badly, if not worse, than you do. Besides, it's so close to your wedding, you don't want to put this off any longer than is necessary."

"I don't." Faith looks down at her hands folded in her lap. "There's still so much to do, and then to have this hanging over our heads. It's just a lot right now."

"So, help yourself and take one less very stressful thing off of your plate. Is there anything that I can help with?" Jackie asks.

Faith looks up at her friend. "You have helped in so many ways, Jackie. Thank you."

"You're welcome. It's what I'm here for!" She starts heading for the door. "I've got to get to my classroom. I'll see you later." She calls out as she walks into the hallway.

By the time the end of her work day comes around, Faith is convinced that she'll talk to Jonathan at dinner tonight, or maybe after dinner. Either way they'll talk tonight. Jackie is right, this can't be hanging over their heads any longer.

She has no idea what time he's going to get home tonight, but she'll start making dinner and when he gets home she'll pour them each a glass of wine.

She pushes the button in her Range Rover to lift the garage door and she sees Jonathan's car is already parked in his parking spot. She's quite surprised and somewhat curious as she walks in through the service door. There are candles lit at the banquet style seating by the island and Jonathan is standing at the Viking range with a grey apron on covering the fitted suit he wore to work.

She can be mad at him and still admit to herself how absolutely hot this man is. She watches as he turns to look at her while he dries his hands on a towel.

"Hi." She says softly.

The stress in his face is released instantly at the sound of her voice. Jonathan rushes over to her and envelops her in his arms. He kisses the top of her head and says, "That's the best thing I've ever heard out of your mouth. Can we talk?"

"I'd like that."

"Dinner is just about done, we can talk and eat if that's OK?"

"That sounds perfect." She smiles softly and he hugs her even tighter.

"I don't like this, I don't like fighting, but not talking is even worse." Jonathan says as he walks back over towards the range.

Faith sees two wine glasses full on the banquet table waiting for them.

Jonathan nods towards the glasses. "You can go ahead and start drinking that if you'd like."

"I'd like." Faith says smiling again.

Jonathan takes a moment to look at her. He inhales deeply and lets it out. "I'm so glad you're home and talking to me again. I've missed your sweet voice."

"You might not like what this sweet voice has to say, Jonathan."

"I want to hear everything it has to say, Faith. If it's bothering you and has you upset and angry enough to not talk to me or even want to look at me I need to hear it so we can fix it."

"I agree." Faith says as she takes a drink from her wine glass. Jonathan has quickly reminded her how incredible he is. His patience with her and the way he's trying to understand her feelings is making her feel so loved and cared for. The anger she feels towards him is dissipating.

Jonathan plates their dinners and brings them to the table. Faith scooches over so he can sit down beside her where he normally does.

"You can start, if you'd like. I'd like to hear about everything that's bothering you, Faith."

Faith takes a deep breath trying to figure out where to begin and what to say. She went over this at least twenty-five times in the short drive home, but now it seems like the words don't want to come out. Her throat feels tight and slightly dry so she takes another drink from her glass. Jonathan does the same.

"Well, as you know, we started at Lee's pub." Faith pauses.

Jonathan waits and then says. "Right, I thought that was an interesting choice."

"We needed to face it. I haven't been in there since that happened and I needed to do that first in order to be able to enjoy my time anywhere else. Jackie had gotten us all drink covers which helped." She pauses again, takes a deep breath and then continues. "I'm getting off topic. When we got there Tracy was working. She felt the need to apologize about everything that happened and she mentioned that you had come in there the night after it happened and that Hector showed you the video." Faith pauses again, but Jonathan doesn't say anything. "It bothers me that you never told me you saw the video. It upsets me that you went behind my back to do that."

"I didn't want to bother you with it especially right after it happened. Faith, you were so groggy and not yourself that day, I was worried and wanted to see if there was anything on the video that would help me help you."

"If you wanted to help me, why didn't you mention seeing the video? We sat in that police station talking to those officers and you never once made it seem like you knew anything more than what I'd told you."

"Because I didn't, Faith. The videos didn't show me more than what you and Jackie had said already."

"But you knew what they looked like. You got to see what he did when we weren't watching."

"It was very strange watching it. I didn't like it. It pissed me off and made me want to hunt them down. I didn't want to share those feelings with you when you were already going through so much."

"But in the past year plus you never thought to mention it?" She asks in a slightly accusatory tone.

"I kind of felt like if I did it would upset you and make you think I'm hiding things from you."

"Are you?"

A shocked expression flashes on Jonathan's face before it softens. "I understand why you feel that way, Faith, but I'm not. You're going to be my wife in less than five days. I'm not going to hide something from you that could possibly jeopardize this and what we have." He moves his hand between the two of them.

"But this is exactly what it does! It does jeopardize us, Jonathan. It makes me think that you're lying and hiding things and it worries me that the nights you're working late isn't work related at all. It makes me question literally everything."

"I'm sorry, Faith. I should have told you. I should have been upfront with you. I just didn't think that when you were so out of it was the best time, and then the more time passed the more it seemed like a horrible idea. Maybe I was being selfish, I didn't want you to be upset with me, but I swear there is nothing going on that I'm hiding from you."

"The biggest problem I have is that I found that out at Lee's pub, and then I find out at the Stellar Amphitheatre that you've hired someone to follow me after I explicitly told you not to do that. Do you realize how disrespected that makes me feel?"

"I do. I mean I can see that now. In the moment I didn't. In the moment, I was being selfish again, and wanted the peace of mind to know that you're safe. It was hell watching you in that hospital bed, and seeing how weak and out of it you were the next day. I couldn't bear to watch you go through that again."

"Jackie tried to tell me your heart was in the right place and I knew she was right, but it still doesn't change the fact that you again went behind my back and did something without telling me about it."

"Jayce is a good guy and I knew he could use the money, but more importantly I knew he wouldn't let anything happen to you. I couldn't be there and I needed to make sure someone was to keep an eye out and make sure you're safe."

"I understand that something bad happened to me, it was terrible, and it was mostly my fault and lack of due diligence. I let my guard down because I felt like we were in a safe place. That feeling of safety has vanished, Jonathan. It took me a while to even feel safe going anywhere that resembles a bar. Remember when we were on vacation last year? I had a hard time when we went to the little barbeque place because of how much it resembled a bar. I'm not letting my guard down any time soon. You didn't need to hire someone, especially when I told you not to. Did you think I wouldn't be pissed off and hurt if I found out?"

"Honestly? I didn't think you would. I thought Jayce would be better at keeping out of sight."

"I was being diligent in keeping track of my surroundings no matter how drunk I was. The concert had barely started when I saw him there and a red flag flashed in my brain telling me he was also at Lee's. I was paying attention, Jonathan."

"I guess you were, Faith. I'm sorry I went behind your back and disrespected you. You had made it clear to me that you didn't want a body guard type person for the night and I disregarded your feelings and I'm sorry. I won't do it again. Instead, we will talk more about it so my peace of mind can come through our communication instead of an outside source."

Why does this man have to be so damn perfect? "That sounds good. It doesn't mean I'm going to forgive you right away, and it doesn't mean that things are just automatically going to go back to how they were. I'm still upset and there is still anger inside of me for all of this."

"I understand. I'm so sorry, Faith. I never wanted to make you feel like this. I love you." He wraps his arms around her pulling her head tight to his chest.

"I love you too, Jonathan."

Once they're finished eating dinner, they curl up together on couch and watch a movie with Zeke sleeping on the floor right next to Faith's feet. When the movie is over Jonathan goes into the basement bedroom and brings the suitcase back upstairs and unpacks.

"I'm sorry about that." Faith says.

"No, you needed some space. I can't expect you to want to share a bed with someone you're angry with. Luckily we have a few spare bedrooms for me to pick from."

"Yeah." She smiles at him, grateful for his understanding.

Chapter 41

Beatitude

Noun; a state of utmost bliss

Faith holds her smoothie while curled up on the couch thinking about the heartbeat they first heard a year ago today. The sun streams in from the large windows on either side of the massive double front door which floods the room with peaceful morning sunlight.

She had woke up at five am, alone, unable to sleep any longer. The day is here! It's her wedding day, and even with the craziness of the last week she is so incredibly excited for it! This morning, however, in the stillness that only it can provide, she feels the need to take a moment and remember their angel baby before being able to celebrate the big day. It only feels right.

Jackie, Hope, and Diane will all be at Faith's house around seven. They're going to meet Trey's team of hair and make-up people at the Amethyst Hotel at nine. Carmine and Jackson will be there soon after to begin taking pictures and video.

Jonathan had suggested they spend the night apart to make seeing one another all dressed up at either end of the aisle even more special. It felt strange sleeping without him. The bed felt colder, she was missing his warmth. Faith had thought about inviting Zeke into bed with her, but she had second thoughts about that, not wanting him to expect to be able to do that all the time. Jonathan would not be happy at all.

She is unsure of what to do until everyone gets there. When she finishes her smoothie she'll go shower so there's enough time for her to dry her hair, based on the instructions given to her by Trey, but that won't take long and she still has plenty of time to kill.

Zeke curls up on the floor by her feet and looks up at her expectantly.

"I know, buddy, I wish you could come to the wedding too, but the hotel doesn't allow dogs. I'm sorry."

Zeke's head tilts and Faith gives him a scratch behind the ears. She takes a drink of her smoothie and watches out the window as birds flit this way and that for a moment before checking her phone.

There's a text message. She unlocks it to see that it's from Jonathan.

Jonathan: Good morning my Bride! I can't wait to see you walk down the aisle to me today! I love you! I hope you slept well!

Faith: Good morning my groom! I love you! It was OK, I was missing you! I can't wait to see you either! Why are you up so early?

Jonathan: Couldn't sleep.

Faith: Me either. Zeke wants to come to the wedding.

Jonathan: I'm sure he does, it's too bad they won't allow it.

Faith: Yeah. I'll see you soon!

Jonathan: I'll be the guy waiting for you.

Faith smiles to herself. That was sweet of Jonathan, but then again he's always been really sweet to her and he treats her so well. Today at least, she can't imagine being so mad at him like she was last weekend.

She takes a deep breath in, hoping to never be that upset and hurt by him again. She thinks of her beautifully specially designed and crafted just for her wedding dress hanging in the pink bridal suite at the Amethyst Hotel and how slipping into that will feel. Then she imagines how she'll feel walking down the aisle seeing Jonathan waiting for her, smiling that smile that gets her every time.

It's going to be a wonderful day.

Just then her doorbell rings. She's confused since it's not seven yet. When she checks on the app she sees Jackie's smiling face looking back at her from the doorbell camera.

As she opens the door Jackie has gifts and a large tote bag she sets down beside her right before pulling Faith in for an embrace.

"It's your wedding day!"

"It is!"

"How are you feeling?"

"Like I woke up too early, but really good other than that!"

"Good! Were you planning on showering?"

"Yes, I just need to finish this." She says holding up her smoothie.

"Well, guzzle that shit down! When you're done showering I can blow dry your hair for you."

"Really?"

"Of course! I'd love to!"

Faith looks over at the gifts. "What are those for?"

"You, silly!"

"You didn't have to get me anything. You being my maid of honor is all the gift I need!"

"That's sweet, but there's no way I could not get you something for your wedding! Go ahead and open them!"

Faith walks over to the two wrapped packages and takes the card from the top one. As she opens it she sees Jackie's beautiful handwritten note on the inside. As she reads it tears begin to form in the corner of her eyes then they spill onto her cheeks when she blinks.

"I'm really glad you had me do this now and not in the bridal suite after we've had our hair and makeup done."

"Yeah, there's a method to my madness sometimes." Jackie laughs.

Faith begins to unwrap the top gift. The box is relatively small and light. She lifts the lid to reveal a small trinket inside. The tears that were only a slow drip has turned into a steady flow.

"I can't believe you have this after all these years!" Faith says.

"How could I have gotten rid of it?"

"I don't know! You could have lost it." She says giving Jackie a sideways glance.

"I couldn't possibly lose the ring you planned to give your future husband."

"It was so silly. I don't even remember why I gave it to you."

"It really was, but you were convinced it would be like Cinderella or something and it would fit him just right. And if I remember correctly, you gave it to me after you lost something else and you were sure you would lose this too. I still remember when you gave it to me, you were so serious.

'Jackie, you have to remember to give this to me on my wedding day. You have to.'."

Faith holds it up examining it. "I don't believe it would fit any man now." She laughs.

"No, we were little and didn't know how big men's fingers really are."

Faith smiles at Jackie. "This is so amazing." She holds the ring in her hand tightly and brings it up to her chest, embracing it.

"I was thinking, we'll have to check, but a lot of times there are ways to tie something like this into your dress or maybe even your bouquet."

"That is the best idea, Jackie!" Faith says enthusiastically. "Thank you again! Thank you for remembering! You're the best!" She hugs Jackie tight.

"And the best part! It can double as your something old and something blue." Jackie says pointing to the navy blue stone in the center.

"What's the other one we need then?" She asks trying to remember the rhyme.

"Something new." Jackie says, nodding to the next box.

Faith unwraps the next box that is a rectangular shape.

"I know you said you have your jewelry already, but when I saw this I thought it was a perfect match with everything! The dress, and your earrings and necklace."

Faith pulls open the box to reveal a bracelet that, just as Jackie said, goes seamlessly with the accessories she's already picked out to wear. "Where did you find this?" Faith asks.

"I went into Riteger's."

"I didn't see it when I picked out the other set."

"From what the sales person told me they had just gotten it in."

"Jackie, it's gorgeous! You didn't have to do this!"

"I know, Faith. I wanted to."

"Thank you!"

"Now, we're going to run out of time! Go get in the shower!" Jackie demands jokingly.

Faith takes the last few sips of her smoothie and goes to get in the shower. She turns some music on and gets in.

While Jackie is waiting, Hope and Diane come over as well.

"How's she doing?" Diane asks Jackie.

"She's doing really well. She's eaten something, so that's good."

"Right."

Hope walks over to the cupboard and grabs a glass. "Does anyone else need anything to drink? I'm getting myself some water."

"No, thank you, dear." Diane says.

"I'm OK too, thanks though Hope."

"You're welcome. How much longer do you think she'll be in the shower?"

"Maybe ten more minutes. I'm not sure what all she needs to do in there. I assume she's shaving and everything."

"I'd hope so." Hope Scoffs. "It is her wedding day after all."

"Yes, it is."

Fifteen minutes later, Faith walks into the living room in a white silk robe. Her hair is pulled up into a wet messy bun. She holds her blow dryer in her hand. Looking at Jackie she says, "I thought it might be easier to do out here."

"That's true, and then we can be with everyone too."

"Yeah."

Diane pulls Faith in for a hug. "I'm so happy your day is finally here!"

Hope blurts in. "Hey, Doubt, it looks like you forgot something this morning."

"What's that?" She asks as she sits down for Jackie to start blow drying her hair.

"To change the number on your count down."

"I guess I did. Would you like to do the honors?"

Hope opens her eyes wide with feigned excitement. "Really? Can I?"

Faith laughs. "If you want to. You can be my guest."

Jackie turns on the blow dryer drowning out whatever smart ass comment is going to come out of Hope's mouth next. Faith smiles up at her best friend.

These three women are her lifeline, and have been almost all of her life. She can't imagine this day without including all of them in significant roles. They're here now, supporting her, earlier than they were told. Which is a feat mostly for Hope, but impressive still for everyone else to want to be there for her in this way. It speaks volumes to who they are, but also to what Faith means to them and she feels so grateful for their presence and their assistance, today especially.

Faith drives them all to the Amethyst Hotel and is greeted by Brenda as they pull up to the front door. Brenda has someone from the courtesy staff grab all of their belongings and take them up to the bridal suite while Brenda shows Faith and the other ladies the ballroom area quickly before escorting them to the suite.

Faith was worried about accidentally running into Jonathan, but Brenda assured her he is already in the Groom's Suite with his groom's people.

When they enter the very pink room Hope whispers to Diane, "I might end up with quite the headache if we have to stay in here too long."

"The pink isn't that bad." Diane offers.

"It's as if the Easter bunny, Pepto-Bismol, and bubblegum all had a baby."

Diane laughs. "That's not entirely wrong." She tilts her head to one side as if contemplating what that would actually look like.

Faith immediately goes to the window where her dress is hanging on an old cast iron hook. She takes a deep breath and unzips the bag it's in. Her breath is taken away with how stunning it is. It's as perfect today as it was when she first saw it after it was delivered to the bridal shop. Mr. Caltroney did an amazing job. She never had a doubt about his talent, she only questioned if it was going to be exactly what she wanted because she couldn't see it in person until it was done.

Now the day is here, she's seen it in person, and tried it on, she can't wait to get it on and wear it down the aisle to marry Jonathan.

"It's absolutely gorgeous." Jackie says walking up behind Faith.

"It is, right? I can't believe it's mine."

"I can. It's perfect for you."

Faith smiles. "Thank you."

Just then the hair and makeup crew knock on the door and enter pulling their wheeled luggage type bags behind them.

"Hi, everyone! I'm Trey and this is Randi and Christina who will also be taking care of your hair and doing your makeup. We also have Sharon who is our helper, getting us everything that we might need."

Faith greets them all. "It's so great to see you guys! Thanks for coming!"

"We're happy to be here! Happy Wedding day, Faith! We're going to start with your mom and the other ladies so that your hair and makeup is as fresh as it can be before the ceremony."

"That sounds great!"

Faith sits on the soft pink velvet sofa in front of the white marble fire place while the other women have their hair and makeup done alternately.

Frank knocks while Diane is sitting in the chair getting her makeup done. "Beautiful as always, my love." He says as he leans in to kiss the top of Diane's head.

"Thank you, dear." She says. Then lowering her voice to a whisper she asks, "How's Jonathan doing?"

"He's eager to get the show on the road."

Diane's smile broadens. "Good." She says simply. "Hopefully he can be patient."

"He'll be as patient as he has to be." Frank says as he walks over to Faith and sits beside her on the sofa. "How are you doing, pumpkin?"

"I'm good." She smiles at him. "Excited for the day to finally be here. It was starting to feel like it wasn't ever going to come. How are you doing?"

"I'm also good. I feel confident in the capabilities of the man I'm giving my daughter's hand to. That's all a father can really ask for."

Faith holds up both of her hands turning them, she says, "I still have both my hands, dad." She smirks.

"Yes, you do." He leans in and kisses her forehead. "I wouldn't want it any other way."

He stands to look at Faith's dress which has now been taken out of the bag. "You are going to look so breathtaking in this." He says as he reaches to feel the fabric of the dress.

"Thanks, dad. It's one of a kind!"

"Just like you." He turns to look at Faith with a smile.

Hope is sitting in the chair getting her hair done. Frank leans in and kisses her cheek. "You look beautiful as always."

Then he looks from Diane to Faith and back to Hope. "My lovely ladies. I am one lucky man." He takes Diane's hand in his. "Thank you for marrying me and giving me daughters that are just as kind, and thoughtful, and beautiful as you." Then he kisses her hand.

He gets up and starts towards the door a few moments later to go back into the Groom's Suite. "I'll be back when it's closer to time to walk down the aisle."

"Sounds good!" Faith calls after him.

After the door closes again Christina leans down to Diane and says, "You really hit the jackpot with that one! I wish we could all find one like him."

"I have been very blessed! Especially since he's only gotten better with age."

"Like a fine wine." Randi says.

"Exactly." Diane laughs.

Two hours later, Faith has her hair and makeup done and has gotten into her dress. Carmine and Jackson have been in both the Bridal Suite and the Groom's Suite taking photos and videos. Carmine even showed Faith a few of the shots he took in the bridal suite and it brought tears to her eyes. It's almost as if seeing those photos made her feel like it's really real now.

The door opens and music from the seating area spills into the room. Frank comes back in with Brenda and suddenly Faith feels the realness even more.

"Are you ready?" Brenda asks with a huge smile.

"I've never been more ready for anything."

"Great because your, very soon to be, husband is waiting patiently for you."

"I'm ready."

"OK!" Brenda speaks up so that all of them can hear her. "I'm going to have you all line up in the hallway, the best man and groom's person will be meeting you there to walk down the aisle together. Remember how we practiced last night."

Everyone follows Brenda out the door with Frank and Faith behind them all. Music fills the air as they walk towards the open wall of sliding doors. Frank sneaks up to the front quickly and walks out with Diane down the aisle to her seat before going back to line up with Faith and wait for the procession to begin.

Hope and Andy walk down the aisle together. Andy smiles at their sister as they walk past the piano and through the open wall to the rooftop terrace. The sun is shining brightly with only a few fluffy bright white clouds in the sky. The bay sparkling in the background is making the perfect back drop.

Once Hope and Andy reach Jonathan, Jackie and Rowen start slowly down the aisle. Next is Frank and Faith. They stay hidden from Jonathan's sight so that only the people seated towards the back can see them as they wait.

Andy's sister, Maggie, begins playing the traditional wedding march. Brenda nods her head and Frank takes a step with Faith falling into step with him. When she first takes in the sight of Jonathan she's surprised to see that his face is quite red and he's overtaken by emotion. As they get closer she can see tears gathered at the corner of his eyes just waiting to fall.

Frank releases Faith's hand and shakes Jonathan's. "Son, she's your responsibility now." He laughs and continues, "No, seriously, I know you'll take good care of her. Thank you for being so wonderful to her. She deserves every ounce of it."

"That she does, sir."

Frank takes Faith's hand once again and places it in Jonathan's. Faith smiles at her father and then she and Jonathan lock eyes. She fights to keep herself from kissing him. A huge smile spreads on Jonathan's face, the tears are still threatening to fall. Then they turn to the officiant still holding hands.

"It's a glorious day for a wedding! We're gathered here today to witness the love shared between Jonathan Michael Hall and Faith Victoria Brandt and to witness the joining of their lives together as one. Love is the home we find in another person where all of our pieces fit seamlessly. Love brings us places we couldn't have found without it. We find parts of ourselves we've lost, and others surface because we feel safe enough to be who we truly are. Our lives are more meaningful because of it. When we've found the one we're meant to spend the rest of our lives with, everything else begins to make sense in an entirely new way.

Jonathan and Faith have done just that. Their lives are forever changed for having found one another and in some ways, all of our lives have changed for having witnessed and shared in their love in some aspect.

Marriage is the ultimate partnership. It requires patience and perseverance as well as reverence for the love and life you share with one another."

The officiant turns towards Jonathan. "Do you, Jonathan Michael Hall, take Faith Victoria Brandt to be your wife, to respect her, love her, and only her for eternity?"

"I do!" He says enthusiastically.

The officiant then turns towards Faith. "Do you, Faith Victoria Brandt, take Jonathan Michael Hall, to be your husband, to respect him, love him, and only him for eternity?"

"I do!" She smiles broadly.

"And now, Jonathan take the ring and place it on Faith's finger as you repeat after me. I, Jonathan, take you, Faith."

"I, Jonathan, take you, Faith."

"To be my lawfully wedded wife"

"To by my lawfully wedded wife."

"I give you this ring as a symbol."

"I give you this ring as a symbol,"

"Of my love with the pledge,"

"Of my love with the pledge,"

"To love you today, tomorrow, always, and forever."

"To love you today, tomorrow, always, and forever."

The officiant turns to Faith. "Faith, take the ring and place it on Jonathan's finger as you repeat after me. I, Faith, take you, Jonathan."

"I, Faith, take you, Jonathan."

"To be my lawfully wedded husband."

"To be my lawfully wedded husband."

"I give you this ring as a symbol,"

"I give you this ring as a symbol,"

"Of my love with the pledge,"

"Of my love with the pledge,"

"To love you today, tomorrow, always, and forever."

"To love you today, tomorrow, always, and forever."

"By the authority vested in me by this beautiful state, I now pronounce you husband and wife. Jonathan, you may now kiss your bride."

Jonathan pulls Faith into him tightly as he brings his lips to hers. While still kissing her he dips her back and there's a hoot of celebration from a handful of wedding guests.

As he pulls her back up, Maggie begins playing and the officiant announces, "I present to you Mr. and Mrs. Hall!"

Jonathan holds Faith's hand up with his in celebration as they walk back down the aisle together as husband and wife. Carmine and Jackson are walking around getting different shots from every angle. Rowen and Jackie are close behind, followed by Andy and Hope. They form a receiving line for guests to greet them at the back of the large room.

Faith and Jonathan meet people from one another's lives they've never met and will most likely not remember the names of. Towards the end of the line of people Faith sees an older frail looking woman. Jonathan freezes next to Faith, his gregarious greetings cease as soon as he sees the woman as well.

For a moment Faith wonders who she could be, until it hits her that it's his Aunt Suz. She's short in stature, with her wiry silver hair done up tightly in a bun. She's wearing all black making her pale skin look even more washed out.

As she approaches she doesn't seem to sense Jonathan's demeanor has changed at all. Faith is certain she didn't send this woman an invitation, she wouldn't have even had the address to mail it.

"Jonathan," Aunt Suz begins, "I'm so glad to see you so happy. You never come to see your old Aunt Suz anymore so I had no idea what was going on in your life until I overheard someone say you were getting married. Surely my invite just got lost." Aunt Suz turns to Faith. "You must be Faith, you are quite a beautiful young lady. I'm sure Jonathan has mentioned me. It's great to finally meet you. I'm his Aunt Suz, the woman who raised him after my baby brother and sister-in-law died tragically in a car accident."

Faith feigns a smile only to be polite. "It's great to meet you too. We'll have to catch up later." Faith says nodding to the line still waiting behind Aunt Suz.

"Oh where are my manners, yes, of course!" Aunt Suz says then hugs Jonathan and Faith and walks over to the table that's being filled up with hors d'oeuvres.

Jonathan is visibly uncomfortable and the hugs were awkward for them both. Faith touches his arm, "Are you OK?"

"Let's get through this receiving line and then I'll need to retreat somewhere for a few moments. I can't believe she did that." He looks at the person walking up to them and says, "OH, Jack, it's so great to see you!"

The line continues for another five minutes. When Faith and Jonathan finish, Faith grabs Carmine, Jackson, and Brenda and they all meet in the Groom's Suite.

Faith takes charge. "There is an uninvited guest here." Faith turns to Brenda. "I'm not sure what we can do or even what we want to do at this point, but she was not invited for a reason and somehow she has just shown up."

Jonathan is sitting on the leather sofa with Faith by his side. His one hand is on her knee, the other is holding his head. He picks his head up and says in an almost menacing tone, "She is a miserable woman and I don't want her here."

Brenda quickly steps up and says, "We'll have her escorted from the premises and if she tries to return we will call the police immediately."

"That sounds good. Thank you, Brenda." Faith says then turns to Carmine and Jackson. "Please be sure not to include her in any photos or videos. It's tainted enough of today, we don't want this to be more than a lasting memory."

"Understood." Carmine says. "There will be no evidence from either of us that she was ever here. We can either edit her out or just delete any files she might have already corrupted." He smiles.

"If only I could do that." Jonathan says flatly.

Faith's heart breaks for him. This was never supposed to happen. It was supposed to be the happiest day of their lives and this woman had to go and ruin it for him. She had to have known she'd have a negative effect on Jonathan. There's obviously a reason he doesn't see her or want her in their lives.

"I'm so sorry, Jonathan." Faith says wrapping her arms around him. He collapses into her and she feels like for once she's his strength.

Brenda calls over the walkie talkie for security to come up to the terrace. "We'll get this taken care of! Don't worry!"

Carmine and Jackson follow Brenda out of the suite leaving Faith and Jonathan alone.

Faith rubs his back for a few moments before pulling his head up to look at her. "Hey, look at me, please?" He does as she asks. A small smile spreads on her face. "We're married! We did it! I'm your wife and you're my husband. Let's focus on that right now."

"You're right."

"It's OK to be upset and hurt and feel those feelings right now, but you also shouldn't dwell there, Jonathan. Not today."

"I'll try not to."

"We're going to go back out there once she's gone and then we'll have pictures taken with the wedding party and my family."

"That sounds really good."

"We're going to try to forget, just for now, that this even happened."

"Yes, we are." Jonathan nods in agreement.

They both stand and Faith straightens her dress.

"You are so astonishingly beautiful, Faith. I'm such a lucky man."

"Thank you!"

"That is one hell of a dress." He says standing back to take it all in.

"Mr. Caltroney absolutely out did himself."

"You were his muse, Faith. It has more to do with what you asked for than his talent."

"It's a good mixture of both." Faith says.

Jonathan takes her hand in his and twirls her around. "So gorgeous." He says.

"Thank you." She says feeling her cheeks getting warm.

Jonathan pulls her in and kisses her deeply. When he pulls away he says, "That is helping me forget." Then leans in to kiss her again. When he pulls his head back he pulls her in for a tight hug and says, "Thank you for everything, Faith. You're more than I could have ever hoped to have."

"Thank you, Jonathan. You're incredibly sweet and I'm so grateful to have you, and to be married to you now."

"We should probably head out. Do you think it's safe?"

"It did seem like Brenda was on top of it."

"Yes, it did."

"I think it'll be OK."

Jonathan takes her hand in his and leads the way out the door and back to the cocktail hour.

Carmine and Jackson find them right away and then gather the rest of Faith's family and their wedding party and go out onto the terrace for photos.

When they've finished there, Carmine leads them down to the lobby of the hotel, then to the ballroom, and finally outside.

"They don't usually let us take photos out here, but Brenda gave me the OK for you two."

"That was sweet of her!" Faith says.

"Yeah, she is incredible at her job, but once you get on her good side you get some of the added perks of that."

"Good to know we're on her good side." Jonathan says.

Carmine gets the whole crew together in different poses and then does some with the bride and groom and each one of the wedding party separately. Faith is so excited to see how these pictures turn out! So far they've been incredibly fun to take and she's sure that's going to convey through the lens.

Jackson is in the background following them around and taking footage. It's funny for Faith to see how all of them have coupled up. Most weddings the party barely know one another, but with theirs, they're either dating or sleeping together instead.

Tom is here, but Jonathan had forewarned him that Jackie was obviously going to be in the wedding. Faith isn't sure if he knows that Rowen and Jackie are sleeping together or not, but she won't be the one to tell him.

When they've finished with the pictures, they go back up to the terrace level to mingle during cocktail hour. Dinner will be served shortly and then drinks and dancing.

When they get into the cocktail hour, everyone seems to be having a wonderful time, talking and listening to Maggie play the piano. She's switched from classical to jazz and it's made the whole ambiance of the room change.

There was a heaviness that Faith felt after everything happened with Aunt Suz that has completely vanished now. Jonathan and Faith walk around the room hand in hand talking with various guests and thanking them once again for coming.

Chapter 42

Splenditude

Noun; the quality or state of being splendid

Brenda leads everyone downstairs to the ballroom an hour later for the reception to begin. Some guests take the elevator while others take the stairs. Faith and Jonathan wait with Hope, Andy, Jackie, and Rowen right outside the entrance to the grand room. The DJ will announce them all before dinner is served.

They didn't plan a special entrance dance or anything like that. Hope wanted to chug a beer, but Andy said to save it for their wedding. Rowen and Jackie were up for anything, but if Hope and Andy weren't going to do anything then they wouldn't either. Today is about Jonathan and Faith and their love.

Diane and Frank have already taken their seats near the head table when the DJ starts the music.

"I have the honor and the privilege to present to you Jonathan and Faith's wedding party! We're hitting you hard with the best man, Rowen Mitchell and maid of honor, Jackie Stafford! Give them both a big round of applause! Coming up next we have groom's person Andy Walsh and bridesmaid and little sister, Hope Brandt! Give them both a big round of applause too!"

The guests clap and the lights begin to go down in the room. The heavy wooden double doors Hope and Andy just walked through close and a spot light is shone on the doors moving about to create suspense for Jonathan and Faith to come through the door.

The DJ starts again, "And now, the moment you've all been waiting for!" The doors open and Faith and Jonathan step forward holding their hands high in the air. "Mr. and Mrs. Jonathan Hall!"

All of the guests applaud with a couple hoots and hollers. The two of them walk into the room, Jonathan spins Faith once they reach the dance floor. The various lights from the DJ's stand make Faith's dress shimmer. The sequins Mr. Caltroney had sewn into the fabric are so subtle that they were nearly unnoticeable until the light hit them in the dimly lit ballroom.

Once they get to the head table the lights come back up and the DJ continues his announcement. "We're going to have a few toasts to the couple and then dinner will be served and once we're done eating we'll get to the bride and groom's first dance!"

Frank stands up and takes a mic from the DJ.

"Hi everyone! If you don't know me, I'm Frank, Faith's father. It's so great to see you all here today! As a parent you watch your children grow throughout the years and by the time they're adults you remember so many little details about their childhood and their likes and dislikes, or the funny way they used to say balloons. It can be easy to forget that they're not that little kid anymore. They grow up, seemingly overnight, they get an adult job and they excel. You see that they're succeeding and you're so happy for them and proud of them, but in a way, you also wish you could just make them be little again. Just to have the small things back again like when they would bring you a book you've read five hundred times already, asking you to read it 'just one more, daddy?' and then promptly sitting so comfortably in your lap you'd think they'd fit there forever, but they don't. They grow so quickly and the years fly by in what seems like the blink of an eye.

We're here today because Jonathan and Faith grew up, found one another and fell in love. It is the cycle that has been going on for millennia and will continue long past our time on this Earth. I am so happy for them, and I wish them all of the happiness this life has to offer. I'm so happy Faith has found someone who makes her heart so happy. To Jonathan and Faith!" Frank holds his glass up as everyone else does the same and then they all drink.

Frank passes the mic to Jackie.

"Whew, OK! I'm Jackie Stafford. I've been Faith's best friend since forever! We've got some stories, let me tell you!"

She looks over to Frank and Diane and then says, "On second thought, I think I'll hold onto those a bit longer." The crowd laughs. "I'm the reason these two are even together." They laugh again. "I'm serious! It's kind of like what Mr. Brandt was saying…it's all because I was born. You see, they met at my birthday party, so had I not been born, they wouldn't have met!" The guests all laugh. "OK, seriously though, these two are special. I'm sure a Maid of Honor or two have said that about other brides and grooms, but actually I mean it. They truly are. I've never seen two people take care of each other the way that these two take care of one another. Faith and Jonathan both, are always trying to make sure the other is happy and doing well. If Faith needs something, she knows Jonathan is going to provide it, and vice versa. They're an incredible team and their love knows no bounds. I feel lucky simply to be a witness to their love, honestly." Jackie looks over to Faith. "We'd all be so lucky to find what these two have. To Faith and Jonathan, congratulations!"

Jackie raises her glass and everyone does the same and then drinks. When she's done, Jackie hands the mic down to Rowen.

"I'm not sure how the hell I'm supposed to follow that!" He says in the mic smiling at Jackie whose beaming back at him. He looks back through the ballroom at all of the faces looking back at him. "I see a handful of familiar faces, but if you don't know me, I'm Rowen Mitchell. Jonathan and I go way back. We first met just before high school started and I was so grateful for Jonathan's friendship. We were new in town, my family and I, and I didn't know anyone. Jonathan befriended me and with it I became like instant friends with everyone he knew. It was great, really! Now he's getting married and I feel lucky to be a part of it. Like Jackie said, what they have is special. I would know too, I'm a lawyer, I've seen plenty of divorces, including my own. I've never seen any of those couples look at one another the way Faith and Jonathan do, or treat each other with the respect and care that Jonathan and Faith do. It's magical to see that relationships like this can still happen." He looks at Faith and Jonathan. "Thank you for giving us all hope!" Everyone takes another drink!

Just as he finishes his sentence the waiters and waitresses come through doors on either side of the room with enormous platters full of plates. Everyone raises their glasses again and take a drink. The waiters and waitresses begin passing out the plates according to the guests choices. The head table is served first. Meanwhile, the DJ is playing soft music in the background.

When everyone has finished eating, the DJ announces it's time for their first dance as husband and wife. Jonathan leads Faith out to the dancefloor, holding her hand. He spins her into him and then embraces her as the music begins playing. They sway together, stealing kisses and talking about how the day has gone so far.

Neither of them mentions Aunt Suz for obvious reasons, but Faith is sure she's still in the back of Jonathan's mind too. The more she thinks about it the more the audacity of that woman gets under her skin, but she tries to move past those feelings to focus on the happiness of the day.

"Thank you for the dance, Mrs. Hall."

"You are so very welcome, Mr. Hall."

Jonathan pulls her into him kissing her and quickly slipping his tongue in between her lips to find hers. Then he dips her and the guests cheer. The song finishes and Jonathan goes back to sit at the head table.

"Now, Faith and Frank will have their Father Daughter dance." The DJ announces.

The music starts and Frank and Faith begin to dance. It brings back memories of the numerous weddings of family and friends that they went to when Faith was little and she would dance with her father. She would envision her wedding someday and how she and her dad would dance together then too. It's such an interesting thing to reconcile memories and your current state of reality. How your visions of what the future could look like and the differences in actuality compare.

"I hope today was everything you hoped it would be, pumpkin."

"It was more than I could have hoped for."

"Good. That makes my heart happy to hear."

Frank and Faith finish their dance and Jonathan heads over to the table where Diane is sitting. Faith and Jonathan wanted to keep it a surprise for Diane, but he decided to ask her to dance with him for the mother and the groom dance.

"I would be honored if you would dance with me during the mother and groom dance."

Diane's eyes instantly tear up and her hand goes to her heart. "It would mean so much to me, Jonathan."

He holds out his hand for her to take and then he leads her out to the dancefloor. The song begins and they dance. Faith watches as the two spin around the dancefloor. Jonathan is talking to Diane and she's laughing. It warms Faith's heart to see them like this and to know how much Jonathan cares about her family. She knows that Diane has felt the need ever since meeting Jonathan to be a mother figure.

As the song comes to an end, Faith see's Diane wipe tears from her eyes then she gives Jonathan a tight squeeze.

"Now, we're going to have the bride and groom as well as the wedding party on the dance floor." The DJ says into the microphone.

Rowen and Jackie start walking out onto the dancefloor followed by Hope and Andy. All four of them stand there looking at Faith and Jonathan who are both wearing huge smiles.

"You didn't tell us we'd be doing this." Hope says.

Faith shrugs her shoulders.

Guitar fills the room as the song begins to play followed by a funky beat and Jackie begins to laugh loudly. Rowen looks at her. "What's so funny?"

"We used to dance to this at every single sleep over we ever had!"

Faith shouts over the music, "I thought this would be the perfect song for all of us to dance to tonight!" She leans in to Jackie. "I hope you don't mind sharing it, just this once, with everyone."

"No, not at all!"

"Good, because it's kind of already happening!" Faith shouts and starts laughing.

"It is a classic!"

Jackie and Faith hold hands and start dancing like they always do to 'Play That Funky Music'. When the chorus starts they all sing it together while they dance around.

Throughout the rest of the night, Jonathan and Faith spend time mingling and dancing. Brenda lets them know when it's time to cut the cake and Carmine and Jackson are right there waiting to get the perfect shots.

Jonathan is loving and gentle when he feeds Faith the first bite of cake, just like he always is when they share their food.

"I love the way you clean that fork off." He says softly in her ear.

"I love the way you feed me." She says and she kisses his cheek.

The whole while, Carmine and Jackson are moving around getting plenty of footage and photos. When Faith and Jonathan take their pieces of cake and sit back down at the head table, waitresses and waiters start to serve everyone their pieces as well.

When they've finished their cake they head back onto the dancefloor where they're joined by Frank and Diane, Rowen and Jackie, and Hope and Andy.

"We're so glad to have you all here! Thank you for helping make our day amazing! It wouldn't have been nearly as special without all of you!" Faith tells them all.

The end of the night comes quicker than Faith was anticipating that it would. The wedding party help them get all of the gifts into their honeymoon suite. They'll bring them home and open them sometime tomorrow. There are more physical gifts than Faith thought there would be.

"Thank you guys for helping bring this stuff up." Faith says motioning towards the gifts.

"Of course, Faith! I'm glad we could help!" Rowen says.

"You mentioned that you got a room here too, right?" Jonathan asks him.

"Yeah, I didn't want to drive back to Caulfield after drinking the majority of the day."

"That's smart!" Faith says.

Rowen puts his arm around Jackie. "Did you want to stay with me?"

"I would." Jackie says raising her eyebrows. They begin to walk towards the door.

"Thank you both again!" Jonathan calls after them.

"See you tomorrow." Jackie calls back.

After they hear the door close Faith asks Jonathan, "What do you think they're going to do?" She can barely finish the sentence without laughing.

"I know what we're going to do." Jonathan says picking her up in his arms. When he sets her back down on her feet he gently turns her around and asks, "How the hell do I get this thing off of you."

Faith laughs. "It's quite the contraption."

Jonathan nods in agreement.

"You'll need to start by unbuttoning all of these little buttons on the back." She says pointing to the line of buttons down the back of her dress.

Jonathan begins unbuttoning the numerous buttons that line Faith's spine. Once those are undone, Jonathan sees a zipper. He unzips it to find hooks inside. "How many different closure apparatuses does this thing have?"

"Probably at least one too many." She giggles.

"I'm so ready to see you naked." He says into her ear.

"You're almost there." She says leaning into him.

Jonathan unhooks her dress while kissing her neck.

"That's a good start." Faith says softly.

His lips follow his hands down her back as he unhooks her bra and then up to her neck once again.

She takes a step forward and slips her dress off taking the time to gently place it on the sofa in the living room area of the suite.

When she turns around, Jonathan has already gotten his suit off and is standing there wearing nothing but a smile.

"Aren't you a sight to behold?" She says as she saunters over to the end of the bed where he's standing.

Jonathan pulls her into him. Feeling her bare skin against his makes his desire for her grow stronger. He runs his hands down her sides to the waist band of her lace panties. Then he moves his fingers in between the elastic and her skin feeling goose bumps begin to form on the trail his fingers left.

She runs her fingers through his hair as he kisses her fiercely gripping her ass firmly in his hand as he uses the other to remove her panties.

When they're around her ankles Faith steps out of them and Jonathan scoops her up in his arms. Faith wraps her legs around him and he walks over to the side of the bed, sitting down with her on top of him.

He takes one of her breasts in his hand and brings his mouth closer to lick her nipple. His tongue flicks it as Faith lets a soft moan escape her lips.

She grinds against him feeling his excitement harden even more. She grips his shoulders as she lowers herself onto him. Another moan fills the room.

"You feel so damn good, Faith."

She grinds harder. "So do you."

"I've been waiting for this all damn day."

Faith moans in response and rocks back and forth her pleasure nearing its peak. She feels Jonathan's warm heavy breath against her shoulder as her breasts press against him.

He lowers his face to bury it in them, kissing and sucking as she keeps rhythm.

She begins to feel her ecstasy build until she's coming down on the other side, with Jonathan unable to hold his pleasure back. Both of them are blissfully loving every minute of their bodies being one.

Faith collapses against him as the waves of her orgasm slow. "Today was so fucking magical."

"It really was." Jonathan says craning his neck to try to look at her. Instead he places his hands on her face and lifts so he can see her then pulls her into him and kisses her fiercely.

Chapter 43

Finitude

Noun; finite quality or state

The past week has flown by, both Jonathan and Faith went back to work on Monday. They won't be taking their honeymoon until next month since school will be out then. Faith is hoping Jonathan's work will slow down a bit since this week he's been working late nearly every night.

Neither of them have brought Aunt Suz up since their talk in the groom's suite on their wedding day. Faith is being patient hoping Jonathan will bring it up when he's ready. Her fear is that he won't broach the subject at all and bury those feelings, which is the last thing he should be doing.

"Have you seen my black sling back heels?" Faith asks Jonathan wearing only a towel.

"I haven't, but you should probably wear something other than that towel. While I love the way you look in it, I'm not sure it's appropriate for Hope's graduation."

Faith laughs. "Are you sure? I thought this was the newest trend?"

"I haven't seen it, but I'm pretty sure you have better options in your closet."

"You're probably right." She says.

Jonathan closes the space between them as he walks into her closet and pulls her into him, placing his lips on hers. Then he says, "I might want to help you take this off though." He tugs on the fabric making it fall to her feet.

She smiles. "I'm not sure we have time."

"No, we don't. I don't want to try to be quick either. I would much rather savor you."

"Savor is a great word for it." She says with a smirk.

"It's accurate too. You're delicious."

Faith feels the heat in her cheeks. She shakes her head and begins to gently push Jonathan away. "Go on now, I need to get ready!"

"Are you kicking me out?" He says surprised.

"Yes, yes I am." She giggles. "Otherwise we're going to be late, and I'm sure it's going to be crazy busy."

"I think you're right."

Faith turns to look at the dresses hanging in her closet. Tucked in the corner behind all the others is her wedding dress still in the bag. She will be dropping it off in a couple of weeks to get it cleaned and prepared for storage. She slides each dress over to get a better look as she tries to figure out what she's going to wear today.

They have Hope's graduation ceremony this morning, followed by Jackie's graduation ceremony in Caulfield in early afternoon. Then guests will be coming over for Hope's graduation party around three this afternoon. Frank and Diane will be going to Jonathan's and Faith's house while they're attending Jackie's graduation to help get everything set up for the party.

Faith finally decides on a floral flowy dress and a pair of white kitten heel sandals. The weather is absolutely perfect and they've already opened the pool for the season which works well for the party.

As she walks out of her closet, Jonathan is sitting on the bed dressed and ready to go. Zeke gets up from his favorite spot at the end of the bed and sits in front of her looking at her admiringly. Faith giggles. "You clearly approve." She says as she pats the top of his head.

"We both do." Jonathan says looking at her lovingly. "You look incredible as always."

"Thank you, so do you." Faith says smiling widely at him.

They sit beside Frank, Diane, and Andy on the bleachers in the large field house. The center of the room is lined with rows of chairs which the graduates will all fill once they file in. The bleachers are packed full twenty minutes before the ceremony begins and there are still people trying to find seats while the graduates are lined up to take their seats, they end up standing near the back of the room.

Faith leans into Diane. "Thank you guys for saving us seats."

"It was actually Andy that got here first."

Faith leans forward to see Andy. "Thank you for saving us these seats!"

"You're welcome! It helped that Hope and I got here so early."

They sit and watch a couple of inspirational speeches followed by hundreds of graduates who walk up onto the stage, shake some hands, and receive a rolled up slip of paper. Diane, Faith and Andy are taking tons of photos of Hope as she walks across the stage.

When the ceremony finishes, they manage to find Hope in the crowd and take more pictures.

Andy gives Hope flowers and embraces her. "I'm so proud of you!"

"Thank you!"

Frank and Diane wait their turn and hug her as well. "Are you happy to be done?"

"Incredibly happy to be finished! Does this mean I get a raise?"

"You're the manager, Hope. The budget is up to you to figure out."

Hope smiles as Faith goes in to hug her. "I'm proud of you little sister. You looked great walking across that stage!"

"Thanks! It felt amazing! I wanted to do a kick off the stage or something, but figured that might get me kicked out."

"If there's a day to do that then I guess today would have been it." Jonathan offers.

"That's true, Jonameister. I should have talked to you before the ceremony."

"Probably should have." He shrugs.

"Do you think Rowen will be there?" Faith asks as they drive into Caulfield.

"I wouldn't hold my breath. When I mentioned something to him about Jackie at my bachelor party he made it clear that they were only sleeping together."

"Yeah, Jackie made that pretty clear too, but then sometimes when I see them together it seems like it could be more."

"I don't think Rowen is the 'more' type of guy."

"He got married before."

"He thought she would fix him. I'm pretty sure he doesn't have those illusions anymore."

"Well, that's good I guess." Faith shrugs.

Jonathan looks over at Faith. "You look so beautiful, Faith."

"Thank you." She says beaming at him.

"I love going everywhere with you on my arm."

"I love going everywhere with you, Jonathan."

He pulls into the nearly full parking lot and attempts to find parking.

"I'd suggest dropping me off at the door so I can get seats, but I'm afraid you'd never find me in there!"

The auditorium this one is being held in is absolutely gigantic.

"They need all this space for the number of graduates they have every year?"

"Yeah. This one is probably going to be even more crowded than Hope's was."

Faith is proven correct when they walk through the auditorium doors. She knows that Jackie's parents won't be in attendance so she doesn't even bother looking for them. It makes her sad for her friend. It's got to be tough to have parents who aren't a part of your life. Whether it's your choice or their doing, Faith doesn't think that makes much of a difference in the way it makes a person feel.

Jackie has been successful in spite of her upbringing and what she went through as a child and adolescent. It's not always easy to overcome those things, and if she had lived in a different place and perhaps didn't have Faith as a friend her life could have very easily been quite different.

They find seats near the back of the room and Faith is grateful for the zoom on her phone's camera when she begins taking pictures of Jackie as she walks across the stage. Aside from the professional photos taken, Faith is pretty sure these will be the only other ones Jackie will get.

"Life isn't fair." Faith blurts out.

"No, it isn't. I'm curious as to why you're bringing that up now, though."

"Well, I have great parents. Your great parents died when you were still pretty little, and Jackie's parents weren't great at all. Hell, they weren't even good."

"Some people shouldn't have kids and certainly not given to them by the courts or the state or whoever handles all of that."

"No, they shouldn't."

"You're right, Faith. Life isn't fair, but we all manage to make it somehow."

"Not everyone does though. Some people take an entirely wrong turn somewhere and they never find their way back."

"That's true too. Sometimes I wonder how I managed to not do that." Jonathan reaches for Faith's hand, squeezing it gently.

"I'm sure you do too."

Just then the last graduate walks across the stage and the auditorium erupts with flying graduation caps. Faith and Jonathan wait to find Jackie after the mass of people slowly make their way through the numerous exits.

"I'm going to call her and tell her where we are."

Faith pushes a few buttons on her phone's screen and Jackie answers.

"Reception is shitty! Where are you guys?"

Faith explains it as best she can. Once they find each other Faith gives Jackie a beautiful bouquet of flowers and Jonathan takes some pictures of Faith and Jackie together.

"My parents wanted to be here, but they went to our house to get everything set up for the party."

"I know. It's OK. I'm just glad you made it."

"I'm proud of you, Jackie. You've worked your ass off for this and you deserve everything good that's to come!"

"Thanks, Hun. That means a lot."

"Are you ready to go to Hope's party?"

"Absolutely! I'll follow you guys!"

When they pull into their driveway, Jackie is close behind. Frank and Diane's truck is parked and so is Faith's old SUV that Hope has been driving since she was cleared after her accident.

Zeke and Orpheus are running around the yard as they pull into the garage. The two dogs come bounding over. Faith walks into the house and the dogs follow. When she sees Diane she says, "I'm glad you guys decided to bring him. He looks like he's having a blast."

"They're loving being able to go outside whenever they want." Diane says rolling her eyes as she places carrots into a veggie tray.

"What do you need help with?"

Diane doesn't answer because she sees Jackie walk through the door behind Jonathan. She swiftly walks over to her and wraps her in her arms. "I'm so sorry we couldn't be there! I want you to know how proud of you we are." Diane pulls a card from her apron pocket and hands it to Jackie.

"Thank you, Mrs. Brandt. I completely understand. You didn't have to do this." She says holding the card and gently shaking it.

"It's the least we could do. Go ahead and open it."

Jackie does as she's told finding a check for a thousand dollars within the heartfelt card. A tear comes to her eyes. "You definitely didn't need to do this." She says as she pulls Diane in for a hug.

"No, but you've always been like a daughter to us, and such a great friend to Faith and Hope too when she's needed it. We all feel very lucky to have you in our lives." Diane kisses Jackie's cheek.

"Thank you Diane."

"You are so welcome." Diane releases Jackie and starts back over to the island where Faith is standing beaming at her mom and best friend.

Frank and Jonathan head out to the back patio to start getting tables and things set up out there.

"Where are Hope and Andy?" Faith asks curiously.

"I'm pretty sure they're outside already."

"Oh, OK. I didn't see them."

Jackie says, "I think I'll go see if there's anything I can help with out there. Thank you again, Diane."

"You are so very welcome, dear."

As guests begin to arrive, Faith feels more at ease than she has with any other party they've thrown at their home. Maybe because she's doing it for her little sister. Carmine and Jackson stop by for a bit and take a few photos. They can't stay long, however due to a wedding that evening.

"I'm glad you two came, thank you so much for coming." Hope tells them appreciatively as she and Faith walk them to their car.

"We'll get the photos to you later this week!"

"You really didn't have to do that!" Hope says.

"No, it's our pleasure! These accomplishments should be celebrated and remembered beautifully!"

Faith smiles at them. "You two are incredibly thoughtful! Thank you so much!

"Yeah, thank you so much!" Hope echoes as they get into their car.

Jonathan is manning the grill when they get back to the patio and about half of the guests are enjoying the pool including Jackie and Rowen.

Faith walks up behind Jonathan and places a hand on his shoulder. Leaning into him she says, "You look so incredibly sexy flipping that meat."

"You should see what else I can do with my meat." He says as he turns around and picks her up playfully.

She lets out a squeal gaining everyone's attentions.

"Newlyweds." Hope says in a joking tone and everyone laughs.

After they all eat, Hope sits and opens her gifts which are mostly cards filled with money. Most of the guests go home after Hope is done opening her gifts, but for the few that stay once it starts getting dark, Faith builds a fire in the fire pit on the far patio overlooking the bay. The evening brings with it a chill. So Faith and Jonathan grab blankets and s'mores ingredients.

There's a full moon high in the sky by the time Frank and Diane decide to head home. Rowen and Jackie aren't too far behind, but they help clean up a bit before they go. Hope and Andy thank Jonathan and Faith profusely for hosting.

"It was no problem at all!"

"But you guys just had the wedding last weekend. I'm sure it was a lot of work and I want you to know I'm grateful."

"Honestly, aside from cleaning, Mom and Dad did most of it since we were at Jackie's graduation Ceremony."

"I know they helped a ton, but you guys still did a lot."

Jonathan leans in. "And we're happy to do it, Hope. You deserve a party and our house works best, plus we enjoy it."

They walk with them to Hope's SUV.

"So, where are you guys going on vacation?" Faith asks.

Andy smirks. "It's still a surprise. She won't know until we're at the airport. That's my goal anyway."

"How in the world am I going to know what to pack?"

"I'll guide you." Andy says simply.

"Jonathan did that when we went to Napa Valley last year. It was pretty awesome! I had no idea where we were going or what we were going to be doing. It worked out fine." Faith reassures Hope.

"I don't need to do anything on vacation besides lay on the beach or near a pool and I'll be just fine."

"Good to know." Andy says still smirking.

"I didn't think this would bother me as much as it does." Hope laughs as she gets into the driver's seat.

"What's that?" Andy asks.

"Not knowing what you're planning."

"It's an exercise in trust." Andy says.

"They're right, you know." Jonathan says.

"Bye!" Faith says as Hope begins to back out of the drive way.

Faith turns to Jonathan. "I'm exhausted. Can we finish cleaning up in the morning?"

"I'm good with that."

Faith smiles happy he agrees. As they walk back into the house and work on getting all the doors closed and locked Faith says, "I still feel bad for Jackie."

"I get it, but all you can do is be there for her. Which you are. You're a great friend to her, Faith. She's lucky to have you. We all are."

"Thank you, Jonathan. We're all lucky to have you too! Thank you for all of the hard work you put into this party."

"You're welcome, Faith. I think it turned out pretty good."

"It did." Faith smiles. "I know I've said it before, but I'm so glad we did the patio back there overlooking the bay. It's perfect for nights like tonight."

"I am too." Jonathan wraps his arms around Faith, making her feel so safe and loved.

Chapter 44

Definitude

Noun; precision, definiteness

Faith fills the empty room with laughter while she holds a paint brush and looks at the paint mark she just left on Jackie's ass. Jackie is currently spinning around trying to see it and failing.

"What did you do that for?" Jackie demands.

"For fun." Faith laughs some more.

"It's only fun for you." Jackie says trying not to let out a chuckle.

"No, it's fun for both of us. I see your smile." She teases.

They're currently in the first bedroom upstairs that initially was staged as a nursery in the architect's rendition. Unfortunately, that use never came to fruition. The original color of the walls was white, it was clean and crisp and easy to paint over, that's what Faith told herself when they initially chose it.

This time Faith has chosen a beautifully rich sea blue green color. When Jonathan and she had first gotten everything painted they went with light and neutral tones. At that point they hadn't picked out their furniture yet so it seemed like the best option.

Now though, Faith wants to be surrounded by color. She wants to feel happy in every space she walks into in this home and the white and neutral greys aren't doing it for her. Rich tones in both paint selection and accent colors is what she's going for now.

"Thank you for helping me, Jackie."

"I don't have anything better to do." She says as she runs the roller up and down the wall. "I do really love this color."

"I do too, I'm thinking about using it in a couple of other rooms in the house."

Jackie stops rolling for a moment. She starts. "Are you," Pauses, takes a deep breath and then starts again. "Are you sure you want to stay here? Like inevitably? Can you even stay here? I'm asking because I'm not sure if I could."

"I don't want to leave." Faith says as she pulls another strip of blue tape from the roll. "This is my home. Yes, it was the home I literally built with Jonathan, and it's enormous and too much for me, but it's mine. It's entirely paid for, all I have to do is pay taxes. Besides, I don't want to go through the hassle of finding a new place and selling this one. Plus, who's going to want to buy a house that was owned by a potential serial killer?"

"He didn't actually kill anyone here, right?"

"No, I'm pretty sure he didn't, but then again the list of things I'm sure of when it comes to him is getting shorter every day."

"There are people out there who wouldn't care who owned this house."

"That's true."

Jackie refills the roller and begins rolling paint on the wall in front of her again. "I don't think you should make a decision yet, I just had to ask. What happens when you start dating again?"

"I appreciate you asking. I wouldn't say I've totally made up my mind. My feelings towards this house could change, but I'm hoping with making the changes that I am it begins to feel better in here. As far as dating goes, my mind is so far away from even thinking about that right now. I guess if I were to date they'd have to be OK with living here, or we start over somewhere else."

Jackie nods her head then asks, "Why did we start in this room?"

Faith looks around the brightly lit room. "This is the room that made me fall in love with the house when we first saw it on the architect's computer screen. It gave me hope for our future and it made me believe anything was possible. I'm hoping to be able to tap into that again."

"The hope is still there, Faith. It's just going to be different now."

"I know. That's what takes getting used to, I think. The fact that it's going to be different. My life is forever changed. Even if he's not convicted."

Just as Faith finishes the sentence Jackie gives Faith a disbelieving look. "Do you think that's possible?"

"I don't know what I think. One minute I'm sure he's guilty and the next I can't imagine him doing those heinous things so of course he can't be. I wrestle with that a lot."

"Has Rowen given you any updates on how Jonathan is doing or what to expect when this all goes to trial?"

"Nothing yet."

"I'm surprised he agreed to represent him, honestly."

"I'm not. They've been friends for so long. I'm sure Rowen felt a sort of obligation to do it."

"Jonathan can afford anyone he wants."

"That is true, but he trusts Rowen." Faith says as she dips the paint brush into the cup of paint and brushes it on the wall along the baseboard and then around the uncovered outlet.

"I really do like this paint color." Jackie repeats.

For the next couple of hours they paint the room as the sun moves across the sky making the light in the room shift. As the sun begins to go down Faith suggests they head into the kitchen for something to eat.

"I'm going to have some wine. Would you like some?" Faith asks as she reaches for the glasses.

"Yes, please." Jackie smiles.

"Thanks again, Jackie. I couldn't have gotten that room done so quickly by myself."

"I don't mind painting. Especially when you're the one doing the precision work." She laughs.

Faith pours them both glasses of wine and then she turns on the burner on the range placing a pot filled with water over it.

"I hope you don't mind spaghetti."

"It's a classic for a reason. I don't mind it at all."

Faith continues making dinner, but as she moves through the kitchen she's blindsided by a feeling that this room must be next. It's fine to do rooms they hardly ever spent time in, but the rooms that Faith really needs to do are the ones where they spent the majority of their time together.

Jonathan is more a part of this kitchen than nearly any other room in the house, with the exception of their bedroom. In order for these changes to make the biggest impact on how she's feeling, she'll need to erase him from these rooms first. It just sucks they are also the ones that require the most work.

"What are you thinking about?" Jackie pries.

"Just that I think this room needs to be next. I'm sitting here cooking in it and all that's doing is reminding me of him."

"See, that's why I wouldn't be able to stay."

"That's exactly why I've decided to do the refresh. I know that I won't be able to erase the memories, but I feel like if the rooms look different they won't bring the memories on as much."

"It's a good theory and one worth exploring, I think."

"That's good since you're the one helping me."

Both women laugh and Faith begins plating their food.

When they've finished eating Faith says, "You know what we haven't done since you've been sleeping over?"

"No, what's that?"

Faith says, "I'll give you a hint." Then begins to sing, "Play that funky music…"

"Really? You want to? I can't tell you how many times I've thought about it, but was worried you weren't in the mood."

"Of course I want to!" Faith says as she types 'Wild Cherry Play that Funky Music' into the search bar in her music app.

"I don't even remember what made us use this song to begin with." Jackie admits.

"I think we found some music my dad downloaded on the computer or something."

"That's it. We were going through playing random songs one night when I was sleeping over and we just thought it was a super fun song."

"I think we were like eight or nine."

"That seems so long ago now!"

The first bars of guitar fill the kitchen and dining area. Jackie's face lights up.

The two of them hold hands dancing together. "I don't think we've danced to this since your wedding." Jackie shouts.

"Nope. It's a shame too! Good thing we're fixing that now!"

The two women dance around laughing and remembering all the times in the past they've done this.

When the chorus starts they sing and shout along with it. Zeke is following them around as they spin and dance. At one point, Faith lets go of Jackie's hands and picks up Zeke's paws. He stands on his hind legs as she dances back and forth with him singing the song. His tail is wagging wildly and Jackie laughs at the sight.

This is how Faith wants to feel. These are the new memories she needs to make. Wallowing in self-pity and negative thoughts isn't what will help her through this and she knows that. Her new wardrobe and décor in her home are simply the start of all of it. Faith is on the precipice of figuring out that she can make it through anything and this is just the beginning of the most powerful years of her life.

Please consider leaving a review at your retailer of choice to help other readers find books they'll love! Up next in the series… Servitude!

Also By J.S. Wik

You can scan or click depending on which
format you're reading.

Find more to read from J.S. Wik!
https://linktr.ee/JSWik

About the Author

J.S. Wik lives in Wisconsin with her incredible husband, their amazing children and numerous pets of various species. When she isn't writing, you'll most likely find her out in the garden, or curled up on the couch with a good book, or possibly with a paintbrush in hand and a colorful canvas in front of her.

www.ingramcontent.com/pod-product-compliance
Lightning Source LLC
Chambersburg PA
CBHW031641200726
48289CB00004BA/1107